Barbara Taylor Bradford

Emma's Secret

HarperCollinsPublishers

This novel is entirely a work of fiction.
The names, characters and incidents portrayed in it are
he work of the author's imagination. Any resemblance to
actual persons, living or dead, events or localities is
entirely coincidental.

HarperCollins*Publishers*
77–85 Fulham Palace Road,
Hammersmith, London W6 8JB

www.harpercollins.co.uk

This paperback edition 2004
1 3 5 7 9 8 6 4 2

First published in Great Britain by
HarperCollins*Publishers* 2003

ISBN 0 00 651441 3

Typeset in Sabon by Palimpsest Book Production Limited,
Polmont, Stirlingshire

Printed and bound in Great Britain by
Clays Ltd, St Ives plc

For Bob, as always, with all my love

THE THREE CLANS

The Hartes shown in line of descent

Emma Harte: Matriarch: Founder of dynasty and business empire

HER CHILDREN

Edwina: *Dowager Countess of Dunvale*: Emma's daughter by Edwin Fairley (illegitimate). *First born*

Christopher 'Kit' Lowther: Emma's son by her first husband Joe Lowther. *Second born*

Robin Ainsley: Emma's son by her second husband Arthur Ainsley. *Third born*

Elizabeth Ainsley: Emma's daughter by her second husband Arthur Ainsley. Robin's twin. *Third born*

Daisy (Ainsley): Emma's daughter by Paul McGill (illegitimate). *Fourth born*

HER GRANDCHILDREN
Shown in line of descent

Anthony Standish: *Earl of Dunvale*, son of Edwina and Jeremy Standish, Earl of Dunvale

Sarah Lowther Pascal: Daughter of 'Kit' and June Lowther

Jonathan Ainsley: Son of Robin and Valerie Ainsley

Paula O'Neill: Daughter of Daisy and David Amory

Philip McGill Amory: Son of Daisy and David Amory; brother of Paula

Emily Barkstone Harte: Daughter of Elizabeth and Tony Barkstone; half-sister of Amanda

Amanda Linde: Daughter of Elizabeth and Derek Linde (Elizabeth's second husband)

EMMA'S GREAT-GRANDCHILDREN

Tessa Fairley Longden: Daughter of Paula and Jim Fairley (Paula's first husband)

Lorne Fairley: Tessa's twin, son of Paula and Jim Fairley

Toby Harte: Son of Emily and Winston Harte II; brother of Gideon

Gideon Harte: Son of Emily and Winston Harte II

India Standish: Daughter of Anthony Standish

and Sally Harte, Earl and Countess of Dunvale

Linnet O'Neill: Daughter of Paula and Shane O'Neill (Paula's second husband)

Chloe Pascal: Daughter of Sarah and Yves Pascal

Fiona Amory: Daughter of Philip McGill Amory

Emsie O'Neill: Daughter of Paula and Shane O'Neill

Desmond O'Neill: Son of Paula and Shane O'Neill

THE HARTES continued

Winston Harte: Emma's older brother and business partner

Randolph Harte: Son of Winston and Charlotte Harte

Winston Harte II: Son of Randolph and Georgina Harte

Toby Harte: Son of Winston and Emily Harte; Brother of Gideon

Gideon Harte: Son of Winston and Emily Harte

Frank Harte: Emma's younger brother

Rosamunde Harte: Daughter of Frank and Natalie Harte

Simon Harte: Son of Frank and Natalie Harte; brother of Rosamunde

THE O'NEILLS

Shane Patrick Desmond O'Neill ('Blackie'): Founding father of dynasty and business empire

Bryan O'Neill: Son of Blackie and Laura Spencer O'Neill

Shane O'Neill: Son of Bryan and Geraldine O'Neill

Linnet O'Neill: Daughter of Shane and Paula O'Neill

Emsie O'Neill: Daughter of Shane and Paula O'Neill

Desmond O'Neill: Son of Shane and Paula O'Neill

THE KALLINSKIS

David Kallinski: Founding father of dynasty and business empire

Sir Ronald Kallinski: Son of David and Rebecca Kallinski

Michael Kallinski: Son of Ronald and Helen 'Posy' Kallinski

Julian Kallinski: Son of Michael and Valentine Kallinski

Contents

PROLOGUE

2OOO

'In my end is my beginning.'
                Mary, Queen of Scots

PROLOGUE

She sat very still in the chair next to the bed, holding her grandmother's hand. It was so quiet in the hospital room she could hear her breathing, the breath coming in soft little intakes and exhalations.

The old woman's face was relaxed, the tension gone from it as she dozed, and she appeared to be younger than her years, younger than she had looked in a very long time.

Perhaps she *will* get better, Evan thought, her eyes on her grandmother, the person whom she loved most in the whole world except for her father. She wished he would get here. He was driving into Manhattan from Connecticut and had left several hours ago; she couldn't imagine what was making him this late. Evan glanced at her watch, and when she saw the time she realized he was probably snarled up in the late afternoon traffic of Manhattan ... rush hour was imminent and Thanksgiving was next week. Too many cars in the city today, she decided, trying to relax. A moment later Evan focused on her grandmother once more, and a small sigh escaped her; she couldn't imagine her life without her beloved Gran in it. The prospect was bleak.

She had been suffering with a kidney infection and had gone into kidney failure. It was only a question of time.

Glynnis Jenkins Hughes. The Welsh girl from the Rhondda Valley, who had arrived in America fifty-four years ago as a GI Bride. Come to these shores to join her GI husband Richard Hughes, and bringing with her their small son Owen, conceived and born in England when Richard had been stationed there in the Second World War.

And she's been as much a mother to me as she has to Dad, Evan decided, leaning back in the chair, closing her eyes, allowing a fund of childhood memories to come flooding back . . . Gran always there for them . . . always laughing, full of fun and gaiety, her warmth and love so abundant, her capacity for caring boundless.

Her mother had been ill for as long as Evan could remember, and still was, a manic depressive living in a world of her own, out of reality, out of their lives in a certain sense.

One day, many years ago, her Gran had come up to Connecticut from New York City and had taken over, muttering that they were all too little to fend for themselves. And adding, in a quieter voice, but not so quiet Evan didn't hear, that a man needed a hot meal to come home to at night, as well as loving arms to hold him, a good woman to give him comfort and warmth and understanding. To boost him, when he needed it, to bolster his confidence.

Gran had spent several years sheltering her and her two sisters, Elayne and Angharad, taking care of them, running their young lives. She had been full of robust energy, enthusiasm and good will, a happy woman, comfortable in her own skin, who wanted only to share her joy in living with them and their father, her only child. Which she did so profoundly, Evan thought, and she is the best part of me. She made me what I am.

Finally opening her eyes, Evan glanced towards her grandmother. A smile broke across her troubled face when she saw that Glynnis was awake.

'You were dozing, Evan,' Glynnis said weakly, her voice whispery.

'Not really. Just resting my eyes and thinking, Grandma.'

'About?'

'You, and how you took care of us so well when we were little girls. And Dad, too.'

A smile touched Glynnis's lips, and quite unexpectedly her rheumy old eyes cleared, became alive, very bright and shining, the blueness remarkable in its intensity.

Squeezing her grandmother's hand, Evan exclaimed, 'You'll be out of here soon! You'll see.'

'Where's Owen?' Glynnis murmured, her voice querulous, barely audible.

'Dad's on his way. He'll be arriving any minute . . . he's probably caught in traffic.'

'Leave here,' Glynnis instructed hoarsely.

'I can't leave you alone, Gran!' Evan protested, shaking her head. Wondering what this was all about, she frowned and added, 'I *want* to be here to take care of you, and so does Dad.'

'Leave New York . . . that's what I meant . . . you're twenty-six . . . should be out . . . in the world . . .' Glynnis's voice trailed off wearily. And she sighed, seemed to sink further into the pillows.

Evan leaned closer to her grandmother, her eyes fixed on her unwaveringly. 'I'm happy here, I love my job at Saks . . . and anyway, I want to be near you.'

'I'm dying.' Glynnis's lids fluttered, and she stared back at Evan, held her granddaughter with her own steady gaze.

'Don't say that, Gran! You're going to get better. I know you are.' Evan's eyes filled, and she tightened her grip on Glynnis's fragile fingers.

'Old,' Glynnis whispered, 'too old now.'

'No, you're not! You're only seventy-nine, that's not old these days,' Evan protested, her voice rising.

Glynnis sighed, and her heart clenched. It was unbearable for her to see her granddaughter's tears, to witness her pain. My one true love, she thought, well there was the other, but that was so long ago it doesn't matter any more. Evan was always mine.

Like my own daughter, the daughter I never had with Richard. Dearest, dearest Richard. The truest husband a woman could ever want. Such a good man. The best man I ever knew; the right man to spend a lifetime with, after all. So much to say to Evan. So little time left. I must get my thoughts unscrambled . . . get them straight. I should have told her before . . . but I was afraid . . .

'Gran! Gran!' Evan cried. 'Please, Gran, open your eyes!'

Slowly Glynnis's eyelids lifted, and as she gazed at her granddaughter again, a sudden radiance flooded her wrinkled face. 'I was thinking of your grandfather, Evan. Such a good man, Richard Hughes.'

'We loved him too, Grandma.'

'Do you think he's waiting for me? Do you believe in an afterlife, Evan? Is there a heaven, do you think?'

'I don't know, Gran.' Evan brushed her eyes with her fingertips, flicked away the tears. 'I hope so, I really do.'

'I think perhaps there is . . . don't weep for me, Evan, I've had a good life . . . sad at times . . . painful, too . . . But I've enjoyed it all . . . there's always the bad along with the good . . .' Glynnis drifted off once more, lost in her thoughts, trying to summon the last vestiges of her strength.

Evan bent closer, touching Glynnis's cheek very gently. 'I'm here, Grandma.'

'I know, dear.' Glynnis sighed, and a faint smile

flickered on her wide and generous mouth.

Evan said, 'Dad'll be here any minute now,' and she hoped that he would. She pushed her spiralling anxiety away.

'I loved him too much,' Glynnis muttered suddenly.

'You can never love a child too much – you said that yourself, Gran.'

'Did I?'

'Yes, long ago, to me, when I was a little girl.'

'I don't remember. *Evan?*'

'Yes, Gran?'

'Go to Emma.'

'Emma? Who's *Emma?*'

'Emma Harte. In London. She has . . . the key. To your future. Oh, Evan—' Glynnis stopped speaking abruptly, stared at her granddaughter with enormous intensity as though committing her face to memory, and then she closed her eyes. A long, fluttering sigh rippled through her before she lay absolutely still.

'*Gran,*' Evan said in a low, insistent tone. '*Gran.*' There was no response, not even the flicker of an eyelash. Evan glanced down at their hands clasped together on top of the sheet and she saw that her grandmother's hand had gone slack in hers. She felt her throat closing. Her eyes welled.

Gran's gone, Evan thought. Gone to another place. She's out of her pain and suffering, at peace.

Bending forward, Evan kissed Glynnis's still-warm cheek; the tears spilled out of her eyes and

slid down her face as grief engulfed her. So dis-
traught was she that Evan did not hear her father
come into the hospital room. It was only when she
felt his loving hand resting lightly on her shoulder
that she became aware of his presence.

'She's gone?' Owen asked, a catch in his voice.

'Yes, Dad, but only a second ago.' As she spoke,
Evan smoothed her hand over Glynnis's silver hair,
and then she got up, turned to her father. When she
saw the tears in her father's blue eyes, the anguish
on his face, she stepped into his arms, wanting to
comfort him and needing his comfort in return.

They clung together for a few seconds. Finally,
Owen said, 'I tried to get here before she died.'

'I know Dad, and Gran knew that too.'

'Did she have any last word for me?'

'She said she loved you too much.'

Her father was silent, a reflective look crossing
his face. A moment later he released Evan and went
to sit beside his mother, his dark head bent over
her, his sorrow apparent.

Evan, watching him, concerned for him, did not
immediately think of her grandmother's last words
to *her*. When she did, she was baffled.

And some time later she went to London. To
find Emma Harte. To find her future.

PART ONE

Dynasty

2001

Hold your friends close,
Your enemies closer.

ANONYMOUS

Be not forgetful to entertain
strangers: For thereby some have
entertained angels unawares.

Hebrews 13: 1–2

CHAPTER ONE

It was a blustery morning.

The penetrating wind blowing in from the North Sea was laden with moisture, and the dampness was heavy on the air, and icy. Linnet O'Neill felt as though it were seeping into her bones.

She huddled further into her thick, loden-green wool coat and tied her scarf tighter around her head. Then, thrusting her gloved hands into her pockets, she trudged on, doggedly following the winding path which would bring her to the crest of the moors.

After a moment she lifted her head and glanced up.

Above her, the arc of the sky appeared hollowed out, resembled the inside of a vast, polished bowl. It was the colour of steel, its metallic greyness relieved by a few scudding clouds, pale and wispy in the clear crystalline light so peculiar to these northern climes. It was an eerie light that seemed to emanate from some hidden source below the horizon.

When she first set out to walk up into the high country which soared above Pennistone Royal, Linnet had anticipated rain, but the massed black clouds of earlier had been scuttled by the gusting wind.

Since she had lived here all of her life, she knew about the weather and its unpredictability, knew that the skies of Yorkshire were ever-changing. By lunchtime the sun could easily be creeping out from behind the greyness to fill the heavens with radiance, or rain might be slashing down in a relentless, unending stream.

You took your chances when you went walking on the Yorkshire moors, she knew that. But she didn't care. Ever since she had been a small child, these moors had been irresistible to her; she had loved to come here with her mother when she was little, to wander amongst the heather and the bracken, content to play alone with her stuffed animals in the vast emptiness surrounding her. It was her world; she had even believed it belonged to her when she was growing up, and, in a way, she still did.

It was quiet on the moors this morning.

In the spring and summer, even in the autumn, there was always the splash and tinkle of water as it tumbled down over rock formations into pebble-strewn becks, and the whistling of little birds, the rapid whirring of their wings, was ever present.

All were absent on this cold January Saturday.

The birds had long ago flown off to warmer places, the becks had a layer of ice, and it was curiously silent as she climbed higher and higher, the land rising steeply.

Linnet missed the sounds of nature so prevalent in the summer months. To her there was nothing sweeter than the twittering and trilling of the larks and linnets as they wheeled and turned in the lucent air.

On those lovely, balmy days it was a treat to come up here just to hear the musical choruses of the linnets, often delivered with gusto from an exposed branch of a bramble bush. They loved those bushes, these little birds, as well as the gorse that grew on the moors where they often made their nests or searched for seeds.

And on those days, in the sunlight and under cerulean skies, there was the scurry of rabbits, the calls of larger birds, the scent of warm grass, wildflowers, bracken and bilberry mingling, all so sweet and redolent on the air. Then the moors were at their most beautiful, except for late August and September, when the heather bloomed and transformed the dun-coloured hills into a rolling sea of royal purple and soft muted greens.

Suddenly the wind became fiercer, buffeted her forward and, taken by surprise, she almost stumbled on the path but quickly regained her balance. No wonder the wildlife has gone to ground, or gone away, she thought, and she couldn't help asking herself if she had been foolish to come out in this bitter cold weather.

But whenever she returned to Pennistone Royal, even after only a short absence, she usually headed for the moors at the first opportunity. When she was walking across them she felt at peace, tranquil in her mind, and at ease with herself. Up here she could think clearly, collect her thoughts and sort things out. And most especially if she was troubled. These days her troubles centred on her sister Tessa who had become her rival in various ways. And especially at the store where they both worked.

It pleased her to know that she was home again, in the place where she truly belonged.

Her mother also loved the moors, but only in the spring and summer months; Paula did not entirely share her feelings about this wild and desolate landscape in the winter, considered by some to be the bleakest county in England at this particular time of year.

It was her father, Shane O'Neill, who had a deep affinity for the high country all year round, and a rare, almost tender love of nature. She always thought of her father as a true Celt, a throwback to a much earlier century, and it was he who had nurtured her own love of the outdoors, of wild things, and the flora and fauna which abounded in Yorkshire.

She knew from her mother that her great-grandmother had been just as passionate about

the moors as she was, and had spent a considerable amount of time on them throughout her life.
'Whenever she was troubled, Grandy headed for
her beloved moors,' her mother had once told her,
years ago. Linnet fully understood why they had
given Grandy such solace; after all, she had been
born in one of the moor villages, had grown up
in the Pennine hills.

Her great-grandmother was the renowned Emma
Harte, a legend in her own time; people who had
known Emma said *she* was like her, and made com-
parisons between the two of them. Linnet simply
laughed somewhat dismissively, but secretly she
was thrilled. Who wouldn't want to be favourably
compared to that most extraordinary woman, who
single-handedly had created a great family dynasty and an enormous business empire circling
the globe?

Her mother said she was a chip off the old
block and equated her with Emma, because she
had considerable business acumen and a talent for
merchandising and retailing. 'Just like Grandy,'
Paula would point out constantly, with a proud
smile.

Linnet felt warm inside when she thought about
her mother, Paula O'Neill. She was a very special
person, fair and just in her dealings with everyone,
whatever others might believe. As for her father,
he was awesome.

Linnet had always enjoyed a perfect and most
harmonious relationship with Shane, and they had

drawn even closer after Patrick's death ten years ago. Her elder brother had died of a rare blood disease when he was seventeen, and they had all mourned the sweet-natured Patrick, retarded from birth but so loving and caring. He had been everybody's favourite; each of them had protected and nurtured him in their own way, especially Linnet. She still missed him, missed mothering him.

As she tramped on, moving ever upward, Linnet noticed tiny icicles dripping from the bramble bushes. The ground was hard as iron. It was becoming colder now that she was almost at the summit, and the wind was raw and biting. She was glad she was wearing warm clothes and boots, and a woollen scarf around her head.

Just as she knew it would, the path suddenly rose sharply, and she felt her calves tightening as she climbed higher. Within minutes she was puffing hard, and she paused to rest. Peering ahead, she realized she was only a few feet away from the crest; there, a formation of huge, jagged black rocks jutted up into the sky like some giant monolith erected as a monument to an ancient Celtic God.

Once she had suggested to Gideon Harte, her cousin and best friend, that the monolith was possibly man-made, perhaps even by the Celts themselves. Or the Druids. But Gideon, who was well-informed about a lot of things, had immediately dismissed that idea.

He had explained that the black boulders piled

so precariously on their limestone pedestal had been carried there by a vast glacier during the Ice Age, long before man had existed in Britain. Then he had pointed out that the rocks had been sitting there for aeons and aeons, and therefore were not actually precariously balanced at all. They merely looked as if they were.

Anxious to reach the top, Linnet now set off again, and suddenly, there she was, stepping onto the plateau to stand in the shadow of the immense monolith floating immediately above her. Its pedestal of limestone, formed by nature millenniums ago, was an odd shape, with two pieces protruding out on either side of a tall, flat slab which was set back. Thus a narrow niche was created, a niche protected from the strong winds that blew at gale force up here on the high fells.

Years ago Emma had placed a boulder in the niche, and this served as a makeshift bench. Linnet sat down on it, as she always did, and gazed out at the vista in front of her. And her breath caught in her throat; whenever she was seated here she never ceased to be awed by this panoramic spread of the land. It was magnificent.

Her eyes roamed across bare, untenanted fells, windswept under the lowering sky, stark, implacable and lonely, and yet she never felt lonely or afraid up here. The wild beauty of the moors captivated her, filled her with such wonder, and she relished the solitude.

Far below her, Linnet could see the fields and

pastures of the pastoral Dales, their verdant summer lushness temporarily obliterated in this harsh weather.

The fields and meadows were gleaming whitely, covered as they were with winter frost, and the river flowing through this bucolic valley was a winding, silver rope that glittered in the cold northern light.

And there, in the centre, sitting amidst the peaceful meadows punctuated by drystone walls, was Pennistone Royal, that ancient and stately house acquired by Emma Harte in 1932, almost seventy years ago.

In the years she had lived there, Emma had turned it into the most magical of places. The grounds were extensive and picturesque. Lawns rolled down to the river, and in the spring and summer months the masses of flower beds and flowering shrubs were ablaze with riotous colour.

But there were no roses anywhere in those lovely rambling gardens. It was a family legend that Emma Harte had detested roses, because she had been spurned by Edwin Fairley in the rose garden at Fairley Hall. On that day so long ago, when she was just a young girl, she had told Edwin she was carrying his child. In his panic, and fearing his powerful father, Adam Fairley, he had repudiated her, made it clear she was on her own in her terrible predicament. He had offered her a few shillings; she had asked to borrow a suitcase.

Emma had run away. From her family and Fairley village nestling in the shadow of the Pennine chain of hills. Courageously, Emma had travelled to Leeds to find her dear friend Blackie O'Neill, whom she knew would help her.

And of course he had. He had taken her to live with his friend Laura Spencer, later his wife, who had looked after her until Edwina was born. It was then that Emma Harte had made a vow: she would become a rich and powerful woman to protect herself and her child. She had worked like a drudge to accomplish this, and as it happened everything she touched had turned to gold.

Linnet's grandfather, Bryan O'Neill, had told her that her great-grandmother had never once looked back. As a young woman she had surged ahead, gone from success to success, reaching even higher, always attaining the impossible, finally becoming a true woman of substance.

According to her grandfather, Emma had apparently never forgotten that horrible day in the rose garden at Fairley Hall. Her senses had been swimming, and feeling nauseous she had vomited violently when she was alone. Emma had blamed her attack of nausea on the roses, and thereafter, for the rest of her life, she had felt overcome whenever she smelled them. The flower held such terrible memories for her she could not abide it.

Out of deference to her beloved Grandy, Paula had never permitted roses to be grown at Pennistone Royal, nor were they ever used in floral arrangements in the house. Emma's ruling still held: roses were forbidden in her homes.

Linnet had been born in her great-grandmother's house twenty-five years ago, in the middle of May. Her grandmother, Daisy, Emma's favourite daughter fathered by Paul McGill, had inherited Pennistone Royal from Emma. But she had immediately gifted it to *her* daughter, Paula, because she preferred to live in London, and also to save death duties later. Paula had lived there since Emma's death. The house meant more to Linnet than any other place on earth; even though she worked in London during the week, she came up to Yorkshire every weekend.

This past November Paula had taken Linnet into her confidence about a matter close to Paula's heart. 'Grandy made a rule years ago,' she explained. 'And it was this . . . Pennistone Royal must go to the one who loves it the most, as long as that person has the intelligence and the knowledge to look after the estate properly. I know that Tessa, as the eldest, believes I'm going to leave it to her, but I just can't, Linnet. She doesn't even like the house and grounds; they're meaningless to her. She's only concerned with what they represent in terms of power and prestige in the family. That's certainly not what Grandy wanted or intended.' Paula had shaken her head and gone on: 'Lorne has no interest in the house, and Emsie cares only about her stables.'

A loving smile had crossed her mother's face as she had continued. 'I doubt she'll ever change, bless her heart. And as for Desmond, he'll have his grandfather's house in Harrogate one day, when Grandfather Bryan is gone.'

At this juncture in the conversation, her mother had reached out and taken her hand, saying, 'And so I am planning to leave Pennistone Royal to you, Linnet, because I know how much it means to you, how much you really care. But not a word to anyone about this. Understand, darling?'

Linnet had nodded and thanked her mother profusely, and promised not to betray her confidence. She fully understood all of the ramifications involved. But Paula's words had startled her; it was the last thing she had ever expected. Deep down she was thrilled; on the other hand, she did not like to dwell on anything she might one day inherit, especially if it involved her mother and father. She was very close to them and wanted them to have long lives.

Leaning back against the limestone slab in the niche, Linnet sighed, still dwelling on Paula's words, the decision she had made. There would be trouble with Tessa if she ever found out about their mother's intentions.

It was true that Tessa did not have any genuine feelings for the house and the estate, but she did covet them, excessive greed being one of her least attractive traits. And her mother was correct, Lorne wouldn't care at all. London was his bailiwick, and he rarely if ever came north any more, except for special family occasions and holidays. He was very much caught up in his own world, the world of the West End theatre, where he was a success-ful and very popular young actor. He was truly dedicated to his theatrical career and, unlike his twin, Lorne was not avaricious or combative. He had a loving, gentle heart and had often been her fierce and loyal champion against Tessa in the past. This did not mean he did not love his sister, because he really did. Like most twins he and Tessa were very close, and saw a lot of each other. Very simply, Lorne was not particularly interested in his mother's business, nor did he have any desire to inherit any part of it. Tessa was welcome to it.

As for the two youngest of the O'Neill brood, they didn't figure in the scheme of things, as far as Tessa was concerned. Emsie was a dreamy-eyed girl, rather fey and whimsical with an artistic nature. Linnet thought of her as another true Celt, like their father Shane. Possessions were of no consequence to her; she loved her horses and her dogs more than new dresses and pretty things.

'Nonsenses,' she called the latter, rather disdain-fully, preferring to muck out the stables in a pair of jeans and an old sweater, rather than dress up to go to parties.

Linnet smiled inwardly, reflecting on her sister, of whom she was extremely protective and whom she loved dearly. Emsie, at seventeen, was a vulnerable, sensitive girl, but also riotously funny when she wanted to amuse the family. Named for Emma Harte, she had become Emsie a few days after her birth, her parents suddenly realizing that there was no room for another *Emma* in the family. The Emma who was dead still dominated them all from the grave.

The last-born child of the O'Neills was the son her father had yearned for, especially after Patrick's death. Desmond, who was now fifteen, was the spitting image of Shane: six feet tall, dark haired and ruggedly handsome, he was looking very grown-up already.

Linnet had always thought Desmond was the most gorgeous child, and he was turning into a stunning young man. There was no doubt in her mind that women were going to fall at his feet like ninepins, as they apparently had at her father's, before he was married to their mother. Desmond was the apple of Shane's eye, and of his grandfather's, the much-desired heir to the O'Neill hotel empire founded by Blackie, and built up into a worldwide company by Bryan and his son Shane, who ran it today.

Funnily enough, Tessa had always been rather taken with Desmond, favouring her youngest half-brother more than her other O'Neill siblings. 'Mostly, that's because he doesn't represent a threat to her,' Linnet had said to Gideon recently, and her cousin had nodded, agreeing with her. 'But he *is* irresistible,' Gideon had thought to add.

For a few seconds Linnet focused on her older sibling, and her face changed slightly, took on a grim aspect. Tessa, her half-sister, had been born to her mother and Jim Fairley, Paula's first husband. But Jim had been killed when the twins were small. He had died, tragically, in a massive avalanche in the town of Chamonix.

Because Tessa had been born a few minutes before Lorne, she was the eldest, and never allowed him, nor anyone else for that matter, to forget this fact. She forever reminded them she was Paula's heir apparent as the first of her six children, only five of whom were now living.

Suddenly contemplating Tessa's competitiveness and rivalry, Linnet cringed inside. She hated confrontation and in-fighting, and was usually the peacemaker in the family. Now perhaps this was no longer a viable role.

She and her cousin Gideon had discussed Tessa's attitude just the other day, and he had reminded her that Tessa was jealous of her, and envious.

Although she loathed the thought of this, Linnet had found herself in agreement with her cousin. He had pointed out how mean-spirited Tessa had been when they were children. She had also been a troublemaker at times. 'A leopard doesn't change its spots that easily,' he had muttered.

A feeling of dismay now lodged in Linnet's stomach. Nothing had changed really, even though she and her sister were now grown-up. Tessa had bullied her, bossed her around when she was little, and in some ways she was still attempting to do so, however indirectly.

Quite unexpectedly, Linnet remembered how she had stood up to Tessa when she was only five, surprising everyone, herself included, and Tessa most of all. Certainly she had shown her independence, that she was feisty, and had the spirit of Emma Harte in her. Her twelve-year-old sister had finally backed off after Linnet had proved she was a match for her.

Linnet laughed out loud, her laughter floating out across the empty fells, reverberating back to her in a series of echoes. She had just remembered an incident with Tessa's bright yellow sunhat, of which Tessa had been so proud. It had been ruined in the swimming pool at the Villa Faviola in France, and Linnet could see it now, in her mind's eye, floating so serenely in the pool. Where *she* had deliberately tossed it . . . how pleased with herself she had been.

And how angry Tessa had been with her that day, screaming that she had wilfully destroyed her expensive, brand-new hat, purchased with a whole week's pocket money at the open-air market in Nice.

On that particular morning, Gideon had roared with laughter, and so had his brother Toby, much to Tessa's annoyance, since Toby was usually one of her drooling sycophants, yes-ing her to death and fawning all over her. As he still did to this day.

As for Tessa, it had been obvious that she was so startled by Linnet's courage and audacity that she was totally flabbergasted. Their mother had been secretly amused by these goings-on, and had had a hard time smothering her laughter.

Tessa was now thirty-one and a married woman. Her husband, Mark Longden, was a well-known architect who had made something of a name for himself with his ultra-modern buildings. They had a three-year-old daughter Adele, named in honour of Tessa's great-great grandmother, Adele Fairley. Tessa was very proud of her connection to that aristocratic family, and this was another point she liked to ram home to people, at least those who were interested and would listen.

In spite of her age and position in the world, Tessa could still be mean, often for no apparent reason. The family was conscious of this, and appalled at her behaviour which they deemed to be immature, and frequently rather ugly.

Linnet and Tessa worked for their mother at Harte's in Knightsbridge, the chain's flagship store. But Tessa had a much more important job than she did; her sister managed a number of departments, while she ran only the fashion floors, and assisted her mother with merchandising and marketing. There was no question that Tessa had more power, and yet in the last few months her sister had grown increasingly hostile towards her.

Only the other day, Linnet had experienced a peculiar feeling, a premonition really, that trouble was brewing and would soon erupt. The mere idea of this was alarming, especially since the cause of Tessa's recent animosity eluded her.

The distant rumble of thunder brought Linnet out of her reverie and, startled, she sat up straighter on the boulder, lifted her eyes to the sky. It looked curdled, suddenly darker, and there was no denying that a storm threatened.

Not wanting to be caught up here in the rain, or perhaps even a blizzard since it was so cold, she jumped up. Turning away from the extraordinary view of the upper fells, she headed down the steep path at once, making for her home just visible below her in the valley.

It had been a long steady pull on the way up, but it was much easier going down, and she moved at a fairly rapid pace. Thoughts of her elder sister continued to preoccupy her. Linnet was baffled by Tessa's coldness in these last few weeks. Normally she was much friendlier. There seemed to be no good reason for the change in her demeanour ... unless she knew, somehow, about their mother's intentions regarding Pennistone Royal and who would inherit it one day.

But how could she know?

The question hovered there. Linnet pondered on it, casting her mind back to the meeting she had had with their mother in November.

The conversation had been held in private, in her mother's inner sanctum at the Leeds store. They had been entirely alone, and in any case Tessa was in London at the time. No, she couldn't possibly have any inkling of it, Linnet decided.

And yet . . . she thought of the way Tessa had directed some of her hostility towards their mother in December – at least that was the way Linnet had read it, and she was surprised at the time. Unexpectedly, Tessa had announced that she would not be coming to Pennistone Royal for Christmas. This was tantamount to sacrilege in the family, and everyone was taken aback.

For years and years the Hartes, the O'Neills and the Kallinskis had celebrated the important holidays together at Pennistone Royal. It was a tradition that had begun in 1933, just after Emma Harte had purchased the grand house and its vast estate outside Ripon.

'The gathering of the three clans,' her grandfather called it, and that was exactly what it was. Emma Harte, Blackie O'Neill and David Kallinski had become friends very early in the twentieth century, and had remained friends throughout their lives, as had their growing families. And the Hartes and the O'Neills were now joined in marriage and by blood.

'Ninety-five, ninety-six years, Linnet,' her grandfather had explained to her this past Christmas. 'That's how far our relationships go back. Spending Christmas together is mandatory. As David Kallinski used to say, we're *mishpocheh* . . . family.'

Not unnaturally, their mother had been very upset with Tessa when she had learned of her intention to remain in London over the holidays.

Dismayed and hurt, Paula had finally laid down the law as only she could, in her inimitable Emma Harte style.

Of course Tessa, in the end, had had no alternative but to acquiesce, commit to the visit, no doubt encouraged to do so by Mark Longden, who knew a good thing when he saw it. Like any smart gambler, he always had his eye on the main chance.

Ever since he had slithered so skilfully into their lives five years ago, Linnet had been scrutinizing him surreptitiously.

And she continued to observe him, saw how obsequiously attentive he was to their mother. It was quite apparent to her that he obviously regarded Paula not only as the matriarch to be kow-towed to, but Mrs Moneybags to be endlessly flattered.

Linnet had been suspicious of Mark from the beginning; had considered him to be an opportunist and a gold-digger. And she had often wondered what the beautiful Tessa had ever seen in him. For beautiful her sister was, and she could exhibit enormous charm and grace when she wanted, and considerable intelligence. And there were many other qualities in Tessa which balanced her less attractive traits. Linnet cared about Tessa; her sister was nobody's fool, she knew that. And yet she had chosen Mark. It troubled her that Tessa had married someone not quite up to par.

Eventually, and somewhat grudgingly, Tessa had agreed to spend Christmas at Pennistone Royal.

Even so, it had been a clever compromise. She had explained that they would arrive on the afternoon of Christmas Eve, in time for tea and the lighting of the tree, and depart after lunch on Christmas Day. Her excuse for such a short visit was the necessity of spending Boxing Day with Mark's parents in Cirencester.

But in essence, Tessa had given her family only twenty-four hours of her time, and Grandfather Bryan, in particular, had been very put out, mainly on Paula's behalf. He had made a few adverse comments to Linnet, after Tessa had left with Mark and Adele. He frequently confided his thoughts to her, and in this instance he had said that Tessa was as manipulative now as she had been as a child.

Despite the Christmas activities, and the presence of the other clans as well as the O'Neills, Tessa had acted rather strangely, in Linnet's opinion. Temperamental by nature, especially in her childhood when she had been prone to throwing tantrums, this characteristic seemed to get the better of her at Christmas. During the short time she was in Yorkshire, she had not even bothered to disguise her moodiness or ill temper, much to Linnet's surprise. Furthermore, she seemed hell-bent on doing battle.

Now, as then, Linnet wondered why. There appeared to be no valid reason for this curious combativeness, and she thought Tessa was being reckless in the way she constantly annoyed their mother.

Paula had not said anything to Linnet at Christmas, nor since then, regarding Tessa's questionable behaviour. But understanding her mother the way she did, Linnet knew Paula had not missed a trick. She was merely biding her time. It was unlikely that Paula would put up with Tessa's moods for very long. She was a practical woman with her feet firmly on the ground, and emotional outbursts for no apparent reason usually left her totally unmoved.

So be it, Linnet muttered to herself. What will be, will be. I'll just have to tackle things as they come at me ... if indeed they do. And in the meantime, I'm not going to worry.

But despite this promise to herself, Linnet *did* worry as she continued her trek down into the valley. She was far too astute to underestimate her sister, and she also knew that Tessa could fight a mean fight.

She hoped it wouldn't come to that. But if it did she would have to defend herself. She had no other choice.

CHAPTER TWO

Linnet was glad to be off the moors for once, and she experienced a sense of relief as she crossed the long meadow behind Pennistone Royal. It was going to snow, and very soon; she knew from experience that the worst thing that could happen was to be caught on the moors in bad weather.

When she finally arrived at the old, wrought-iron gate that led into the estate she pushed it open, hurried past the vegetable gardens, and only slowed her pace when she came to the parterres cut into the back lawn.

She stood there for a second surveying the intricate designs, as always intrigued by their geometric precision. 'Best seen from the air, them there parterres,' Wiggs used to say to her when she was a little girl and he was a young gardener. 'But I don't have an aeroplane,' she would protest, staring at him perplexed. 'An upstairs window then?' he would suggest with a big wink. And she would wink back, the way he had taught her, run into the house, up the stairs and into a back bedroom. From there she could see the parterres from high up, just as Wiggs had said. She had always had a soft spot for him; now he was head gardener at Pennistone Royal and in charge of the whole estate.

On this cold morning she thought the parterres looked a bit sad. But in the spring and summer the geometrical patterns would be bristling with tender young leaves and the small, flowering plants that brought vivid colour to the dark earth. And elsewhere on the estate the many fountains would be spraying water high into the bright sunlight, and the famous Rhododendron Walk, which her mother had created over thirty years ago, would be in full bloom. That was the time of year she loved the gardens best of all, when there was such renewal, and everything was bursting with life and the air was fragrant with mingled scents.

Linnet shivered under the sharp wind and hurried on, huddling down into her coat, wanting to get home to stand in front of one of the roaring fires, to warm herself until she was thawed out.

Within a few minutes the front façade of the house loomed up in front of her, and she came to a stop, gazing up at it with admiration. There was a timelessness about it that never failed to move her . . . how much this house must have seen over the hundreds and hundreds of years it had been standing. The dramas of families and so many lives. Happiness and joy, pain and suffering, death and loss, love and marriage and the bearing of children. An endless, enduring cycle, her grandfather was prone to saying, always adding, 'If only these venerable old stones could talk, what stories they could tell.'

Rooted in the seventeenth century, Pennistone Royal had a majestic dignity with its mingling of Renaissance and Jacobean architecture. The grey stone walls were intersected with many mullioned windows and topped with crenellated towers, whilst tall chimneys punctuated the roof. When she had been a very little girl she had thought of those chimneys as sentinels standing guard over the house and everyone in it – especially her family.

She smiled at the remembrance; she had been such an imaginative, fanciful child.

As her eyes roamed over it she realized just how much she loved this ancient house. It was her safe haven, her home, just as it had been Emma's home for so many years of her long life. Linnet felt her great-grandmother's presence in every corner of it, and this was another reason she cared about it so much. Grandy Emma would want me to have it, when my time comes, Linnet mused, but I hope that's not for years and years . . .

She lifted her eyes and glanced up at the sky as she began to walk on at a brisk pace. As usual it had changed yet again: bloated, heavy with cloud, it looked curiously luminous, streaked with pale, silvery light. Suddenly her face was thoroughly wet . . . it had started to snow and the flakes were whirling around her in great flurries, settling on her scarf and her coat.

Not wasting another moment, Linnet began to run, her loden coat flying out behind her.

Bryan O'Neill had arrived at Pennistone Royal over an hour ago, and once he had looked in on his grandson, Desmond, who was recovering from the flu, he had made his way to the upstairs parlour.

Positioning himself at a window, he had stood there ever since, looking out at the moors, anxiously waiting for Linnet to return, worried about her.

Now, as he saw her sprinting along the path, he relaxed for the first time since entering the house. Convinced that she was going to get lost in a blizzard, as she had once before, he had been on tenterhooks.

With her suddenly in his direct line of vision, his spirits lifted considerably, and he felt his taut shoulders relaxing. A small sigh escaped. He tried so hard not to have favourites amongst his grand-children – he loved them all – but there was no denying he loved this one the best, even though Desmond happened to be the apple of his eye, the long-awaited male heir-apparent.

Linnet was a wonderful young woman in so many different ways, but then so were his other granddaughters. However, there was a special reason why she was close to his heart and precious to him, and it was bound up with so many of his memories and his childhood.

Bryan strode across the room and went out into the corridor, making for the central landing. In December he had celebrated his eighty-fourth birthday, but he looked nowhere near that old. Vigorous and strong, and in robust health, he was a fine figure of a man, tall and broad-shouldered, with a shock of silver hair and the same merry black eyes his father Blackie had had, and which his son Shane had inherited from them both.

As he headed towards the grand staircase, Bryan heard the front door slam, and by the time he reached the top of the stairs Linnet was standing in the Stone Hall, struggling out of her coat and scarf.

Unobserved, he watched her as she put them away in an antique armoire near the front door.

It was her colouring, of course, that so captivated, so drew the eye to her: the glorious red hair shot through with golden lights, the translucent skin, the oval-shaped face with its fine, chiselled features, the wide-set eyes of a green so deep their colour appeared almost unnatural. She had been endowed with the famous Harte colouring, the famous Harte looks, and he thought she was the embodiment of true beauty.

Unexpectedly, in the inner recesses of his mind, he heard Edwina's voice reverberating, and he instantly fell down into the past as he recalled her comments uttered thirty years ago or more. 'All the Hartes have is pots and pots of money. Oh, and their looks, of course. There's no denying they are a good-looking family. Each and every one of them.'

Bryan had never forgotten what she had said that day, and with such awful disdain it was chilling to the bone. It had been at the party after the christening of Lorne and Tessa at Fairley Church, in the little village at the foot of the moors. He had been shocked by her tone, and truly angered by her attitude.

Edwina was a Harte herself, Emma's first-born child, and yet all she had ever wanted was to be a Fairley. Blackie had frequently said that her attitude was an insult to Emma, and Bryan had fully agreed with his father.

Yet what Edwina had said all those years ago did have a certain ring of truth to it, inasmuch as their looks were concerned. The Hartes *were* good looking, and they had been for four generations. Even the men were beautiful, and there were others in the family with Linnet's colouring. But it was she who resembled Emma Harte *exactly*, was the spitting image of her right down to the widow's peak so dramatic above her broad, smooth brow.

'Grandpops! What are you doing here so early? You weren't expected until tea time!' Linnet cried, having suddenly spotted Bryan on the landing. As she spoke she ran to the bottom of the staircase, stood looking up at him, her face ringed in smiles.

These two had been confidants since her childhood, and they were still close.

'I was bored and lonely rattling around in that big old house in Harrogate all by myself, don't you know,' Bryan answered, and started down the stairs towards her, his step firm and steady as he descended.

'There's nobody here but us chickens! Well, except for Desmond, who's still sick in bed,' she informed him, laughing. 'Paula and Shane are out.'

It still startled him when she called her parents by their first names, even though she'd been doing it for years, and he asked, 'And where are your *mother* and *father*?'

'Dad's gone to Harrogate to meet Uncle Winston for lunch—'

'At the Drum and Monkey, I've no doubt,' he interrupted.

She grinned. 'That's right, and Mummy's at the Harrogate store.'

'I looked in on Desmond,' Bryan said. 'Your father told me he was under the weather, but where's Emsie on a nasty day like this? Margaret said *she* was out too.'

'Emsie went down to the village to see her friend Anne's new horse, and she mumbled something about staying there for lunch. But you've got *me*, Gramps, and we can have a nice cosy lunch together. Margaret will be able to rustle up something special for you.'

Smiling, his black eyes sparkling, Bryan stepped

into the hall and pulled his granddaughter to him, gave her a big bear hug, holding her close, loving this girl. Releasing her, he held her away from him for a moment, and said, 'You're looking especially bonny today, mavourneen.'

Linnet smiled up at him, linked her arm through his, and led him across the Stone Hall to the grand fireplace where a pile of huge logs were blazing up the chimney back.

'Now, Gramps, how about a drop of your favourite Irish whiskey before lunch?' she asked, patting his arm, giving him a wide, warm smile.

'I wouldn't say no, Linnet, thanks, me darlin'.'

'It'll warm the cockles of your heart . . . just what you need on a day like this,' she remarked, gliding across to a chest in one corner, where an array of bottles, glasses and an ice bucket had been lined up on a tray.

Bryan remained standing with his back to the fire, enjoying the warmth from the logs. His eyes followed Linnet, and he couldn't help smiling to himself at the way she mothered him. She had been doing it since she was a child, just as she had been a little mother to her brother Patrick. It was instinctive with her, he supposed, and came quite naturally. One day, when she married, she would make a wonderful parent.

Instantly his thoughts veered to Julian Kallinski. Good-looking young man. Clever, too. Heir to the Kallinski empire. Now if he and Linnet did tie the knot, then Emma's greatest wish would be fulfilled.

The *three* clans would finally be united in marriage. He wanted that, so did Ronald Kallinski and the rest of the Kallinskis, Hartes and O'Neills.

It would be a perfect match, and he was just about to ask her about Julian when he remembered Shane's warning of only last week. Apparently there had been too much pressure put upon them, and they were 'cooling it', to use Shane's expression. No, better not mention Julian today, he decided. No point in fanning the fire.

Instead, he shifted his stance and glanced around the Stone Hall. It was large with a high ceiling criss-crossed with dark wood beams. It took its name from the local grey stone which was used everywhere – on the walls, the ceiling, the floor and the fireplace façade.

He had been sixteen years old when he had first stepped into the Stone Hall with Emma and his father. She had wanted to show them the house, which she had just bought, and they had been impressed with its grandeur. 'Wasted space,' she had muttered to Blackie that day, glancing around the great hall. And in the end she had turned it into one of the most splendid living rooms he had ever seen.

Despite its grand size, it had warmth and intimacy, because Emma had used large pieces of handsome Jacobean and Tudor furniture made of dark mellow woods, and comfortable oversized sofas and chairs.

To Bryan it looked exactly the way it had the day

Emma had finished it, although he knew Paula had done a lot of refurbishing over the years. But she had kept Emma's basic style, as she usually did in these things. And like Emma she had filled the room with flowering plants, which were housed in blue-and-white pots and copper buckets. Today, the tops of the polished wood tables and consoles were alive with pink, amber and yellow chrysanthemums, orange-red amaryllis, and many of the white orchids that Paula loved and nurtured in the greenhouse.

A moment later Linnet was back with his whiskey and a small glass of sherry for herself. After handing him the whiskey, she clinked her glass to his. 'Cheers,' they said in unison.

Bryan took a sip, then murmured in a reflective tone, 'I suppose you were up on those Godforsaken moors because something is troubling you.'

Linnet nodded, but did not volunteer anything.

He wondered if she was worrying about her relationship with Julian, and he asked, as casually as possible, 'Want to talk about it?'

Linnet hesitated fractionally, then answered in a slightly hesitant voice, 'It's Tessa. I'm worried about her. What I mean is, I'm concerned about her attitude towards me, Gramps. She's so hostile these days.'

'Nothing new about that, is there?' he asked, a snowy brow lifting quizzically.

'Not really . . . I suppose. She's often been odd with me at different times. Somewhat bullying when I was little, as you well remember. And bossy since we've been working at Harte's.'

'Competitive with you, Linnet, wouldn't you say?'

'I suppose so,' she agreed finally.

Bryan was silent for a moment, ruminating, and then he remarked softly, 'Ants in her pants, I'm afraid.'

Linnet threw her grandfather a puzzled look. 'What do you mean?'

'Mentally she has ants in her pants; can't be still in her mind. And I'm quite sure that's because she's full of anxiety about her position at Harte's. She desperately wants to be reassured that she will one day succeed your mother.'

Linnet nodded vigorously. '*Absolutely*. She thinks she will. She expects to, actually.'

'And what do you think, mavourneen?' Bryan probed, his dark eyes resting on her with great interest.

'I don't know what my mother plans to do. But Tessa *is* the eldest of Paula's children, and I suppose she's entitled to inherit my mother's job when she retires.'

Bryan shook his head vehemently. Then, taking hold of her arm, he led her towards the sofa placed nearest to the fire. 'Let's sit down,' he murmured, and after settling himself in a corner against the tapestry cushions, he continued: 'Your mother doesn't operate that way, she's not into those kind of rules, or the law of primogeniture as far as inheritances are concerned. I'm certain Paula will choose someone *she* wants to be her successor in the family business. After all, she is the largest single stockholder, not to mention CEO.'

When Linnet made no comment, Bryan added, 'Let's not forget she was trained by Emma Harte for many, many years, and that was *her* policy. *She* gave the key jobs to those who deserved them and could handle them. Paula will do the same.'

'I guess you're right, Gramps, but Tessa does very well at Harte's, you know. She's a pretty good executive.'

'Could she run the store in Knightsbridge? And the whole chain as well?' Bryan asked, looking at her keenly.

Linnet bit her lip and glanced away, acutely aware of her grandfather's penetrating gaze, thinking of the discussions she'd had with Gideon about this very subject. And with her cousin India Standish, who worked at Harte's. They believed that Tessa would never be able to cut it, but she fully acknowledged they were prejudiced, having suffered at Tessa's hands in the past. Especially when they were children.

Clearing her throat, Linnet said, 'As an executive Tessa's very good, well organized, practical, and she handles the daily problems with skill . . .' Linnet's voice suddenly trailed off as she thought of the rows her mother had with Tessa about the future and planning ahead. She stared at Bryan, then sighed. 'Oh gosh, Gramps, Tessa's my sister and I love her . . .'

'There's a big *but*, I suspect, when it comes to certain things to do with her work.'

'I think so. She's great on a day-to-day basis, as I said. But Tessa never considers the future or plans ahead.'

'No real vision, perhaps,' Bryan pronounced. 'There's got to be vision in any business, but especially in retailing, otherwise the stores will go nowhere. Except down the drain eventually. That's always been one of your mother's strong suits, Linnet. Paula has had tremendous vision over the years, still does, and Emma often commented on it to me. It made your great-grandmother very proud, and she felt secure about leaving Harte's to her.'

'Mummy's a genius in so many ways. You know, she's really been annoyed about Tessa's attitude regarding my project. Tessa thinks my idea for a fashion retrospective is ridiculous, that it won't succeed. But I know it will, and Mummy's given me her blessing.'

Bryan frowned and shook his head, his expression startled. After a moment's thought he murmured, 'But your fashion retrospective is a natural. It's bound to bring in hundreds of women, and when they're in the store they'll spend money on the fashion floors.'

'Exactly, Gramps! That's the whole idea, but Tessa doesn't get it.'

Or doesn't want to, Bryan thought, but said, 'The main thing is that it's going to be a big success. You mustn't worry about what Tessa says or

36

thinks . . . only your immediate boss, and that's your mother.'

She nodded. 'Mummy's thrilled I'm using such a lot of Grandy's *haute-couture* clothes. Vintage clothes are very *in* these days, and the retrospective does cover eighty years. It'll be fabulous and will pull in a lot of young women. India agrees.'

'I do too, as I just said. And tell me, how is little India working out?'

'Very well, grandfather, and she's not so little either. She's quite the dashing young woman.'

'So I noticed on New Year's Eve.' He chuckled. 'I always think of India as being little. You know, in the sense of petite, dainty, very delicate and feminine.'

'That she is. But getting back to Tessa, Gideon says she doesn't know how to handle people, that she has no empathy or compassion.' Linnet sat back and made a small grimace. 'Mummy's always said it's important to feel compassion for people if you're an employer, and Gideon thinks Tessa lacks that quality.'

'Do you?'

When Linnet was silent, Bryan knew the answer. But she was a fine young woman and he knew how much she disliked criticizing others. Deciding not to press for an answer, he leaned back against the cushions once more, and studied her for a moment, and quite unexpectedly his throat tightened with emotion. For he saw not Linnet O'Neill, his twenty-five-year-old granddaughter but Emma

Harte when she was twenty-seven and his surrogate mother. He had been born in December 1916, and his biological mother Laura O'Neill had died almost immediately after his birth. With his father Blackie away fighting in the First World War, there was only Emma Harte, his parents' best friend, to look after him. And so she had taken him home from the hospital and brought him up as her own. And it was *her* face he had gazed up at from his crib, *her* face he had learned to love at such a tender age.

And now, eighty-four years later, he was staring into that same face at this very moment. Of course it was not Emma he was looking at, it was Linnet, but to him she was Emma Harte reincarnated, and the resemblance between them was uncanny.

'Gramps, are you all right? You've got such a funny look on your face,' Linnet said, sounding concerned about him.

Sitting up straighter, Bryan blinked several times, then smiled at her. He coughed behind his hand, and after a moment replied, 'I have some photographs at home of your great-grandmother when she was about your age, maybe a couple of years older than you are now. And you *are* her, Linnet. Why, it's as if Emma has been reborn in you. It's not only that you're the spitting image of her physically, as everyone tells you these days, but you have so many of her facial expressions and her gestures, and you think like her. Certainly you have her drive, energy and talent for retailing, and you're a good businesswoman. You'll get even better, too, with a bit of age on you.' He smiled at her. 'You're the best, in my opinion.'

'You're prejudiced, Gramps.'

'Perhaps. But nonetheless, you're going to be fine . . . another Emma Harte.'

'I'll try to live up to all of the things she was, and stood for. I know she had great integrity, that she was a most honourable woman, one who knew right from wrong, and was just and fair in all her dealings.'

'That she was indeed, and you'll do her justice. I've no qualms about you, mavourneen.' He reached out, took her hand in his. 'My money's on you, Linnet, and in my opinion it's *you* who should take over from your mother when she retires. Harte's should be yours.'

'I'd like that very much, but it really is up to my mother.'

She's probably chosen you already, Bryan thought, but for once he did not confide in his granddaughter. Instead he said, 'I want you to have those photographs of Emma. I'll bring them with me the next time I come over.'

'Oh, thanks, Gramps, I'd love to have them. I'll treasure them.'

A moment later Margaret came hurrying into the Stone Hall, and in her usual quiet and efficient way, she said, 'Lunch is ready, Mr O'Neill . . . Linnet. If you'd like to come into the morning room, I'll serve it in there, it's much cosier than the dining room, with the fire an' all.'

'Thanks, we'll come right away, Margaret,' Bryan said, pushing himself to his feet. 'Linnet did tell me that you'd be rustling up something special for me. Well, that's the way she put it. So what's for lunch?'

Margaret laughed and explained, 'Oh, some of your *real* favourites, Mr O'Neill. I had a crock of Morecambe Bay potted shrimps put away for lunch tomorrow, but I thought you'd like to have them today with some of that nice thin brown bread and butter of mine, and I've made your real favourite, a cottage pie with fresh ground beef and a crust of mashed potatoes, puréed parsnips and peas. And for pudding you can either have freshly baked apple crumble with warm custard, just the way you like it, or trifle.'

'Goodness, Margaret, you've done me proud! Everything sounds delicious,' Bryan answered, smiling at the housekeeper. Then, turning to Linnet, as they walked together across the hall, he added, 'I'm seriously thinking of moving in here.'

'I wish you would, Gramps!' Linnet exclaimed, tucking her arm through his, meaning every word she said.

'The idea is tempting, mavourneen, but I think it's best I remain in Harrogate. After all, Blackie built that house, and I've lived in it forever it seems, and I'm keeping it warm for Desmond, so to speak. It'll be his one day, when I'm gone.'

'Let's not talk about you going anywhere!' Linnet cried, bustling him forward in the direction of the morning room. 'You've got lots of years ahead of you.'

'I hope so, Linny, but as Blackie used to say, when you get to be over eighty, a man's living on borrowed time.'

The two of them sat down for lunch at the round walnut table which stood in the bay window of the morning room. Until very recently this had been an office, rarely used, which Paula had considered wasted space. A few months before Christmas she had turned it into a spot for intimate casual meals, such as breakfast and light lunches, or tea in the afternoon. Now everyone used it.

The morning room had a springlike feeling because of Paula's decorative scheme based on pale apple-green and white: green walls, green-and-white-striped balloon shades at the windows, green-and-white-checked fabric on the chairs around the table. Accentuating this look were a collection of thirty-six botanical prints hanging on one wall and jugs of yellow and white chrysanthemums which stood on a long, carved wooden sideboard and a Queen Anne chest placed in a corner of the room. Adding a welcoming, cosy touch on this snowy day was the blazing fire in the hearth; a small loveseat and armchairs covered in rose-coloured linen were arranged around a coffee table in front of the fire, and it was here that tea was often served.

As always, Bryan admired Paula's decorating. His daughter-in-law had a way of making a room look elegant, but it was never intimidating because she had the happy knack of creating a sense of comfort in the midst of the elegance.

Linnet said, 'A penny for your thoughts, Gramps.'

He smiled at her. 'Wasn't thinking of anything much. But . . .' He paused, leaned across the table and asked in a conspiratorial voice, 'Any more information about Paula's plans for Shane's birthday?'

Linnet nodded. 'Mummy spoke to me about it the other day. Uncle Winston's also going to be sixty in June, and she said she was considering making it a joint birthday party for the two of them. Actually, she told me she was going to speak to you about it, Grandfather.' Linnet gave him a hard stare and her brows pinched together in a frown. 'I guess she didn't.'

'No, she—' Bryan broke off as Margaret came hurrying in with a tray; a moment later she was placing a plate of potted shrimps in front of him, then brought one over for Linnet. 'The brown bread and butter is already on the table, Mr O'Neill,' she said, then glancing from one to the other, she asked, 'Do you need anything else?'

'We're fine, Margaret, thank you,' Linnet replied. 'Thanks very much.'

The housekeeper nodded, then flashed a smile and disappeared.

Bryan picked up a fork and plunged it into the

tiny pale-pink shrimps encased in the round of hardened butter. 'Mmmm. They're delicious,' he said after a moment. 'A *joint* party, eh? And where does your mother plan to have it?'

'Here at Pennistone Royal . . .' Her voice faltered as she noticed that his expression seemed to change. 'Don't you like the idea of a party for the two of them?'

'Sure an' I do, I think it makes great sense, Linny, darlin'. Your father and Winston have been best friends all of their lives, since they were boys, and then as young men they shared Beck House in West Tanfield. What rascals they were when they were little,' he said, chuckling, '*and* when they were young spalpeens chasing after the girls. Handsome they were, too.'

'They still are,' she shot back, laughter echoing in her voice.

'True, only too true. But they got their wings clipped all right, that and they did! And by Emma's favourites . . . your mother and Emily.' Bryan grinned at her. 'Fell like ninepins, the two of them, when those beautiful Harte girls batted their eyelashes.' He shook his head, still smiling, and continued to spear the blush-pink shrimps with his fork.

Linnet confided, 'Mummy wants to make it quite a fancy bash, Grandpops. You know, a marquee in the garden, dancing under the stars, and all that stuff. I suppose the only thing that's really worrying her is the weather. June can be cool, and sometimes rainy.'

'Yes, it can, but the house is big enough for a grand party, sure an' it is, mavourneen,' Bryan murmured. 'Emma gave a dinner-dance here in the fifties and it was wonderful. *She* did the whole bit with a marquee outside, just like your mother is planning, but Emma used it for cocktails, and dancing later. It was the Stone Hall that was set up for dining, and, as I recall, there was another band indoors in case of rain. It all worked well . . . such a lovely night it was.'

'Mummy said she'd heard Grandy talk about that party once. She thought you'd know all about it and that you'd be able to help her do something similar.'

'I will that,' Bryan replied, a look of pleasure settling on his face. 'I do believe I have some photos from way back then. I must look them out.' He stared off into the distance for a moment, recalling this event of long ago, and obviously he was filled with happy memories from the beatific smile on his face.

Margaret cleared their plates, served the steaming hot cottage pie and vegetables, and then slipped out of the room quietly. Linnet and her grandfather went on to discuss her brother Desmond and his many talents, but eventually they fell silent as they finished lunch. These two had always been comfortable in each other's company, were at ease with each other, and words weren't always necessary.

At one moment Bryan sat back and stared across the table at Linnet. In the cool northern light coming in through the bay window her colouring was so very vivid it startled momentarily. Yet there was a paleness, a translucent quality to her skin today, and she looked suddenly quite fragile.

Yet Bryan knew how strong she was both mentally and physically. She had enormous willpower, as well as stamina and energy, even though she was a slender girl.

She is going to need all the strength she has, he thought, just as she'll need her wits about her. Tessa wants it all, has convinced herself she's entitled to it all, and she'll fight for what she believes are her rights. Intuitively, he knew that Paula would give everything to Linnet. This was her child by Shane, the great love of her life, the hero of her childhood, her true soul mate, and Linnet was their love child, very much desired, and conceived in great passion. Furthermore, she was cast in the image of the woman who had founded the Harte family dynasty and a great business empire. Yes, there was no question about it, Linnet was irresistible to Paula. Also, she was best suited to take Paula's place one day. She was level-headed, steady as a rock, with a cool nerve, and an insight quite remarkable for her age.

All this aside, Tessa did not have Linnet's business acumen, her vision or her stamina ... all necessary attributes required in the person running Harte stores. Paula, shrewd, calculating, and with a mind like a steel trap when it came to business, knew this. She might not discuss it with anyone, but Bryan *knew* she knew what Tessa's shortcomings were.

He had been resistant to Tessa's charms when she was little, long before Shane and Paula were married. Even then he had been wary of Jim Fairley's child, detecting in her vanity, duplicity and a tendency to lie. And later it had irritated him that she had been so envious of Linnet. Now that they were grown up Tessa was not only envious but she resented Linnet, most especially her looks. Those were simply an accident of birth, to do with genes, and there was nothing anybody could do about them.

Tessa's other resentments were bound up with the Fairleys, with Shane who had been a loving father to her, but was, nonetheless, still perceived as the stepfather, and with Emma Harte. The last was easy enough to fathom; at least he had fathomed it all out finally.

There'll be tears before bedtime one day very soon, he thought, taking a sip of his water. His instincts told him trouble was brewing and that Tessa had Linnet in her line of fire. It was going to be nasty. He wished it could be different, but he knew that was not possible.

The die was cast. It had been cast long ago.

CHAPTER THREE

'It's only the flu, Dad, I'm not dying,' Evan said, balancing the phone between her ear and her shoulder, reaching for the box of tissues on the beside table. 'I'll be better in a couple of days,' she added, then blew her nose several times.

'It doesn't sound like it to me,' Owen Hughes responded swiftly, then exclaimed, 'Oh, just a minute, honey! A couple of customers have walked in.' Putting the phone down on his desk, he stepped out from his office into the main room of his antique shop in New Milford, Connecticut, to greet the two women who had entered. But when he saw that his assistant Darrell was already moving forward to look after them, he retreated and returned to his desk. He picked up the phone again and went on, 'Sorry about that, Evan.'

'It's okay, Dad. How's Mom?'

'Not much change . . .' His voice, suddenly deflated, trailed off.

Instantly she wished she hadn't asked the question.

Her mother had gone into one of her depressions about ten days ago, just before she had left for London, and when her father had come to New York to take her to Kennedy Airport he had been worried about his wife, and down in the dumps himself.

Summoning a cheerful voice, Evan said, 'As I told you when I called you on Wednesday night, George was so nice when I arrived, and he's been very kind to me since. As soon as he knew I was ill, on Friday, he had a doctor here to see me within a few hours. So try not to worry about me, Dad.'

'I can't help it,' Owen answered, and then had the good grace to laugh. 'And I know, before you tell me, that you'll soon be twenty-seven. But I can't change the way I feel about you. I guess you're still my little girl. And listen, honey, I'm glad George is there for you: he's a great guy, and he thought you were the cutest kid on the block when you were little. He'll help you any way he can, and so will Arlette. You only have to ask them.' A small sigh escaped. 'I just wish you'd waited until spring to go to London. January's such a lousy month. It's snowing, I've no doubt.'

'It's going to be a rainy Sunday tomorrow, Daddy. But I don't care, I won't be out in it. And I'm very cosy here in the hotel.'

'At least I don't have to worry about you missing meals, not eating. I know George keeps a good kitchen, and the hotel has room service.'

'It does, but I'm not hungry. Arlette has poured

a lot of soup and hot tea down me, though, these last few days.'

'Just take care of yourself, Evan.'

'I will, and thanks for calling, Dad. Have a great weekend, and I bet you'll have a big crowd for your lecture tomorrow.'

'I hope so, but not *too* big a crowd. As you know, the shop only holds about sixty,' he answered with a laugh. 'Don't go out until you feel better, honey. That English dampness can be treacherous. *Promise.*'

'I promise, and give my love to everyone.'

'I will. Bye, sweetheart.'

'Bye, Daddy.'

When she hung up, Evan slid down in the bed, pulling the covers up to her chin. She had started with the flu the night she arrived from New York. That was Wednesday. Now it was Saturday, and she still didn't feel all that much better, even though the doctor had prescribed various medicines which she had been taking religiously.

But better to be sick *here* than in some awful commercial hotel, Evan thought glumly. Once she had made the decision to come to London, her father had insisted she stay at the small family hotel in Belgravia owned and run by his old friend George. Her father had met George when he had gone to live in London as a young man, and they had been friends ever since. She was glad now that she had agreed. George Thomas, whom she barely remembered from her toddler years, was a lovely

Welshman, and his wife Arlette was one of those completely competent, take-charge Frenchwomen who seemed to know everything about everything. They had been warm and welcoming when she had arrived and given her a most comfortable room that was both inviting and full of real charm.

It was on the top floor, one level down from the attics under the eaves of this grand Victorian townhouse, which they had turned into a small but attractive hotel some years before. The room was decorated with lovely, colourful floral chintz fabrics and handsome Victorian furniture, including this wonderful four-poster bed where she now lay cocooned in two feather-light duvets. She felt coddled and cared for, thanks to Arlette's expert ministrations and motherly interest.

Despite this tender loving care, Evan would have given anything not to be sick. Her plan had been to go to Harte's department store in Knightsbridge when she arrived without wasting any time. Once there she had intended to seek an appointment with Emma Harte, using her grandmother's name as an introduction. But the flu had laid her flat. Next week, she thought. I'll go next week to see Emma Harte.

Ever since Glynnis Hughes had died last November, Evan had felt lost. That cheerful, encouraging, stalwart woman had always been there for her as long as she could remember. Her gran was forever boosting her morale, cheering her on, telling her she could do anything she wanted, as long as she put her mind to it and worked hard. Evan had always believed that Glynnis had been more of a mother to her than her own mother.

An image of her mother suddenly insinuated itself into her mind, and Evan's thoughts turned to her. Marietta Hughes had been a talented artist once, but something awful had gone wrong, and she had given up, given up on life in so many different ways.

When Evan had told her father she was considering going to London for a year, he had been instantly enthusiastic about it. But almost immediately she had noticed the look of sorrow enter his eyes, saw a sudden dulling of their brightness, and she had realized at once that he, above all others, would be the one to miss her the most. Her mother wouldn't miss her. Marietta hadn't even noticed her absence after she had left home and moved to New York, and that had been nearly ten years ago.

But on that day in the middle of December she had quickly backtracked, had told her father that perhaps she wouldn't go after all. But he had insisted she take this sabbatical, as he called it, reminding her that he had done the same thing himself over thirty years ago, had gone back to visit London, where he had been born during the Second World War. It was at this time that he had met her mother, then an art student studying at the Royal College of Art. Marietta Glenn. A beautiful blonde girl from California with whom he had fallen madly in love. He had married Marietta in London. 'And don't forget, *you* were born there,' he had reminded Evan that particular afternoon.

After they had talked about London and her impending trip, Evan had then confided her grandmother's last words to her father. He had been just as startled and baffled as she had been. 'But Emma Harte must be very old now. I vaguely remember my mother once saying that she had met her during the war, just before she married her wonderful GI Joe, as she called my dad, and came to America. As you well know by now . . . it's family history. I doubt my mother's name will mean anything to her, Evan, so don't be disappointed, honey, if you don't get a reaction.'

She had promised him that she would not let anything disappoint her on this trip to England, and she meant it. Her father had hugged her and told her how important she was to him. He had then explained that she would have no problem working in London because she had dual nationality, as he did. Born in England to a British-born American father and an American mother meant that she was a legal citizen on both sides of the Atlantic.

Finally a date had been set for her departure and her father had made all of the arrangements with his old pal George, and he had gone on to say that she should think of George and Arlette as family, but without infringing on their time or abusing their good will. 'Have fun, and most of all be happy, Evan,' Owen had said with a big smile, hugging her to him again. 'Life's too short for misery.'

That day she had thought what a wonderfully courageous and positive man her father was. He was cheerful, and had an even temper most of the time, despite the burden of her mother, a woman who might as well be dead for all she cared about living. What had gone wrong in her mother's psyche? How often Evan had asked herself that, for years now, but she had no answers for herself. There were women, she knew, who enjoyed being ill, but surely no woman could enjoy this. There were so many things Evan didn't understand. After all, her mother had doctors, and they prescribed medication all the time, and her mother took them. Yet she was still wrapped in a cloak of depression. Or was she?

Evan had often asked herself if her mother faked it at times, in order to retreat from her husband, from them all, from responsibility, from the world. What an awful thing, if that were true.

I want to live my life to the fullest, Evan thought. I want to follow my dreams, fulfil my ambitions. I want a career in fashion, just as I always dreamt of having. I want to meet a wonderful man, get married, have children. I want a life. *My own life.*

Evan, curled up under the duvets, half dozed, half drifted with her thoughts.

Her father had wondered out loud if she would

be happy in London when they had discussed her impending trip in December. She wasn't sure, but it was worth giving it a try. That was why she had come: to meet a challenge, seek her destiny.

This was the city of her birth, and she had lived here until she was almost four. It was then that her parents had returned to New York; soon after they had settled in Connecticut, where Elayne and Angharad had been adopted, just a year apart.

And it was there that Owen Hughes had raised his family in a rambling old house in Kent, sometimes with the help of his mother, whilst launching himself into his own antique business. He was following in the footsteps of his father; Richard Hughes had taught his son everything he knew, and Owen had studied on his own, learning more, enhancing his knowledge to the fullest.

It was her grandparents who had brought her back to London when she was twelve years old. Her grandfather, Richard, had been coming to London on a buying trip, and he had invited Glynnis and Evan to accompany him.

Part of the time she and her grandmother had gone with him in search of beautiful antiques, for his shop on East Tenth Street, making trips to the country towns just outside London, or driving down to Gloucestershire and Sussex in search of all manner of precious things. It had been an adventure for her and she had loved every moment.

The two of them, she and her gran, were sometimes alone, when Grandfather was off making important transactions with other dealers. It was then that Glynnis had taken her out to see Windsor Castle, Hampton Court and Kew Gardens. And she had learned about British history, especially Welsh history, from her grandmother, who knew a lot and was articulate in the telling of it all.

It had been lovely weather that particular summer, and the three of them had enjoyed the time they spent together. Her grandfather loved the theatre, and so they had gone to see plays in the West End, and one night they had even had supper at the Savoy Hotel, in the elegant dining room overlooking the River Thames. Another evening, after a play, Grandfather had taken them to Rules, the old and very famous restaurant which her grandparents had favoured for years. These treats had been special for a girl of twelve, and she had never forgotten them.

After almost two weeks in London they had crossed the English Channel to France, where her grandfather had hoped to find other interesting items and small treasures for the shop. He had been an expert in English Georgian furniture, and had also specialized in English and European china. That was the real reason for their trip to France: the quest for rare porcelains in perfect condition.

It was from his father that Owen had learned all about English and European porcelains, as well as furniture. 'I studied at the knee of the master,' he often said, and he was now a leading expert and dealer in the field today. Over the years Owen had made something of a name for himself as an antiquarian; he frequently gave lectures at his shop, and people came from all over to hear him speak, and to learn.

Evan knew how much her father loved antiques, and she was well aware that his work had been his great saviour over the years, especially when they were growing up and their mother was incapacitated.

Angharad, the youngest, had shown a talent for spotting 'the good stuff', as her grandmother had called it. Knowing that she had what he called 'a good eye', Owen had taken his daughter into the business when she was old enough, and she worked with him at the New Milford shop for part of the week, and on Sundays.

Elayne, who was the middle child, was an artist and painted very well, Evan thought, and she had a small studio near the family home in Kent. Her paintings were shown in a gallery their father had created within his New Milford shop, and sold very well. People liked her evocative landscapes and sun-filled beach scenes, most especially her mother-and-child studies, which touched a chord in everyone.

In a certain way Evan had thought Glynnis was her best friend when she was growing up, and especially when she was in her late teens. She had gone to live with her grandparents in Manhattan at the age of seventeen, and after six months, when she became eighteen, she had enrolled in the Fashion Institute of Technology on West 27th Street, where she had studied fashion design, her true vocation.

Now, suddenly, her thoughts went to her grandmother's will. She and her father had been taken aback by it. Glynnis had left almost four hundred thousand dollars, and the amount had taken their breath away momentarily.

'Where did it all come from?' Evan had asked her father, once they had left the lawyer's office a few days after Glynnis's funeral.

Owen had shrugged, looking nonplussed. 'Damned if I know, honey, but my mother was always frugal, and also a good businesswoman. She kept my father's books at the shop for years and she had a good head for figures, he told me. I know she liked to dabble in the stock market a bit. Over the years she did quite well, but your gran was prudent, cautious, and she also tended to scrimp and scrape. I guess that's where her money came from – her own thrift and prudence.'

Her father had received the bulk of the money and his mother's apartment, which Glynnis had inherited from Richard after his death several years earlier. There had been nice bequests to Elayne and Angharad, and she herself had received the sum of thirty thousand dollars, much more than the other two girls. But she was the eldest grandchild, and they had understood. Their grandmother's few pieces of jewellery and small trinkets had been left to her sisters and herself. Very generously, Glynnis had passed on several of the really good pieces to their mother, obviously not wanting to leave Marietta out, or slight her daughter-in-law.

Follow your dreams, Owen had said to Evan. She would try. Certainly her grandmother had made that possible. Evan had been able to come to London under her own steam, without asking her father for money, and for this she was grateful.

Her grandmother's dying words again reverberated in her head, and she couldn't help wondering why Emma Harte was her future. What had Glynnis meant by that? Evan had no idea. And she wouldn't know until next week, when she was well enough to go out.

Rousing herself, Evan got up, went over to the chest of drawers near the fireplace. On top of it she had arranged a selection of family photographs. She picked up the one of her grandparents and herself when she was twelve, taken here in London on the famous trip.

She stared at the photograph for a few moments, studying it. In the background were the gates of Buckingham Palace. It had been a sunny day and she was squinting into the sun, and looked sedate in a plaid skirt, a white blouse, white ankle socks and patent-leather shoes gleaming in the sunlight, their shine very visible in the picture.

She half smiled at the youthful image of herself, thinking she looked so gangly and awkward with her long legs and skinny shoulders. Her hair had been cut in bangs, a straight dark line across her forehead, and the hairstyle did not suit her. She recognized that now, but she had known it then as well.

Her grandfather, tall, straight backed, almost military in his bearing, was wearing a dark blazer and grey trousers, and looked very smart with his pale blue shirt and navy tie. His hair was pepper-and-salt, and his light grey eyes twinkled in his lean, craggy face. Still a handsome man, just as he had been in his younger days.

Her grandmother was quite amazing looking in the photograph. She had been sixty-five at the time, and she had stopped tinting her hair long before. It was a cloud of silver around her still-youthful face, and the blueness of her eyes appeared very sharp in the picture. That wide smile Evan had known and loved all of her life was in place on Glynnis's face, which as usual reflected her loving nature.

Grandparents were important, she was fully aware of that. It was only through them that you really knew who you were, where you came from, what you were all about. In a sense, great-grandparents were of even more importance, for what you gleaned about *them* gave you considerably more insight into your grandparents, your parents, and your-self. You carried their genes, their blood, and also their hopes and dreams and aspirations. All of these elements were there in you, inherited, flowing down through the bloodlines over several gen-erations. Knowing about your family background gave you a sense of direction, and of purpose, she thought, and told you so much about who and what you could become. It gave you and your life meaning.

It was because of her grandmother that she was here in London. And next week she would come face to face with her future on the day she went to Harte's in Knightsbridge. If her grandmother was to be believed . . . She had faith in Glynnis; she had always had faith in her.

CHAPTER FOUR

Once lunch with her grandfather was over, Linnet made her way to the attics in the East Wing of Pennistone Royal. She had been working up there at weekends for several months, and had almost finished cataloguing Emma's couture clothes.

After opening the door with her key, she stepped inside and switched on the light, then stood for a moment, glancing around, a smile of pleasure flitting across her face.

These attics were special to her, more than ever since she had arranged everything the way she wanted. What made them unique was their size; they were not at all like the small, low-ceilinged rooms usually found under the eaves of most houses.

Spacious, with fairly high ceilings, they had been remodelled by her great-grandmother many, many years before. Emma had had the walls lined with cedar, the floors covered with carpeting stretching wall to wall, and she had installed excellent lighting, comparable to that used in the Harte stores. Cupboards with deep shelves had been specifically designed to hold boxes of varying sizes, where all manner of things could be safely kept free of dust. Emma had created a series of splendid storage rooms for all of her clothes, and for fashion accessories such as shoes, hats and handbags, and costume jewellery as well.

As she moved forward, Linnet couldn't help congratulating herself on the reorganization she and her cousin India Standish had done in the last few months. When her mother had asked her to sort out the muddle in the attics, it had not taken her very long to realize there was no *real* muddle. The basic problem was that many racks had been pushed close together and filled with innumerable dresses, gowns, and all kinds of outfits and ensembles.

She and India had decided there was only one way to organize the clothes, once the racks had been properly spaced out. They did it by designer name rather than by category of clothing, as her mother and Aunt Emily had done some years before. Designers now had a rack, or racks, with his or her name posted in bold letters.

It had always been something of a wonder to Linnet that so much had been kept. Even as a child she had liked to roam amongst the racks of clothes, admiring the beading and the embroidery, touching the beautiful fabrics – the chiffons, satins, silks and velvets.

Her great-grandmother had had perfect taste,

and everything had been kept in excellent condition by her, and later by Paula and Emily. Some years earlier her mother had installed air-conditioning, which was kept on low the whole year round, so that there was total climate control to preserve the clothing.

Normally the ensembles were kept in dust-proof, zip-up garment bags made of cotton, but she and India had taken many of the outfits out of the bags in order to make decisions about them. She glanced at them now as she walked along an aisle in between the racks; it struck her that she could use almost all of her great-grandmother's clothes in her retrospective, especially since she was covering eighty years of fashion.

Emma's ensembles dated back to the 1920s and featured many great designers. In particular she had favoured three French designers in their heyday: Pierre Balmain, Cristóbal Balenciaga and Christian Dior. But she had bought from Vionnet and Chanel in Paris; Hardy Amies in London; the French-American designer Pauline Trigère, based in New York, and the Russian designer Valentina. Her couture house had also been in New York until her retirement in 1957. The clothing aside, there were all those wonderful accessories. It was an enormous treasure trove of elegance and style.

Linnet knew she could easily finish the last of the cataloguing tomorrow. Now she had a specific purpose – finding a missing evening gown which her aunt had told her about last week. Emily had discovered it years ago in Emma's Belgrave Square flat, and had used it in a display of fashion Paula had once put on in the early 70s, which her mother had called Fashion Fantasia.

'It's a *must*, you have to use it,' Emily had told Linnet. 'It's really not lost, just mislaid. I'll bet you anything it's in the attics at Pennistone Royal, since it's not in London. Look for a very large flat box, a dress box, and I think it has a Harte's label on it, rather faded. I found it in that box and I put it back there, as far as I remember. As you well know, beaded dresses are heavy, the weight of the beads pulls the fabric down and makes a mess of the shape. So I know it's not hanging in a dress bag.'

Emily had gone on to describe the dress: 'A sheath of pale blue chiffon covered all over with thousands of tiny bugle beads of pale blue and emerald green. It's simply gorgeous. Oh, and there's a pair of emerald-green silk evening shoes by Pinet of Paris.'

When Linnet came to the end of the first aisle of racks, she headed for the long work table she used for different jobs, and put her shopping basket of tools down on it. Dragging the stepladder closer to one of the tall, built-in cupboards, she opened its doors and climbed the steps. As she leaned forward and pulled out a large box, a number of others tumbled to the floor. Backing down the ladder, she put the box she was carrying on the table. It was very heavy, and when she lifted the lid she saw it contained lots of shoe boxes neatly lined up next to each other.

At this moment her mobile began to ring; reaching into her basket, she grabbed it. 'Hello?'

'It's me,' her cousin Gideon announced.

'Hi! Where are you, Gid?'

'At the stables in Middleham. When I phoned the house, Margaret told me to call you on your mobile. Where on earth are you? You sound as if you're on the moon.'

She laughed. 'Not quite. But I am up in the attics of Pennistone Royal.'

'Good Lord, it's years since we've been up there . . . playing with all those old toys.'

'Not those attics, silly. I'm in the East Wing where all of Grandy's clothes are stored. I'm actually looking for an evening gown your mother told me about last week.'

'Oh gosh, that's right. Your big project is in the works. Eighty Years of Elegance and Style,' he said, laughter in his voice.

'Don't make fun of me, Gideon. The retrospective is going to generate a lot of traffic in the fashion department, and that means sales.'

He was suddenly chagrined, knowing how seriously she took her work. He would never tease her about that, and swiftly he exclaimed, 'Now *you're* being silly. You know how much I respect you, and your work, Linny. Would I ever do that to you?'

'I don't suppose you would, Gid. You *are* coming to dinner tonight, aren't you?'

'Course I am. That's why I'm phoning, actually . . . Listen, do you think it will be all right for me to bring a guest? Will your mother mind?'

'I'm sure she won't. You know how she likes to play Mother Earth, invites the whole world to partake of her food. Who do you want to bring?'

'Actually, Linnet, it's Julian.'

'*Kallinski!*?'

'Is there another Julian in your life?'

'No, and he's not either. Mummy won't mind if you bring him to dinner, but I certainly will.'

'Oh come on, Linnet, you know how you feel about him.'

'And how's that, Gid?'

'You love him.'

'Yes, that's true . . . in the way I love you. Like a cousin, or a big brother.'

'Liar!'

'I'm not a liar, and it's true. Since we grew up together, as you well know, we have a very fraternal relationship.'

Gideon did not respond, and she was wondering if she had lost him, if the connection had just gone dead, when he said, 'It's not the way Julian portrays your relationship.'

'I think you're fibbing, Gideon Harte.'

'No. I'm not. I *know* he loves you, *and* in the most romantic, man-woman sense.'

'Is that what he said to you?'

'Yes, it is. More or less. Scouts' honour,' Gideon answered, sounding suddenly serious.

66

'I knew men were worse gossips than women,' Linnet muttered. 'What else did he say?'

Ignoring her jibe, he answered, 'I believe he wants to tell you *that* himself.'

'When?'

'Tonight.'

'He's not with you now?' she asked, riddled with curiosity.

'No, he went to see his grandfather. Sir Ronald's not been feeling well, a bit under the weather. But Julian's staying with us in Middleham.'

She was silent, her mind racing.

'Well, can he come to dinner or not? Come on, you know you want to see him.'

Linnet hesitated then said, 'I guess it'll be all right. My mother's having a bit of a crowd, I think.'

'She is?' Gideon sounded alarmed. 'Who's coming?'

'Well, Gramps is here for the weekend, so that's another O'Neill, making six of us altogether *if* Desmond and Emsie join us for sups. And then there's Emily and Winston—'

'I know my parents are coming,' he cut in.

'India said she might fly up from London to help me with the last of the cataloguing and the packing of the clothes, but she hasn't appeared so far. Oh, and Mummy said something about Aunt Amanda coming too.'

'She was supposed to be staying with us, but she's not arrived either.'

'The blizzard didn't amount to anything much after all. So Amanda's probably just late, not lost in a snowdrift somewhere. Oh, and by the way, Gid, I think Mummy invited Anita Shaw, just to even out the numbers.'

'Good God, I hope not!' Gideon exclaimed. 'I can't bear that girl . . . I do wish your mother would stop trying to fix me up with women. I'm quite happy as I am, the proverbial bachelor.'

Linnet laughed. 'Somebody's going to catch you one day, Gid.'

'You will tell your mother about Julian coming, won't you?'

'Yes. And listen, I was teasing you about Anita. She's not invited. I think my mother's given up on trying to get you married. I suppose we're going to have to rely on a total stranger to sweep you off your feet.'

'That'll be the day!' he shot back, chuckling. 'I'll see you later then, and don't work too hard.'

''Bye, Gid,' she answered.

Linnet stood leaning against the stepladder for a moment, her mind on Julian. She wondered if she had made a mistake, allowing her cousin to bring him to dinner. In the last year she had felt totally mixed up about their relationship, which is why she had pulled away from him six months ago. Julian had agreed they should have some breathing space, and they had stopped seeing each other by mutual consent.

Despite the closeness of their families, they had only run into each other once since, and that was at Christmas here at Pennistone Royal. But like Tessa, Julian had fled as quickly as he could without appearing rude.

She closed her eyes, saw him in her mind's eye. Tall, slender, darkly handsome, with the most penetrating blue eyes she had ever seen. His cold blues, she called them, when he got angry.

Linnet felt a sudden and terrible longing for him, and she was momentarily startled. He had been part of her life for as long as she could remember, from the time they were toddlers, and an indispensable part of her existence since she was fifteen. She missed him . . .

'I'm sorry I'm so late.'

Linnet snapped her eyes open with a start, and straightened against the stepladder. Her cousin, India Standish, was hovering in the doorway, carrying her own shopping basket, her tortoiseshell glasses pushed up on top of her mass of curly, pale blonde hair.

India was twenty-seven but looked much younger, and was pretty in a soft, delicate way. She had large, luminous, silvery-grey eyes and an expressive, sensitive face, reminiscent of the Fairleys. She had their blood running through her veins. Without a doubt, India was the most popular person in the family. She was considerate, gentle in her ways, and had an understanding heart. Everyone loved her.

Walking into the attic, India asked with a small frown, 'Is something wrong, Linnet?'

'No, I'm fine. Why?'

'You're rather pale, and you look . . . well, slightly troubled.'

'Oh, it's nothing of any importance, India,' Linnet answered and, pushing her mobile into the pocket of her loden-green trousers, she continued more briskly, 'I pulled out that very big box over there on the table, and a lot of others fell down. We'd better pick them up. Maybe the missing dress is in one of them.'

'Don't worry, darling, we'll find it,' India murmured in her soothing voice which held a lovely lilt, a hint of her upbringing on the estate at Clonloughlin, which belonged to her father Anthony, the Earl of Dunvale.

Placing her shopping basket of tools on the table, India added, 'I'm quite sure we can finish everything by tomorrow night, so don't worry.'

'I hope we can. We have to go back to London on Monday morning. Early. We've a lot to do at the store, India.' As she spoke, Linnet carried one of the larger boxes to the table; India did likewise.

Together, the two great-granddaughters of Emma Harte sorted through the flat boxes which contained so many things that had belonged to their famous forebear. But after an hour's search the beaded dress had not turned up.

'It can't have walked away. It must be somewhere,' Linnet remarked to India, and then hurried off down an aisle between the racks. 'Let's look in that big built-in cupboard in the smaller attic next door. Maybe we'll be lucky,' she said, disappearing from view.

India hurried after her. 'I think that built-in is full of suitcases; old leather suitcases that belonged to Grandy.'

'I don't remember seeing any there,' Linnet answered, sounding puzzled. 'I wonder who could have put them there?'

'Who knows. But certainly Aunt Emily might easily have packed the evening gown in one of them,' India suggested.

'She was positive she'd put it back in the box she'd found it in, one with a faded Harte's label on the lid. But she could be mistaken,' Linnet said over her shoulder. 'After all, it was years ago.'

'To be sure it was,' India murmured.

A moment later the cousins stood in the smaller attic staring at the shelves in the tall cupboard. It was stacked to the hilt with boxes. But just as India had said, there were also a number of leather cases on the lower shelves.

The young women lost no time in taking out all of the boxes, and as soon as Linnet saw one with an old Harte's label attached to the lid, she shrieked. '*Voilà!* I bet it's in here!' At once she pulled the lid off, and was staring down at a glittering mass of pale blue and emerald-green bugle beads. 'We've found it!' she exclaimed triumphantly, then lifted the gown out of the box, held it up to the light,

71

gazing at it. 'Isn't it beautiful, India?' She pressed the beaded sheath against her body, stood looking down at the dress.

'Grandy must have been a sensation when she wore it, don't you think?' India said. 'What with her red hair and green eyes. And you don't look half bad yourself, the way you're holding it against your body. The colours are wonderful for you. You know, Linnet, it has a sea-like effect, all those blues and greens mingling.' India gave Linnet a big smile. 'The gown seems to undulate when you move. Maybe you should keep it for yourself. You love vintage clothes more than anyone I know.'

'It's too valuable,' Linnet responded, laughing. 'And the beading has been very cleverly worked, that's why it undulates,' she explained, then carefully laid the dress on top of the long table. She began to examine the embroidery and the overall workmanship, marvelling at both as she scrutinized the gown intently. She was amazed at its condition, realized how well it had been preserved over the years, which was the reason it looked almost new.

In the meantime, India had made a discovery of her own, and she was excited by her find. She exclaimed, 'Linnet, come over here and look at this.'

'What is it?' Linnet asked without turning around, her attention on the lining of the evening gown.

'It's a suitcase that belonged to Grandy. I just opened it up and there's a smaller case inside marked *Private and Confidential*. And her name is on the same luggage label. Oh, and here's a little key attached with a bit of string to the handle.'

'What's inside the smaller case?'

'I don't know, I haven't looked. After all, it is marked private and confidential . . .' India's sentence trailed off as she untied the small key and opened the case, murmuring, 'Since our great-grandmother has been dead for many years, I suppose I can lift the lid at least.'

'Of course you can,' Linnet said confidently.

'Linnet, please do leave that dress and come and look at what I've found. *Please*.'

Struck by the excitement and urgency in her cousin's voice, Linnet jumped up and went to join India on the floor in front of the built-in cupboard.

She crouched down on her haunches next to India and followed her gaze. 'Oh my God!' Linnet's hand flew to her mouth as she stared into the large suitcase. It contained the smaller one, which India had just opened, and Linnet couldn't believe what she was looking at. Her eyes widened, and she reached out, touched the leather-bound books lying there side by side. What she was seeing made her heart miss a beat. And she was speechless all of a sudden. At last she said in an awed voice, 'Emma Harte's wartime diaries. Oh, India, what a find!' She lifted one out and read the date embossed in gold on the black leather cover. 'Nineteen thirty-eight. Long before we were born, and even before our parents were born. Gosh . . .'

'This is a treasure trove, you know,' India volunteered. 'They run right through to nineteen forty-seven. Did you notice that?'

Linnet nodded, then tried the lock on the 1938 diary, which was still in her hands. It opened easily. Linnet was about to look inside the diary, but hesitated, then very resolutely she closed it again.

India, sounding nervous, said, 'I'm glad you didn't read anything. I know Grandy's been dead longer than we've been alive, but I think it is rather an invasion of privacy, reading her diaries, don't you, Linny?'

'I do, and I think it's my mother's decision. After all, she was Emma's chief heir. My mother should see them first. I'll take them down to her when we've finished up here.'

'Yes, yes, that's the wisest thing, to be sure,' India agreed.

Linnet put the diary back in its given place in the small case, and then slowly smoothed her hand over the ten books, her expression reflective, her eyes suddenly far away, as if she saw something no one else could see. After a moment or two, she focused her attention on the diaries. All of them were bound in black, the year embossed in gold, and she was sure none of them were locked. She could not help being curious about their contents, wondering what secrets they contained, and she longed to read them.

But her integrity, bred in the bone, would not permit her to violate her mother's trust in her.

The golden rule in the family was that anything pertaining to Emma Harte first passed through Paula, head of the Harte dynasty.

Linnet was honour-bound to abide by that rule.

CHAPTER FIVE

Although she was fifty-seven, Paula McGill O'Neill looked younger. Her head of thick, luxuriant dark hair, coming to a widow's peak above her smooth brow, was still the colour of jet, although she was the first to admit that it got a little help from her hairdresser these days. Her eyes, her most spectacular feature, were still that amazing deep violet, thickly fringed with dark lashes. They had always reflected her intelligence, but wisdom and compassion dwelt there now as well.

She sat in the upstairs parlour at Pennistone Royal with her cousin Emily Harte, but her thoughts were on her daughter Linnet, and Julian Kallinski, whom at one time she had thought Linnet would marry. She wished her daughter had confided in her more; wished that Linnet had not made such sweeping and drastic moves without at least one discussion. But when she herself had been in her twenties she had been headstrong, too; had believed she knew everything.

Oh, what it was to be young and impulsive, and so convinced of the rightness of what one did. She had married Jim Fairley when she was very young, and lived to regret it, as she had come to understand that it was Shane O'Neill who held her heart. But at least things had eventually worked out for her and Shane. They had been married now for almost thirty years, their love growing deeper and deeper with the passing of time.

Eventually, Emily said, as if reading her thoughts, 'I think Linnet and Julian were made for each other, as you and Shane were—'

'And you and Winston, too,' Paula interrupted, as she roused herself from her thoughts of her daughter.

'*True*. Anyway, I was going to say I hope those two begin to realize this, and very soon. Wouldn't it be nice to have a lovely family wedding in the summer with the three clans present?'

'You see, there you go, Emily!' Paula exclaimed, shaking her head. 'Bringing the clans into it. But yes, you're right, it would be nice. In the meantime, there's Gideon for us to worry about. He's still a bachelor.'

'He doesn't settle down with any of the women he dates. Brief encounters, I call them,' Emily muttered.

'He just hasn't met the right woman yet, that's all,' Paula asserted. She pushed herself up from the chair, walked across the floor of the upstairs parlour where they were sitting.

Emily's eyes followed her. She thought her cousin looked beautiful tonight with her new short hairdo: sleek, stylish and youthful. She was wearing a long, straight, amethyst wool skirt and a matching turtleneck sweater that brought out the colour of her eyes and was a foil for her dark hair. The outfit was simple, even a little severe in a way, but it suited Paula, who was tall and slender.

Emily wished she had a figure like Paula's, but try though she did she always looked slightly plump in comparison. No wonder Paula had affectionately dubbed her Apple Dumpling when she was little. She was still fighting the childhood propensity to put on weight.

In all the years of their growing up together they had never exchanged a cross word or had a quarrel, although sometimes the eight-year-old Paula had reprimanded Emily when she was five and they were staying at Heron's Nest, Emma's summer home in Scarborough, and she had been what Paula called 'a pest'. Cousins, best friends and confidantes, they had been each other's rock in times of trouble and adversity.

For the most part, these two had been brought up by Emma, were trained by her, and today they ran a large part of her empire between them, and did so with great skill. They were devoted to their grandmother's memory, and in a sense they were the keepers of the flame.

Pausing at the door of the bedroom which adjoined

the upstairs parlour, Paula said, 'There's something I want to show you before the others arrive.'

'What?'

'Linnet and India found it in the storage attics and—'

'The famous beaded dress!' Emily declared triumphantly.

'No, not the dress. Oh, they found that all right, but they came across something else, something much more important.'

'Hurry up then, I'm intrigued.' Emily sat back, an expectant look on her face.

A moment later Paula came back carrying the old brown leather suitcase, the small one which contained the diaries. She placed it on the coffee table in front of Emily, and then, leaning forward, she lifted the lid.

'This is it,' she said, glancing over her shoulder to look at her cousin.

'What's in it, actually?' Emily asked, full of curiosity.

'Grandy's diaries. From 1938 to 1947. Ten of them, and they're all in the most beautiful condition. I suspect she stored them in this case for years, and that's why they're so well preserved.'

'Oh my God, what a find!' Emily cried, leaning forward, staring at the set of black leather, gold-embossed diaries placed side by side in consecutive order within the case. 'But where on earth have they been all these years? And how is it the girls just found them? I mean, why didn't *we*?' She glanced at Paula, frowning. 'How could we have missed them?'

'You're going to have a good laugh when I tell you where they were stored for years, Emily.'

'*Where?*'

'In that walk-in closet in the ground floor office.'

'Not the one which is now called the morning room?' Emily asked, her eyes wide with surprise.

'Exactly. They'd been there for years. This one and five others, all part of a matched set of luggage from Asprey. Grandy used that office every day when she was at Pennistone Royal, and for years and years. So it was definitely she who put them there. This small case was actually inside a larger one, otherwise I would have noticed the luggage label marked confidential. Anyway, I moved them when I revamped that room a few months ago.'

'And you never looked inside any of the cases?' Emily asked, incredulity echoing in her voice.

'No. Why would I? They weren't heavy. I just assumed Grandy had kept them there because there was no space left in the luggage room. Which there isn't. And it was a convenient place. Actually, I never gave them a second thought, not even when I used that office myself. I had Margaret put them down in the basement when I redecorated.'

'So how did they find their way to the attics?'

'Margaret took them up there. We had a dreadful flood in the basement two weeks ago, and she remembered the cases when she was taking other

80

things out to safety. She knew they were good, hardly used, and she put them in the smaller attic, in the first cupboard where there was space.'

'Thank God she did. If she hadn't, the cases and the diaries would have been totally ruined, destroyed.'

'You're right, we're lucky she acted so promptly.'

Emily glanced at the open suitcase again, and then turned to her cousin. 'Have you read any of them?'

'I haven't. Linnet only gave them to me a couple of hours ago.'

'Are you going to?'

'Eventually, I suppose.'

'Shall we look inside one now?' Emily asked. 'I'm very curious.'

Paula hesitated, and then nodded. 'All right, if you want to, Emily.'

Reaching into the case, Emily pulled out the diary dated 1938, opened it and glanced at the first page, then she handed it to Paula silently.

After scanning the page in the same cursory way Emily had done, Paula put the diary back in the small suitcase. 'I don't think we should be reading these . . .'

'I know what you mean, they're very private. On the other hand, Paula, I have the feeling Gran wouldn't mind *us* looking at them. I think she'd want us to read them, actually.'

'Perhaps you're right. But for now I'm going to lock the case and put it away somewhere safe. And maybe in a few weeks or so we can read them together. If you'd like that, Emily?'

'Oh yes, I would, that's a good idea. Gran was articulate, you know, and actually she wrote rather well I thought. She expressed herself most eloquently at times.' Emily paused, and then leaning toward Paula, she said quietly, 'I'm sure there are a few secrets in there, don't you agree?'

'I don't really know . . . did she have any during the war years? Paul was dead and she was grieving, coping with our uncles being in the services, running a big business under wartime conditions. What kind of secrets could she possibly have had?'

'Well, I didn't mean sexual, or anything like that! I bet she never wrote that kind of thing down. Really, Paula, Gran was very proper.'

'She also had a number of husbands, let's not forget that.'

'Only two. And two lovers.'

'And that was that. So I'm sure there are no secrets buried in those diaries.'

'You never know. Anyway, everyone has secrets,' Emily pronounced.

'They do?' Shane said from the doorway, startling them both, making them jump as he strolled into the room. 'Are you quite positive of that?' He was smiling broadly as he came to join them by the fireside.

Paula said, 'I didn't get a chance to tell you earlier, Shane, but India found a case full of Grandy's diaries in the attic. I was just telling Emily about their discovery, showing them to her.'

'How wonderful,' he said, glancing at the case on the coffee table. 'I see they're her private diaries.'

'Yes, it's a great find, but we've decided not to read any of them. At least not now.'

Shane looked down at her, his eyes loving as he said, 'You've made a good decision . . . wait for the right moment. After all, these are sacrosanct . . . a woman's private thoughts and feelings. Those should be treated with great respect.'

Later, as she sat near the fireplace in the great Stone Hall, Paula glanced around at her family, as always pleased and happy to have them gathered around her at Pennistone Royal.

Everyone had finally arrived. Shane had mixed drinks for those who wanted whiskey or vodka, and Linnet and India had poured champagne into tall Venetian flutes and passed them around.

Although she rarely drank, Paula had elected to have a glass of champagne tonight, and she sat sipping it, her eyes roaming around the room. They came to rest on her cousin . . . and staunchly devoted ally, Emily. She was currently engaged in deep conversation with Emsie, the two of them sitting in a corner near the fireplace. Those two had bonded early in Emsie's young life, and they were particularly close. When Emily had been a teenager, she had loved horses, and had been a champion rider in all manner of equestrian events in Yorkshire.

Mucking out stables had been fun for Emily, just as it was for Emsie. They had a lot in common, in many areas, quite aside from loving each other. How pretty Emily looks, Paula thought. Her cousin was wearing a sage-green silk tunic over fir-green wool twill trousers, so narrow and well cut they might have been tailored for a cavalry officer. The green emphasized the loveliness of her eyes, and her soft blonde colouring, while the outfit made her look slimmer, Paula noted.

She experienced a sudden, wonderful surge of warmth and love for Emily, who had been her stalwart companion since childhood. There was nobody like Emily in the whole family, not really. Loving, kind and sincere, she was also a tough businesswoman, direct, with no frills attached, and outspoken to the point of bluntness. There were times, at meetings, when she took Paula's breath away with her pithy comments, most of which usually made Paula laugh hilariously.

Even Emsie had made a big effort tonight, Paula realized, as her eyes lingered on her seventeen-year-old daughter. *Emsie* . . . another original, Paula thought, smiling inwardly. Usually she looked dishevelled and grungy in unattractive clothes that Paula wanted to rip off and burn. In fact, the only time she looked halfway decent was when she wore her riding clothes. But tonight there had been a sudden reversal, and Emsie was attractively decked out in scarlet wool trousers and a matching turtleneck sweater, which Paula recognized. Didn't they belong to Linnet? Well, she'd obviously borrowed them. Red was a marvellous colour for Emsie with her black hair and black eyes.

No mistaking who *she* is, Paula thought, scrutinizing her intently. She was Black Irish, a true Celt, the epitome of an O'Neill. Her eyes swept over the three men in her life: Shane, Desmond and Grandfather Bryan. They were standing together talking near the big armoire, obviously engrossed in some topic, horses and racing, no doubt. Tall, long-legged, broad shouldered all three of them, descended from Shane Patrick Desmond O'Neill, known to the world as Blackie. They had inherited their looks and their colouring from him. Bryan's hair was pure white now and Shane's tinged with silver at the sides, but Desmond, at fifteen, had hair as black as coal. Her three devoted men, how she loved them. Like Emsie, the youngest of the clan, they were unmistakably O'Neills right down to their boots.

And there was her other child, Linnet. She was a true Harte, no two ways about that, with red hair shot through with gold and green eyes. She had chosen to wear black trousers and a black sweater with a scooped-out neck, and she looked taller than ever and very slender, her hair a fiery halo around her pale face. Tonight she appeared quiet and reflective, unsmiling. Paula was certain it was because of Julian's presence.

Shifting slightly in the chair, Paula's eyes scanned the Stone Hall, and finally she spotted her great ally,

Gideon. He was standing at the far end, engrossed in conversation with India, his first cousin and close friend. Like Linnet, Gideon was pure Harte, with dark russet hair and light green eyes, very white teeth in his lean, tanned face. He loved sports and had recently been to Switzerland for five days' skiing, where he had caught the sun. He was good looking, like his father Winston, and just as stable; devoted to the family in the same way Winston had always been.

Her eyes settled on her cousin Anthony's daughter, India. Lady India Standish. She had an honorary title as the daughter of an earl. Another blonde in the family, a dainty, fragile-looking girl, with delicate bones and soulful eyes. Soft, gentle; but Paula knew that India had a great deal of strength, and was a true and loyal friend to Linnet. She carried the Fairley blood through her grandmother Edwina, and there were those who said she had a strong look of *her* when *she* had been young. Paula felt protective of India, although Shane laughed at her when she said this, reminding her that India had the courage of a lion and could easily stare down an army without flinching. She was the family's favourite because of her loving kindness, her tenderness and compassion for others. Paula knew that she was also very brave.

Paula spotted another family favourite, and her great friend and colleague, Winston. Her cousin, Emily's husband. He was travelling across the Stone Hall in long strides, intent on joining his best friend

Shane. Winston's red-gold hair had faded and was touched with grey, but just as the O'Neills were stamped with a particular look, so were the Hartes, passed down from Emma and her brother Winston. This Winston, the one walking across the stone floor tonight, had been very special to Emma, a great favourite, perhaps because he had looked so much like her. 'The salt of the earth,' she had called him, and it was true. He was very charming, dashing. Emily had been smitten with him when she was sixteen, and no wonder. These days he was a commanding figure, her staunchest supporter in all things, whether business or family matters. She loved Winston like a brother.

As she sat back in her chair, sipping her champagne, Paula let her gaze finally rest on the son of one of her dearest friends, Julian. He had, in the last few minutes, edged closer to Linnet, and now they were speaking to each other quietly, standing a little apart from the others. How she wished she could hear what they were saying. Oh to be a fly on the wall, Paula thought, and hoped they were ending their silly separation, which had been Linnet's idea. And not a very good one at that. Julian was already a member of the family by the very nature of his birth, and a full-blown member of the third clan; everyone liked and admired him.

He was a truly nice young man – perhaps too nice in some ways – and he had many excellent qualities. He adored Linnet and always had, and because of this he was a little too submissive to her will, Paula thought. He's so right for her, though, and he understands that she will have so much responsibility one day. Just as he will. And they have a shared history, the past, and their childhood that binds them together irrevocably. He *is* admirable, thoughtful, kind, intelligent, even a bit of an intellectual, and fun loving. The latter is so important for Linnet, who tends to be a workaholic.

Suddenly, there he was, moving in her direction, coming across the floor in rapid strides, looking hell-bent and determined about . . . something. And something important at that, she decided, if the look on his face was anything to go by.

Then he was hovering over her, tall, dark-haired, just like his father Michael, his eyes clear, bright blue and unblinking. Filled with the honesty and sincerity she had first seen there when he was only a child.

Julian was a pleasant-looking young man, lean and slender . . . perhaps a little too thin right now, Paula thought. He was, as usual, well dressed in a dark blazer worn with dark grey trousers and a black turtleneck sweater.

'I need to talk to you for a moment,' Julian said, smiling down at her. 'In private,' he added softly.

Paula nodded, stood up instantly, her hopes soaring unexpectedly. Perhaps he was going to speak to her and Shane about Linnet, about becoming engaged, and was testing the waters with her first before jumping in the deep end with Shane. But surely he knew they were all for this match . . .

He interrupted her thoughts as he placed his hand under her elbow and led her across the Stone Hall to a quiet corner away from the fireplace, where everyone was gathered, talking amongst themselves as they sipped their drinks.

'Let's sit here for a moment.' He indicated two straight-backed chairs, covered in tapestry, placed near a circular table.

Once they were settled, she stared at him expectantly.

Always straightforward and direct, Julian got right to the point. 'My grandfather wondered if you could pop over to see him tomorrow? If you're not too busy.'

'Why, of course I'm not. But is something the matter? I know he's not been feeling well.' Her face clouded over with concern.

'Oh he's all right, suffering from a bit of rheumatism, and he's had a bad cold. But Grandfather's a tough old bird, don't you know, and as sharp as he ever was. He actually wants to talk to you about . . .' Julian broke off, leaned closer, lowered his voice and murmured *sotto voce*, 'Jonathan Ainsley.'

Paula stared at him disbelievingly, her body instantly stiffening. '*Jonathan*,' she repeated. 'What on earth could Uncle Ronnie have to say about him?'

'Apparently your cousin has returned to England.

Permanently. Grandfather heard through his bankers in the City that Jonathan plans to open a business in London.'

For a moment she could not respond. She felt a trickle of apprehension run through her, and although she did not know it, she had turned considerably paler.

'But is Uncle Ronnie sure of this?' she asked at last. As the words left her mouth she knew the question was a foolish one. Ronald Kallinski, her wise rabbi ever since Emma's death, always knew exactly what he was talking about.

Julian nodded. 'Oh yes, he's *quite* sure. He feels for you and he needs to talk. He's obviously not very happy about this sudden turn of events.'

'Jonathan Ainsley can't hurt me, or create problems with the company. I own fifty-four per cent of the stock, and that's what matters in regard to the Harte stores. Even if he bought some of the stock that's being traded on the London Stock Exchange it would be meaningless because I own the majority of the shares and control many more. And as far as the other companies are concerned, they're all controlled by me, Winston, Emily and Amanda, privately held by the family. And as tight as a drum. Emma saw to that before she died. We are invulnerable. But you know all this, Julian,' she pointed out, sounding confident and sure of herself. 'We've never had any secrets within the three clans.'

'I know, and I agree with you. On the other hand,

Grandfather did sound rather concerned about the return of the dreaded Mr Ainsley.'

Paula laughed, then responded, 'I'll go and see him tomorrow, if only to reassure myself that he's all right.'

Julian gave her the benefit of a wide smile. 'You've always worried about everyone for as long as I can remember. Linnet's right when she says you're a genuine earth mother. And look, I can come and get you tomorrow, drive you over to Harrogate to see Grandfather.'

'Well, if you're sure it's no trouble.' It suddenly occurred to her that she might easily use the opportunity to speak to him about Linnet.

'It's no problem at all. And anyway, it will give us a chance to chat about Linnet.' He threw her a coolly calculated look and added, with a small smile, 'I bet you were thinking exactly the same thing, weren't you?'

He's astute, just like his grandfather, she thought, and then nodded. 'Well, yes, I was,' she admitted.

Leaning even closer to her, Julian said in a low, confiding voice, 'It's all going to be fine, so don't worry. I know Linnet better than I know myself. She wanted to step away from our situation to take stock; she thought we were being pressured into marriage. We weren't, not really, but ...' He paused, shook his head, finished, 'Please don't worry.'

'I can't help it,' Paula answered, and then hesitated.

'You know, life does have a way of taking care of itself,' he announced in a firm voice, before she had a chance to say anything else. 'Tell me later what time you want me to come and fetch you tomorrow, and I'll be here.'

He moved away; Paula watched him return to Linnet's side, and then at once her thoughts went to Jonathan Ainsley, her cousin. He had betrayed the family and tried to steal the stores from her, but she had outwitted him, and in a certain sense she had destroyed him. He called her his nemesis and she was. He had vowed to wreak his revenge. And she knew he would. A cold chill settled around her heart.

CHAPTER SIX

Harte's was the most imposing edifice in Knightsbridge, an important landmark ever since the first day it was finished, and its glamour and prestige were renowned the world over. Almost everyone who visited London felt compelled to make a stop at Harte's, always to browse and marvel, usually to buy . . . *something*, however small.

On this cold Tuesday morning in the middle of January, Evan Hughes was finally hurrying towards the magnificent store, filled with excitement and anticipation. It was acting like a magnet, pulling her forward, and she couldn't wait to enter its stately portals.

Evan paused, but only for a moment, to peer into the beautifully dressed windows that fronted onto Knightsbridge. How imaginative and tasteful they were, and she felt a little frisson of anticipation as she pushed open the doors and went inside the vast and impressive establishment.

She stood for a moment blinking in the bright lights and glancing around. How spectacular it all was. She was in the cosmetics department and there was a glitter and shine to everything, from the products themselves to the decorative elements which added their own unique touches.

Slowly Evan walked through the department, admiring the flair that was very much in evidence in the displays of creams and lotions, lipsticks, powders and perfumes, breathing in the scented, rarefied air as she strolled along.

Suddenly she caught sight of her own reflection in one of the counter mirrors and she stopped, paused to check her appearance before moving on, satisfied that she looked well put-together. Her make-up was perfectly applied, her hair fresh and glossy, and she felt better than she had in days.

After her bout with the flu, which had lasted ten days in the end, she had been drained, a bit weak in the legs. But last night she had decided she did not want to put off visiting Harte's any longer, and she had made the decision to come to the store today.

Earlier that morning she had washed her hair, done a skilful make-up job and dressed with care. Her choice was a stylish black trouser suit which emphasized her slenderness and height, and black leather boots. Over the suit she wore a long, black wool coat that came down to her ankles, and was not only well tailored and elegant but had a certain dash to it. Adding a flash of bright colour to the ensemble was a long red wool scarf which she had thrown around her neck. Other than this accessory her only adornments were gold earrings and a watch.

Although Evan did not realize it, she cut quite a swathe as she strolled on through the cosmetics department; a number of people turned to look and admire.

But she was totally oblivious to the attention she drew, endeavouring to feel more at ease and relaxed. She was lost in her thoughts as she headed towards the information booth.

The young woman in the booth looked up and smiled as Evan came to a standstill in front of the window, and asked pleasantly, 'Can I help you, madam?'

'Well. Er. Yes. What floor are the management offices on?'

'The ninth,' the young woman answered.

'I'm assuming Mrs Harte's office is on the same floor,' Evan ventured, staring at her questioningly.

'*Mrs Harte*,' the young woman repeated and frowned, shook her head. Then she exclaimed, 'Oh, you must mean Mrs O'Neill . . . Mrs Paula O'Neill. A lot of people get her confused with her grandmother.'

'And her grandmother is Emma Harte?'

'*Was*. Mrs Harte is dead. Has been for quite a while.'

Taken aback though she was, and instantly

dismayed, Evan said quickly, 'Yes. Yes, I was getting them confused, that's true. And Mrs O'Neill's office is on the ninth floor, isn't it?'

'It is.'

'Thanks very much,' Evan murmured, and with a quick nod she hurried away, not quite sure where she was heading in the store. But it certainly wasn't towards the bank of elevators which would whiz her up to the management offices.

At this moment what she really wanted was to sit down and have a cup of coffee and think about her grandmother's last words to her. Because the words uttered by the girl at the information desk had just negated her grandmother's instructions to 'go and find Emma . . . your future is with her.'

Emma Harte was dead. Had been for quite a while, the young woman had said. That could mean anything. A few months, a year, or maybe even a few years.

It struck her now that her grandmother and Emma Harte must have been about the same age, since they had seemingly known each other in the Second World War. Mrs Harte had probably passed away recently, just as her gran had. Well, so much for that, she muttered, and glanced around.

Evan had been walking without paying much attention to her surroundings, and now she realized she was in the jewellery department. Approaching a sales person she asked politely, 'Excuse me . . . Is there a restaurant on this floor?'

'There's the Coffee Café on the other side of the

food halls. Just keep walking straight ahead, you'll come to it,' the young man told her with a smile.

'Thanks,' Evan said, and walked on. Within a couple of minutes she had traversed the huge, well-stocked food halls and was standing in front of the Coffee Café. Pushing open the opaque-glass doors she went inside, glancing about as she did so.

The café was small and attractive, and redolent with the smell of coffee. It was almost empty; she made for a booth where she sat down and took off her scarf.

A moment later she was ordering a pot of coffee, and as she waited for the waitress to bring it, Evan pondered on her predicament. She had come to the store hoping to see Emma Harte and hoping to get a job; without this important contact there was no possibility of that now.

Sighing, she leaned back against the banquette and closed her eyes, filled with dismay again. Her thoughts were on Glynnis. Almost two months ago now, as she lay dying, her gran had told her to come to London to seek out Emma Harte, and she had implied that Emma Harte had something to do with her future.

Had her grandmother been delirious? Or living in the past? Didn't that sometimes happen to people when they were dying? Didn't parts of their past lives flash before them like a reel of film unravelling? She'd read that somewhere. She had believed her grandmother that day, because she had no reason not to do so. And yet just before she had left, her father had pointed out that she might not get a reaction from Mrs Harte, since Glynnis had known her in the Second World War. And that had been sixty years ago, after all. Over half a century ago. Too long.

How foolish she had been to take everything on face value. Why hadn't she checked things out? Because she had trusted Gran. Irritation with herself swept over her and she experienced a rush of frustration. Here she was in London, with nothing to do, no prospects. The trip had been a waste of time, and, more importantly, money.

No, that's not really true, she thought, sitting up straighter on the banquette. The pot of coffee had materialized while she had been lost in her thoughts, and she poured herself a cup, added milk. As she sipped it she decided she deserved a vacation, and she also reminded herself she had no real reason to worry, at least not for the moment, thanks to the money her grandmother had left her.

Immediately she zeroed in on the legacy that she, her siblings and her father had received from his mother. The overall amount Gran had left was enormous, at least to them it was, and was something of a mystery. Her father had attempted to explain it away, yet it did seem incredible to her that Gran had accumulated such a princely sum.

Her grandparents had lived comfortably, but there had never been any great wealth. In fact, it struck her that they had always lived rather modestly. *Why?* They could have indulged themselves a little bit with the kind of bank balance Glynnis had obviously had. On the other hand, perhaps Gran had been hoarding the money for her son and granddaughters.

Suddenly her father's puzzled expression flashed before her eyes . . . how truly surprised he had been in the lawyer's office that day. Startled and confused. Just as she had been. Her grandmother had been a dark horse.

Her father deserved this windfall from his mother, deserved to inherit his parents' apartment, which Glynnis had left to him. Evan was glad he had finally decided to keep it, rather than put it on the market, something he had been contemplating doing. The apartment was on East Seventy-Second Street and Madison Avenue, a great location; real estate was bringing excellent prices at the moment, so the idea of selling it had been tempting to him.

Evan regarded the apartment as an escape hatch for her father, much to be desired, and she was relieved when he said he planned to use it instead of unloading the place. It pleased her that he now had somewhere to stay overnight when he went into Manhattan; also, it was his own private space, a safe haven away from her mother, and to Evan that was of immense importance. Marietta had become a depressed and lethargic woman, listless and without any interests, and she had turned into a recluse. But *why*?

Evan bit her lip, shook her head sadly. So many mysteries in her life . . . so many questions . . . and no answers. She pushed these thoughts away from her. Mysteries were for another day.

The cup of coffee had warmed her, given her a boost, and she felt much better, more relaxed. And slowly she began to formulate a plan.

She had given up her job in New York, so why go back? There was no reason. Why not stay in London for a few months? The weather would get better soon, and she'd always wanted to come back here . . . after all, this *was* the city where she was born.

But what to *do*, how to occupy herself? Her kind of sightseeing would be finished in a couple of weeks, then what? Get a job, of course. And why not a job here at Harte's? She liked the look of this grand store. No, it was more like an emporium, she decided, and somehow it had a connection to her gran, however tenuous that was.

So why not go up to the management offices and apply for a position here? There was nothing to stop her, was there? No, nothing at all, a voice whispered in her head; go for it, girl. Evan smiled to herself. Glynnis would have said exactly that, and she would have added, 'You've nothing to lose and everything to gain.' Another smile flitted across her face as she thought of her grandmother.

If she was absolutely truthful with herself, Evan knew she had seized on her grandmother's dying words, had taken them to heart – in order to leave New York and her family. She loved them all, most especially her father, but she needed to be on her own. She needed to be free.

London had beckoned her, suddenly beguiling, and she was here. And here she would stay, at least for a while. And you never knew what was going to happen. As her gran had always said, 'Life is full of surprises, Evan, make the most of the good ones.' Perhaps her future *was* here after all, she thought, her face brightening.

Evan stepped out of the elevator on the ninth floor and found herself in a small lobby. To her left was a blank wall, to her right a pair of wooden swinging doors with glass windows set in the upper panels.

Only way to go, she thought, as she turned to her right and pushed through the doors into the vast corridor. Slowly she walked along, looking from side to side at the various doors, reading the different names on each of them.

Halfway down the corridor, arched alcoves on each side broke up the flow of doors, and Evan paused, stood staring at a large oil painting hanging above a narrow side table in one of the alcoves. She stepped closer, marvelling at the beauty of the woman in the portrait, who had red hair shot through with gold that came to a widow's peak on her forehead. She had expressive eyes, very green, and small hands clasped in her lap.

The woman wore a pale-blue silk dress, with an emerald bow pinned on one shoulder and large, square-cut emerald earrings on her ears. The ring on her left hand was a large emerald which matched the others. There was a lovely warm smile on her face and her eyes were alive and sparkling with intelligence. She looked to be about fifty years old in the painting.

Evan knew exactly who it was before she leaned forward and read the small engraved plaque attached to the elaborate gold picture frame. *Emma Harte: 1889–1970*.

Momentarily dumbfounded, she read the plaque again. And finally it sank in . . . *Emma Harte had been dead for thirty-one years*. Surely her grandmother had known this, if they had once been friends? Someone would have informed her. So what had made Gran utter those words on her deathbed? What had possessed her? Evan shook her head, more baffled than ever, not understanding what her gran had been trying to accomplish.

After several seconds staring at the painting, Evan turned away. It was then she noticed the second painting hanging in the alcove on the opposite wall. As she stepped up to it she thought the woman in the portrait seemed vaguely familiar, but she couldn't quite place her. The plaque on this simply gave the name of the subject: *Paula McGill Harte O'Neill*. Emma's granddaughter, Evan murmured under her breath, looking at it more closely.

She studied the portrait for a few minutes, very taken with it, and struck by the dominant widow's peak obviously inherited from Emma. But here the resemblance stopped. Paula O'Neill's hair was jet black, brushed back and worn in a pageboy style that ended at her strong and determined jawline. Her complexion was pale as ivory, and she had a broad brow, high cheekbones, dimples, and large expressive eyes the colour of pansies. Truly beautiful eyes, Evan thought – unusual – and she then decided Paula looked about forty-five in the portrait. She was striking in a dark, exotic way. In the painting she was wearing a silver-grey silk dress and Emma Harte's emeralds were very much in evidence.

Standing totally still, Evan discovered she was completely mesmerized by this painting; it was extraordinary, an accomplished portrait of—

'Can I help you?'

Evan almost jumped out of her skin, startled by a male voice, which had broken the silence in the corridor. She swung around, came face to face with a tall, good-looking young man.

A surprised look was flashing across his face as he stared at her and then he said again, 'Do you need some assistance?'

'Yes. Yes, I do. I'm looking for the management offices.'

He nodded. 'They're at the end of the corridor. I'm heading in that direction, I'll show you where they are.' Stepping closer to her, he held out his hand.

Evan took it, smiled up at him.

'Gideon Harte,' he announced, shaking her hand.

'Oh!' she exclaimed and automatically her eyes swung to Emma's portrait. 'And that's your grandmother!'

'No, it isn't, actually,' he answered. 'That's my great-grandmother.'

'I see.'

'And you are?'

'Oh excuse me, I'm forgetting my manners. I'm Evan Hughes.'

'A Welsh name. A *boy's* Welsh name, to be precise,' he responded.

'My grandmother was Welsh, and she told her son, my father, that she expected him to name his first child Evan. She was sure I was going to be a boy. I turned out to be a girl.'

'So I can see,' he said, giving her a swift appraising look.

'But now I think the name Evan is used for a boy or a girl,' she went on, ignoring his gaze, and then very gently extricated her hand from his.

He said, 'Let's go along to the management offices,' and began to walk slowly down the corridor.

Evan fell into step with him.

After a moment's silence, Gideon said, 'You're an American, aren't you?'

'Yes, I am. From New York.'

'Great city.' He glanced at her. 'And are you in London on business?'

'Well, no, not exactly. I decided to come to London for a year or so,' she quickly invented.

'And that's why I'm here at Harte's today. I'm looking for a job.'

'Are you now? In what area?'

'Fashion. I studied design in New York, and worked in the fashion departments of several stores. I also did a year's apprenticeship with Arnold Scaasi, the American couturier.'

He nodded, seemed about to say something, then merely cleared his throat. 'Here's where you want to be . . . Human Resources,' he explained, indicating the door. 'But Miss Hughes . . .' He stopped, cleared his throat again, and then said, 'Do you have a work permit?'

'No, I don't, but I don't need one. I was born in London. I have an English passport and dual nationality.'

'Well then, that's fine,' he answered, giving her a broad smile.

Opening the door for her, he ushered her into a large office. A young woman seated at a desk looked up as they entered.

'Oh hello, Mr Harte,' she said.

'Hello, Jennifer. This is Miss Evan Hughes. She's come to apply for a job at Harte's. In fashion.' Looking at Evan, he added, 'I wish you lots of luck, Miss Hughes.'

'Thank you, Mr Harte,' she answered, smiling up at him again. 'Thanks for everything.'

CHAPTER SEVEN

Gideon Harte walked down the corridor, thinking of the young woman whom he had just ushered inside.

Evan Hughes. Unusual name. Unusual woman.

From the moment he had set eyes on her he had been intrigued, instantly struck by her amazingly fine looks, and not the least by her curious likeness to Paula O'Neill. For a second he had thought this uncanny. Their facial characteristics were very similar, as was their colouring, and he had recoiled in surprise when she had swung around to face him.

But then he had realized the likeness between them meant nothing. A lot of people resembled each other without being in any way related. In any case, how could this young American woman be related to Paula, of all people? There was no way.

Moving away from the door, Gideon walked on, heading for Linnet's office, where he had been

going when he had come across Evan Hughes looking lost in the middle of the corridor. But, in fact,
she had been studying the portrait of Paula, he
realized that now. Maybe she herself had noticed
her likeness to the boss of the store.

Opening the door to the executive offices from
which this venerable old store was run, he crossed
the small central foyer and turned right.

Linnet's outer office was usually occupied by
Cassie Littleton, her secretary, but this morning
Cassie was nowhere in sight. His cousin's office
door was wide open and he strode toward it, but
paused in the doorway when he saw she was busy.

Linnet was on the phone, staring out of the window as she talked, and he hovered on the threshold,
not wanting to intrude on her privacy. Suddenly
she swung around, saw him and beamed, then
beckoned. Immediately, she hung up the phone,
exclaimed, 'Gid, come in and sit down!'

He hesitated.

'What's the matter?' she asked, frowning, seating
herself behind her desk.

'I'm not sure where I *could* sit, nor how I could
possibly navigate myself through this—'

'Don't you dare say *mess*,' she cut in peremptorily.

'I wasn't going to,' Gideon answered, strolling
into the room, being careful not to knock over any
of the precariously balanced boxes. 'I was going to
call it a minefield, because I know if I did acciden-
tally tangle with something you'd explode.'

'Ha! Ha! Very funny, Gid. But seriously, just

manoeuvre your way through and come and sit here.' As she spoke, Linnet leapt to her feet, ran around the desk and lifted a pile of manila folders off the chair on the other side. 'You'll be comfortable here,' she remarked as she stacked the folders on the floor near the window.

'Thanks,' Gideon said as he stepped warily around the many boxes, sat down, crossed his legs and continued, 'What did you think about the pictures I had them dig up in the photo morgue at *The Gazette*?'

'They're great. Grandy Emma gave some party in the fifties, by the look of the pictures anyway, and they'll be helpful to us. So, we're in charge it seems.' She threw him a quizzical look.

'We are indeed, but I don't mind, do you? Stupid question!' he exclaimed, answering himself. 'I can see very well what's going on here, and your Fashion Retrospective has become somewhat demanding, according to Julian.'

Linnet nodded. 'Too true. I just haven't had a chance to see him, and before you start chastising or criticizing me, I will have dinner with him, as I promised I would. But I've got to get some of this work under my belt first.'

'I know that. By the way, where's Cassie? She's usually keeping guard out there.' He half glanced towards the door as he spoke.

'She has the flu. And so does India. Actually, poor old India sounds awful. Very chesty, and she has a nasty cough. I hope she doesn't get bronchitis again. She's prone to that, as you know. It's a Fairley characteristic, at least that's what Mummy says. Tessa's got a weak chest, too. Anyway, not to digress . . . I'm trying to cope on my own while they're both off nursing their ailments.'

'So I can see.'

'It's going to be a super show, I can promise you that, and I know my mother's going to be pleased. It'll be a great boost for the store.'

'I know it will, I've always said that to you. But listen, Linnet, getting back to the birthday party for our respective fathers for a moment, have you come up with any ideas yet? Ideas about a theme, that kind of thing?'

'No, not really. But I haven't had much time to focus on it. Are you going to Yorkshire this weekend?'

'Yes, I am. Why?'

'I'm staying in London for once, to work through this lot, and I was thinking we might have supper on Saturday or Sunday, and brainstorm the party. But if you're going to Middleham . . .' Her voice trailed off and she gave a small, dismissive shrug.

'I'm sorry, but I promised Dad. We have to work on some business papers. I really do have to go, especially since I wasn't up there last weekend.' He gave her a rueful smile. 'But I promise I'll put my thinking cap on and brainstorm by myself. We can get together next week, if you can manage it.'

'That'll be okay. Is Julian going with you?'

'No, as a matter of fact he isn't. But if he were,

and he knew you were staying in town, I can assure you he would cancel *me* out immediately.'

She laughed, then said swiftly, 'Well, I'm going to have to dig into this pile, no matter what, however long it takes. What *I* need, actually, is two assistants, and right *now*.'

Gideon sat up straighter in the chair, a knowing look crossing his face, and he exclaimed, 'How about one assistant right *now*? Would that help?'

'Are you joking, of course it would!'

'Then I think I might have just the right person for you.'

'Who?'

'Evan Hughes.'

'A man. Oh, I'm not sure—'

'No, a woman,' he cut in. 'And yes, before you say it, I am fully aware that Evan is a Welsh boy's name. But apparently in America it's often used as a girl's name as well.'

'Oh, she's an American?'

'Yes. And well trained, I think. Studied fashion, worked for a well-known American couturier. She comes from New York, and she's about twenty-six, or around that. And she's very personable.'

'And she's a friend of yours, Gid?'

'Not exactly.' He cleared his throat, gave Linnet a faint smile. 'Actually I just met her in the corridor on her way to the personnel office.'

'You mean you picked her up in the corridor, you Don Juan, you!'

'Don't be so ridiculous, Linnet. She was looking

rather lost, and I asked her if I could help her,' he shot back in a slightly injured tone, wondering how he had managed to acquire the reputation of being a womanizer in the family. He wasn't that at all.

'I bet you did.' Linnet leered at him, and added, 'Well, one thing's for sure, if she grabbed *your* attention—'

'What's that?' he interrupted.

'She must be good looking.'

Gideon began to laugh. 'Well, yes, she is. I must admit that.'

'And where is she now?'

'I think she must be in Human Resources.' He glanced at his watch, nodded his head. 'Definitely. She has to be still there.'

Linnet, always decisive, picked up the phone and dialled. 'Jennifer, it's Linnet,' she said when the phone was answered. 'Do you still have a Miss Evan Hughes with you?'

'We do, Linnet. She's in with Maggie right now, who wanted to talk to her. Her application read very well, and so did her résumé,' Jennifer explained.

'Very good. Transfer me to Maggie, would you, please, Jennifer.'

'Right away.'

A second later Maggie Hemmings answered her phone with a crisp, 'Human Resources here.'

'It's Linnet, Maggie. I understand Evan Hughes is with you.'

'Correct.'

'Jennifer says her papers are good.'

'That's right.'

'I'm looking for an assistant. Would she fit the bill? Is she worth seeing?'

'I don't know.'

'Oh, well, once you've finished your interview, I'd appreciate it if you would bring her along to my office. I'd like to talk to her myself.'

'No problem,' Maggie said. 'See you shortly.'

'I'll be waiting,' Linnet replied and hung up. Looking across at Gideon, she remarked, 'Apparently your Miss Hughes has made a reasonable impression.'

'She's not *my* Miss Hughes. She's not even an acquaintance.'

Linnet nodded. 'Don't be so snarly, Gid. I'm teasing.'

'I'm not being snarly. Merely factual.' He smiled at her; his expression was loving.

She stared back at him, also smiling, thinking how well he looked today in his impeccably-tailored Savile Row suit, dark grey with a white pinstripe, pale blue shirt, and a silk tie. There were moments, like now when he was looking serious and intent, that he reminded her of his father, Winston. The Harte looks were predominant in them both, except that Uncle Winston's vivid colouring had begun to fade. Gideon's hair was a rich russet colour, his eyes light green, and he had clean, sharply defined features.

She and Gideon looked a lot like each other, and strangers often thought they were brother and sister. Certainly their relationship was very close, and had been since they were small. But then their parents were cousins and best friends, in each other's company constantly, and in consequence as children they had been thrown together a lot, along with his brother Toby, and Tessa and Lorne. Her other siblings were not yet born at that time.

At the thought of Toby, Linnet winced. He was not one of her favourites in the family, and she had always believed he was her enemy. He had been forever allied with Tessa, one of her half-sister's sycophants, constantly paying court and drooling all over her, which Tessa blatantly encouraged. Perhaps now that he was a married man things had changed somewhat, although she doubted it.

'Penny for your thoughts,' Gideon said, breaking the silence.

'I was thinking how smart you looked today. Very dashing, actually.'

'Thanks for those kind words, my pet.'

'And then Toby jumped into my head . . . What's *he* up to at the moment? He's been awfully quiet of late, wouldn't you say?'

'Yes, he has. But he's very busy with work; he's got a hugely demanding job, as a matter of fact. I know he's not your favourite, Linny, and sometimes I have problems with him myself – always did, as you know only too well. Still, I've got to say he's good at what he does. Brilliant. He loves working in television, and Dad's pleased with the way he's been managing the television company. None of us can possibly fault him there, you know.'

Gideon shifted in the chair slightly, and continued, 'And of course, he's a newly wed . . . I suppose he's rather preoccupied with his bride.'

'You're right . . .' Linnet paused, threw him a direct look, her head on one side. 'Do you like Adrianna Massingham, Gid?'

'She's all right. Not *my* type, but that doesn't mean anything really. Even though her appearance is very contrived – it's all that make-up, I guess – she's still a beautiful young woman, and pleasant enough, I suppose—' He cut his sentence off abruptly, and sat back in the chair, looking thoughtful, his face growing more serious than usual.

'But what? There's definitely a *but* here,' Linnet asserted.

'True. Look, to be honest, I'm not sure that the marriage will weather the storms that are bound to erupt. Toby's not easy, we know that, and he wants kids, wants to start a family, whilst Adrianna doesn't, is very intent on pursuing her acting career. Everyone's aware of that at home, especially my mother. No children for Adrianna, at least not right now. Maybe her attitude will change in time. What does Tessa think? Whoops, that's a stupid question!' he exclaimed. 'Of course *you* don't know what *she* thinks, because she never confides in you.'

'No, she doesn't, she never did. However, I suspect her nose is out of joint because he got married.'

'But she's married herself!'

'Tessa's a bit odd, Gid. She's always thought of

Toby as her property, from when we were kids growing up together. Have you forgotten that?'

'Not really, but I was certain she'd outgrown her possessiveness.' Shaking his head, merriment filling his eyes all of a sudden, he began to chuckle.

'Why are you laughing?'

'Don't you remember, when we were kids I always told you that Tessa had what I used to call ETS.'

Her auburn eyebrows drawing together in puzzlement, Linnet said, 'I must've forgotten. What does it mean, ETS?'

'ETS means Elizabeth Tudor Syndrome, something I dreamt up. Our famous greatest monarch forever clung to her favourite men, even when she replaced them with *new* favourite men.'

'Except for Lord Robert Dudley. She never ever replaced him in her affections,' Linnet responded, staring at her cousin pointedly. 'And you were the one who told me that.'

'Of course I did, come to think of it. Yes indeed, her Robin Two Eyes, as she called him, was always special. She promoted him to be her Master of the Horse, elevated him to the peerage by making him the Earl of Leicester, and he was her only true love. Actually, he was her one true *favourite* for her entire lifetime, even after he was dead.'

'And Elizabeth was *his* one true love, don't you think?' Linnet murmured.

'I do. Even though he did carry on a bit with some of her court ladies – had sexual liaisons, because men will be men you know – it was only Elizabeth he ever truly loved. He may have married Lettice Knollys, but it was his queen he *loved* and most devotedly.'

'Funny, isn't it, when you consider that it was Lettice Knollys' son, Robert Devereux, the Earl of Essex, who became a favourite of the queen's many years later; then he betrayed her most horribly and lost his head on the block for treason.'

'Very ironic, I'd say,' Gideon agreed. 'And even stranger that it all played out within the one family so to speak. Sort of incestuous.'

'Just like us, all muddled up together and the other two clans thrown into the mix for good measure,' Linnet pointed out. 'Anyway, I'd forgotten about ETS. Preoccupation with work.' A sudden thought occurred to her, and leaning forward, she exclaimed, 'Gideon, you said your Miss Hughes was an American. So how could I employ her immediately? A work permit has suddenly loomed large in my mind. Oh God, all that red tape to go through!' she groaned.

'Not necessary, my pet. I should have mentioned that she was born in London, has a British passport and dual nationality. No work permit required.'

'That's good to know, and I must say, you certainly found out a lot about her in only a few minutes.'

He grinned. 'You are now in possession of the sum total of every blessed thing I know about Miss Evan Hughes.'

CHAPTER EIGHT

Two things were instantly apparent to Linnet, after Maggie Hemmings had introduced Evan Hughes and then left her office.

Firstly, the young woman was the same type as her mother – slender, willowy, dark-haired, pale of skin and exotic looking, just as Paula was. And, by an odd coincidence, Linnet thought, there was a curious likeness between the two of them.

Secondly, Gideon and Evan were transfixed in the middle of the room, staring at each other as if mesmerized, completely oblivious to her presence. They were very taken with each other, that was patently obvious. But hadn't she known that because of the way he had spoken about Evan earlier?

Certainly she had never seen this particular look on Gideon's face before: it was a dazed look, and she felt a sudden twinge of jealousy, of possessiveness. He was her favourite cousin, her best friend since childhood, the closest to her in the family, closer even than India. And he belonged to her.

No, stop thinking like that, she told herself, immediately pushing these unexpected and destructive emotions aside. She wasn't like her sister Tessa; she did not suffer from ETS, as Gideon called it. For a moment she was stricken that she could be so . . . petty . . . so self-involved and selfish, she who took pride in her kindness and understanding, her fair-mindedness and integrity. Silently, she chastised herself.

She loved Gideon, only wanted the best for him, and of course he *would* meet someone special one day, someone that mattered, and he would get married. It hadn't happened thus far, and so he was available. And she had come to rely on him more and more of late, ever since she had put her relationship with Julian on hold.

Linnet reminded herself that Gideon had never been jealous of Julian, but then the three of them had grown up together, and Julian was Gideon's greatest male friend. Her father had called them The Three Musketeers when they were kids, because they were always together, inseparable, and devoted to each other.

Julian. He had been part of her life for as long as she could remember, part of her, and he was always there, hovering at the back of her mind, however much she tried to block him out. Was he her one true love, just as Robert Dudley had been Queen Elizabeth's soul mate? Had she made a terrible mistake in turning away from him for, well, for so many reasons actually? Perhaps those reasons were not quite as valid as she thought. She couldn't help wondering about this from time to time. But not now, an inner voice suddenly cautioned. Now it's time to concentrate on this young woman, to concentrate on work, on the retrospective.

Linnet dropped her eyes to the folder that Maggie had just left on her desk, opened it and looked at the application forms and the detailed résumé.

But, riddled with curiosity as she was, she glanced up after only a split second, focusing her eyes on Gideon and Evan Hughes.

Now he was solicitously shepherding the young American to the chair near Linnet's desk, the glazed expression having been replaced by a most beatific smile. Evan was looking slightly flushed, a little shy, perhaps even flustered, but her eyes held a distinct sparkle.

Clearing her throat somewhat noisily, Linnet looked directly at Evan as she came over to the desk, and said pleasantly, 'I'll finish reading your résumé and application forms later.'

Evan nodded, looking pleased. Inside she was thrilled, excited to be sitting here; she could scarcely believe her luck.

Returning Evan's steady gaze, Linnet noticed that the young woman's resemblance to her mother was stronger than she had realized a moment ago. Evan's face was the same shape as Paula's, finely sculpted and the dark brows sweeping along the broad forehead were identical. But her eyes were not the colour of pansies, as her mother's were.

Evan's were a light, bluish-grey, large and translucent. At this moment those eyes were full of eagerness, and there was a sense of earnestness about her that Linnet couldn't help liking. In fact, there was something truly appealing about Evan Hughes, and Linnet smiled at her warmly, approvingly.

Evan smiled back, and was just about to say something when she was cut off by Gideon.

Hovering behind Evan's chair, his hand resting on the back, he exclaimed, 'Well, I'd better skedaddle, leave you both to get down to the nitty-gritty.' Striding purposefully towards the door, he finally swung around before exiting. Blowing a kiss to Linnet, he said, 'I'll give you a ring later, so that we can discuss the big bash in June. And Miss Hughes, I wish *you* lots of luck at Harte's.'

Before either woman could make any kind of response, the door closed softly behind him.

'I've been looking to hire another assistant,' Linnet explained to Evan, once they were alone. 'I already have one, actually. Her name's India Standish, and she's my cousin. We work well together, we run the fashion floors and we have for several years. Unfortunately, India's off sick right now, she has the flu. So does my secretary, Cassie Littleton.' Linnett stopped, shook her head helplessly, and then, making a face, she glanced around the room. 'Hence this *mess*. It's not usually like this, I'm a fairly tidy person. Anyway, I don't think either of them will be in this week. I just hope *I* don't come down with it. I can't afford to be sick right now.'

'I think there's a bit of an epidemic,' Evan warned in a worried voice. 'I've just recovered from a bout of the flu myself.'

'I'm glad you're better,' Linnet murmured. 'Anyway, not to digress. I understand from Gideon and Maggie that you studied design, and had a career in fashion in New York.'

'That's correct. I was a student at the Fashion Institute of Technology in Manhattan, and then later I was an apprentice with the couturier Arnold Scaasi for a year. I even worked in the fashion department at Bergdorf Goodman for a while.'

Evan shifted slightly in her chair, and continued, 'I also helped Pauline Trigère with a retrospective of her couture which she was putting on. That was about six years ago, when I was still at F.I.T. She's a friend of my father's, and he asked her if I could help her with the exhibit, just to gain experience, and she said yes. I learned a lot from simply being around her. She has great personal style, and her clothes are marvellous.'

'That I know. My great-grandmother was a fan of hers, according to my mother, and the clothes I found in storage are proof of that. There are a number of Trigère gowns, suits and coats in Emma's vast collection.'

Evan's face lit up as she exclaimed, 'That's wonderful. They will be in the fashion retrospective, won't they?'

'Yes, they will. Obviously Maggie Hemmings told you about the exhibit which India and I are planning.'

'She did touch on it, yes. How comprehensive is it going to be?'

Leaning across the desk, Linnet explained in an enthusiastic voice, 'Very comprehensive. We're going to be showing eighty years of fashion, going all the way back to 1920 and coming forward to the year 2000. We're basing part of the exhibit on the clothes which belonged to my great-grandmother. She was Emma Harte, the founder of the Harte stores.'

'Yes, I know,' Evan said, and then, before she could stop herself, she blurted out, 'I saw her portrait in the corridor. You certainly look like a younger version of her.'

Laughing, Linnet opened the centre drawer of her desk, and murmured, 'Oh yes, I know . . . everybody tells me that. I just hope I'm a little bit like her in other ways, particularly in character. She was pretty special; a very brilliant woman.'

Bringing out a sheet of paper, Linnet handed it to Evan. 'These are some of the designers we're planning to feature. The clothes that belonged to Emma are also listed, and they're from her *haute-couture* collection.' She laughed. 'Actually, I think I've taken *all* of the collection.'

Quickly scanning the list she was holding, Evan read out some of the names in an awed voice. 'Pierre Balmain, Coco Chanel, Cristóbal Balenciaga,

Christian Dior, Trigère, Lanvin, Vionnet, Hubert de Givenchy, Yves Saint Laurent, Scaasi, Cardin. Heavens, what fantastic names. Your great-grandmother must have had wonderful taste,' she finished, looking across the desk at Linnet.

'*I* think she did.'

'I notice you're also listing separately Valentino, Oscar de la Renta, Karl Lagerfeld, Zandra Rhodes, Lacroix, Versace and many other designers. Do you have their clothes already?'

'Only some. We have Emma's collection, of course. That's recently been brought down here from Penni-stone Royal, my mother's house in Yorkshire where they are stored. And we do have a certain number of items by other designers. However, I think we do need to find more clothes, additional vintage pieces, and I was hoping that you could handle that. Naturally I'm assuming that you would like to work on the retrospective, if you come on board at Harte's.'

Leaning forward urgently, her face full of that engaging eagerness Linnet had noted before, Evan exclaimed, 'I'd love to work at Harte's, and I'd be thrilled to be involved with the retrospective. A project like this is always challenging, Miss O'Neill.'

'And very hard work,' Linnet pointed out, giving her a direct look. 'I hope you don't mind long hours.'

'Not me. I've been told I'm a workaholic by most people I've worked with.'

Linnet burst out laughing. 'That's good to know,

and join the club! India and I suffer from that same ailment, I'm afraid. Though I think I'm worse than she is sometimes! Anyway, do you have any thoughts about where and how to acquire vintage clothes for the exhibition?'

'Yes, I do. There are several good vintage clothing shops in New York. The best I think is Ken Valenti. He's a private dealer of vintage couture, and he has about ten thousand pieces, as well as accessories such as shoes, bags, scarves and jewellery. He has quite a lot of Yves Saint Laurent, I do know that. Anyway, he has an Internet site, and we can pull it up on the computer so you can see some of the clothes. Then there's Didier Ludot in Paris. He has three shops, but the best is the one in the gardens of the Palais Royal, which is dedicated to vintage *haute couture* dating from the 1920s up to the 1980s. Your time span for your exhibit.'

'That's good to know! We do have to investigate, look at web sites. There are auction houses, of course, such as Christie's and Sotheby's here in London. In fact, we've already bought quite a lot at auction in the past year, which is how long we've been working on the retrospective, putting it together.'

'The William Doyle Galleries in New York also specialize in vintage *haute couture*. There's probably an auction coming up sometime soon.'

'You mentioned accessories a moment ago,' Linnet remarked. 'And I forgot to tell you that we have shoes and bags from Emma Harte's collection, which we'll be putting on display.'

'That's always a great idea, to give the whole picture,' Evan answered. 'Also, some fashion designers are willing to loan clothes from their archives for a retrospective like the one you're planning. Have you contacted any of them?'

'Yes we have, and the clothes have already been lent to us. All those wonderful original models the designers have kept for posterity, which is great. And we have a number of current *haute-couture* pieces in the fashion department which we're planning to include. But we still need more items to make the exhibit really impressive . . .' Her voice trailed off, and she shook her head. 'It's quite a task, you know.'

After a moment's thought, Evan said quietly, 'I have an idea. Why not pick out six or eight, or better still, *ten* really chic women in London, and honour them at the retrospective as Fashion Icons. They'd be a wonderful vehicle for publicity, especially if they're well known. And they'd probably agree to lend us some of their own couture clothes to put on display. If we had *ten* icons and each loaned the store five or six pieces, that would mean we'd have fifty or so garments in one fell swoop.'

'Brilliant!' Linnet exclaimed, her eyes lighting up. 'Let's take it a step further . . . why don't we have a best-dressed list? Create one of our own. That would engender some publicity for the retrospective—' Linnet stopped abruptly, suddenly looking concerned. 'I can see from your expression that you don't like *that* idea one bit,' she muttered.

Evan responded swiftly, 'It's a good idea, but I must admit I am worried about the use of the phrase "best-dressed list". I'm not sure whether that's a registered trademark. The Best-Dressed List was started by Eleanor Lambert in New York, as far as I know, many years ago. It just might—'

'Belong to her,' Linnet interrupted. 'I understand your concern. Point well taken. So let's skip it then. I don't want complications, and certainly I don't want to work on something that might prove to be a waste of time. Let's go with the Fashion Icons, though. I love it. India will help with the right names, and so will I. We'll need a long list, a lot more women than ten, because not all of the women we approach will agree to participate. Let's do some research on that.'

Evan agreed and, encouraged by Linnet's enthusiastic response to her suggestion, she went on, 'I can talk to Arnold Scaasi. I'm sure he would lend us a number of his evening gowns. He has a magnificent collection of his own designs, a great archive.'

Linnet nodded. 'That'd be fantastic. But we will have to buy some of the vintage couture that's around. Very simply, we just *need* it, no two ways about that, to round out certain years in fashion.' She sat back, deciding that Evan Hughes was going to be invaluable to her. How lucky it was that Gideon had noticed her in the corridor. But who could fail to miss her? She was an arresting-looking young woman. Unexpectedly, Linnet felt considerably better about properly completing all of the work on the exhibition. The young American woman had been in her office for what? Only half an hour, at the most. Yet she had a truly good feeling about Evan, a positive reaction to her. And in the most peculiar way she felt as if she had known her for a very long time. There was something vaguely familiar about Evan Hughes.

For her part, Evan, who was quick, intelligent and acute, knew she had made a good impression on Linnet, and now she said in that lovely quiet voice of hers, 'I guess you're planning to have the retrospective in June, from what Mr Harte said.'

'No, no, it'll be in the middle of May,' Linnet responded swiftly, and then thought to explain, 'My cousin was referring to a birthday party we're helping to plan with my mother. It's for his father and mine. That's what Gideon was talking about when he mentioned the big bash in June.'

Evan merely inclined her head, hoping she didn't look foolish for assuming something, and then voicing it so readily without knowing the facts.

Linnet went on, 'The retrospective will be on view for about four months, perhaps even six. The longer the better, and so I do want it to be something really smashing. Sumptuous clothes, elegance all the way.'

Evan asked, 'Where will it be housed in the store?'

'On the top floor. We have an auditorium up there, which my mother carved out of a number of different defunct departments a few years ago. She demolished and remodelled, she's very good at that. It holds about eight hundred people, so it's very spacious, as you can imagine. The clothes will be displayed to great advantage there.'

'There's a lot of preparation involved in this kind of show,' Evan murmured, thinking out loud, her mind racing when she thought of all that had to be done by May. It was the middle of January already. Yes, it was a big challenge indeed.

'I agree with you,' Linnet was saying. 'But the clothes we already have are in perfect condition now. They've been cleaned, and repaired, whenever that was necessary, and also steamed or pressed. Touch-ups can be done once the clothes are on the mannequins and in position in the auditorium. But all that aside, there's still an awful lot to finish. That's why I need extra help. Would you be interested in the job?'

'Oh yes, I would!' Evan's voice echoed her enthusiasm.

'When could you start?'

'Whenever you want me to.'

'I'll talk to my mother and get back to you tomorrow morning?' Linnet said.

'Thank you, Miss O'Neill.'

Once she was alone, Linnet looked at Evan's résumé again, and she liked what she read. She also liked Evan. There was something open and honest about her, and certainly she was enthusiastic about working at Harte's; Linnet had detected in her a desire to work. No shirker here, she thought, as she stood up, and walked out of her office.

Hurrying down the corridor, she headed in the direction of Maggie Hemmings's office.

Jennifer looked up as she went in, and smiled. 'Hello, Miss O'Neill. Can I help you?'

'I was looking for Maggie. Is she in her office? Is she free?'

Jennifer nodded.

Linnet smiled, crossed the room, knocked on the door, and went in. 'Do you have a few minutes, Maggie?'

The older woman looked up, gave Linnet a warm smile. 'Certainly.'

Linnet sat down, looked across at the head of Human Resources. 'I wanted a word with you about Evan Hughes. I thought you seemed a little reluctant about her, not as enthusiastic as I would expect after reading her résumé.'

'The résumé does read well, I can't argue there. But I wasn't sure if she was quite right for Harte's.'

'*Oh*. Why not?'

'I can't really put my finger on it . . .' Maggie shrugged. 'It's just a feeling. And anyway, I thought it was odd, the way she was introduced by Mr Gideon, and then she denied knowing him to me. There's another thing,' Maggie leaned over the desk, and added, in a lowered voice, 'Don't you think she looks like your mother?'

Linnet laughed. 'They're similar types, that's all. And I don't think it's odd, no. As for my cousin, he ran in to her in the corridor when she was looking for this office. He simply guided her here. He *doesn't* know her, Maggie.'

'I see.'

'And even if he did, why would it matter? I think she has excellent credentials, and certainly she would be very helpful to me at this particular time.'

'Are you going to hire her?' Maggie asked, her voice neutral now, her expression cautious.

'I'm certainly going to think about it,' Linnet answered, and with a nod and a smile, she rose. 'Thanks, Maggie,' she murmured as she left the office.

What was *that* about? Linnet asked herself as she went back to her own office, baffled by the attitude of the other woman, but determined not to be influenced by anyone. Evan could be of great help to her in mounting the retrospective. Perhaps she would hire her on a trial basis.

The following morning Linnet spoke to Evan on the phone. 'I'd like you to come in and see me again, Miss Hughes. Around eleven. We can talk some more, and I'll take you to see the collection of clothes we've already assembled.'

Evan was thrilled. 'I'll be there, Miss O'Neill, and thank you very much.'

Always punctual, Evan arrived at Linnet's office exactly on time.

After chatting to Evan about the retrospective

and her needs, Linnet said, 'I'd like to offer you the job, on a trial basis, Evan.'

Evan beamed. 'I accept, Miss O'Neill. Thank you.'

Linnet took Evan to a storage room on the seventh floor, behind the *haute-couture* fashion department. Pausing at a large metal-clad door, she took out a set of keys, and turned to Evan. 'Only India and I have keys to this room. That way we're the only two people responsible, and only we can be blamed if anything goes wrong. Or goes missing.'

'I understand.'

Linnet unlocked the door, pushed it open and stepped inside. She paused for a moment on the threshold until she found the light switch on the wall. A split second later many overhead lights came blinking on; she beckoned to Evan to follow her and walked into the cool, temperature-controlled storage space.

There were dozens and dozens of racks of clothes hanging in cotton bags, and when Linnet saw Evan's face she exclaimed, 'Oh, don't worry, I'm not going to show you everything right now. There's far too much to look at. But perhaps you'd be interested to see a few choice pieces that belonged to Emma.'

'Yes, I'd like that.'

Hurrying to the far end of the room, Linnet moved a rack or two around and explained, 'There are a couple of outfits here that are just knock-outs.'

As she spoke she began to untie the drawstring at the top of a cotton bag which held the garment.

Evan watched her taking out a black suit on a padded hanger, and she remarked, 'What a marvellous idea these cotton bags are. Did you have them made?'

Linnet swung around. 'Not these, no. They came from Paris. But we have had similar ones copied for the other clothes hanging here. Actually, the bag is called an "*oooss*".'

'An *oooss*,' Evan repeated slowly. 'What a strange name.'

'That's the way it's pronounced, but it's spelt *h-o-u-s-s-e*. It's the French word for "cover", in fact.'

'They're certainly effective for storage purposes,' Evan replied, thinking they looked like voluminous tents.

'Look at this suit.' Linnet held it out. 'It's by Cristóbal Balenciaga. Emma had it made in 1951.'

Evan inspected the suit closely, and nodded her head. 'There's nothing like a piece of *haute couture*, is there? The cut, the shoulderline, the overall silhouette. It's simply impeccable, a masterpiece of workmanship.'

Linnet pulled a dress out of another cotton bag. 'And this is a cocktail dress by Balenciaga. Emma also bought it in 1951. I happen to think it's fantastic. Here, Evan, hold it against yourself.' She handed her the cocktail gown on its padded hanger; Evan did as she instructed and held it against her body, looking down at the dress, which was made of black tissue taffeta. 'I love the way the skirt is flounced in tiers and the bodice wrapped around. It's unique. And the wonderful thing is that, like the suit, it's not a bit dated.'

'I agree with you. There's a picture of Emma in the dress, and it looks as if it was taken only yesterday. Over there –' Linnet swung her head, gestured toward more racks – 'are some couture outfits lent by my mother, India's mother, and my aunts Emily and Amanda. Their pieces will also help to flesh out certain years in design.'

Evan helped Linnet put the two garments back in their cotton covers and, as they stood at the rack, Linnet remarked, 'I think you're going to enjoy working on the retrospective, Evan. Even though we have a tough road ahead, I believe that the three of us will be able to pull it together most effectively.'

'I know we will,' Evan answered, crossing her fingers, stepping away from the clothes rack and picking up her purse.

'Let's go and see Maggie and get you properly hired as my assistant,' Linnet said, leading the way out of the storage room.

CHAPTER NINE

Evan felt as if she were walking on air when she left Harte's several hours later. She was not aware of the cold, frosty weather and the biting wind, nor did she feel hungry, even though it was turning two. I'm on cloud nine, she thought, hurrying towards the cab she had hailed, and which had suddenly slithered to a stop close by.

Once inside, she sat back against the leather seat, her thoughts on her father. All she wanted now was to get back to the hotel so that she could put in a call to him.

Since today was Wednesday she knew he would be at the antique shop in New Milford; he always did his books when business was slower. She could hardly wait to tell him her news; he would be surprised, she was certain of that. She could scarcely believe it herself: that she actually had a job at Harte's was something quite incredible to her.

Once she was in her quarters at the hotel, she

shrugged out of her red scarf and long black coat and put them away in the cupboard. And then, after turning on the electric fire in the small sitting room, she sat down next to it in the big easy chair. Picking up the phone, she dialled his Connecticut number and waited for it to ring through. A couple of seconds later, her father answered the phone.

'Good morning. Hughes Antiques.'

'Hi, Dad! It's me, Evan.'

'Evan, honey, you sound great! You've made a good recovery, I can hear that.'

'I'm feeling like my old self, more or less. But listen, Dad, I've got some great news. I've got a job.' She paused for maximum effect, and then cried, 'At Harte's! I've got a job in the fashion department at Harte's.'

There was a moment's silence at his end of the phone, but in her excitement and enthusiasm Evan paid no attention.

'Well,' he said, at last and rather slowly. 'That's good news.'

It struck her then that his voice was flat. Certainly there was no enthusiasm in it, and she exclaimed, 'You don't sound a bit excited, and I thought you'd be thrilled for me . . .' Her voice died away on her, and she clutched the phone a little tighter, frowning.

'Oh I am, Evan, I am. I was simply taken aback, that's all. I hadn't realized you'd already been there and applied for a job.'

'I didn't. What I mean is, I hadn't been there

135

before, I just wasn't up to it until yesterday morning. But I felt so much better that I got ready and went to the store. Basically to see Emma Harte, as Grandma told me to do.'

'Yes, I know what she told you. And did you see Emma Harte?'

'Dad, she's *dead*! And for thirty-one years. So I don't know what Gran was going on about. If they'd been friends she must have *known*. Anyway, I was startled. And upset. But, you know me, I bounced back after I'd had a cup of coffee and time to think. I liked the look of the store, it's very beautiful, so I decided to go up to management and apply for a position. I mean, what did I have to lose?'

'Nothing. And so they hired you just like that. Is that what you're saying, honey?'

'I was lucky yesterday, *very* lucky. I happened to be in the right place at the right time.'

'Were you now,' he murmured. 'So go ahead, tell me all about it.'

'What happened was this . . .' Swiftly, but graphically, Evan told her story, finally finishing, 'And before I knew it, Maggie Hemmings, of Human Resources, was taking me to see Linnet O'Neill. She's the head of fashion and the great-granddaughter of Emma Harte.'

'It does sound very fortuitous,' Owen remarked softly. 'And this Linnet O'Neill was impressed enough to hire you on the spot, is that it?'

'Not exactly, I had to go back today for another

chat with Linnet O'Neill and then she hired me on a trial basis.'

'Congratulations, I'm pleased for you. And who was the nice young man you mentioned?'

'His name's Gideon Harte, and I found out later that he works at the family's newspaper company. He runs the *London Evening Post*.'

'I see. Well, Elayne and Angharad *are* going to be thrilled when I tell them the news later.'

'Give them my love. I'll be helping Linnet put on a fashion retrospective for the next few months, and hey, Dad, guess what? Some of Miss Trigère's clothes are going to be in the retrospective. Emma Harte was a fan of hers.'

'I'll tell Pauline. She'll be pleased to hear it,' Owen replied.

'Dad?'

'Yes, honey?'

'Do you think Grandma *knew* Mrs Harte was dead?'

There was total silence at his end of the phone. Evan said insistently, 'Dad, are you still there?'

'Yes, I'm here.'

'So . . . what do you think? *Did* Gran know? If so, why did she tell me to go there?'

'I've no idea. She never mentioned anything about Emma Harte to me, except that she'd known her during the Second World War. Look, Evan, my mother could've been wandering in her mind, or delirious, in her last moments. I told you that before you left for London.'

'I know. At least she pointed me in the right direction . . . as it turns out.'

After another short silence, her father agreed, saying quietly, 'That's true, yes.'

Evan asked, 'How's Mom?'

His voice brightened as he answered, 'She's better; she's come out of herself a bit. And she cooked a nice dinner for me last night. I think the new medication's started to kick in.'

'Oh I'm so glad! That's great. Give her my love.'

'I will. When do you start at Harte's?'

'Tomorrow morning.' She began to laugh, and quipped, 'They really do need me there, Dad.'

She expected him to laugh with her, which was usually his way, but he did not. 'Perhaps,' he answered in the same low voice, and rapidly changed the subject.

They talked for a few minutes longer about other things, and then said their affectionate goodbyes.

After Evan put the receiver down she leaned back in the chair, thinking about her father's reaction to her news. It wasn't what she had expected at all, and she felt oddly disconcerted, even irritated by his low-key response, and somewhat baffled by his attitude. The more she thought about it the more she came to realize that he hadn't sounded pleased about her job. She couldn't help wondering why. Like her grandmother, he had always cheered her on, been her greatest booster. But not today.

*   *   *

Pondering this in London, Evan Hughes had no way of knowing that, thousands of miles away, her father, seated at his desk in his New Milford shop, was staring absently into space. He was wondering what exactly his mother had set in motion on her deathbed, admitting to himself that he should have known Glynnis would have been unable to resist pulling a few strings at the end. Under his breath Owen cursed himself for having so enthusiastically encouraged Evan to go to London, to take a sabbatical there as he himself had once done years ago. Instead, he should have discouraged the trip. But in December he had not known what he knew now. Anyway, it was too late. Evan was already there . . . and the wheels had begun to turn . . .

Evan liked the public rooms at the little hotel in Belgravia, which George and Arlette had decorated in the manner of an English country house. Not that she had ever been in an English country house, but she had seen photos in magazines, and she was partial to that particular look: the vivid floral chintzes, the mellow woods, the fine antiques, the beautiful porcelain lamps with their cream silk shades, plus the big vases of flowers loosely arranged in the English style.

Of all the rooms downstairs on the main floor, her favourite was the sitting room with its walls painted terracotta and glazed with light peach, the red-rose patterned chintz curtains at the three windows, and the overstuffed sofas and chairs upholstered in russet-red linen. On the floor, a wonderful old Persian rug had a similar background colour to the draperies, with a pattern of deep blues, pinks and greens. It helped to pull the entire scheme together, and acted as the perfect anchor for the seating arrangement.

The room was empty when Evan went down for afternoon tea, and as she walked in and headed for the fireplace, her spirits lifted. The atmosphere was rich, warm, welcoming, and the huge fire blazing in the hearth added to its overall cosiness, its lovely roseate glow.

She seated herself on one of the big sofas near the fireside, sat back and relaxed against the over-sized needlepoint cushions, mentally pushing aside her preoccupation with her father's odd manner on the phone. She let herself drift, staring at a painting of a moorland scene with a waterfall, heather and several sheep. It was restful to look at.

A moment later, her eyes roamed around, taking in the other traditional oil paintings, most of them landscapes obviously executed long ago. She liked them; the room had a particular style which made her feel comfortable, at ease, at home.

The grandfather clock in the corner began to strike four, and a few seconds later one of the young waitresses came bustling in, pushing a three-tier trolley laden with teapots, plates of finger sandwiches and scones, bowls of strawberry jam and clotted Devonshire cream.

The young woman was closely followed by a

colleague, also behind a tea trolley, this one stacked with a variety of cakes on antique silver stands.

The two waitresses were dressed in Edwardian style, wearing long black dresses, white frilly aprons and caps, and they looked most effective in the period setting. Both women busied themselves at a long, mahogany sideboard at the far end of the room. The cake stands, plates of sandwiches and scones were soon deposited there, along with the numerous teapots.

Clara, one of the waitresses Evan was acquainted with, came hurrying over when she saw her sitting by the fire. 'Good afternoon, Miss Hughes,' she said with a bright smile. 'Here for tea, are you?'

'Hi, Clara, and yes, I am.' Evan flashed her a friendly smile in return, and added, 'I didn't have lunch today, so I think I'll go for the whole works.'

'The full afternoon tea, then. Sandwiches, scones, and cake. Right away, Miss Hughes. Oh, and it *is* English breakfast tea you like, isn't it?'

'Yes, it is, thanks, Clara.'

It was her gran who had introduced Evan to afternoon tea when she was a child growing up in Connecticut. Glynnis had made quite a ceremony out of it, serving the tea from a silver pot with a silver strainer over the cup, and thin slices of lemon, or milk for those who preferred. The tea had always been Twinings brand from London, usually the English breakfast tea preferred by Glynnis, but sometimes replaced by Orange Pekoe. Never Earl Grey, because Gran didn't like the flavour. *Smoky*, she had called it.

Evan and her sisters had loved the finger sandwiches filled with egg salad, slices of cucumber or tomato, occasionally thin slivers of chicken, sometimes sardines, or wafer-thin pieces of smoked salmon between the crustless bread. Because Gran had liked to bake, there were always fresh scones right out of the oven, served with strawberry jam and clotted cream, and for the finale, a caraway-seed cake.

On special occasions her grandmother would make a light sponge cake, which she sliced through the middle into two flat pieces, and filled with whipped cream and raspberry jam. And when she had grown older Glynnis had taught *her* how to make the sandwiches, the scones, and the various cakes; in fact, it was her gran who had taught Evan how to cook any number of things, and over the years she had become quite accomplished in the kitchen.

Evan thought of this now as she munched on a smoked salmon sandwich, wondering what to do about an apartment. Should she look for a small one in this area? Or should she stay on at the hotel? She had meant to ask her father about this earlier, but she had been so distracted by his lacklustre response to her news that it had slipped her mind.

In many ways the hotel was more convenient because she was so well taken care of here; on the other hand, she did not have a kitchen and had to eat in the hotel dining room, which added to her expenses.

After wrestling with the problem for a few minutes, she made a decision. She would stay on at the hotel for the moment, very simply because she did not have time to look for an apartment.

In any case, Evan already had a good picture of what working at Harte's was going to be like: back-breaking routine, long hours, and total devotion and dedication to duty. She had already perceived that Linnet would be a hard taskmaster, and that she would expect everyone to work as hard as she did. And especially a newcomer like her, who was bound to be on trial. Evan had discerned that Linnet, for all her sweetness and beauty, was at heart a tough businesswoman. This did not trouble her; rather, she admired that trait.

Yes, it's better to stay here, Evan told herself, where I'm comfortable and have every convenience. Later, once the retrospective is set up and things are rolling along smoothly, I'll think about finding my own place, one with a decent kitchen where I can cook; an apartment where I can do a little entertaining, even. This thought pleased her, and she reached for a scone, spread it with strawberry jam and added a large dollop of cream.

As she ate the scone she realized just how hungry she had been, but she also reminded herself how fattening scones and rich cream cakes were. Not too many of these afternoon teas, she vowed to herself, and then smiled. She would be at the store most of the time anyway – and how she was looking forward to it! All of her life she had found challenges enormously appealing.

Leaning back against the cushions once again, Evan let her thoughts wander, reviewing the events of the day. And eventually they came to settle on Gideon Harte.

He had been pleasant and helpful in the corridor when she was looking for the management offices. But later this pleasantness had turned to genuine masculine charm and much solicitousness. When she had walked into Linnet's office with Maggie Hemmings, he had hurried across the floor to greet her. Once she had been introduced by Maggie to his cousin, he had not hidden his interest in her. In fact, he had been so attentive to her that she found herself staring back at him, as intensely as he was staring at her.

His light green eyes had gazed into hers, and she found she could not look away, mesmerized by him. Now she remembered how her heart had skipped a beat, and that his long, penetrating look had made her legs go slightly weak at the knees. Nothing had ever happened to her like that before; but then no man had looked at her quite like that, not ever in her entire adult life. A moment later, when he had taken hold of her arm to lead her over to the chair, his hand had seemed to scorch through the fabric of her jacket. She had been momentarily thrown, so attracted to him was she—

'Evan. How are *you*?'

At the sound of Arlette's lilting, lightly accented French voice, she sat up with a start and exclaimed, 'I'm fine, Arlette. How nice to see you. And how're you?'

'I am well. Busy, busy. George is away on the business, so I am in command, as he calls it. And one needs the *bon courage* to be in charge of a hotel. Even a small one such as this.'

'But you do everything so well, so I'm sure you run it exactly the same way George does.' As she spoke Evan smiled at Arlette, her face dimpling.

Arlette, as always, was completely captivated by that warm, wide smile, which she found so infectious, and she smiled in return. There was something unique about this friendly, open, out-going American girl who was full of such charm and grace. Now she asked, 'Are you all right? Are you feeling better?'

'I'm back to normal, thank you,' Evan reassured her, and then she leaned forward from the waist, looked up at Arlette. 'Can you sit for a minute? I've got some news for you.'

'*Mais oui, cherie*.' Arlette lowered herself onto the sofa next to Evan.

'I got myself a job today, a wonderful job. At Harte's store in Knightsbridge.' Once again, Evan enthusiastically launched into the retelling of her experience at the store, explaining in detail about the events which had taken place. 'And Linnet O'Neill hired me,' she finally finished, settling back, a look of pleasure lighting up her lovely face. 'I will be working in fashion with her.'

'*Très bien*, Evan! It is wonderful news. I know you like the fashion. And what made you pick Harte's? Out of all the stores here?'

'I've always wanted to work there. It's the finest store in the world, in my opinion.' Evan had no intention of confiding to Arlette her grandmother's dying words; she would appear ridiculous if she did.

Arlette Thomas sat studying Evan for a moment or two, thinking how stunning she looked. The black hair was glossy, the complexion translucent, the blue-grey eyes huge pools in her delicate face. She was a beautiful woman, very feminine, yet compelling. Alluring to men, Arlette had no doubt, and there was also an air of refinement about her that the Frenchwoman admired.

'And this young man?' Arlette asked now. 'The one who helped you this morning . . . will you be meeting him again soon?'

Evan gaped at her. 'Oh, but he doesn't work there.'

'I didn't mean seeing him at *work*.' Arlette gazed at the younger woman indulgently, shaking her head, pursing her lips.

Evan saw the merriment in Arlette's dark eyes, noticed the hidden laughter twitching on her pretty mouth, and for a moment she wondered if this attractive and motherly Frenchwoman was teasing her. After only a moment she realized that she was not. Evan took a deep breath. 'He was just trying to be helpful, that's all,' she protested.

Arlette sat up a little straighter, and crossed her legs, arranging her full red skirt over highly polished brown boots. After a moment's consideration, she explained. 'I was thinking of a *rendezvous* . . . a date with him?' Those wise brown eyes lingered on Evan's questioningly.

A deep pink flush spread from Evan's neck up to her face, and she almost stuttered as she said, 'I – I don't think I will be meeting him again. Not in the way you mean, Arlette.'

'No? You do not think so?' The Frenchwoman sounded surprised and shook her head vigorously. 'But I do. *Ah oui*. I am sure. You will have a *rendezvous* with him, *ma petite choux à la crème*. And in the not too distant future.' Her lilting laughter rippled on the warm air once more. 'It is . . . obvious . . . he had a hand in cutting through the red ribbon. At the store. Ah yes. *Absolument*.'

'The red ribbon?' Evan frowned at her, looking puzzled.

'*Ah non, non*. I am stupid! Not the red ribbon. The red *tape*.'

'You're right about that part, Arlette. But I'm not sure about a date with him. I don't think he's interested in me.'

'Trust me, *cherie*. I am *older* than you, *and* I am a *Frenchwoman*. And we know about these things. We know about . . . *l'amour*.'

*   *   *

Unbeknownst to Evan and Arlette, Gideon Harte, at that precise moment in time, was indeed thinking about a rendezvous with Evan Hughes.

He sat in his office at the Yorkshire Consolidated Newspaper Company, in a building on the other side of London, his mind on the young American woman. He had been thinking about her a lot, since meeting her in the corridor at Harte's yesterday. There was something about her that was special. She totally held his interest, and there was no doubt that he wanted to see her again. And as soon as possible. He had discovered that he felt a sense of urgency about her, a need to be in her company, to discover more about her. At once. He was impatient to know more.

Gideon already knew that Linnet had hired her on a trial basis. His cousin had phoned to tell him that a short while ago. Furthermore, Linnet had thanked him profusely, as if he had led Evan by the hand to Harte's, when, in fact, her arrival at the store had been happenstance, pure luck. And she had been enthusiastic about Evan Hughes, gone into minute detail about the meetings they had had. 'She's great for me,' Linnet had just informed him. 'She's going to be wonderful. She's a real find, Gid, and I know India's going to like her as much as I do. Evan came up with some brilliant ideas. She bodes well for me, Gideon, she really does.'

Did she bode well for him? He hoped so. He wished he could call Evan right now, but he had no idea where to find her, and he certainly had no intention of phoning Linnet to ask for her number. He would deal with that tomorrow by calling Evan herself at the store.

Pushing his chair slightly away from the desk, he put his feet up on it, crossing his long legs at the ankles. Closing his eyes, he contemplated the new addition to Linnet's staff.

Since there was a big push on to complete the retrospective, Linnet and Evan would be together a lot, which meant he would have easy access to Evan. In any case, he didn't imagine there would be a problem about dating her. It had struck him that she had seemed interested in him, just as he was in her. He had seen her blushes, noted her fascination with him, felt the tremor in her arm when he had led her over to Linnet's desk. Yes, she was taken with him. Well, he hoped she was.

Although he had never had much trouble with women, Gideon Harte was not a conceited man. In fact, in certain ways it was his lack of male vanity, his gentleness and a degree of diffidence that women found attractive. Although he was tall, good looking, and blessed with an easy charm, there was also a little boy quality in him which appealed to women, made them want to fuss over him, spoil him.

Gideon liked women, respected them, and especially admired those who were accomplished, who were doers and workers. He didn't have much interest in women who wasted their time, had no job or profession. Yet all types of women flocked to him. The problem was he had never really been in love, had never met anyone he had wanted to get serious with. Until now.

Until now! Wow! This unexpected thought brought him up with a start.

Snapping open his eyes, he sat straighter in the chair, and dropped his feet to the floor. Good God! He was thinking about getting serious with Evan Hughes, and he didn't even *know* her! What was wrong with him? He must have gone mad.

After a moment's contemplation he had the answer. He had fallen for her, fallen hard, and in the blink of an eye.

A *coup de foudre*, the French called it, a flash of lightning. Oh God, he thought, I've gone and fallen for a stranger I know nothing about. Maybe she's engaged, or involved with another man. And maybe she's not interested in me. Maybe I've imagined that, maybe it's wishful thinking?

Puffing his cheeks, he blew out air, then settled back in the chair. What was it about her that was so *different*? Not necessarily her looks, even though she was beautiful, because he usually went for tall, slender, dark-haired women, exotic-looking women.

Perhaps it was her manner that had captivated him. She had been forthcoming in the corridor, and yet he had detected a reticence in her, an air of refinement. And then there was her extraordinary smile, which had made his heart do a flip, and those large liquid eyes that had seemed to swamp him. Clear, luminous eyes that were full of honesty, and trust.

I'm behaving like a schoolboy, he chastised himself. And I'm twenty-eight years old. I should know better. I mustn't get carried away. That could be fatal for me, especially if she's caught up with someone else.

She might even be engaged, he now decided. On the other hand, she hadn't been wearing a ring. Still, that didn't really signify anything these days. People were often engaged without a ring to show for it.

But I'll get her a ring, he thought. A sapphire ring. No, aquamarine to match the colour of her eyes. Hey, slow down, he muttered under his breath. You're running ahead of yourself. But he couldn't help it. No two ways about it. He wanted Evan Hughes.

Gideon's eyes shifted to the door at the sound of knocking. 'Come in,' he called, and then instantly jumped to his feet at the sight of his father on the threshold.

'Hi, Dad,' he exclaimed, walking towards him.

'Hello, my boy,' Winston Harte said, giving him a broad smile.

After they had embraced, and Gideon had led his father to a chair near his desk, he said, 'I thought you were in Yorkshire, Dad. What're you doing in London?'

'I came up to town for a meeting at the television studios, and I wanted to see you anyway.'

Gideon raised a brow quizzically. 'What about?'

'Christian Palmer.'

'Oh God, Dad, I knew you were going to say that. Look, I don't seem to make any inroads with him. You know what he's like, so tough-minded. He won't come back, Dad. He's busy writing his book.'

Winston sighed. 'I figured you'd say that, although I knew you'd stay on top of it. I've always said you're like a dog with a bone. But look here, there must be some inducement we can offer?'

Sitting down at his desk, Gideon nodded. 'I think there is, but it's going to cost us.'

'Whatever it is, Christian's worth it. He's the best damned editor we've ever had, and I believe we need him back here. So, what's the price?'

'He loves that house he's renting on the Isle of Man. I'm sure if we offer to buy it for him he'll agree to come back.'

'How much?'

'I'm not sure, Dad. I'll go into it with him, if you're in agreement. It's a nice house, and he's rented it off and on for a number of years. He's become very attached to it.'

'Whereabouts is it on the Isle of Man?'

'Just outside Douglas. In an area where he used to go with his parents as a child. He finds the Manx way of life very easy, very compatible, and of course he has peace and quiet to write his books. Furthermore, it's not difficult to get to, you know, just a plane trip from Lancashire.'

'It's not exactly an easy commute,' Winston pointed out, shaking his head. 'And are you sure the house will be enough of an inducement? He might want something else?'

'I doubt it. Christian's not like that, and listen, he might not even go for the deal. He's hell-bent on doing some serious writing, you know.'

'All I know is that he is the best editor Fleet Street has ever seen, except for Arthur Christiansen, and he was king of the heap sixty years ago. He made the *Daily Express*. Palmer's cut from the same cloth. Editors with their talent and brilliance don't often come along. So, do your best, my boy. Get him to come back, whatever the cost.'

'Okay, but it might mean a bigger contract as well.'

'That's not a problem, Gideon,' Winston said briskly. 'I learned years ago from Aunt Emma that when you want someone or something badly enough, the price doesn't really matter. That's how important Christian Palmer is to this company. So do your stuff.'

'I think I'll have to go and see him,' Gideon said, thinking aloud. 'I'll talk to him on the phone tomorrow, and suggest a visit next week.' Gideon chuckled. 'I wish it were the middle of the summer, not the dead of winter. The Isle of Man is superb in warm weather, but a bit chilly at this time of year.'

'You're right about that. I wish we could tempt Christian to come back to the Land of the White

Rose . . . I always thought he loved Yorkshire, loved his house in Ripon.'

'I think there's another inducement on the Isle of Man, Dad. A particular lady he's very attached to, quite aside from his fondness for that cottage.'

'Oh, it's a cottage is it?'

Again, Gideon chuckled. 'A big one though.'

'Make the deal with him, and the sooner the better.'

'Listen, Dad, hang on a minute. I think we'll have to wait for him until he finishes the book. In fact, I'm sure of it. Once he's delivered to the publishers he'll be lost, bored silly. That's when he'll come back, and only then.'

'So be it. I'll agree to whatever he wants. And dangle a new contract. Make it a good offer, an offer he can't refuse. Now, do you have a date tonight, Gideon? Stupid question, I suppose you do.'

'No, I don't, as a matter of fact. Why?'

'I'm at a loose end, with your mother in Yorkshire. It occurred to me we might have dinner together.'

'Great idea, Dad. I'd love it,' Gideon said, meaning this. But he couldn't help thinking about Evan Hughes. She insinuated herself into his thoughts again.

CHAPTER TEN

Winston Harte had always had a good sense of humour. And now, as they were being driven in his car through central London, pushing through early evening traffic towards the Dorchester Hotel, he teased his youngest son about his reputation with women.

'I couldn't believe my ears when you said you were free this evening, Gideon. A most unusual occurrence for you, wouldn't you say?'

'Not really, Dad. I'm often alone in the evening, you know. I'm not always gadding around the West End with a beautiful woman on my arm.'

'That's not what *I* hear, my boy. Everyone knows how you can so easily charm the ladies into your arms . . . I'm told it's like whistling the birds out of the trees for you. Come on, admit it, Gid.' His father chuckled. 'You've gained a reputation for being quite the ladykiller.'

Gideon had the good grace to laugh. 'It's an exaggeration, believe me. Toby had plenty of girls before he got married, and you know it, Dad.'

'Bah! Don't be daft! Now it's you who's exaggerating. He wasn't half as popular with women as you are.' Winston paused for a moment, and suddenly his voice sounded a trifle more serious when he added, 'Talking of Toby, he's got a bee in his bonnet about Tessa and Paula. Cornered me about them this afternoon, after the meeting.'

Gideon looked at Winston swiftly, and even though the light in the car was dim he detected a troubled look settling on his father's face, a tightening of his mouth. 'Cornered you in what sense?'

'He wanted me to talk to Paula.'

'What about?' As he asked the question, Gideon was almost certain he knew the answer. Unless he was wrong, it was the same old story rearing its ugly head.

Winston answered quietly, 'About the succession, of course. Who's going to head up Harte's when Paula retires.'

Gideon burst out laughing. 'He's crazy, Dad! They're *both* crazy. Paula's only in her mid-fifties. She's no more thinking of retiring than you are, or than I am, for that matter. She's not giving it a thought at the moment, I'm sure. One day she'll step down, maybe in ten years.'

'I beg to differ, Gideon, my boy. But only inasmuch as I think Paula will *never* retire. She'll never relinquish her power. Nor should she. Yes, she's going to be like Emma . . . she'll die with her boots on, at that desk in that store.' He nodded his head to underscore his point.

'But I thought Aunt Emma *did* retire. I remember you telling me that she did so when she was eighty, quite unexpectedly. At her birthday party, you said. I remember the phrase you told me she used. You said she charged Paula to "*hold her dream*" that night. I always thought it was a lovely way of saying she was passing on her mantle.'

'Yes, you're right. But after Aunt Emma returned from her world tour with Blackie, she was soon back at the store. Maybe not running things exactly, giving Paula her head, but nonetheless she was there. And most especially after Blackie died so unexpectedly. She didn't have anywhere else to go. And she was so bored at home.'

'Now I remember . . . she actually died in the store, didn't she?'

'Yes, *and* with her boots on, just the way she wanted. However, getting back to Toby, he thinks Paula's being unfair, that she ought to set Tessa's mind at rest. He believes Paula should tell her that she *will* succeed to the throne at Harte's one day. Whenever that is . . . *I've* certainly no idea.'

'But she's not going to succeed!' Gideon exclaimed, and instantly broke off abruptly, sitting back hard against the seat.

Winston glanced at his son through the corner of his eye, and asked *sotto voce*, 'And how do *you* know this, Gideon? Has Linnet said something? Confided in you?'

'Course not, Dad. Linnet doesn't know any more than you or I do. Or Toby and Tessa, for that matter. I'm simply making a guess. It's my opinion, and mine alone. I know that only Linnet can properly run the stores. Tessa doesn't have a clue; she's just not capable of it. For one thing, she's not employee-friendly, and God knows that's hellish important when you're running a huge retailing empire. Anyway, if I can see this with such clarity, then surely Aunt Paula must have the same vision.' He looked at his father quizzically.

'You're prejudiced, wouldn't you say?' Winston murmured, his eyes narrowing. He tended to agree with his son, but he wanted to encourage Gideon to reveal more, and said, 'You've always been extremely thick with Linnet, so naturally your instincts are to stand behind her. You see only *her* virtues, no one else's.'

'And you have an open mind? Is that what you're saying?' Gideon chuckled softly. 'Oh, *Dad*, come on! You know what Tessa's really like, you've had to deal with her so many times in the past. You used to comment about Linnet being the best of the bunch, except for poor little Patrick. You and Mum said she was the peacemaker, and a dyed-in-the-wool little mother the way she kept Lorne happy and fussed over Patrick. As for Tessa, she seemed out of it most of the time, I thought.'

'That's perfectly true. It *was* exactly the way you say. And she *was* odd, but teenage girls can be very, very strange at certain times. Hormones, your mother used to say. And Tessa may have changed . . . I only see her on family occasions, as you know, but she's a grown woman, married—'

'And just as bad as she always was,' Gideon interrupted.

'*Bad*. What do you mean by that, Gid?'

'I don't mean *bad* as in *wicked*. I meant she's just as difficult as ever. Contrary, bossy, egotistical, and very proud to be a Fairley by descent. I don't believe she thinks much of us Hartes. She looks down on us.'

'More fool she. Tessa's where she is today because she's a Harte through Paula.' There was a moment's silence, and then Winston remarked slowly, 'So, you think Paula's going to make Linnet head of the chain, eh?' He gave his son a hard, very direct stare.

'One day. *Yes*. Very *much* yes. But only when Paula feels it's necessary. It won't be for many, many years. Paula's too young to retire, and she loves Harte's, loves her work. It was what Aunt Emma brought her up to do, Linnet says. But then you surely know this better than I do, Dad.'

'Yes, I do. And you're absolutely correct. I *shall* have a word with her, though.'

'*Why?*' Gideon asked, sounding a trifle irate. 'She'll only tell you it's none of your business.'

'No, she won't. In a sense, it's very much my business. I run our media companies which are a major portion of the Harte empire, whilst Paula, your mother and Aunt Amanda run their divisions.

But we confer on everything. *Always*. Aunt Emma constantly pounded it into us that we had to think of the *whole*, the entire conglomerate, and not just our own separate *divisions*. We've always done that. And been very successful, I'm happy to say. So I know that I must alert Paula to these ... *rumblings*. They affect all of us in the long run. Of course, I'm not going to advise her, only pass on a bit of information, which she can tuck away, or use as she sees fit. Even immediately, if she wants. You do understand that, Gideon?'

'Yes, Dad. You know best ...'

'Paula is the head of the Harte family and all of the businesses. Emma trained her for this lifetime job, and she *is* Emma's great heiress. But Emma told Emily, Amanda and Paula that I was to be second in command ... I've actually never told you this before, but you really ought to know. Not that I ever expect to be running the family dynasty and its empire. Paula is a young, vital, healthy woman, and she's going to be around for a long time yet.'

'I am glad you told me though,' Gideon answered, now suddenly fully understanding how much real power his father wielded in the family hierarchy. It suddenly struck him how foolish Toby and Tessa were, thinking they could buck the system, challenge the old guard, or do whatever it was they were attempting to do.

Gideon said, in a low voice, 'Perhaps you should remind Toby that Paula owns fifty-two per cent of our media empire, and is actually just as much in control of his destiny as you are, Dad.'

'Oh, I don't think I have to remind him, Gideon,' Winston murmured, his brows coming together in a frown. 'He knows that.'

'I hope he knows he should watch his step,' Gideon remarked.

When they arrived at the entrance to the Grill Room in the Dorchester, the maître d' was at the other end of the dining room. They hovered together for a moment, waiting to be shown to a table.

On the way to the hotel, Gideon had decided he wanted to pay for dinner tonight; he realized it would give him immense pleasure to entertain his father, who was so generous with him always, and whom he never got a chance to take out for a meal. He felt around in various pockets, seeking his credit-card wallet.

Preoccupied as he was for a moment, Gideon did not notice that his father had moved closer to the screen that fronted the Grill Room and created a barrier between the room and the entrance. Winston was peering with growing interest into the restaurant through the glass panels of the wooden screen, his eyes widening.

Gideon only became aware that something was wrong when he heard his father curse quietly under his breath, felt the sudden hard pressure of Winston's hand on his arm.

'We can't go in there. Come on,' Winston muttered. Plucking at Gideon's sleeve, he guided him out into the hall.

'Dad, what's wrong?' Gideon stared at his father, and was instantly struck by the bony pallor of his face, the fierce, dark gleam in his eyes.

When Winston did not at first respond, Gideon asked again, 'Dad, whatever is it? You look as if you've just seen a ghost.'

'More like the devil. Jonathan Ainsley, to be exact. He's dining in the Grill with Sarah Lowther. They've always plotted against the family, and their presence together in London doesn't bode well for any of us. Mark my words.'

'You and Mother have always talked about the trouble Jonathan Ainsley and Sarah Lowther caused the family, and I know they were kicked out of Harte Enterprises. But I still don't know exactly *what* it is they did,' Gideon said, staring at his father.

The two of them were seated at a table near a window overlooking Green Park in the elegant dining room of the Ritz Hotel on Piccadilly. At Gideon's suggestion they had come here after they had made a hasty retreat from the Dorchester, Winston in particular being hell-bent on putting distance between his two cousins and themselves.

'Well, it's a long story – two stories, really. I'll tell you in a moment, and I'll make it as concise as possible. But first, let's order a drink. What would you like, Gideon?'

'White wine, I think.'

'And I'll have a glass of champagne.'

'Oh that's a good idea, Dad. I'll join you, forget about the white wine.'

Winston nodded, beckoned to the waiter, and ordered two glasses of Veuve Clicquot, then settled back in his chair. Gideon thought his father now looked better, but at the Dorchester he had been struck by Winston's pallor, worried because he appeared to be so upset.

Gideon voiced this when he said, 'You looked so disturbed at the Dorchester, Dad. I was really alarmed.'

'I was *angry*, Gid. Individually, those two are dangerous. But even more dangerous when they're in cahoots together.' He sighed and shook his head. 'I knew Jonathan Ainsley was in London, but I certainly had no idea Sarah was here from France.' He glanced at Gideon, added, 'Uncle Ronnie warned Paula that Ainsley had come back to live here. He told her a couple of weeks ago.'

'It was the weekend Julian was staying with us, and Aunt Amanda came up too, the weekend of all that snow. And we went to Pennistone Royal for dinner on Saturday. I thought Aunt Paula seemed rather perturbed during the latter part of the evening.'

'Julian gave her a message from his grandfather. I think it shook her up a bit. Uncle Ronnie was concerned about Ainsley's sudden reappearance after all these years, and when Paula went to see him the next day he warned her to be on her guard.'

'But Julian told me Ainsley can't actually do anything.'

'Not as far as the Harte companies are concerned,' Winston said. 'But, intrinsically, he's a troublemaker. And he always was. It's the nature of the beast, and if he could hurt Paula in some way, any way at all, he would. Actually, it would give him pleasure to upset her applecart. He's vicious, and he always was, even when he was a child and we were all growing up together.'

Their drinks arrived and, after they had clinked glasses and each taken a sip of champagne, Winston continued: 'I had a word with Uncle Ronnie, and he told me he'd advised Paula to hire a private investigator to check on Ainsley's activities. Uncle Ronnie explained that his gut instinct tells him Ainsley is out for blood. Paula's blood.'

An involuntary shiver ran down Gideon's spine and he exclaimed, 'I hope Aunt Paula *is* going to put a private eye on him, Dad.'

'Well . . . she's not at all keen, I must admit. Let's say she's ambivalent at best.'

'What do you think?'

'I'm in favour of it. Uncle Ronnie's a wise old bird. And never forget that the most valuable commodity of all is *information*. We all learned this from Aunt Emma, and, as I reminded Paula the other day, forewarned is forearmed, my boy.'

Gideon nodded his understanding, turned to the

waiter hovering and took a menu, as did his father. After a few seconds they ordered Colchester oysters to be followed by grilled Dover sole, choosing exactly the same dishes as they had done for years. Father and son had similar tastes in many things, including food and wine, art, music and books. So much so that Emily had dubbed them 'my two peas in a pod' years before.

After requesting two more glasses of champagne, Gideon turned to his father. 'Enlighten me about Jonathan Ainsley, Dad . . . tell me what he and Sarah did.'

'Ainsley headed up the real-estate division of Harte Enterprises in the sixties and seventies, and he ran the company very well. But suddenly business slackened, and he seemed to be missing a lot of big deals. Later we found out that he had been steering these really valuable deals to a company called Stonewall Properties, and—'

'But why?' Gideon cut in.

'Because secretly *he* owned Stonewall Properties with his old friend from his Eton days, Sebastian Cross. Ainsley was actually cheating Harte Enterprises out of thousands and thousands of pounds by doing what he did. He undermined the financial stability of the whole division.'

'And Sarah Lowther was involved in this too?' Gideon asked, a brow lifting.

'Yes, although somewhat indirectly, I think. She had invested money in Stonewall Properties, but to be honest, Gid, I don't believe Sarah knew of her cousin's treachery to the family. Once Paula and her father had enough evidence against Ainsley, they confronted him, kicked him out of the company and out of the family. And Sarah as well.'

'They didn't have any choice,' Gideon asserted, giving his father a direct look. 'And then *he* went to Hong Kong and made a fortune in real estate.'

'That's true. Ainsley was always quite brilliant at business, we all knew that,' Winston explained.

'Julian told me Ainsley came back later and tried to get control of Harte stores. How could that happen?'

Winston shook his head, his face changing, becoming suddenly saddened. 'It was actually Paula's fault. Ainsley did return to London in the nineteen eighties, just around the time she put ten percent of her shares in Harte's on the market. Naturally he snapped them up. And those shares, combined with what he owned, gave him an advantage.'

'But why did she sell some of her shares?'

'She wanted to buy a chain of stores in the States. Shane and I both understood her desire to create something of her own, but we also knew she was being flawed in her judgement. It's the only mistake she's made, to my knowledge. Other than marrying Jim Fairley, of course. *That* was a disaster.'

Towards the end of the evening, Winston turned to Gideon and stared at him intently for a moment or two.

Gideon frowned and leaned towards his father.

'What is it, Dad? You're looking perturbed again.'

'No, no, I'm fine. I was actually thinking about the great dynasty that Emma and Winston senior created, and I was hoping you might be the one to continue it . . . continue the line of descent.'

'I'm not sure I'm getting what you really mean.'

'Toby's not likely to present me with any grand-children as long as he stays married to the actress. Adrianna doesn't want any children, and I don't think Toby will be able to make *her* change her mind, whatever *he* believes.'

'But there's Paula, Dad, she's got a large brood—'

'True,' Winston interrupted peremptorily. 'And she's a Harte. But her name is O'Neill.'

Gideon nodded, suddenly understanding what his father was getting at. 'We *are* the last of the family to bear the Harte name, that's a fact.'

Winston sat back in his chair, pondering for a moment, a reflective look on his face, and he finally said, 'Far be it from me to prevent you from sowing your wild oats, and admittedly, you're only twenty-eight. But . . . well, I was just wondering if there was anyone on the horizon? A girl you might be *serious* about. A likely prospect, so to speak.'

'Not really, Dad.' When Gideon saw his father's crestfallen expression, he added swiftly, 'Actually, I've just met someone, and I like her a lot. But it's too soon. I don't want to make any wild predictions and then disappoint you.'

'But is she the marrying kind?' Winston probed.

Gideon nodded. 'I certainly don't think she's the

type of woman a man would attempt to sow his wild oats with – no, no, not at all.'

Winston beamed at him. 'I'm looking forward to meeting her, my boy.'

Much later that night, Gideon discovered he was unable to fall asleep. He lay wide awake in the darkness, his mind racing, as he thought of all the things he and his father had discussed.

He had been startled to discover that Paula, the most brilliant person he knew, had actually made such a bad judgement that she had almost forfeited her grandmother's beloved stores. In the same vein, he had been shocked that a member of their family had resorted to such treachery – and for personal gain when he already had so much. 'Ego and greed,' his father had said earlier. 'A fatal combination that has destroyed many other men as well as Jonathan Ainsley.'

And finally there had been the conversation he and his father had had about him settling down, getting married and having children. If Winston had been a little obvious, Gideon had not minded, nor had he been put out. He loved and admired his father, and he fully understood where he was coming from, how much he longed for grandchildren. As did his mother. It was only natural they would feel that way.

Evan Hughes. He had met her only today, yet he had been utterly captivated and a little thrown by his reaction to her. He did not know her, or anything about her, and yet he felt as if he *did* know her. She was beautiful, and she had been warm, outgoing. He found her sexually attractive, very desirable. And yet he discerned in her a refinement that gave her an added dimension.

Tomorrow he would phone her, invite her out . . . He fell asleep thinking about Evan Hughes.

CHAPTER ELEVEN

Tessa Fairley Longden picked up her hand-bag and carry-all, glanced at her desk, then hurried across the room, snapping off the light as she left her office.

She was dressed entirely in white, one of her favourite colours; a soft and flowing long cashmere cape was thrown over her shoulders on top of a white wool suit and matching silk shirt. Her boots were a deep cream colour as were her croco-dile handbag and the leather carry-all stuffed with files. The all-white ensemble underscored her ethe-real appearance, which came from her wonderful head of pale silvery-blonde hair, her silvery-grey eyes and her ivory complexion which was per-fect. Her delicately-wrought face lookcd as if it had been carved by a master sculptor, and to say she was lovely was an understatement. Tessa was staggeringly beautiful, so striking that heads turned wherever she went. She was tall, slender, willowy, and always wore the most beautiful and costly clothes. They were unique, distinctive, and often by lesser-known designers who catered to her wishes and her whims. Tessa knew what she wanted and aimed to get it no matter what, when it came to her clothes, at least.

She didn't always get what she wanted in other areas of her life, particularly when it came to her husband Mark Longden. Of late he had been more difficult than usual, bad-tempered, irritable, and extremely impatient with her. It seemed to her that he only kept his temper when their little daughter Adele was around, or in front of her family. He wouldn't dare be rude or nasty in the presence of her mother and Shane, but he didn't seem to care how he treated her in front of their friends. Not that they went out much any more; he was always staying late at the office, or going to see clients at weekends. It occurred to her now that he didn't have much time for her these days, unless it was to rant and rave at her about nothing of any great consequence.

A couple of times lately she had smelled alcohol on his breath, and he had looked flushed, his eyes glazed. But he had denied he had been drinking too much, and had flown into such a violent temper she had quickly retreated behind the safety of the bathroom door for half an hour.

He was always contrite after his volatile behaviour, almost slobbering over her, asking, begging, her forgiveness. And, of course, fool that she was, she always forgave him. Until the other day when he had raged at her about some chipped paint in the kitchen. He had been so ridiculous she had abruptly stood away, looking at him objectively, and she had begun to wonder what exactly was wrong with him.

As she turned the corner, walking rapidly towards the bank of elevators, she saw her half-sister Linnet, and she immediately called, '*Linnet!* I need to talk to you.'

Linnet paused, swung around, a smile lighting up her face when she saw Tessa. 'You look beautiful, absolutely gorgeous Tess, in all that white!' As she spoke Linnet stepped towards her sister, was about to embrace her. Then the smile slipped when she saw Tessa's face.

Tessa moved closer to the elevators, and said in a cold tone, 'How dare you countermand my orders about the auditorium. You had no right to do that. I am the senior executive here, and what I say goes.'

'But I didn't know—'

'I can't stand here wasting time with you. I'm late as it is,' Tessa interrupted in a strident tone, and stepped into the elevator. 'Just don't do things without asking my permission,' she snapped as the door closed, cutting off her view of Linnet.

That girl goes too far at times, Tessa thought, as the lift carried her down to the ground floor. She was suddenly seething about the younger woman, and once again all of her resentment and jealousy of Linnet rose to the surface. There was no question in

Tessa's mind that Linnet O'Neill was the favourite child of her mother and Shane. *Shane O'Neill*. In her own way she loved him, he had always been kind, had brought her up as his own. But she was *not* his biological child, and deep down that rankled. How could he love her as much as Linnet when she was not of his blood? In a way, though, she was glad she was not an O'Neill . . . *she* was a Fairley, came from an aristocratic line that went back centuries. Why, she herself was an aristocrat. Everyone said she looked like the Fairleys, and she knew she resembled Aunt Edwina, who was also part Fairley and a countess. To hell with Linnet, she thought, and pushed her out of her mind.

As she went through the side entrance of the store, nodding to employees as they, too, left for the evening, Tessa decided to be especially nice to Mark tonight. She did love him, despite his behaviour of late, and she wanted to keep the marriage intact. She had learned that the best way to make sure their time together was absolutely tranquil was to be acquiescent. She had to meet his every demand.

It was cold, and she shivered as she stepped out into the street, but within a second her driver had pulled over, was getting out of the front seat, coming around to her side of the car.

'Good evening, Mrs Longden,' Milton said, opening the door.

'Good evening. I'm going straight home, Milton,

thanks,' Tessa said, as usual scrupulously polite with the help.

Settling back against the seat, Tessa decided she would make pasta tonight. She had a well-stocked larder, because she often worked late herself, and frequently she and Mark did not sit down to supper before nine o'clock. They would eat earlier; she had made a point of leaving at five-thirty, so that she could start preparing their meal. Mark liked food and vintage wine, and she aimed to please.

When Milton pulled into the driveway of the Hampstead house where they lived, Tessa saw at once that Mark was already home. His car was parked outside the front door.

'Thanks, goodnight, Milton,' Tessa said as she alighted. She gave him a faint smile and asked him to come for her at eight the following morning. He said he would and bid her goodnight.

Running up the front steps, she let herself into the house, calling as she usually did, 'Adele! Cooee! Where's my little girl?'

A split second later Adele came running into the entrance hall, shouting, 'Mumma! Mumma! I'm here!'

Crouching down, arms outstretched, Tessa caught her child as she hurtled forward into her embrace. Adele kissed her cheek and snuggled closer.

After a moment, Tessa held the little girl away from her. 'How's my sweetiepie?'

'I'm fine. Daddy's here.'

The words had hardly left the child's mouth

when Mark's shadow fell across them. He stood in the archway that led through into the large kitchen.

Looking up at him, smiling, Tessa saw that his face was cold, his eyes angry. He seemed somehow menacing to her. Although her smile congealed, she said evenly, 'Hello, darling, you're home early.'

'And you're late. As always,' he murmured, his tone quiet but icy.

Standing up, taking hold of Adele's hand, Tessa said, 'It's only six, Mark. Come on, Adele, let's go and find Elvira.' As she spoke she took off her cape and threw it on the bench in the entrance hall.

Elvira, the young nanny, was stacking the dishwasher, and she looked up and smiled at Tessa and Adele as they came into the kitchen together. 'Hello, Mrs Longden, Adele ate well tonight. She's just had a nice supper. Steamed vegetables and a small piece of grilled sole. And raspberries for dessert.'

'It sounds delicious. Thanks, Elvira. You look after her so well.'

'Good nutrition, Mrs Longden.' Closing the dishwasher, Elvira added, 'I'll take her upstairs in a few minutes to get her ready for bed.'

'Oh I can do that,' Tessa replied quickly. Looking down at Adele, she went on, 'Shall I read you a story, darling?'

'Oh yes, Mumma. *Please*.'

'I need to talk to you. Right now, Tessa,' Mark said, suddenly looming over her.

'But I want to read a story to Adele. Can't it wait a few minutes?'

'No, it cannot.'

There was such a nasty undertone in his voice, Tessa nodded, and then bent over Adele, murmured. 'Daddy needs me. I'll come up shortly. Elvira can get you ready and then I'll come and read the story to you before you go to sleep.'

Adele smiled up at her mother, whom she adored.

Taking hold of her arm, Mark led Tessa across the hall into the library, closing the door behind them. This was yet another room in the house that Tessa loathed. She found it cold, dark and depressing, rarely entered it.

'What's so important that it couldn't wait a few minutes?' Tessa asked, looking at Mark, smiling, wanting to keep everything calm between them.

'I want to talk to you about the hours you keep,' he answered. 'You stay at that damned store far too late, and you work too hard. And some good it's all going to do you.'

'What do you mean?'

'She's not going to leave anything to *you*. Paula O'Neill doesn't care about *you*. Linnet's her *favourite*. She's the love child, born out of Shane's loins. Did you know he was her lover before your father was even *dead*? She was screwing him when she was on her business trips to New York . . . when you were left behind in England with the help. And did you—'

'That's not true!' Tessa exclaimed, automatically

defending her mother. 'I know Mummy and Shane were friends then, in fact they have been friends all their lives, since they were children. They grew up together in Yorkshire. You're being ridiculous. I won't have you talk about my parents like that.'

'*Oh*. Shane's suddenly a parent, is he?'

'He did bring me up, Mark, and he was kind and loving. I was only a small child when Jim Fairley was killed in the avalanche.'

'And wasn't *that* convenient for your mother and her lover. An avalanche. An act of God!'

'Oh stop this! You're being disgusting. And God knows where you got that kind of information. Why it's . . . almost *libellous*.'

'No it's not, because it's true. And I got it from a very good source.'

'Who?'

'I never reveal my sources. Rule of the game, you know.'

Tessa glared at him. 'I demand to know who is making these scurrilous remarks to you about my mother and Shane.'

'A little dicky bird. Look, why don't you ask her yourself. Ask her about her weekends in New Milford, Connecticut. The long weekends she spent with Shane in his barn there.'

Tessa shifted slightly in the chair, frowning. She stared at Mark and then looked away, puzzled and disturbed by his stories.

He broke the silence, saying suddenly, 'You won't get to be head of the stores, believe me you won't. And you won't get to inherit Pennistone Royal either. Linnet's going to get it all. Poor little you, you're the one who's going to get a royal screwing.' He laughed coldly.

'I don't believe any of this,' Tessa said, striving to keep her voice steady. But she was upset, shaking inside, and she wondered if there was any truth in what he was saying. Abruptly, she jumped up, walked towards the door. 'I'm going to read to Adele.'

'Not so fast,' he cried, striding across the room, grabbing her arm before she could reach the door. He pulled her into his arms, and kissed her, forcing his tongue into her mouth. With his free hand he locked the door. He walked her over to the sofa, and pulled her down with him, throwing a leg over her, pressing his face against hers. In her ear he said, 'I'm going to give you a royal screwing right now, Tessa, my love.' He fumbled with her white silk shirt, and growing impatient with the buttons he simply ripped it down the front, put his hand in her bra and got hold of her breast. He brought his mouth to it, kissed the nipple, and then suddenly he bit it.

Tessa screamed, struggled with him, pushed him away, and sat up. Slender though she was, she worked out every day and she had amazing strength in her arms. She gave him a sudden hard shove and he rolled off the narrow sofa onto the floor.

'You bloody bitch,' he shouted.

'You hurt me, Mark,' she said quietly, at once

conciliatory, knowing his temper was about to flare up. 'Why did you bite me?'

He struggled to his feet without responding.

Standing herself, Tessa edged toward the door. He caught hold of her arm, almost wrenching it out of its socket. 'Don't spend too much time with Adele,' he murmured, his voice unexpectedly soft. 'I have an urgent need for you tonight. You're going to have to meet your wifely obligations.'

'I always do, Mark darling,' she whispered.

His answer was to grab hold of her hand and press it against his crotch. 'See what you do to me? Come on, Tess, let's have a quickie now. Right there on the sofa. The door's locked. No one can get in.'

'Later, Mark darling.' She leaned into him, kissed him lightly on the mouth. 'Let me deal with Adele first.'

He took her face between his hands, squeezing it hard, so hard it hurt, and tears sprang into her eyes. 'Don't be too long,' he hissed. 'Otherwise I might have to—'

'Have to what?' she cut in.

He did not answer. He merely gave her a cold stare in return, let go of her, walked across to the door and unlocked it. 'Be my guest,' he said, his voice menacing again.

Tessa hurried out and ran upstairs, fastening her jacket. She almost stumbled into Adele's room, and then took a deep breath, calmed herself. With a smile she walked towards the bed, saying, 'And what story shall I read to you tonight, darling?'

'Anything you want, Mumma.' Adele patted the bed. 'Sit here.'

Tessa did as she said, picking up one of the books on the beside table, opening it.

Adele leaned closer to her mother, and touched her cheeks. 'Why are you crying, Mumma?' she whispered. 'What's wrong?'

'Nothing, sweetiepie.' Tessa smoothed her cheeks with her fingertips and then wrapped her arms around her daughter, holding her close.

Twenty minutes later, when Adele had fallen asleep, Tessa turned out the lamp but left on the night light, and slipped out of the room quietly.

Walking slowly downstairs she took total control of her emotions, and went into the library. Mark was sitting at his desk, going through the mail, and he glanced up, instantly smiled at her. 'I'm so sorry,' he murmured, getting up, coming towards her. 'I hope I didn't hurt you?'

She shook her head. It was not unusual for him to be suddenly calm after the storm. He had strange mood swings these days, was erratic, went from being angry to loving.

He said, 'I don't know what gets into me sometimes. I suppose it's overwork, stress, pressures. Forgive me?'

'Yes, Mark. But why did you say those things about my mother? Why did you say I'm not going to inherit?'

'It was just some gossip I heard about your

mother. Forget it, darling. I really shouldn't have repeated it. I was wrong.'

'Why won't you tell me who told you?'

'It's not anyone you know, some American chap who was here from New York. He claims he knew Shane in those days, when Shane was running the American end of O'Neill Hotels International. Let's forget it, okay?'

'All right. But it wasn't very nice, I mean the things he said about Mummy.'

'Oh I know. And as I said, I was wrong to repeat them. Look, let's go out to dinner, shall we? Why don't we go to Harry's Bar? Go and change, and I'll try and get a table for nine o'clock. Please, Tessa.'

'That'll be nice, going out,' she murmured. 'I'll go and get ready.'

CHAPTER TWELVE

'I have only one question for you,' Linnet said, pausing in the middle of Chester Street, staring up at Julian.

'Yes?' he responded, looking down at her, thinking how lovely she looked in the lamplight, curbing the desire to kiss her passionately. 'And what's that?'

'How did you manage to get past security at the back door of the store, *and* up to my office without anybody phoning me?'

Amused by the question, he began to laugh. 'Joe Pinkerton was on duty at the staff entrance, and he's known me since I was a toddler. So obviously he let me through.'

'I see.'

Noting her sudden snippy tone, and not wishing to get a senior staff member into trouble, he quickly added, 'But Joe did ask me to sign the book.'

'I'm glad to hear it.'

'Also, I mentioned I was coming to pick you up,'

Julian thought to add, watching her face carefully.

'And how did Joe react to that?' she asked, her voice a fraction milder.

'He smiled, and winked, and—'

'You *see*! Someone else assuming we're a couple!'

'Well, we are. We always have been and hopefully we always will be, whatever *you* think. And what's wrong with that anyhow?' he demanded, his voice rising sharply, an irate gleam entering his blue eyes.

Linnet continued to stare up at him, looking slightly put out, and she was about to make another sharp retort when spontaneously he grabbed hold of her shoulders, pulled her to him and kissed her fully and deeply on the mouth.

For a moment Linnet resisted, tried to push him away, and then suddenly, unexpectedly, and much to her amazement, she crumbled. Clinging to him fiercely, her arms around his neck, her resistance to him dissolved. She began to return his kisses with a passion which equalled his, surprising herself as well as Julian.

After a moment or two, they reluctantly drew apart, stood gaping at each other, both of them startled, for the same reason: Her unbridled response to him after weeks of cool and forbidding distance was a total turnabout, almost shocking in its own way.

Julian touched her cheeks, lightly, with his fingertips and murmured, 'Come on, I've got a surprise for you.' As he spoke he tucked her arm through his, and they continued down the street in the direction of his apartment. Once they were inside the entrance hall of the remodelled townhouse, he kissed her softly on the mouth again; then, taking her hand, he hurried her up the flight of stairs to the next floor.

'What kind of surprise?' she asked at last, her curiosity finally getting the better of her.

Julian Kallinski simply smiled enigmatically, said nothing, and led her directly to his front door. After unlocking it, he ushered her inside, slammed the door behind them with his foot, and took her in his arms once more, his mouth finding hers.

Continuing to kiss her, he began to pull off her heavy topcoat, dropped it to the floor, then shrugged out of his own, let it fall, and they half-walked, half-stumbled towards the living room, still kissing each other.

The room was in darkness except for a pool of light from a small, silk-shaded lamp and the lambent flames from the fire burning in the hearth.

'Our separation is over,' Julian announced, impatiently taking off her suit jacket, throwing it on a chair, leading her towards the fire.

'But—'

'No *buts*,' he cried, putting two fingers on her lips to silence her, then he took her face between his hands, and stared deeply into her eyes. It was a face he loved, had loved since they were children. Heart-shaped, with high cheekbones and a broad brow, it was perfectly sculpted, the lines fine, delicate. She had sweeping auburn brows above those marvellous, deep-green eyes, balanced by the widow's peak which came down onto her forehead in a dramatic vee. Her colouring was so vivid, so unique, it was heartstopping.

He had always loved her bright red-gold hair, and when her siblings and some of her cousins had called her 'carrot top' and 'red pepper', teasing her unmercifully when they were all growing up, he had angrily shouted rude comments back at them, forever defending her. And he had taken her to one of their secret places, where he had kissed the tears off her cheeks, kissed her small, capable hands, repeatedly told her she was the most beautiful of all girls. It was Gideon who usually came to find them, and he, too, hugged and comforted her, and encouraged her in her defiance of the others. They were her stalwart champions, the two of them.

Now Julian said, very slowly, 'I've loved you all of my life, Linnet O'Neill. I'll always love you. Until the day I die I'll love you, and even after that. And I cannot go on like this. Very simply, I *won't*. We have to be together again, and immediately. I can't bear being away from you, I can't live like this, I just can't tolerate the separation you imposed.'

She gazed at him, saw the sincerity written on his face, the desperation in his eyes. But she remained silent, afraid to say anything, because she knew the wrong word would make him blow up. He was obviously at the end of his patience.

'Tell me you truly want to end our relationship,' he said after a moment, 'tell me to go away forever, and I will. I promise I'll never bother you again. Tell me you don't love me any more, Linnet O'Neill, and I'll go.'

Looking him straight in the eye, she cried, 'Of course I love you, Julian! I always have, but you see, it's—'

'No!' he shouted, more in frustration than annoyance. 'This ridiculous nonsense has to stop, do you hear? I am putting a stop to it right now. I'm taking a stand, Linnet. I just won't accept this from you any longer. *This is an ultimatum.* Either we go back to our normal relationship or I'm getting out . . . I'm jumping ship!'

He had spoken so harshly to her she was taken aback, and she visibly recoiled, startled by the authority in his voice, the look of absolute determination on his face. And suddenly she knew, at this precise moment, that if she continued her campaign to keep him at arm's length, to stall the relationship, to put him off with endless excuses, she would lose him forever.

Julian had just shown her that he was in earnest. Deadly serious, in fact, and she understood deep within herself that he was far too proud to be treated with the kind of indifference she had been meting out. He was too much in love with her to stand for the separation she had imposed, too much of a man, too strong and virile, too self-confident to be bullied by her. No weakling, he.

Unexpectedly, she realized with a sudden rush of clarity that she was risking the relationship, that she somehow had to make amends to him. *Now*. At once. Not tomorrow. Tomorrow would be too late. She had pushed him too far, too hard, to the very limit, and his patience *was* at an end. That was patently obvious from his tone, the stance he had taken, the hard glint reflected in his blue eyes, the tight set of his generous mouth.

Linnet took a step forward and put her arms around him. Standing on tiptoe, she kissed him lightly on the mouth. Holding his hand in hers, she gently pulled him towards the fire.

'Take this off,' she murmured, touching the lapel of his jacket.

He did as she asked, and in one movement threw it to one side, stepped closer, and took her in his arms very forcefully. His mouth sought hers hungrily, and they kissed for a long time, and then they sank down onto the rug in front of the blazing fire, wrapped in each other's arms.

Pushing himself up on his elbow all of a sudden, Julian gazed at her for a long moment, frowning, trying to read her face.

She saw the question in his eyes and asked, 'What is it, Julian?'

'Are you *sure*?'

'What do you mean?'

'Sure about this? Being here with me like this? Are you sure about ending the separation, coming back to me? Sure about *us*?'

'Yes, I'm sure,' she whispered, reaching up, touching his face, her eyes spilling her love for him.

He nodded his understanding; a smile flickered fleetingly on his mouth and was gone. He wanted her so much; he always had. He began to smooth his hand over her breasts. They were suddenly taut beneath the thin silk of her shirt, and her nipples stood erect as they hardened. Just as he himself was erect and rapidly hardening. He bent over her, sucked at her nipple through the silk, staining it, then unbuttoned her shirt, took a breast out of her lacy bra. His mouth came down on her warm flesh, and he kissed her breast tenderly. He breathed in the warmth of her.

Linnet's hands went up onto the nape of his neck, into his thick dark hair, and her fingers felt strong and firm on him.

Julian's desire for her was intensifying, and to such an extent he thought he would burst. They had been apart for weeks now, weeks that had seemed endless, and during that time he had constantly thought about her, dreamed about her; she had rarely been out of his mind. And of course he had fantasized about making love to her, being with her like this.

He was terribly excited, his emotions high, his physical desire flaming through him. He wanted to enter her, to sink into the deepness of her, into her core. And yet he did not want to rush; he wanted to prolong these moments, savour them, and he wanted to pleasure her, just as he had been doing for years, since they had first understood that they were sexually attracted to each other as teenagers.

He began to kiss her mouth once again, and she opened it slightly for him, and he sought her tongue, gave her his. And they were enraptured with each other, joined in great intimacy, becoming part of each other.

Linnet was on fire, burning up, as she always was when they kissed like this, so voluptuously. She wanted him inside her, loving her, making her feel whole once more. She realized now how very much she had missed him, missed their lovemaking, their shared passion, their extraordinary sexual bonding. He had been making love to her since she was sixteen, possessing her constantly, and with great feverishness, and how she loved being possessed by him with such fervour. Suddenly she felt the pulse at the core of her beginning to throb, and she was damp and wild with desire just thinking about him. 'Julian, Julian . . . please. I want you so much,' she moaned softly.

He lifted his head from her breast, looked down at her, and nodded. He began to pull off her blouse, and she unbuttoned his shirt, snatching at it, and finally they shed the last of their clothes.

Julian lay down next to her on his side, fitting his body to the curve of hers. He was silent. Observing her. Absorbing her. He enjoyed looking at her, studying her, devouring her with his eyes.

She thought how marvellously masculine he was. Long and lean, yet muscular, with a broad chest. He was darkly handsome, with high cheekbones, a cleft in his chin, and eyes that were bright blue, but dark now with desire, his longing for her. He moved closer to her and she felt his hardness against her thigh, and it both thrilled and inflamed her; knowing how much he wanted her sexually was an aphrodisiac.

After a moment, Julian raised himself up on one elbow, began to stroke her all over, running his fingers across her breasts, down onto her stomach and then her thigh, until they came to rest on the red-gold hair at the top of her legs. Slowly, tantalizingly, he slid his hand down between her legs, which she parted for him. Linnet sighed and her body began to relax as his fingers fluttered around her core, probed and then entered her. She stiffened and a low moan trembled in her throat. He stroked and caressed her until she was crying out, and he bent over her body, brought his mouth down to join his fingers and he pleasured her until she convulsed, her legs stiffening, and as she came for him she cried out once more.

He could no longer hold back. Gripping her body, he entered her swiftly and hard, thrusting down into the deep darkness of her, loving her. She was part of him, part of his soul, and she had been for as long as he could remember.

Her long slender legs went around his back, and she locked them at the ankles, locked him into her the way she had learned to do so expertly over the years, the way he had taught her. He pushed his hands under her buttocks, lifting her to him, and she began to thrust her body against his, as he thrust into her velvet warmth. And he found himself floating higher and higher, as if he were intoxicated, and he was. With her, with the scent of her red-gold hair, the scent of her womanliness and her sex.

She began to tremble, the core of her suffused with heat and opening up all around him, engulfing him. He crested higher and higher; deep shudders convulsed him as he soared and, dimly, he heard her calling his name as he cried hers, and they were united once more, riding on waves of ecstasy and joy.

The intimacy of their reunion, the power and passion of their coupling after such a long absence left them both shattered, and they lay still for a long time, depleted.

But eventually they began to stir.

Julian watched Linnet as she gathered herself together, smoothed her hand through her auburn curls, settled against the base of the sofa, then reached for her shirt, slipped it on, as always a trifle shy with him after their lovemaking. She had always been that way, modest, aware of her nakedness, needing to cover herself, to be proper.

He smiled inwardly, thinking that there were two of her. The Linnet of this moment, covering her bare breasts, saying little, introverted, lost in herself; the Linnet of a short while ago, soaring with him on a sexual high: hot, wild, passionate. Uninhibited. Joyous. She was the joy of his life. He loved both of his Linnets with all his heart.

He pushed himself to his feet, bent over her, kissed the top of her head, walked across the living room and into his bedroom.

She watched him go, then closed her eyes, let herself drift with her thoughts. She was so happy to be with him again, and their lovemaking had been sublime. How had she ever believed that she could give him up? She must have been mad. He was part of her. The only man for her. The only man she had ever wanted.

Linnet sensed that he had returned, and she opened her eyes, looked up at him. He leaned down, draped a silk dressing gown around her shoulders, and once more joined her on the rug in front of the fire, pulling his own robe around himself, tying the belt.

'You should always wear that shade of blue,' she murmured, looking across at him. 'It matches the colour of your eyes.'

'I know. My favourite woman bought it for me.'

She smiled at him, her eyes crinkling with laughter, then she said softly, 'I love you, Julian Kallinski. I love you as much as you love me.'

'I know that, Linnet.'

There was a small silence; she bent her head, plucked at the dressing gown, then went on, 'I'm sorry . . . sorry I did this to you . . . asked for breathing space, and in the process hurt you so much. I did, didn't I?'

'Yes, you did.'

'Do you accept my apology?'

'I do, but I have a question.'

'Yes?'

'*Why*? Why did you do it, Linnet? I'm still baffled.'

She nodded, let out a deep sigh. 'I felt I was being manipulated, that *we* were being manipulated into marriage by our grandfathers. I really and truly did feel this. After all, the three clans have always wanted a Kallinski to marry a Harte.'

'You're an O'Neill,' he teased.

'You know what I mean . . . a descendant of David Kallinski and a descendant of Emma Harte must marry, because long ago, almost a hundred years ago, at the turn of the last century, David loved Emma.'

'And Emma walked away from him, just as you walked away from me. History must repeat itself, is that it?' he asked, sounding just a little acerbic.

'No, no, of course not! David Kallinski, your great-grandfather, was a married man, and you know that. Emma had immense integrity and she would never break up a marriage, attempt to build a life on someone else's misery. That's why she walked away, but she remained his friend until he died, and he was her partner in Lady Hamilton Clothes for years. Grandfather Bryan's often told me *that* story. I know it by heart by now.'

'And I heard it from Grandfather Ronnie at one point in my life. But feeling manipulated is not a good enough reason, Linnet,' Julian murmured.

'I know. And it was only part of the reason. I wanted us both to be sure of the way we felt about each other. I wanted to let you have a few months of . . . well, freedom, actually, to find out where you stood with me. You could say I set you free, Julian . . . you know what I mean.' She made a small *moue* with her mouth, shaking her head. 'I didn't want you to feel obligated to me. I wanted you to be unattached, in a sense, so you could have a relationship with another woman if you wanted.'

He gaped at her, surprise sliding onto his face. Then he burst out laughing. 'You mean you set me free so that I could . . . *play around*?' he gasped, still chuckling.

'Yes.'

He was so amused he couldn't speak for a moment, and he laughed again.

Linnet frowned. 'Did you?' she demanded.

'Did I what?'

'Have an affair in the last few months?'

'No, of course I didn't! I'm not interested in anybody else but you. Surely you know that by now,' he retorted heatedly.

'I suppose I do. But I did feel we were being pushed headlong into marriage because of *their* pasts, because the three clans wanted it, and I resented that a whole lot. Also, there was another thing. I thought that once we were well and truly married you'd get bored. That does happen, you know. A couple are together for years, happy being with each other, and then once that piece of paper's been signed, *it* comes between them. I began to worry that we'd been together for so long . . . I thought the marriage would break up, and then where would we be?'

'Oh Linnet . . . darling, how could I ever be *bored* with you?'

'Well, we have been sleeping together for ten years . . . that's a long time.'

'That's true, and I've loved every minute,' he said, staring at her, wondering whether to laugh or cry. She had put him through hell, agonies of mind and body for weeks, and all because she was full of preconceived ideas about men and their behaviour with women. But he was not like other men. Their rules didn't apply to him; he didn't follow anybody's rules.

In a way, she was right about the grandfathers, though. They were to blame, if blame could be attached to anyone. They had not let the matter rest for years, ever since they'd realized, and with delight, that he and Linnet were a twosome. And they had stepped up their campaign this past year, so he knew exactly how troubled she was by their manipulation. He had felt it himself, if the truth be known. He had simply been less affected than her, had been able to shrug it off.

And he supposed, if he were eminently fair, that many women might well think that a man could become sexually turned off one day, after spending years and years with the same woman, a woman he had known since her childhood. But he was different. He wished she'd realized that about him. It bothered him, for a moment, that she hadn't understood him better, and then he kicked the thought away, with the force he once used to kick a rugger ball. And then dismissed it completely.

Moving closer to her, he put his arm around her and pulled her to him. 'Do you remember what we did when you were seven and I was eleven? Up in the attics at Pennistone Royal?'

'What *we* did! You mean what *you* did.'

'What did I do that you didn't do?'

'You undressed me, *without* my permission!'

'I don't remember you objecting, you little beast.'

'You didn't think I was a little beast *then*. You were fascinated . . . with every part of me.'

'If I remember correctly, you were very willing and able, and an enthusiastic participant in our little games when we were teenagers. In fact, you once undressed me, and quite forcefully, and examined me, and did a lot more, I might add. You even went as far as to—'

'Don't say it, Julian Kallinski, or I'll—'

'You'll what?' he interrupted.

'I'll do it again, right now.'

'Yes, please.' Smiling at her, he moved even closer, buried his face in her fragrant hair that smelled of lemon verbena and a hint of summer flowers and cleanliness. Such a familiar scent . . . her scent. 'Oh I do love you so very much, my

Linnet, my darling, my sweetheart. How could you ever think I would want to make love to another woman? I've only ever wanted you . . . only you could give me such joy, such satisfaction.'

She smiled to herself. 'I *was* your willing pupil, wasn't I?'

He pulled away from her, winked wickedly. 'But you did have the best teacher in the world, don't you know.'

'Oh I do, I do, only too well!'

He cradled her in his arms, thinking about her, trying to be objective for a second or so. He knew her through and through, better than he knew anyone else, even members of his own family.

She was a complete Harte. She had inherited all of their characteristics: their toughness of mind, their loyalty and generosity, their spirit and energy, their many diverse talents, their extraordinary capacity for backbreaking work. All the Hartes were fierce in their defence of each other and she was no different. Touch a Harte and the rest of the clan would go for the jugular. He knew full well that she had never really liked Toby, but she would fight until she dropped to defend or avenge him. That was the way they were. They were abiding by Emma's rules, as they did in all things. She had set the standards long ago and they still existed for every one of the Hartes.

Yes, Linnet had inherited *all* of their traits, good and bad, and their marvellous looks. Not to mention their hot-bloodedness. Emma's blood ran in her veins, and Emma's had never been icy. To the contrary. Men had fallen at *her* feet, and there had been a number of men she had loved, had had liaisons with, and several of her children had been born on the wrong side of the blanket – tribute to her passionate nature. If he was any judge of character, from what he knew about her, Emma Harte had more than likely been as hot and uninhibited in bed as her great-granddaughter was with him.

But he loved Linnet because she *was* a Harte, because she was all the things she was. He loved her defiance of the rules, her independence, her pithy bluntness that at times reminded him of her Aunt Emily, and made him laugh hilariously. And he loved her for her sweetness, her tenderness, her gentleness with children, her kindness to the elderly in the family. He knew how much she cared for Bryan, even though at times her grandfather had driven her crazy with his talk of the final uniting of the three clans.

For her part, Linnet's thoughts were on her behaviour over the past few months. She was mainly worrying that Julian thought she had been silly. Well, she had been foolish in certain ways; she should have confided her worries in him, instead of insisting on a period of separation. What had been accomplished in the end? Nothing at all. It had only made them both miserable, and been a waste of precious time. No, perhaps not such a waste. Certainly she valued him more than ever . . . now she suddenly understood that. The very thought of losing him a short while ago had terrified her, filled her with dread, and she had been determined to make things right between them. Immediately. And she had.

Their attraction for each other was as rampant now as it had been the first time they had made love. She remembered that night very clearly. They had kissed and touched and explored each other for years, and then, not long after her sixteenth birthday, the petting had gone too far, flared into something much more dangerous one evening. She had encouraged him, enticed him until finally they were carried away by their own feelings, and had gone the whole way. Several times that night, in fact. Then they had worried themselves to death until she had her next period. After that Julian had armed himself with contraceptives until she went on birth-control pills.

Julian Kallinski. Her *first* love. Her *only* lover. She sometimes wondered if she had been his only conquest; she was not sure. He was four, almost five years, older than her, and had gone away to boarding school, then to Oxford. Once she had heard her father and Uncle Winston talking and laughing about Gideon and Julian, and Uncle Winston had muttered something about them being a couple of 'Jack the lads'. Which meant only one thing in her mind.

But she did not care. Those days had ended. He was carrying a great deal of responsibility at Kallinski Industries, and he would have to shoulder much more one day in the future when he took over. They understood each other very well, and she herself had her own load to carry at Harte's. In a sense, they had been lumbered by their ancestors' great successes. Perhaps that was why they were compatible, the shared background and upbringing, the dedication to duty, their acceptance of the circumstances of their lives. No explanations were ever necessary when it came to work and business. Julian was brilliant, hard working and dedicated, and they had identical values. For as long as she could remember she had loved him; she also liked, admired, and respected him. For her, he was a man for all seasons.

She stirred in his arms, and sat up. 'You told me you had a surprise for me,' she exclaimed, remembering what he had said earlier.

'I do.'

'What is it?'

'Close your eyes.'

'Okay. They're closed.'

Julian reached into the pocket of his robe and fumbled around until his fingers touched the object he was seeking. He took it out, got hold of her hand and slipped on the ring.

'Open your eyes.'

'Oh my God, Julian! It's beautiful,' she cried as she stared down at the emerald engagement ring glittering on her finger in the firelight. She looked up at him. 'It's more than beautiful, it's absolutely perfect. Thank you.' Reaching up, pulling him down to her, she kissed him on the mouth.

'It matches your eyes,' he murmured a moment later, enjoying her pleasure. 'Do you accept it?' He drew away, peering at her in the soft light. 'You know what it means if you do?'

'Of course I accept it, and I *do* know what it means, silly. We're engaged.'

'At last.' He began to chuckle.

'What is it? Why are you laughing?'

'The grandfathers are going to take credit for our engagement, you know.'

'Don't you dare mention *them* to me now,' she exclaimed, but she couldn't help laughing with him. 'So this is why you came to the store tonight, appeared at my office unexpectedly and dragged me off, almost by the hair. To get engaged to me.'

'I didn't know what was going to happen, how you'd respond,' he replied. 'But I wanted to be prepared . . . for any situation. I mostly wanted to talk to you, Linnet, to clear the air. You see, I just couldn't stand it any longer. I thought I was going to go insane without you. I wanted to have it out, settle it once and for all.'

'And when you kissed me in Chester Street I knew I couldn't bear to be apart from you any longer. So you see, you were right to come to the store and act so masterfully. And tomorrow I shall thank Joe Pinkerton for sending you up unannounced.'

He hugged her to him, and after a moment he said, 'I could eat an elephant I'm so hungry. Aren't you?'

'Yes. But you never have any food in your refrigerator.'

'I do tonight. This afternoon I did a bit of shopping, and brought dinner home. Mrs Ludlow prepared it all just before she left at six. She put everything on the tea trolley in the kitchen, left the champagne on ice, lit the fire in here. We've nothing to do really, just wheel in the trolley, that's all. How about a picnic on the rug? Courtesy of Harte's, of course.'

'It'll be lovely, but we won't have a fire if you don't put another log on it.'

'Right away.' He jumped up, removed the fireguard, dropped a log on the smouldering embers.

'I'll come and help you in the kitchen,' Linnet said, also rising. 'Now that I'm almost, if not quite, your missus.'

'You've always been my missus,' he shot back, taking hold of her hand and staring at the ring. It was a pool of green fire in the lamplight. 'The mister who gave you this must be crazy about you. It's some ring. And then some!'

'The mister who gave me this ring is terrific in every way, but especially in bed. I've always got the hots for him.'

He put his arm around her, laughing, and they walked across the living room and into the kitchen.

CHAPTER THIRTEEN

Lifting her crystal flute, Linnet touched it to Julian's. 'Cheers,' she said and took a sip. Looking at him over the rim, she added, 'When are we going to announce our engagement? Or shall we keep it a secret for a while?'

'Cheers, darling.' After a long swallow of champagne, Julian shrugged lightly. 'It's really up to you . . . do you want to have a drinks party? Just for the clans. Maybe on Valentine's Day? Or is that too corny?'

'I don't think it's too corny, but Valentine's Day is next week. There's going to be nobody around. Paula and Shane went to Paris this morning. Uncle Winston left for Toronto yesterday, for a board meeting, and Gideon's in the Isle of Man.'

'Oh that's right. He went to see Christian, I understand. Hoping to lure him back to Fleet Street with all kinds of promises. And goodies.'

'If anybody can do it, Gideon can,' she laughed,

and leaned back against the base of the sofa, stretching her legs.

The two of them were sitting on the rug in front of the fire, the picnic spread out between them. There were plates of cold meats and chicken, slices of cold game pie, potato salad in a crystal dish, a bowl of cornichons, plus a baguette cut up in pieces, and a slab of butter on a plate. The bottle of champagne sat in a bucket of ice nearby.

Julian eyed the food, took a slice of the pie, laid it on his plate and speared a fork into the cornichons. 'You used to love these when you were little.'

'Still do,' she said, and also took a slice of pie and some of the small pickled cucumbers. After munching on one, and eating part of the pie, she glanced at Julian. 'Why did you agree to take a breather, as I called it?'

'Because you wanted it so much and I decided I must humour you. But very frankly, Linnet, I'd no idea you'd stretch it out for several months. I thought we were talking a few weeks at the most. It became too unbearable for words.'

'I know . . . I'm so sorry.' She served herself some potato salad, took a forkful, then murmured, 'Gideon's smitten with Evan Hughes.'

'*Very*.' Julian gave her a quick look, drank some more champagne, then stared into the fire, his expression reflective. Finally he turned back to her. 'Actually, Linnet, I've never seen him like this before. He's really fallen hard.'

'I know. I think it happened the moment he set

eyes on her in the corridor at Harte's. He told me
the other day that it was a *coup de foudre*.'

'He told me the same thing . . . and I believe
he's right in that. Has Evan said anything to you,
Linnet?'

'Not a lot . . . she's cautious, but that's only
natural, I suppose. After all, he's a Harte, and she's
my assistant. Maybe she's a bit awkward because
she works for me. But if you want my opinion, I
think she feels the same way I feel about you.'

Julian sat back.

'She's flipped for him, in other words, and she's
got stars in her eyes.'

'So that's how you feel, is it?' He leaned forward,
looking pleased, squeezed her arm.

'Yep.'

There was a small silence.

It was Julian who broke it a short while later
when he said quietly, in a thoughtful tone, 'What
do you know about Evan Hughes, Linnet?'

She met his steady gaze with a puzzled look.
'What do you mean? What are you getting at?'

'I was just wondering about her background,
where she comes from, that kind of thing. I realize
you have her résumé, know all about her previous
work in fashion. I was actually thinking about her
personal background.'

'She's only been working for me for about three
weeks, but I like her a lot. So does everyone else.
And she's good, Julian, really professional. Imaginative, even quite brilliant in certain ways. India's

impressed, and so is Cassie. I haven't asked her a lot of questions about her private life, but I think it goes without saying that she was available – not entangled with anyone – when Gideon first asked her out. I know she was brought up in Connecticut, but lived in New York for about ten years before moving here. Her father's an antique dealer. I gather her mother is a manic depressive. She has two sisters. She's never been married. Well educated, nice manners. Great personality. That's about all I can tell you, really.'

Julian nodded, took a few sips of champagne, put the glass down. He cut a piece of the game pie still on his plate, ate it, the reflective look still in his eyes.

Linnet also ate a little of the pie, took a small piece of chicken, reached over for the bottle and poured herself another glass of the champagne. 'What a good idea this was, darling. So tell me why you're interested in Evan's background?'

'There's something about her that seems . . . well, quite mysterious . . .' He let his sentence trail off because he couldn't quite put into words what he really meant. Also, he didn't want to say anything which would be inflammatory to Linnet or, equally as important, put her off Evan Hughes. God knows she needed another assistant because of the retrospective, and she had for a long time. Evan Hughes puzzled him; she had done so since he had first met her with Gideon. Not the least of it was her uncanny resemblance to Paula, which he found so startling he was actually troubled by it.

Taking a deep breath, Julian plunged in: 'Don't you think there's something odd about her? She shows up at Harte's, out of the blue, and gets herself a job with you . . . and everyone's agog because she looks exactly like your mother. Younger version, of course.'

'I don't think she looks *exactly* like Paula,' Linnet answered swiftly, staring across at him. 'They're the same type, that's all: tall, dark, exotic in appearance. Evan has sort of bluish-grey eyes, my mother's are violet, and Mummy's got dimples and a much broader forehead. And no, I don't think there's anything odd about Evan, I really don't, Julian. As for her *slight* resemblance to Mummy, it *is* just that . . . *slight*. Very slight. And anyway, lots of people look like each other, but it doesn't mean they're related.'

'You're right,' he agreed, not wishing to upset her, or probe further. As far as he was concerned, from her appearance Evan Hughes could easily be Paula's daughter; in fact, she looked more like her than Linnet did. When he had met Evan he had been truly taken aback by her looks, but he *had* liked her; had found her charming, warm, quite lovely in many respects. And he had understood her appeal for Gideon. For any man, actually. And yet . . . well, he might as well admit it, he was quite suspicious of Miss Evan Hughes and her sudden appearance at Harte's. As his grandfather would say, there was something not quite kosher here . . .

'When are your parents coming back?' he asked.

'In a few days. Sometime next week. Dad had some hotel business in Paris, and Mummy just decided to tag along at the last moment. She said they're spending Valentine's Day there. Why?'

'I was thinking about asking your father for your hand in marriage.'

'Go on, don't be so daft, lad!' she cried in a broad Yorkshire accent, and began to laugh uproariously. 'You don't have to ask him, I think he's always known it would happen, that we'd get married one day,' she added in her normal voice.

'But I want to ask him, Linnet. I think it's the proper thing to do.'

Linnet leaned over, kissed his cheek. 'That would be lovely, darling,' she said softly, knowing what a close call she had had with him. She had almost lost him because of her own foolishness.

CHAPTER FOURTEEN

Throwing her long black coat around her shoulders, Evan headed towards the door, but the shrilling of the telephone made her turn back into the little sitting room. She ran to pick it up, exclaiming, 'Hello?' glancing at her watch as she did. She was running late: it was almost seven o'clock.

'It's me, Evan,' her father said from faraway Connecticut, sounding as if he was just around the corner.

'Hi, Dad!' she cried brightly, obviously glad to hear his voice. 'How are you?'

'I'm okay,' he answered in a low mutter. 'But you haven't called in over a week and I started to worry. Are you all right?'

She knew that down-in-the-dumps tone only too well, had always dreaded it, and swiftly she said, 'Oh, Dad, I'm so sorry, and yes, everything's fine. I'm great. It's just that we've been so busy with the retrospective I haven't had a minute to spare. But you shouldn't worry, I'm doing great here.'

'Well, I'm happy to hear it.' He said this in such a grudging voice it was obvious to her that he was not happy at all.

Evan murmured quietly, in a conciliatory way, 'I ought to have called you. I mustn't let the pressure of work get in the way again.'

'I've got to admit, I *do* worry about you. You seem so far away, Evan.'

When there was a small silence at her end of the phone, he said, 'Evan ... Evan ... are you there?'

'Yes, I am. And don't worry so much. I'm almost twenty-seven, for heaven's sake, Dad.'

'I miss you. We all do,' he answered, 'and I can't help worrying.'

'I miss everyone too, Dad. How's Mom doing? How're the girls?'

'About the same, and your mother is a lot more cheerful at the moment. I even got her out to the movies the other night.'

'That's wonderful news!' Evan was startled at this turn of events but pleased. Perhaps her mother was finally coming out of her lethargy and depression.

'So, you like working at Harte's, do you?' her father asked.

'Very much. I'm loving it. The retrospective is going to be something really special, and it's a challenging job. Mounting it properly, giving it cachet and excitement is most important.'

'I told Pauline Trigère some of her clothes are going to be in it, and she was thrilled.' There was a little pause, and then Owen said, in a careful tone, 'And how's your admirer?'

'Admirer?' she repeated, frowning, taken aback by the question.

'I hear you have a boyfriend.'

'Oh. Well, he's just a friend really, Dad,' she responded, knowing at once that he'd been speaking to George Thomas.

'Is it that man you met at the store when you went for the interview?' her father now asked. '*Gideon Harte?*'

'It is Gideon, yes.'

'He's the cousin of your immediate boss, isn't he?'

'That's right. But we're just good friends, as I said.'

'I hope so, Evan. It wouldn't do for you to get mixed up with your employer, you know.'

'He's not my employer!' she exclaimed. 'He's in the newspaper business; he has nothing to do with the store.' She gripped the phone tighter, trying to remain patient with her father. But he was obviously not pleased with her, on various levels. This baffled her, made her feel uneasy.

Owen Hughes said, 'I don't like the idea of you being mixed up with him, Evan. He's out of your league. It wouldn't work.'

'Dad, I told you, he's just a good friend. He's tried to be nice to me, to be helpful. Anyway, who told you about Gideon? George Thomas, I've no doubt.'

'No, Arlette. I phoned the other day to speak to George and she answered the phone in his office. In passing, before she put George on, she told me you had an admirer.'

'What do you mean he's out of my league?'

'All of Emma Harte's offspring are fabulously wealthy, powerful, live a life of privilege. You're not used to their world, Evan—'

'He's not like that,' she interrupted. 'He's a very nice, hardworking guy, and you wouldn't know he was from great wealth or privilege. He's very down-to-earth, committed to work, as are his cousins Linnet and India. In fact, the whole family has a very strong work ethic, Dad, so I don't know what you're talking about. And in any case, I'm *not* out of his league. That's a very strange thing for *you* to say, you've always said I could have any man I wanted!'

It was Owen's turn to be conciliatory, and he said quickly, 'You don't have to get all het up! I'm only being protective of you, honey.'

'I am quite capable of looking after myself. I've been doing that since I was seventeen, when I went to live in New York. Remember, Dad?'

'Yes, I do remember, and you weren't on your own, you were living with my parents in Manhattan. And listen to me, Evan, I don't care how nice this guy Gideon is, I know what his type are like, snobby, class conscious, out to get what they can from a woman—'

'Dad! Stop it. And at once! Gideon's not like that, and in any case, I told you we're just good friends. I'm not having an affair with him, if that's what you're getting at. He's taken me out a few times, a number of times actually, but that's it. We have a lovely friendship, he's tried to be kind, to steer me in the right direction, giving me helpful tips about working at Harte's.'

'I understand. But remember, he's from a very different world than you're accustomed to, Evan, and I want you to be careful. I don't want anyone ever to take advantage of you.'

'They won't,' she said in the steadiest voice she could muster. 'I'm a big girl, you know, a grown-up now, Dad. And you have always said I'm very level-headed. So I just don't really understand this tack you're taking with me.'

'Let's not quarrel, Evan,' he said in a less belligerent voice.

'I'm not quarrelling,' she shot back, thinking he was the one trying to pick a fight, not her.

'All right, honey, I trust you, trust your judgement. Anyway I'd better get off the phone. I have to drive into New York this afternoon.'

'Dad, if I'm not here at the hotel, and you want to speak to me, you can always call me at the store, you know.'

'I don't like to bother you at work.'

'You wouldn't be, honest.'

'All right then. Take care, honey. I love you.'

'I love you, Dad. And give my love to the girls and Mom.'

'I will. Bye.'

She said goodbye and put the phone down, stood for a moment with her hand on the receiver, thinking about the conversation. Her father just hadn't sounded like himself, and she couldn't help wondering why.

As Evan stepped out of the lift she collided with Arlette Thomas, almost knocking her over.

Gripping Evan's arm, steadying herself, the somewhat diminutive Frenchwoman exclaimed, '*Mon Dieu*, Evan, you are in the hurry!'

'I'm sorry, Arlette. I didn't mean to hurt you!'

'I am perfectly all right, *cherie*,' Arlette answered, looking up at Evan, smiling at her, as usual quite entranced by the young American. 'You look *très chic* tonight, but, more importantly, very beautiful. I hope you have the *rendezvous* . . .' She paused, laughing, and her eyes twinkled . . . 'with that nice young man you told me about.'

Evan couldn't help smiling back at her, and she realized then that Arlette had not meant to make mischief by mentioning Gideon to her father. She had merely done what came naturally to a romantic Frenchwoman – she had passed on what she thought was a little bit of harmless information about two young people going out together. Evan had come to know Arlette quite well in the last two months, and she was aware that the charming and motherly woman did not have a bad bone in her body. On the contrary, she was kind, loving, and saw only the best in everyone.

Edging towards the lobby of the hotel, Evan, nonetheless, ignored the remark about Gideon, and said, 'I was just talking to my father. He called me from Connecticut. I understand you told him I had an admirer.'

'*Mais oui, cherie.* I am so happy for you . . . and I told him *that*, too, and I said it was always nice for a young woman like you to have a lovely male companion.'

Evan said nothing, and a tiny silence fell between them.

Arlette, looking at Evan keenly, suddenly wondered if she had done the wrong thing by mentioning Gideon to Owen Hughes, and she frowned, made a small *moue*. 'I hope you did not mind that I spoke in that way . . . I hope I did not speak out of turn to your father?'

Arlette sounded so troubled, and there was such a worried expression in her dark eyes, Evan exclaimed, 'No, no, not at all. He called me because he hadn't heard from me for over a week, I've been so busy with work. I guess he worries. But he shouldn't, Arlette. I'm a grown woman, I'll soon be twenty-seven.'

'That's very old; so old it's downright ancient,' a masculine voice with a lilting Welsh accent said behind them.

The two women swung around as George Thomas,

Arlette's husband, came walking out of the office next to the concierge's small desk. Both of them laughed, and so did George.

The tall, pleasant-looking Welshman drew to a standstill next to Evan and kissed her on the cheek. 'You look bonny tonight, my dear.'

'Thanks, George,' she responded cheerfully, smiling at him. 'I was just talking to Dad. I guess he was on the phone to you during the week, worrying about me as usual.'

'I told him he should stop doing that, and immediately. You're well grounded, Evan, and he ought to know that. He brought you up. And you're level-headed. I think I embarrassed him a bit, actually, because I gave him a lecture.' George began to laugh. 'I told him he was getting to be a fuss-pot, an old lady.'

'He wouldn't like that!' Evan exclaimed. 'Anyway, he was fine when we hung up. To be fair, I suppose he misses me a lot.'

'Yes, he does.' George hesitated, and then he said in a low voice, 'I hope you're going to stay on at the hotel, Evan. The other day Arlette told me you had been thinking of finding a flat.'

'Oh, but not at the moment though,' Evan replied. 'I'm far too busy, and I'm so happy and comfortable here at the hotel. Maybe one day I'll look for a flat, but not just yet.'

'I'm very happy to hear that,' George said.

'And so am I, *cherie*,' Arlette agreed. 'And now we must let you go. I know you are in a hurry.'

'Yes, I am.'

'Have a lovely evening,' George said.

Arlette merely gave her a knowing glance as she smiled broadly, the look in her eyes soulful and romantic.

Evan smiled back, and she couldn't resist winking at the Frenchwoman.

Evan found a cab immediately, and gave the cabbie the address of the newspaper offices. Then she sat back as the taxi swung around and headed towards Belgrave Square. She could not help thinking about the conversation with her father, as she settled back on the seat. He had sounded so unlike himself . . . very odd really. There had been a hint of belligerence in his voice, and his tone had been rather critical when it came to the Hartes. But *why*? He didn't even know them. He had told her his mother had only ever mentioned Emma Harte to him once in passing, years ago, when she had said she had met her in the war years. It's very peculiar, she said to herself, and then wondered if it had merely been her father's possessiveness coming to the fore, and nothing else. Although she was reluctant to admit it to anyone, she had always known that she came before her adopted sisters, that she had always been his favourite, because she was his biological child. He had favoured her in everything, had quietly spoilt her when she was growing up, and even later.

But he had never displayed any kind of possessiveness before, much less shown jealousy when she had brought home her various boyfriends over the years. On the other hand, he had known that none of them had been very serious contenders for her hand in marriage. Except for Willard Cox.

With his approval, she had become engaged to Willard five years ago, but it hadn't lasted very long. Once she had decided to break it off with Will, her father had admitted that he had never thought that wedding bells would ring for them. 'Will wouldn't have been able to handle you, Evan. He's far too weak,' her father had said, and they had never mentioned him again. Owen had never even asked her why she had broken her engagement. If he had she would have told him the truth: one day, it had dawned on her that she didn't *like* Will. Certainly she wasn't in love with him, that was for sure.

She had never been in love. But she knew she might easily fall in love with Gideon. On the other hand, was she simply carried away because of his charm, his savoir-faire, his looks, his uniqueness, his very Englishness? She wasn't sure.

Gideon had made it clear he was keen on her, wanted to pursue a relationship. He had been a devoted friend to her since her first working day at Harte's, had made a point of taking her to lunch a couple of times a week, although it was always in the Bird Cage, the restaurant at the store, because of her tough schedule. And they had been out to dinner a number of times. He had held her hand, kissed her goodnight, but he had never been aggressive; he had handled her with kid gloves, as if he didn't want to scare her off. In fact, he had been the perfect gentleman.

One thing was certain – they got on well, were compatible with each other. They never stopped talking, had many things in common, and similar tastes. She wasn't exactly sure what his true feelings were, but she had stars in her eyes about him . . . he was a very desirable man.

As they entered the Mall and went down towards Trafalgar Square, it suddenly struck Evan that she hadn't liked the way her father had characterized Gideon, without even having met him. It was not like the Owen Hughes she had grown up with and knew so well . . . or thought she knew. Perhaps she didn't, after all.

Looking back over the past few weeks, she realized that he had been churlish about the Hartes from the moment she had found a job at the store. Did he have something against them? But if so, why had he encouraged her to go to see Emma Harte? He hadn't, now that she thought about it. He'd actually made no comment. It was only when she had pressed him that he had said something: that Glynnis had known Emma in the Second World War. He had not volunteered anything else. Had her father always known that Emma Harte was dead and buried for thirty-one years? If that were so he had let her go on a wild-goose chase knowing that her visit to Harte's would come to nothing. He had been humouring her perhaps, because of her devotion to her grandmother. That was the only explanation . . .

Her mobile began to ring, and she fished around for it in her handbag, brought it to her ear. 'Hello?'

'Evan, it's me, Gideon.'

'Hi.'

'Where are you?'

'Just coming down the Mall. I'm almost at Trafalgar Square.'

'That's good. I've finished here at the paper earlier than I expected. Tell the cabbie to take you to the Savoy. I'll meet you in the bar.'

'I'll see you in a few minutes,' she answered, and put the mobile back in her bag.

They sat together in a quiet corner of the bar, sipping their glasses of white wine and talking. At least Gideon was talking, about his work mostly, and Evan was listening attentively. Finally he fell silent. As he had been speaking his eyes had remained on her face, and they were still on her.

She returned his fixed scrutiny steadily, without blinking. His light green eyes looked as if they were flecked with gold in the dim light of the bar, and it seemed to her that he was trying to convey his innermost feelings to her. She realized they were the same as hers: identical, in fact.

After a moment, Gideon said, 'I have a confession to make . . .'

'Yes?' she asked quietly, staring into his face, which was now full of yearning.

'I've never felt like this before . . . the way I feel about you.'

'Neither have I.'

A small smile settled on his mouth.

'I think we both share the same feelings for each other,' Evan said.

'I hope so.' His face filled with sudden happiness. 'I'm not playing around with you. I'm very serious about you, so tell me if you don't feel the same . . . If this is just a *passing thing* for you, then say so now.'

She shook her head vehemently. 'It's not a passing thing. I'm not in the habit of playing around. But we still have a long way to go. We have to get to know each other better, don't you think? We need to spend more time together.'

He nodded his understanding, took hold of her hand again, brought it to his mouth, kissed the back of it. 'There's one way I want to get to know you much better. And tonight. Will you come home with me later . . . so that we can be together at last?'

She nodded.

'I booked a table at Rules for dinner.'

'Oh, you did!'

'You told me you went there with your grandparents when you were twelve. But you don't sound very enthusiastic.'

'I'm not hungry.'

'I know what you mean. Neither am I.' His eyes held hers. 'I want to be with you more than anything in the whole world. Would you like to leave now?'

'Yes, I would,' she whispered.

Gideon Harte paid the bill and they left the bar.

He escorted her through the lobby, his hand under her elbow, solicitous as he always was with her, and they stepped out into the courtyard of the hotel.

A moment later his driver was pulling up alongside them; as they got into the car, Gideon said, 'You can drop us off at home, Harry, thanks.'

Once they were settled on the back seat and the car edged out of the yard, his arms went around her and she brought her face up to his. He kissed her deeply and continued to kiss her for a few minutes longer, and then he moved his face away from hers. Sitting up a little straighter, he still held her tightly in his arms; against the cloud of her dark hair, he murmured, 'I've got to stop this. I can't stand it. I think I'm going to explode.'

'I know, I know.'

Chapter Fifteen

Evan had been to Gideon's flat once before with Linnet and Julian: they had gone for drinks before the four of them went out to dinner. That night she had been struck by its inherent good taste, but now she saw, at a quick glance, that it also had great charm and comfort. The whole was a mingling of greys and soft blues, accented with white, and there were some very good paintings on the walls.

After taking her coat, he led her from the entrance hall into the sitting room, where he turned on more lamps. But they did not linger there. In his usual take-charge manner he ushered her across the room in the direction of his bedroom. 'Let's go in here now, darling. Let's not be coy. All right?'

'Yes,' she answered softly.

Evan knew that she would have been slightly startled if this somewhat cut-and-dried comment had come from anyone else. But not from Gideon; he was so kind and sincere he had meant it in the best possible way. Anyway, she liked his directness. They had come here to make love. Why pretend otherwise?

In the bedroom he snapped on a small lamp in a corner, and then turned to her, kissed her lightly on the mouth and began to unbutton the neckline of her black wool dress. But suddenly he stopped, drew her to him and held her very close. He said, after a moment, 'I can't begin to tell you what this means to me, Evan, having you here with me. And I do want to please you so much . . .' He let the words slide away, held her tighter.

'You do,' she whispered.

Later that night she was to remember how tender and loving he was when they undressed, recall how she realized he was being so true to his nature . . . gentle and thoughtful, concerned for her.

Gideon held her in his arms, kissing her, touching her lightly; and she responded to him ardently. He was as tall as she was, and they fitted well together as they lay alongside each other on the bed. Eventually he began to stroke her, exploring her body, kissing her all over, and then he covered her with his long, lean body, and her arms went around him. Her fingers crept into the hair on the nape of his neck, and then she slid her hands down over his shoulders and onto the small of his back.

He was very still, quiet, hardly speaking at all, except for a few gently murmured endearments.

And she was silent, too, enjoying this intense communion without words, enjoying his hands all over her. His touching, so experienced and knowing, was erotic, sensual.

Bracing himself on his hands on either side of her, he looked down into her face, his eyes on hers. The expression in them was so intense, so penetrating, she felt as if he were seeing into her very soul, and she into his. Unexpectedly his face contorted slightly, and his eyes widened, as if in surprise, as he took her to him finally, sinking deeply into her.

An involuntary moan escaped her as he thrust harder, deeper, and he instantly covered her mouth with his, tasting her. Almost at once they fell into their own fluid rhythm, moving together as one.

Evan, her arms and legs wrapped around him, felt the heat rushing through her. It was rising from the core of her. She was red hot with desire, her face flaming under his touch as he stroked it roughly, then brought his hand down onto her breast, cupping it. The heat flowing through her suddenly seemed to intensify; she knew she was on the verge of climaxing and her body began to tremble under his. She whispered, 'Gideon. Oh Gideon. Please don't stop.'

He raised himself again, looked down into her face, his eyes piercing, overflowing with desire. 'I won't,' he said, his voice still hoarse, rasping with his own pent-up emotions. 'Come to me, Evan, come to me, darling. Be mine, as I am yours.'

Gideon could no longer control himself. Shudders racked through him, convulsed him, and he gripped her body hard, pulled it tighter to him. And they crested together on wave upon wave of pure, unadulterated joy.

They lay together in a mass of tangled sheets, not moving, not speaking. Eventually, Gideon moved closer, half covered Evan with his body and moved strands of hair away from her face. Staring into her luminous grey eyes, he said softly, 'Before, you said I pleased you. I hope I please you even *more* now?'

She smiled up at him, her eyes crinkling at the corners. 'Yes, you do. Very much.'

He nodded, still looking at her intently, and then he let his hand wander down from her breasts, over her stomach towards the vee of black hair at the top of her legs. He caressed her with tenderness, kissed her passionately, slowly found her core and began to make love to her with great concentration. Almost immediately her legs began to quiver, and her whole body stiffened, and she cried out as waves of ecstasy convulsed her.

Eventually she calmed, and he wrapped his arms around her, held her close to him, and said in a low voice, 'I want you to be mine and only mine, Evan.'

'I am, Gideon,' she whispered, and reached up to touch his face.

*　　*　　*

Evan awakened suddenly, snapping open her eyes, glancing about. Disoriented for a moment, she glanced around the dimly lit room, and then she realized she was at Gideon's flat in Belgravia.

Turning, she reached for him, only to discover that his side of the bed was empty. She got up, found the terrycloth robe he had given her last night, and put it on. Padding across the carpet in her bare feet, she found Gideon in the sitting room. Wrapped in a dark blue silk dressing gown, wearing his tortoiseshell glasses, he was seated at his desk, his head down, staring at papers, his briefcase open on the floor.

He must have sensed her presence. He glanced up and instantly smiled at her. 'Darling! It's the middle of the night. Go back to bed.'

She leaned against the door jamb for a second, and then glided over, stood before him at the desk. 'It's three o'clock. Do you always work at this hour?'

'Frequently. But I've already accomplished quite a lot in an hour, so come on, let's get a bit of sleep if we can.'

He rose, came around the desk, took hold of her hand and led her back to the bedroom. They got into bed and he turned out the lamp, took her in his arms, kissed her cheek and held her close. After a moment he said, 'I have to go to the Isle of Man again on business. I want you to come with me. Will you, darling?'

'Yes. If Linnet lets me have the time off.'

'She will.' He nuzzled the back of her neck, and they settled down. And entwined, comfortable with each other, they soon dozed.

But within the hour Evan woke up again. During sleep they had disentangled themselves from each other; Gideon was lying on his side at the edge of the bed, obviously in a very deep slumber, breathing evenly.

She curled against his back and closed her eyes, but sleep eluded her. For a while she thought about every single moment of the last few hours, relived them; she focused on their sexual attraction, their rampant desire for each other, their passionate lovemaking. It seemed to her that they were perfect together, perfect in every way, really. They had discovered, right from the beginning of their relationship, that they were completely compatible; that had been patently obvious to them both. In these last few weeks they had come to know each other well, had become friends and, in a way, allies. She was glad of that; happy that they had such a strong foundation for their relationship. There was no question that she was in love with him. She wanted him. It was apparent to her that he felt the same way.

Unexpectedly, her father's words came back to her. The way he had fitted Gideon into some ridiculous slot in his mind was shocking. How foolish it was to characterize and categorize people. And her father wasn't a stupid man. So perhaps it was something else which made him speak in that awful manner. Dislike of the Hartes? But he didn't even *know* them. Or did he? She was becoming very suspicious of her father as far as Emma Harte's offspring were concerned.

Gideon moved restlessly, made a strange, strangled noise in his throat, as if he were having a bad dream, and then almost at once he settled down again. Gently, Evan smoothed her hand across his back, not wanting to wake him, but wanting, certainly, to soothe him.

Gideon worked so hard. Sometimes when he met her for dinner it was well after nine o'clock, and he looked exhausted, his face pinched, his eyes dull and weary. It took him a while to relax, to let go of that world he occupied all day. It was a world he loved, she knew that, but it took its toll. He was trying to build the circulation of the *London Evening Post*, and he needed to entice Christian Palmer back to the paper. That's why he had to return to the Isle of Man. Last week he had told her he was working on the contract for Christian, and that things now looked positive. She hoped Gideon would succeed.

The entire family worked hard; she had realized this right from her first day at the store. And she had told her father this earlier tonight, but he hadn't seemed impressed. He just wanted to focus on his own view of them; but his view was skewed. She had begun to understand that the Hartes were totally dedicated to the great business empire founded by Emma Harte. 'A legend in her own time,' Linnet had explained the other day. 'Imagine that, Evan. Already a legend when she was only in her early fifties. It's amazing.' But they were all amazing, weren't they?

Eventually Evan fell asleep, curled up against Gideon's back, one arm thrown over his body, one leg entwined with his. Her last thought was that this was where she wanted to be for the rest of her life. With him always.

CHAPTER SIXTEEN

P aula glanced at the full-sized portrait of
Emma Harte hanging over the fireplace in
her office, and said to Emily, 'Grandy would
be very proud of you, Dumpling, you've done a wonderful job the way you've run Harte Enterprises.'

'She'd be proud of all of us, actually, and I do
think you'll have to stop calling me Dumpling. It's
a most unsuitable name for a middle-aged woman.
Quite embarrassing, actually.'

Paula started to laugh. 'I agree, but I can't help
it, darling. I started calling you Dumpling when
you were four or five years old, and I guess it's a
habit that's hard to break.'

'Try.'

'I will.'

There was a small pause, and Emily glanced
around Paula's office, suddenly exclaiming, 'Gosh,
it's like spring in here with all your wonderful flowering plants, and the daffodils look beautiful. I
wish I had your green fingers. You've always

been able to make things grow ever since we were little.'

'It's just luck really. Well, *Emily*, let's go over the guest lists for Winston's and Shane's birthday party. I see you have pretty much included everyone I put on my list, so we're in agreement there. I don't think there's anyone to add.'

'I think there is. One person is missing, Paula,' Emily remarked, settling back in the chair on the other side of Paula's partners' desk, which had once belonged to Emma, as had this office.

With a small frown, Paula asked, 'Who did I miss?'

'Evan Hughes.'

'But she's not family,' Paula began and stopped abruptly. 'Of course! Gideon's been taking her out, so Linnet tells me, and obviously you think he'll want to bring her with him. But will it last until June? It's only March now. Or is this serious?'

'Yes, it's the first time he's ever been serious about a woman in his life. You know the story . . . how he found her looking for the executive offices in January. Well, he's been seeing her ever since. And I think the initial friendship has blossomed into a love affair.'

'Oh! How do you know?'

'Winston told me, and he got it from the horse's mouth, so to speak.'

'What did Gideon say to Winston?'

'A few weeks ago, that night Winston spotted Jonathan Ainsley and Sarah Lowther in the

Dorchester Grill Room, the two of them had a talk about Gideon's love life. Winston point blank asked him if there was anyone serious, and Gideon said he'd just met someone he thought *could* be, but it was too soon really to say. Well, a couple of days ago, he told his father he did have serious intentions about Evan.'

'And what about Evan? Did he say how she felt?'

'That she was very involved with him, but being sensible and cautious she thought they should get to know each other properly before making a long-term commitment to each other.'

'That sounds like her. Linnet says she's very down-to-earth and practical. And a workaholic, which Linnet loves because she's such a slave driver. But I will add this, Emily, India is crazy about her as well. She can't speak highly enough about her. Evan seems to be rather popular all around.'

'So I hear. Amanda thought she had a look of you.'

'I didn't know Amanda had met her.'

'The other day, before she flew to New York, she came to the store to see Linnet – to bring a couple of gowns for the retrospective, actually – and Linnet introduced them.'

'Do *you* think she looks like me, Em?'

'No, I don't, to be honest. Oh yes, she's the same type as you – tall, slender, dark-haired, exotic looking – but that's all it is, really. She doesn't have your widow's peak, and her eyes are grey not violet.'

'That's what Linnet says, but oddly enough, Shane did a double-take the other day when *he* met her.'

Emily shook her head. 'I just don't see it. On the other hand, she tends to dress like you, in very tailored clothes, which adds to the impression, perhaps. But who cares, she's obviously not a relative. On the couple of occasions I met her I liked her, Paula.' Emily leaned forward slightly, and gave her cousin a long hard stare. 'I trust my son, he's a good judge of character, and his happiness is all that matters for me. If he wants to marry Evan, then it's all right by me, and by Winston. But you know he's anxious to have grandchildren. He's banking on Gideon to deliver the goods, because he's certain Adrianna will do her best not to get pregnant by Toby.'

'I tend to agree with that. Well then, let's add Evan Hughes to the list. I see you didn't,' Paula murmured.

'I wouldn't, not until I'd spoken to you. By the way, Mummy's really excited about coming, seeing the family.' Emily started to laugh. 'She's so excited, in fact, I do believe she's thinking about having another face job before she faces the entire family.'

Paula laughed with her. 'Poor Aunt Elizabeth, you do malign her, Em, and I'm sure she's not going to have a face job. She looks half her age and perfectly wonderful.'

'You're right. But she is hightailing it to Paris.

To Balmain on the rue François Premier to be exact. She wants Oscar de la Renta to make her a fabulous evening gown. And she told me she's getting her ill-gotten gains out of the bank.'

'Ill-gotten gains?'

'All the diamonds her husbands and lovers have given her over the years.'

'Emily, that's a downright lie, and you know it! Your mother bought her own jewellery. Remember what Grandy said – that your mother's husbands all had dubious titles and *empty* wallets.'

'Except for my father. Tony Barkstone was a true blue Englishman and so was Derek Linde, Amanda's and Francesca's father. Mind you, they didn't have a bean between them but they were nice. Mummy should have never dumped either one of them. But you're right, she did buy her own stuff, except for some rather nice pieces Grandy gave her, with the understanding they came to Amanda, Francesca, and me when she dies.'

'You've told me that before. Amanda is doing a great job at Genret, don't you think?'

'Yes, I do, and Amanda's getting her divorce moving forward, by the way.'

'I'm glad to hear it. I thought it was a mistake right from the beginning,' Paula replied and added, 'by the way, I spoke to Aunt Edwina in Yorkshire the other day. I couldn't believe how she sounded.'

'Well, she *is* very old, you know. Over ninety.'

'No, no, what I meant is that she was fantastic.

Sounded as if she was about to lead the entire British army into battle.'

Emily grinned. 'That's Edwina. I do believe her favourite granddaughter India gets that enormous energy from her. It's bred in the bone, I guess.'

'I think so. Now, Em, what do we do about Uncle Robin?'

'I think we have to invite him, Paula. He's not responsible for his son's treachery to the family.'

Paula nodded, picking up another sheet of paper. 'I like your suggestion about having various food bars during drinks, but we have to settle on the actual dinner menu. How—' Paula stopped, glanced at her private line as it buzzed, and picked up the receiver. 'Hello?'

'Mother, it's me. Tessa.'

'Yes, Tessa. What can I—'

'I want to see you,' Tessa cut in swiftly. 'Immediately. I *have* to talk to you. It's very important. And it can't wait, so I'm going to come up to your office now.'

'I'm in a meeting at the moment,' Paula responded, her voice cool, contained. 'I can't see you for at least half an hour.'

'Then I suppose I'm going to have to wait until then.' Tessa banged the phone down without any further discussion.

As she replaced the receiver Paula looked across at her cousin and said in a clipped tone, 'The Dauphine is in something of a snit, it seems.'

'She really *does* think she's the heir apparent,

you know,' Emily remarked. 'She has illusions of grandeur. She certainly thinks she's going to take over from you, Paula, sooner rather than later.'

'Grandy often used a wonderful Yorkshire saying in such instances: "You know what Thought did? Followed a muck cart and thought it was a wedding." Rather apt, wouldn't you say? I'm afraid Tessa has a few lessons to learn ... the first one in half an hour.'

'What's my problem, you ask? *Really*, Mother! You should know by now it's Linnet and her ridiculous sibling rivalry. It can't possibly have escaped you that she acts as if she owns this store. It boggles the mind the way she walks about, telling everyone what to do, throwing her weight around. She thinks she's in command of everyone; certainly she bosses enough people about. Not me, of course, she wouldn't dare, but her underlings, oh yes indeed. And now, on top of everything else, she has another assistant, as well as India. It's preposterous. I don't even have an assistant, merely a secretary. And do you know what she did the other day? She countermanded an order of mine, and I was—'

'*Countermanded!*' Paula exclaimed, cutting her daughter off. 'That's a peculiar word to use. This is not the army.'

'You know what I mean, Mother. Don't split hairs.'

'And you watch your manners, young lady. Now

stop it! You're whipping yourself into a fury for no reason at all and dancing around like a whirling dervish gone mad. Calm down, Tessa, and let's get to the bottom of all this nonsense.'

'Yes, let's do that!' Tessa exclaimed, glaring at Paula. But, nonetheless, she was wise enough to flop into the chair opposite her mother on the other side of the desk.

Paula said, 'First of all, Linnet doesn't have one ounce of sibling rivalry in her. *That* exists simply in *your* imagination, and yet you are using the idea of it to come in here and make trouble.'

'That's not true!' Tessa cried, leaping to her feet. Her voice had risen and she looked angry.

'Sit down! And shut up!' Paula admonished sharply. 'I won't tolerate this kind of behaviour. Now, you listen to me, and listen very, very carefully, because I'm only going to say this once. Linnet does none of the things you suggest. Nor does she throw her weight around or boss people about. She gets on with her work and confines herself to that work. If you have the need for an assistant, or even *two* assistants, do some hiring. I have never ever prevented you from employing the help you need to do your job efficiently. Do you understand me?'

'Yes, Mother. I'll start looking for an assistant tomorrow,' Tessa announced coldly, but at least her voice was lower.

'Let us get to the core of the matter, to the reason you demanded to see me,' Paula said, staring at her eldest daughter steadily and very intently.

Tessa squirmed slightly under this unwavering stare, but made no comment. She shifted in the chair, and clasped her hands tightly in her lap, trying not to show her nervousness.

Paula continued: 'Your agitation springs from your need to know about the succession . . . who will one day have my job.'

'No, Mother, it's not—'

'Do not deny it, Tessa. Lying doesn't become you. I know that you've been talking about it to members of the family—'

'Toby!' Tessa exclaimed. 'I was talking to Toby, my dearest friend in the family, and no doubt his father told you. It was Winston! Don't pretend otherwise.'

'I wasn't going to do that, and you might as well know that under no circumstances will I designate a successor. I have no intention of abdicating! I would be in dereliction of my duty if I did, and I would be breaking a promise I made to Emma Harte over thirty years ago. When Grandy retired on the evening of her eightieth birthday, at her party, in fact, she charged me to hold her dream. I promised I would. And the next day when we had lunch together she asked me to promise her something else, and I did. And it was this: that I would not retire from my job as head of the Harte stores unless I was desperately ill and no longer able to execute my duties properly and with due diligence. And so, because I am only fifty-six, and in excellent health both mentally and physically, I fully intend to remain as head of Harte Stores. Since I'm a Harte I will more than likely have Grandy's great health for many years, and I'll probably retire when I am eighty, as she did, and not before. So you can shelve any ideas you might harbour about taking over from me.'

Tessa was so taken aback she was speechless, and she simply sat staring at her mother, unable to think of a suitable comment to make. But she was boiling inside.

'I hope you really do understand, Tessa, that I will not name a successor for the future. I will not name you and I will not name Linnet. I will only announce who's taking over from me on the day that I actually do retire.'

'But why, Mother?'

'Because I don't know who it's going to be.'

'But surely you have some idea—'

'I certainly do not,' Paula cut in peremptorily in a stern voice. 'You both have a lot to learn; much more experience to gain. Anyway, it might not be either of you. It could well be somebody else in the family.'

'*But who*? Surely you're not thinking of silly little Emsie. She's dopey and only interested in horses.'

'Emsie is not silly, and she's your loving sister, so please refrain from bad-mouthing her. But for your information, no, I'm not thinking of Emsie.

I'm actually not thinking of anyone. I just told you that. Stop trying to pin me down, it's not going to work. I'm a young woman, and I fully intend to keep my promise to Emma Harte for as many years as I can.'

'What about Pennistone Royal? Who's going to inherit that?'

Paula gaped at her daughter, flabbergasted. 'Good God, Tessa, not only do you want my job, you apparently want my home. I'm not dead yet, and I will not discuss my will, or my intentions, with you or anyone else. You've gone too far today. I'm appalled at your behaviour. How dare you broach the subject of Pennistone Royal?'

Tessa stared at her mother, her lip quivering, and then she burst into tears, suddenly sobbing into her hands.

Instantly Paula leapt to her feet, went around her desk, bent over her daughter, and put her arms around her. Tessa flinched slightly, then recoiled. Aware of this at once, Paula drew away, and looked down into Tessa's tearful face.

'What's the matter? Why did you flinch like that? Surely I'm not *so* repulsive to you?'

'No, no, I have a bad arm, Mother, that's all.'

'And I hurt you as I got hold of you, is that what you're saying?'

Tessa nodded, her large eyes brimming.

'What happened to it?'

'I – I – er, well, I fell.'

'Here at the store, darling?' Paula asked.

'No. At . . . well, at home.'

'Have you seen the doctor?'

'It's not necessary, Mother.'

'Come on, take your jacket off, let me see it,' Paula murmured, trying to be conciliatory, but also concerned about Tessa's injury.

'It's nothing, really it isn't,' Tessa muttered, reluctant to remove her jacket. But Paula insisted and finally Tessa stood up, slipped off the black cashmere blazer and allowed her mother to look at her arm.

'Tessa, this is dreadful! You must have fallen very hard to get such huge bruises. They must be awfully painful. No wonder you recoiled the way you did. Are you sure you haven't broken any bones?'

'No, there's nothing broken. I thought at first my shoulder had been damaged, but I had an X-ray and it's fine.'

Paula frowned, still staring at the purple and black bruises on Tessa's upper arm. 'How did you say you fell?'

'I didn't. But I fell down the stairs at home.'

'You must be more careful, darling. So many dangerous accidents do happen in the home.' Paula shook her head. 'Are you sure you don't want Doctor Gill to take a look at it?'

'No, honestly, Mother, I'm okay. But . . . well, thanks for being concerned,' she answered, her voice suddenly grown quiet, even meek.

Taking hold of Tessa's other hand, Paula gently

pulled her daughter closer, kissed her on the cheek. 'I'm *always* concerned about you, Tessa. I love you very much. And we mustn't quarrel like this, it's just not right. I meant what I said, you know, I'm not going to designate a successor for many, many years. So you must relax about it. Enjoy your job here, move up the corporate ladder, and enjoy your husband and your child. Everything's all right at home, isn't it?'

'Oh yes, yes, of course it is.'

'I'm glad . . .' Paula sighed as she walked back to her chair, and then added softly, 'Marriage is relentless . . . no matter how much you love someone.'

CHAPTER SEVENTEEN

Tessa paused on the top step and took a deep breath. And then she arranged a smile on her face before putting the key in the lock and opening the front door of her house in Hampstead.

It was a smile she had donned for years – her fraudulent smile, she called it, because it concealed her true feelings. As a child it had been a useful tool because it disguised so much – hurt, pain, sorrow, anger or discontent. And over the years she had become adept at hiding her real feelings behind that dazzling smile.

'Cooee, cooee,' she called as she stepped into the hall, and a moment later she heard Adele's fast-flying little feet as her baby daughter came running from the direction of the kitchen, calling, 'Mumma! Mumma!'

Tessa swept Adele up into her arms and hugged her tightly, and then deposited her on the floor carefully. Leaning forward, kissing the child's smiling face, she hunkered down next to her, and said, 'I've brought you something special, Adele. I know you're going to love it.'

The child's face lit up and she excitedly cried, 'A present, Mumma.'

'Yes, a present, darling.' Reaching for one of the Harte shopping bags she had brought in with her, Tessa pulled out a gift-wrapped package and showed it to her three-year-old daughter. Adele's large, silvery grey eyes became even larger in her delicate face, and she reached out small plump arms for the package.

'It's too big for you to carry. Come along, let's go to the kitchen and we can unwrap it there.' As she spoke Tessa stood up, took hold of Adele's hand, and the two of them walked across the glassy, black granite floor in the direction of the kitchen.

'Oh, hello, Mrs Longden,' the young nanny said, closing the dishwasher door and swinging around as mother and daughter walked in together.

'Good evening, Elvira,' Tessa replied, ushering Adele towards the small breakfast area which opened off the spacious modern kitchen. 'I've brought a present for Adele, and now we're going to open it, aren't we, darling?'

Adele nodded, her face full of smiles, her eyes sparkling.

'Aren't you a lucky girl?' Elvira said and then addressed Tessa. 'I'm sorry I've got to take the night off, Mrs Longden, but as I told you on the phone my mother's fall was a bad one. Fell off a stepladder, she did. A broken arm and a broken leg, both in casts. Thank goodness her next-door neighbour happened to come in to see her about something. Mrs Abel found her and was able to get Mum to the hospital. But now she's sort of . . . well, stranded there at home alone.'

'I understand, Elvira, and I'm sorry this happened to your mother. Do you know how long you'll be gone?'

'Oh, only tonight, Mrs Longden. I've been on the phone and my sister Pearl is driving up from Sussex. She'll be arriving about midnight, and she'll stay with Mum until my other sister, Moira, comes back from her holidays in Spain. Between them, Pearl and Moira can handle everything.'

'As I said, I'm sorry your mother hurt herself, Elvira. Broken bones are a nuisance and very painful. But I must admit that, rather selfishly, I'm relieved you'll be back tomorrow.'

'I know you need me to look after Adele; you work so hard, Mrs Longden. I should be here by lunchtime. But you'll have Mrs Jolles in the morning, and she loves Adele. She can look after her until I arrive.'

Tessa nodded, and followed her daughter into the breakfast area. After placing the package on the table, Tessa lifted Adele into a chair, and said, 'Come on, let's untie the ribbon and take off the paper.'

Eagerly, the child pulled at the bow of ribbon, tore off the paper, and Tessa helped her to finally reveal the golden cardboard box. Lifting off the lid, Tessa then tipped the box up on its end so that Adele could see its contents.

'Oh! Oh!' she exclaimed a little breathlessly. Her face was a picture of delight. 'A doll, Mumma! Pretty doll!'

'Yes, it *is* pretty, just like you.' Tessa took the exquisitely crafted and beautifully dressed porcelain baby doll out of its box and handed it to Adele, who immediately kissed its cheeks and hugged it to her.

'Do you like her?' Tessa asked, sitting down in a chair opposite her daughter.

'Yes,' Adele said, nodding, smiling at her mother and patting the doll's head.

'What's her name?' Elvira asked, as she came to join them.

Adele looked from Elvira to her mother. 'Name, Mumma?'

'She doesn't have a name, not yet. You have to choose one for her, Adele.'

'*Oh.*' Adele's silver grey eyes opened wider, and she looked at her mother in a puzzled way, then dropped her eyes to the doll she clutched in her arms. She stroked its bright blonde hair and touched its face and then she looked up at her mother and said, 'Daisy.'

'That's a pretty name for a pretty doll,' Elvira said, smiling at her young charge, who was such a beautiful child she was breathtaking.

'Gan-Gan's name,' Adele suddenly announced.

'Gran-Gran Daisy *will* be pleased,' Tessa murmured, somewhat startled that the child had chosen the name of her great-grandmother. But of course Daisy did have blonde hair and a pretty face. She spent part of her time in England again, after the death of her husband Jason Rickards in Australia. And she was a frequent visitor here to see her granddaughter and her great-granddaughter, especially adoring little Adele the way she did.

Glancing at her watch, Tessa rose. Turning to Elvira, she remarked, 'It's well after six, so you must have given Adele her supper.'

'Yes, I have, and I thought I'd start getting her ready for bed in a short while. I was just waiting for you to come home so you could spend a bit of time with her.'

'Thanks, Elvira, I do appreciate that. Will you help me to bring the shopping bags into the kitchen, please? Mr Longden's getting back from his trip later this evening, and I'm going to cook dinner for him.'

'That's nice, Mrs L. What're you going to make?'

'*Coq au vin*, it's one of his favourite dishes.'

It was peaceful in the kitchen.

The only sound was the music playing on the radio, turned low so that it was merely a background hum. Pleasant but not distracting.

Tessa moved between the stove and the long central island, where she had prepared most of the ingredients for the chicken dish, one of her specialities. After browning the chicken and frying the chopped bacon and chopped onions, she brought all three pans to the island counter, and emptied the contents into a large enamelled pot. She liked cooking, and she worked easily, as always relaxed when she was preparing food.

Once she had opened a bottle of Beaujolais, she poured herself a glass and then added half of the bottle of wine to the pot. Into this also went a tin of tomato paste, a small jug of chicken broth and two cupfuls of sliced mushrooms. The *bouquet garni* she had made earlier and tied with a piece of cheesecloth was added, and then she carried the pot to the stove and turned on the gas, setting it at medium.

Tessa stood stirring the contents of the pot with a wooden spoon and, when everything was well mixed together, she put the lid on and went back to the island. After taking a sip of red wine she glanced at the ingredients to be added later – a small bowl of pearl onions and another one of button mushrooms. She began to clean up after herself, being a very tidy cook. Within seconds all of the dirty dishes, pans and utensils were stacked in the dishwasher, and finally Tessa sat down on a stool at the island to enjoy the glass of wine.

Her eyes roamed around the kitchen, taking everything in. She liked this spacious room with its high-flung cathedral ceiling and the skylights cut into each end, the wide French doors opening onto the patio and the garden beyond. It was light-filled and airy, and the perfect space for cooking because it was properly planned and its proportions were excellent.

To Tessa the kitchen was the best room in the house. She thought the rest of it was cold, a little banal even, and far too modern for her liking. But that was Mark's great claim to fame: ultra-modern buildings soaring upward, with great empty spaces inside. Cold, empty spaces without colour or life and a minimum of furniture. Uncomfortable furniture, she thought, and poured herself a little more wine, focused on the home she shared with Mark. She hadn't realized until she moved into this house that she truly detested it. She had watched Mark strip the lovely old Edwardian house down to its bare bones, and then rebuild the interiors the way he wanted. It was not what she wanted, she had vociferously protested, but he had swept her concern and opinions to one side, telling her she would love it once it was completed, that she had no vision.

But she had not loved it, and the upsetting thing was that her mother had bought the house for her and it belonged to her, and not to have a pleasing place to live affected her badly at times. And the money he had spent remodelling had been enormous – *her* money.

She had been brought up at Pennistone Royal and her mother's Belgravia house, which had once been Emma Harte's, and she was used to the warmth and comfort of both places. Pennistone Royal, stately home though it was, with so many huge and soaring spaces, nevertheless had its smaller rooms which were intimate, charming and cosy, and lovely to be in, to live with.

There were those who thought Mark was a genius. Of late she had come to understand this was not the case at all; she had suddenly realized that much of what he designed was plagiarized from other more famous architects, most of them dead. These designs he modified and changed until they were bastardizations of the originals. Thus he could claim them as his own, although Tessa often wondered why he would want to do so. She thought that most were monstrosities.

Recognizing that he was not what she had originally thought him to be had come as something of a shock. And yet hadn't she always known deep down inside that he was a bit of a fraud, a blowhard and a boaster? Good looking yes, but not as good a catch as she liked to make out to others. And if she were really truthful with herself, their marriage was suddenly not working quite so well any longer. However, there was Adele to think of, who adored her father; anyway, she did not want to leave him, even though he was becoming increasingly difficult and at times verbally abusive. The ridiculous thing was that she still loved him.

What was that remark her mother had made this afternoon? 'Marriage is relentless,' she had said.

Well, yes, that was true. Absolutely true. And *he* was relentless, forever on her back about so many things to do with her mother and the stores, her power, her inheritance, her future in the hierarchy, and her money.

Tessa sighed to herself and got up, carried the remainder of the ingredients over to the stove. Her eye caught the clock on the kitchen wall, and she was startled to see it was well past eight. But then she had taken a long time preparing the various ingredients for the *coq au vin*. She wondered where Mark was as she added the rest of the items to the pot, stirred them, poured in the additional chicken broth and a bit more of the Beaujolais.

The *coq au vin* smelt delicious. It was going to come out well and Mark would be pleased. Replacing the lid, she set the table in the breakfast area before returning to the island in the middle of the kitchen.

Sitting down on the stool once more, Tessa poured the last of the red wine into her glass and took a sip absently, thinking of her mother and other aspects of their conversations of earlier that day. It suddenly struck her that Paula had looked upset, rattled when they had been discussing the succession, and she reflected on this for a while.

Tessa could not deny that Paula had been a good mother to her, because she had, and to all of her children, in fact. But there were times when she resented her attitude. How easy it would be for Paula to make *her* life easy by simply naming her as the heir apparent . . . the Dauphine, as she liked to call herself. How she loved that word; it sang with power. But obviously her mother was not going to do this. She had made that clear. But at least she wasn't going to name Linnet. Or anyone else for that matter.

But wasn't her mother being a bit unfair? After all, she *was* the eldest of Paula's children and also a Fairley. It was family lore that Emma Harte had taken much of what had once belonged to the Fairleys, and so in her opinion she was entitled to oversee those family businesses later, just as her mother did now.

The problem was her mother favoured Linnet above all others, because she was her child by Shane . . . their love child. Tessa blew out air in a whoosh, suddenly irritated. Her mother blamed *her* for the sibling rivalry that existed between them, but it actually emanated from Linnet, aided and abetted by India Standish and Gideon Harte. They egged her on, as they always had.

But she had Toby on her side, and they had their plans well laid, and one day . . .

The sound of the front door slamming brought Tessa up with a start, and she looked eagerly towards the kitchen door, which stood ajar.

In spite of his difficult personality and the problems he now created between them, Tessa was determined to save the marriage, make it work . . . because that was what she wanted.

CHAPTER EIGHTEEN

'Hello, darling,' Tessa said as Mark walked into the kitchen. Giving him her most brilliant smile, she went on, 'I was beginning to worry, you're so late.' Sliding off the stool, she went to meet him, gave him a hug, but he was so unresponsive she let her arms fall to her sides, suddenly deflated. 'Where have you been?' she now asked, her voice very quiet.

Pulling away from her, he answered gruffly, 'On a bloody train, where the hell do you think I've been?' Making a face, he added, 'Public transport is diabolical in this country these days.'

'Yes,' Tessa murmured, retreating to her stool at the island counter, realizing he was in one of his belligerent moods.

His dark eyes followed her and instantly settled on the bottle of Beaujolais. He was at the island in two or three long strides, and he picked it up, shook it. 'This bottle's *empty*! You've been drinking again!' he exclaimed, staring at her, his eyes suddenly full of icy disdain.

'You say that as if I'm an alcoholic, for heaven's sake. All I've had is a glass and a half. Most of that bottle of wine is in the *coq au vin*.' Hoping to avert another outburst of nastiness, she flashed her winning smile again, and explained, 'I've made a big pot. I know how much you like it, darling.'

Ignoring her words, he waved the bottle in front of her face rather dangerously and intoned in a dire voice, 'It's a Fairley problem, *drink*. You don't want to end up like your father. Or worse still, your great-grandmother, Adele Fairley. She was so soused one night she fell down the stairs at Fairley Hall and broke her bloody neck.' He shook his head, his expression more disdainful than ever. 'What a family I've married into.'

Tessa was gaping at him, totally taken aback. 'Where on earth did that particular story come from? I've never heard it before, and if it were true I would have. So come on, who told you such a terrible lie about my great-grandmother Adele? And who impugned my father's reputation?'

Mark Longden ran his hand through his already rumpled brownish-blond hair, and shrugged carelessly. A look of sudden indifference crossed his disgruntled face, and he muttered. '*I don't know*. I heard it from someone. But it doesn't matter who told me, it's a well-known fact the Fairleys were huge tipplers, renowned across the county for their drinking, apparently. So just watch yourself, do you hear? I won't have my daughter brought up by a drunken mother.'

'Mark, stop this! And immediately. I've not even had two glasses of wine, and I rarely drink. And you know it. So stop it right now!' Tessa was on her feet, regarding him intently, aware of some kind of implied threat behind his words. She was alerted to trouble, suddenly on her guard, asking herself if *he* had been drinking. And where had he been? This morning he had told her he was going out of town for the day. But where had he been *exactly*? And who with?

Mark had seated himself on one of the other stools, and he glanced at her, and said in a lighter and more normal voice, 'I'd like a vodka. Please fix one for me, darling.'

Wanting to be conciliatory, Tessa smiled in relief, nodded and hurried across to the drinks cupboard at one end of the kitchen where the liquor was stored. She returned with a bottle of Russian vodka, put it on the counter, took ice from the refrigerator, then stood at the island mixing a drink for him.

'Cheers,' he said as he lifted the glass to his mouth and took a long swallow.

'Cheers.' Tessa picked up her glass which was now empty except for a few drops of wine. 'Who was the client you went to see today?' she asked, trying to sound casual, not wishing to start another row.

'A chap up North,' he muttered, staring into his drink absently, as if preoccupied.

'*Up North*. Were you in Yorkshire?' she asked, instantly suspicious, especially after his ramblings about Adele Fairley and her father.

'No, I meant the Midlands,' he corrected himself, looking across at her. 'I'm designing a house for him. Lots of money in it. For the firm.' A strange ironic smile struck his mouth and he asked, 'And what about your day? How did it go? Any quarrels with little sister? Did you talk to your mother? About the bloody succession? I know the answer to those questions. Rows with Linnet, I'm certain, just as I'm certain you haven't spoken to your mother. About when you're taking over as CEO.'

Tessa was on the verge of telling him what had transpired, and instantly changed her mind. It would cause trouble, she was suddenly very sure of that. He was in a strange mood, and if he had not been drinking then he was definitely on something. His eyes were slightly glazed, and although he was not at all slurred or unsteady, she detected a change in him. It was ever so slight but it was there. He was not quite himself.

Clearing her throat, she lied when she said, 'My mother had important meetings with the board today. I didn't get to see her at all. But I will, darling. Anyway, there's no problem, really, it's obvious I'm going to be the boss. I'm the eldest.'

'Let's hope so.' He swilled some of the vodka,

then put the glass down, and looked at her intently. 'Is something burning?'

'Oh my God!' Tessa ran to the stove, lifted the lid on the pot and peered inside. 'No, nothing's burnt. It's all right. And the *coq au vin* looks great. You're going to enjoy it,' she said, turning to him.

'I'm not hungry.'

'Come on, Mark, you must eat something. You've been gone since dawn, and if I know you, lunch got skipped.'

He did not respond. He simply stared at her morosely, his eyes glassy.

It took her a few minutes, but Tessa cajoled him with a certain adroitness, and finally he went into the breakfast area and sat down at the table, nursing his vodka with both hands.

As she served spoonfuls of the *coq au vin* onto the plates which had been warming on top of the stove, he called out, 'Bring a bottle of Beaujolais and I'll open it.'

Muttering under her breath, she did as he asked and then continued to serve their dinner. Once she had put the plates on the table, she went into the kitchen again for the bread basket and butter dish. Finally she sat down with him.

He was struggling with the bottle opener but managed, awkwardly, to pull out the cork at last. He poured the wine sloppily, splashing some of it onto the table as he did, his hand a trifle unsteady.

Observing him, Tessa thought of the way he had chastised her about drinking a short time before.

Now he had obviously forgotten that, since he had filled her glass to overflowing. What's wrong with him? she wondered, observing him acutely. Is he drunk? Or drugged? Her guard went up once more, and she decided to remain silent, listening to an inner voice that warned her to protect herself.

Earlier Tessa had been hungry, but now her appetite had totally disappeared. Nonetheless, she began to eat, putting a forkful of chicken into her mouth. It was delicious, but he was making her feel so nervous she could barely swallow the food.

The slamming down of his fork, the sound of metal hitting glass made her sit up with a jerk, alarm flaring in her. Swiftly she looked across at him. 'Mark, what's wrong?'

'This is foul. I don't know what you've cooked but it's disgusting. *Pig swill!*'

'But it's delicious,' she exclaimed, and then instantly stopped speaking, not wanting to inflame him further. She felt a surge of panic inside, and an internal shaking took hold.

'Don't argue with me, you bitch!' he yelled, his face growing red and contorted. He pushed the plate away so ferociously it slid across the glass table and fell to the floor with a crash.

Tessa did not dare move a muscle. She simply sat there staring at him, her large eyes growing wide with surprise.

'Clean it up!' he shouted angrily. 'Or I'll give you a thrashing you won't forget.' He half rose in his chair, raising his hand, and she leapt to her feet before he could touch her and flew into the kitchen. She found the dustpan and brush and ran back to the breakfast area.

Kneeling down, she swept the food and the shattered plate into the dustpan, and fled again, still shaking inside. A moment later, she returned with a wet dishcloth, knelt again, and washed the sticky mess off the polished parquet floor.

Unexpectedly, and so suddenly she went into a state of shock, she felt his hand gripping the back of her neck. He was standing over her, and she sensed, rather than saw, the menace in him. He tightened his grip on her neck, squeezing it roughly.

'Please let go of me, Mark,' she said, her voice soft, cajoling.

'What's going on between you and Toby Harte?' he demanded. 'You'd better tell me, bitch!'

'Nothing's going on. We're family, we've always been best friends since childhood, you know that,' she answered as evenly as possible. Staying calm and controlled was important, she realized that.

'What I hear is that you're more than friends,' he hissed, squeezing her neck even harder. 'What I hear is that he's in your knickers and has been since you were kids.'

'That's not true, and you know it,' she cried. 'He's my cousin, for God's sake.'

'Ha! Fat lot that means! Par for the course, I'd say, the way your bunch marry each other. Talk about an incestuous lot: your bloody family takes first prize.'

'Don't be ridiculous. There's nothing between Toby and me—'

'Daddy! Daddy!' Adele squealed, running into the breakfast area in her nightgown, dragging her rag doll Aggie by its arm.

Instantly Mark let go of Tessa and rushed to his daughter. He gathered her up in his arms, held her close to him. 'Hello, sweetheart,' he whispered against her softly curling blonde hair.

'How's Daddy's special little girl? Are you all right, my pet?'

'Yes.' She nuzzled her face against his, then said, 'Come see my doll, Daddy.'

'But I can see her,' he responded, taking hold of the rag doll she was dangling in one hand.

'No, new doll,' Adele said.

Tessa, who had immediately jumped up and retreated to the safety of the kitchen, explained quickly, 'I bought her a doll today. It's upstairs in her bedroom.'

Mark glanced at Tessa. 'I'll be back in a few minutes,' he murmured, and once more his voice sounded much more normal.

That's for the benefit of Adele, Tessa thought, as she watched his retreating figure, wondering how long he would be gone. For the first time in her life she was afraid. And she did not know what to do. Her initial thought was to flee, to run out of the house and go to Toby's flat. But Mark had Adele with him and she could not leave her child behind. Her eyes flew to her handbag on the far counter. Her mobile phone was in it, and she went to get it. But who should she call? Toby would come over immediately, and if she called Shane he would be here as fast as possible. And yet she did not want either of them to know about Mark and his treatment of her. It would humiliate her to confide in them.

Wait it out. See what happens, that inner voice told her. But she understood that she must be cautious, wary, and very alert.

After fifteen minutes, when Mark had not returned to the kitchen, Tessa went out into the hall and climbed the stairs, being as quiet as possible. As she crept down the corridor stealthily, she saw that the door of Adele's room was open, light shining out, and she held her breath until she got there. All was quiet, perfectly still inside the room. When she finally tiptoed in she saw that Adele was already fast asleep, clutching the rag doll to her and sucking her thumb.

Bending over her daughter, Tessa smoothed the fair hair from her face, turned out the bedside lamp but left the small nightlight burning.

Once she had closed Adele's door behind her, Tessa continued down the corridor to their bedroom. The door was half open and she pushed it, peered inside. Mark, half undressed, was sprawled across the bed. Lost to the world and snoring, he was in a drunken or drugged sleep: which she did not know.

After closing the bedroom door, Tessa stood

in the corridor, hesitating, debating what to do. Finally she decided to sleep on the single bed in Adele's room, which had been put there for her or Elvira to use if there was ever a medical problem with Adele. She knew Mark would never harm their child, and so she deemed it the safest place to be tonight.

Tessa lay on top of the single bed under the duvet cover, fully dressed except for her blazer and shoes, and clutching her mobile phone in one hand.

Although she had locked Adele and herself in the child's room, she found it impossible to relax, but over the next hour Mark did not emerge from their bedroom and everything was quiet. Silence reigned throughout the entire house.

Eventually she dozed off from sheer exhaustion; it was only at dawn, when a glimmering of light began to seep in through the windows, that she suddenly awakened with a start, for a second feeling out of sorts and disoriented. And then she remembered the events of the night before, and her husband's strange behaviour, and she became fearful for a brief moment.

Mark had always had a tendency to be volatile – he was excitable and even abrasive at times – but it was only in the last six months that he had become verbally abusive, and this had both startled and alarmed her.

As she lay there thinking about Mark, she remembered that there had often been unspoken criticism in his attitude towards her, plus a superiority in his manner in the last few years. The latter had amused her because she was nothing if not self-confident, a trait which she knew she had inherited from her great-grandmother, Emma Harte, via her grandmother Daisy and her mother. She was not easily cowed; intimidation rolled off her back like water, and she could be wonderfully articulate if she had to defend herself. The only thing that could make her truly apprehensive was physical violence directed at her daughter. Or her.

Last weekend a quarrel had erupted between her and Mark about who would succeed her mother. It was an old subject, and they had wrangled, and in the heat of the moment Mark had lunged at her, as if to punch her in the face. She had adroitly sidestepped him, but then she had tripped and fallen down the six steps that led to the lower-level larder, situated immediately above the basement.

He had been at once chagrined, had rushed to pick her up, looking scared and worried. The result of the fall had been her heavily bruised shoulder and upper arm, which her mother had looked at yesterday, appalled, and concerned.

This was the first time her husband had gone for her in that way during their entire marriage, and she had been shaken to the core and mentally thrown off balance. Mark had a quirky personality which seemed to be coming to the fore more and more. He was not the easiest of men, but he had never displayed the slightest hint of violence in the past.

Now she contemplated the events of the night before. He might well have become really violent if she had not remained calm and in control of herself, and if little Adele had not walked into the breakfast area precisely when she did. The unexpected appearance of his adored child had evidently brought him to his senses; certainly it had pulled him up short, prevented possible mayhem.

Tessa was certain he had been drinking earlier in the evening, and also convinced he was on something else as well, some sort of designer drug, perhaps. He was definitely *off*, not himself in a variety of ways, and this had unsettled her. Normally he held his drink extremely well, which is why she had become so alarmed at his erratic behaviour. His eyes were glassy, actually glazed over, and he had gone through several mood swings in a very short period of time. Last night she had seen a whole new Mark.

She would have to ask Toby about drugs. As a high-powered media executive running a television network, he probably knew quite a lot about them, and if *he* didn't, Gideon surely would. She knew that neither of her cousins would go anywhere near drugs. They had always needed to be in control, of themselves and others, and anyway they were too ambitious, driven and work-oriented to indulge in substances of oblivion. But in their line of business they would have a certain amount of information at their disposal.

She wondered, suddenly, if she ought to confide in Toby, after all. He was the closest to her, except for Lorne . . . but *they* were tight because they were twins, and Lorne might easily tell their mother about Mark and how he was behaving if she took him into her confidence. A still tongue, a wise head: that had been her motto for years. Tell no one . . .

Little Adele murmured in her sleep, and turned over restlessly, and Tessa threw off the duvet, swung her feet to the floor and almost stepped on the mobile phone which must have fallen out of her hand during the night.

After looking down at Adele, smoothing her hair gently from her face, smiling with pleasure, and filled with love for this gorgeous child of hers, Tessa covered her with the eiderdown then stepped across the room.

Unlocking the door, she went along the corridor, being scrupulously careful not to make a noise. It was unusually quiet. Glancing at her watch, she saw that it was just a few minutes past six.

Moving carefully, Tessa paused at their bedroom door, opened it gently, and looked inside. Mark was still passed out on top of their bed, sprawled diagonally across it, almost in the same position as last night. Hardly daring to breathe, she closed the door as quietly as possible and continued down the corridor to her own suite.

This was a set of private rooms she had insisted on designing herself. She had fought Mark about it, finally winning. It consisted of a fully equipped office, a small gym, a large and luxurious bathroom, plus a huge dressing room where her clothes hung in well-organized perfection. Also housed there were her shoes, handbags, scarves, shawls, and other accessories. It was her private domain and it gave her a great deal of pleasure; she loved to have everything neat, orderly, and scrupulously arranged, being a perfectionist in all things.

After a quick shower, Tessa blow-dried her hair and then sat down at the dressing table to put on make-up. A short while later she went to one of the closets and selected a tailored grey pin-stripe suit and a pale blue man-tailored cotton shirt. Within minutes she was hurrying downstairs to the kitchen. After putting on the coffee, she quickly stacked the dishwasher with a few remaining items from last night's cooking, turned it on, threw out the *coq au vin*, which had congealed overnight, and then made herself a slice of toast.

She was halfway through her first cup of coffee when Mark suddenly appeared in the kitchen. His blondish-brown hair was still damp from the shower, and he was freshly shaved, dressed in a white shirt, which was open at the neck, and dark blue trousers. He carried the jacket of his suit and a dark blue tie as well.

He hesitated fractionally when he saw her, his step seeming to falter, and then he recouped and came towards her, a feeble smile playing on his face.

After putting the jacket and tie on one of the stools at the island counter, he came around to her side, and stood looking down at her, forcing the smile to become a little wider. 'Good morning.'

When there was no response from her, he said in a low, contrite voice, 'I'm sorry, Tessa darling. I can't remember exactly what happened last night, but when I woke up not long ago I realized I'd probably behaved badly.'

Still she remained silent.

He stared at her, all of his attention on her. 'I did, didn't I? Behave badly, I mean. Please tell me what happened? I'm so troubled . . . we had a row, didn't we?'

'No, we didn't,' she said, speaking at last, levelling her steady gaze at him, her face icy cold, her eyes the colour of steel.

'*Oh*,' was all he could say, obviously taken aback. He moved away, went and poured himself a cup of coffee, and carried the mug back to the island. He stood next to her, drinking it. After a split second, he murmured, 'I thought we'd had a quarrel, because I found myself on top of the bed, almost fully dressed, and obviously the bed hadn't been slept in . . . and you were gone.'

'Only too true.' Tessa let out a sigh. 'However, we didn't have a row, Mark, but you did behave very badly indeed. You came home in an extremely belligerent mood, and tried to pick a fight. Your behaviour was extraordinary, very strange, in fact, and I thought you were not only drunk but *on* something. You were, weren't you?'

He shook his head vehemently. 'No, no, not at all. I'd had a couple of drinks, that's true, but if you're implying I'd taken drugs, or some kind of . . . *substance*, then you're totally mistaken. *Totally*.'

'But there *was* something terribly wrong with you! Your eyes were glazed over and your manner was most erratic.' Deciding to let him have all the gory details, she told him everything that had happened the night before. And when it came to his physical attack on her, how he had held her neck in a vice-like grip when she was on the floor, she pulled no punches.

It was quite apparent to Tessa that he remembered bits and pieces, because he nodded his head several times, obviously recalling certain things but not others.

His shame and remorse hung heavy on him. 'Oh my god! Tessa, I'm so sorry, so terribly sorry. All I can think of is that I took some cold pills on the train. Perhaps they had a bad effect on me, especially since I did have a few drinks afterwards. You see, I thought I was coming down with the flu, and I bought some cold pills at the station . . . swilled them down with Scotch. It was stupid. *I was stupid*.'

Although he was obviously upset and ashamed, and wanted to make amends to her, Tessa instinctively knew that he was lying. About the cold pills, at least. It was such a phony story it took all her self-control not to laugh out loud. But she remained absolutely cool, and unresponsive to his protestations of innocence and his sudden abundance of contrition.

'Who did you meet yesterday?' she asked after a few sips of coffee. She stared at him over the rim of the mug, her silvery-grey eyes penetrating, challenging.

'I told you, darling. A client.' Mark went and sat down opposite her and put the coffee mug on the countertop.

'But you didn't say who the client is. What's his name?' she pressed.

'Oh, I thought I told you before. His name is William Stone, and he's apparently filthy rich. I've designed a house for him . . . he calls it the house of his dreams.'

'And where is this dream house?'

'In the Midlands. I thought I'd told you that.' He frowned at her.

'Did you drink with him before you left? Maybe that would explain your disastrous condition.'

'What do you mean?'

'If you drank with your Mr Stone and then drank on the train, maybe you were drunker than you realized.'

'Possibly.' He shook his head, and leaned across the counter, taking her hand in his. 'Listen, Tessa, I'm truly sorry. This whole thing has been painful, very painful indeed, for me to listen to. Please, darling, say you accept my apology. I promise it won't happen again. You know I adore you. Upsetting you is the last thing I want to do. I love you, Tessa.'

She stared into his face, remained absolutely silent. Despite his bloodshot eyes he looked surprisingly boyish this morning. Perhaps it was the pink flush on his cheeks or maybe his open shirt, but he did look young and appealing. It had always been part of his charm, that collegiate look of his, and his sincerity. Although she was never quite sure if that was really genuine; sometimes it struck her that it was entirely fraudulent.

Finally nodding her head slowly, Tessa said, 'I forgive you, Mark.' But will I ever forget? she asked herself, and then to him, she added, 'But it can't happen again. If you ever become physically violent with me, as you did last night, I'll leave you. Divorce you. I won't stand for that, you know. And neither will Paula and Shane.' She had thrown their names into the mix just to remind him of exactly who she was, and who it was that stood behind her. If nothing else, he understood the meaning of money and power, of immense clout, as he usually referred to it.

Mark smiled in relief, and reached out. He took her hand again, brought it to his mouth, kissed her fingers. 'I'm truly, truly sorry. And it will never, *ever* happen again, I promise you, Tessa.' His eyes did not leave her face, as he added, 'I'm so utterly ashamed of myself. Contrite.'

The sound of the key in the back door made them

both sit up a little straighter, and Tessa exclaimed, 'Oh it's Mrs Jolles. Elvira asked her to come in early today.'

'Why's that?' Mark asked, frowning.

'Because I have to go to work, and so do you, and Elvira had to go home last night to look after her mother.'

'What happened to Mrs Wilson?'

'She broke her arm and a leg. Fell off a ladder, apparently.'

'Oh dear,' Mark raised his eyes to the ceiling and rolled them in mock horror.

'Good morning, Mrs Jolles,' Tessa said, turning around. 'Thanks so much for coming in at the crack of dawn.'

''Morning all,' Mrs Jolles answered in her bright and cheerful voice. 'Don't disturb yourselves; finish your breakfasts. I'll go and see to Adele.'

CHAPTER NINETEEN

Gideon sat waiting for Evan in the large sitting room of the small hotel in Belgravia where she lived. From the moment he had walked in he had been struck by the decor, the refinement and good taste that abounded in the entrance hall and here.

Now, as he sat on the sofa near the fire, he glanced around, thinking how charming and well appointed the sitting room was. There were some lovely landscapes on the walls, and the entire ambiance was pleasant and restful.

Gideon sighed and stretched out his long legs. He was feeling a little weary today. It had been a trying week, and he had been burdened by so many different problems at the newspaper. The only good thing was that Christian Palmer was becoming more amenable about working for the *London Evening Post* again. It was all a question of negotiation, and settling the problems of the time off which Christian needed. His book was practically finished, and after that he would be at liberty to work for them. Possibly it would have to be part time, but Gideon and his father knew this was better than not having him on board at all.

His thoughts turned to Evan. She was such a special young woman he could hardly believe his luck. That he had found her was something of a miracle to him. He had fallen heavily, and he knew she had too; he had laughed the other day when she had called their coming together a *coup de foudre*, because he had thought the same thing earlier. When he had told her this she too had been amused. 'Well, great minds think alike,' he had murmured, squeezing her hand. She was not only lovely to look at but charming, and bright and intelligent, and they always had fun together. He never felt bored with her, as he had with so many other women; they were compatible on every level.

There was one thing that worried him about her and this was her occasional sadness. It seemed to him that a strange melancholy overtook her at times, and he couldn't help asking himself what caused that sudden change in her. Though they had not discussed it, Gideon thought it had nothing to do with them, but sprang from another area of her life.

A moment later she was walking into the sitting room, her face full of smiles, her cheeks dimpling prettily as the smile grew wider.

Gideon jumped to his feet as she stopped. She kissed him on his cheek, and then said, 'I'm sorry I kept you waiting. I was late at the store.'

'That cousin of mine is a genuine slave-driver!' he murmured, squeezing her arm.

'She is a bit, but I don't mind,' Evan replied. 'I'm inclined to be a workaholic, as you well know. I'm late because I decided to change after all, even though you said it didn't matter.'

He smiled, glanced at her appraisingly. 'You look wonderful, but then you always do. Come on, I'm starving, I can't wait to get a knife and fork into some wonderful roast lamb.'

'Where are you taking me?' Evan asked as he led her out of the sitting room, through the hall and out into the street.

'The Dorchester. They have the best roast leg of lamb and roast beef in London.' Gideon raised his hand, flagged down a taxi, and helped her in. After giving the cabbie the name of the hotel, he took her hand in his and kissed it. 'I've missed you.'

Evan turned to him, raising a dark brow. 'But you saw me yesterday.'

'I know. But I've still missed you in the meantime.'

Smiling to herself, she leaned back against the leather seat, wondering if she should tell him she had missed him too. She missed him whenever they were not together; it was, in fact, a state of affairs that was entirely new to her. But she remained silent.

Within a few minutes they were pulling up in front of the hotel, and the doorman, dressed in green with a tall hat, was opening the cab door and helping her out. 'Evening, madame,' he said in a friendly voice.

'Good evening,' Evan answered, and went up the steps, stood waiting for Gideon as he paid for the taxi.

Inside the hotel, he guided her to the cloakroom, and once they had checked their coats they went across the hall to the Grill Room. Instantly, they were seated, and Gideon looked at her and asked, 'What would you like to drink?'

'A glass of white wine would be nice, thank you.'

Beckoning to a waiter, Gideon ordered her a glass of white wine, and a vodka and tonic for himself. When they were alone he confided, 'I've had such a heavy day, I need a good strong drink. But I'm happy to say I think Christian Palmer is now seriously thinking about coming back, if only part time. We'll be glad to have him.'

'Oh that's wonderful. I'm so pleased for you, Gideon. You've wanted this so much.'

'And Dad has, too. We're kind of chuffed about it ... that means, well ... *pleased*, in case you didn't know.'

'But I did. My grandmother often used it, especially when I was growing up and did something she deemed was wonderful. That's when she would tell me she was *chuffed*.'

Their drinks materialized; Gideon lifted his glass, touched hers, and said cheers. And so did Evan.

The Grill Room was busy tonight. Gideon glanced

around, but there was no one there he knew. Turning to Evan, he said, 'The trolleys over there have the best roasts. Are you going to join me in the roast leg of lamb?'

'I think I will.'

'And to start?'

'Oysters.'

'Snap. I'm having the same.'

Now it was Evan's turn to look around, taking in the surroundings. She liked this room with its dark wood furniture, large tapestries hanging on the walls, its sense of timelessness, its very Englishness. 'You come here a lot, don't you, Gideon?'

'Yes, I do. I like the English food they serve – the roasts, the wonderful soups, the potted shrimps and the oysters. But quite aside from the food, it's sort of . . . well, a family hotel. I don't mean it belongs to the O'Neill hotel chain that Shane owns and operates, but *family* in the sense that we've all favoured the Dorchester for donkeys years.'

'Oh really, why is that?'

'From what I understand, it goes back to the years during the Second World War. My great-grandmother used to come here all the time, as did most of the elegant uppercrust Londoners. My father told me that it was considered to be the safest hotel in London because of the way it was built. In any event, she came often, and so did her brothers, and the O'Neills. It's kind of—'

'A home away from home,' she suggested, cutting across him.

'That's right,' he answered with a laugh.

The waiter came and Gideon ordered for them both, and then he turned to Evan and said quietly, 'There's something I've wanted to talk to you about, Evan, but I haven't really dared. Now I think we know each other well enough, and it *is* something that troubles me.'

'But what is it? And of course we can discuss it, Gideon.' She stared at him intently, a worried expression settling in her eyes, wondering what it was that troubled him. When he remained silent she touched his hand lightly, and said, 'I've felt right from our first date that we could talk about anything, tell each other anything . . . say what you're thinking, Gid.'

'There are times when I seem to lose you, Evan,' he began, taking her hand in his. 'What I'm trying to say is that there are occasions when you become pensive, melancholy really, and you seem to drift off to a faraway place. I don't seem able to reach you for a while. In fact, it's only when you come out of it that we're normal again. It *is* troubling, and I was wondering . . . well, is there something worrying you?'

'Not about us, or you, if that's what you mean,' she was quick to reassure him. Clearing her throat, she added, 'I do worry about my mother quite a lot. Perhaps that's what you're detecting in me.'

'Possibly.' He looked puzzled. 'Why do you worry about your mother? Is there something wrong with her?'

Taking a deep breath, Evan answered, 'My mother suffers from depression. She's on medication all the time.'

'Oh Evan, I'm so sorry,' he murmured, his voice sympathetic. 'Is this a recent ailment?'

'No, Gideon, it isn't. Mom's been depressed for as long as I can remember, from when I was a small child. It was after my parents adopted Angharad . . . that's when her mood swings began. At least, that's how I remember it. And that's why my grandmother, Glynnis, used to come and stay, to look after us, and look after my father. I worry about him a lot too.'

'I'm sure you do. That kind of illness is hard on a family, as well as on the sufferer.'

'Do you know something about it?' she asked.

'Not really, but I do know a couple of people who are manic depressives, old friends of mine, and of course I've read about famous people who were sufferers. Sir Winston Churchill for one. He called his depression Black Dog. He fought against it all of his life . . . that's why he had such a rigorous routine, kept himself extremely busy, hoping to sidestep his depression, I guess.'

'I understand.' Evan shook her head, looked away for a moment, and then told him in a low, confiding voice, 'I often worry that I might get to be like my mother . . . do you think that's why I keep myself so terribly busy, why I'm a workaholic?'

'Out of fear?' he asked. 'Fear that you might have inherited it, that you might become a depressive too?'

'Yes.'

Gideon made a face, shook his head. 'I've got to admit I don't know the answer. But my family are all workaholics, over-achievers, and none of them suffer from depression. I don't, and I'm just like you when it comes to work.' He squeezed her hand. 'Try not to worry so much about your parents. They have each other, and presumably take care of each other. Your mother's not in hospital, is she?'

'Oh no, she's at home. And there are days when she's much better—'

Evan broke off as the waiter arrived to serve their plates of oysters. When he had done so and they were alone, Evan murmured, 'I hadn't realized I was drifting off like that when I was with you, Gid, I'm sorry.'

'No need to be sorry. Anyway, talking about it has cleared the air. Now that I understand it makes everything easier.'

Between swallowing the delicious Colchester oysters they talked about other things, but at one moment Gideon said, 'Is Tessa still being difficult with you?'

Evan shook her head. 'It's not that she was ever difficult. Well, to be honest, she was a bit uppity. These days she just sort of . . . ignores me.' Evan began to laugh. 'I don't care. It worries India at times, and Linnet also, but I told them her attitude is not important. I don't work directly with her. And Linnet and India are both wonderful to me.'

'I know. Tessa's like that with everybody. She has a superiority that is most annoying,' Gideon explained. 'It doesn't mean anything, so don't *personalize* it. Mind you, I bet she's a bit jealous that Linnet has another assistant.'

'That's what India said the other day.'

'I'm glad you're enjoying working at Harte's, enjoying my cousins.' He grinned at her. 'They're the best – kind, loving, nice to be around, aren't they?'

'I'll say! And we have a lot of fun together when we're working. They've made me feel at home. I hope Linnet's going to keep me on after the retrospective's finished. It would be hard for me to work anywhere else after being with them at Harte's.'

'I'm sure you don't have to worry,' Gideon reassured her.

CHAPTER TWENTY

Toby Harte sat listening most attentively to everything his cousin Tessa Fairley was saying. He always thought of her as Fairley rather than Longden, and he suspected this was because he was not a huge fan of her husband Mark Longden.

When she finally paused for breath, Toby asked with a frown, 'Why are you suddenly so interested in drugs? You of all people, Miss Goody Two Shoes. Do you have a suspicion Mark is on something? Is that it, Tessa? There can't be any other reason.'

Although she was taken aback by this statement, she realized she ought not to be. Toby was one of the shrewdest people in her orbit, and he knew her intimately, better than anyone.

Clearing her throat, she said, 'I'm not really sure that he's on drugs, to be honest, Toby. But he could be. He came home a couple of nights ago in a very strange state. Glassy-eyed, erratic, extremely belligerent, trying to pick a quarrel. He'd been drinking, I knew that. He was quite drunk, I'd say—'

'In *vino veritas*, eh?' Toby cut in, raising a dark brow.

'Perhaps. And yet I was suspicious because he was somehow . . . well, *different*.'

'Did you question him about his behaviour the next morning?'

'Oh yes. He said something ridiculous about having taken cold pills, and that he had then had several drinks on the train. He suggested the combination must have created a problem. I certainly didn't believe *that* story.'

'I don't blame you. Neither do I.' Toby stood up, walked across Tessa's office, stood looking out of the window which fronted onto Knightsbridge far below. After a moment contemplating Mark Longden, he swung around, and said, 'You mentioned he'd had drinks on the train. Where had he been?'

'To see a new client. In the Midlands. He sounded rather chuffed about that. It's a big architectural job for him. A grand house, apparently, according to what he told me. The client's filthy rich, so Mark said.'

'What's his name?'

'William Stone. Some sort of tycoon, I think.'

'Never heard of him.' Toby shrugged. 'Not that that means anything. There's a lot of wealth around these days that nobody knows anything about.'

Toby strode back to the chair opposite Tessa's desk, sat down and continued, 'If he *was* on something, it was more than likely a designer drug rather than anything else. Probably ecstasy, that's still very popular.'

'What exactly *is* it?' Tessa asked, riddled with curiosity.

'Ecstasy's a party drug, and popular because it creates a rush, a high, very quickly, so I'm told. But it can be hallucinogenic, and even creates paranoia in some people. Basically, it's a stimulant.'

'Is it hard to get?'

'Not if you know where to go.'

'Mark doesn't seem a likely candidate for drugs. He works very hard, and he's made the firm a success.'

Toby nodded, then smiled at her, aware of how troubled she was. 'Perhaps he was just very, very drunk, darling,' he suggested, wanting to make her feel better.

'Maybe you're right. Nevertheless, he was awfully weird.'

Gazing across the desk at her, it occurred to Toby that she did not look well this afternoon. Her delicately wrought face was drained of all colour; this combined with the halo of silvery-blonde hair made her look like a pale ghost, extremely frail. But perhaps it was the black suit she was wearing; the colour certainly emphasized her extreme pallor and delicacy. And yet there had always been a certain fragility about Tessa, which is one of the reasons he had fallen so easily into the role of protector when they were children. Despite this physical frailness, however, she was strong mentally.

Toby knew how tough Tessa could be, and she had a will of iron. He admired his cousin and he had always loved her. To Toby her *only* fault was her inability to disguise her true feelings in certain instances, most especially when it came to her sister Linnet. She was competitive with her, seemed to have no idea how to conceal this. The art of dissimulation, apparently one of their great-grandmother's most important assets, had seemingly escaped Tessa.

'You're suddenly very quiet, Toby.'

'I was thinking about Mark. He wasn't abusive, was he?' Toby sounded worried and his dark eyes reflected a sudden fierceness.

'Oh no, nothing like that!' she lied. It would embarrass her to tell Toby the truth. Knowing him as she did, she was aware he would seek Mark out, take him to task, or worse, beat him up. Toby had always defended her and nothing had changed there. They were not only cousins and best friends, but cohorts in business, with many well-laid plans for their future together in the Harte empire.

'Now *you're* suddenly quiet,' Toby remarked, staring hard at her.

Tessa gave him the benefit of a wide and loving smile. 'You know how mad you get when someone reminds you that you don't look like a Harte?'

'Oh yes, the changeling, that's me,' he muttered sarcastically.

'I saw a photo recently of Emma's father, Big Jack Harte, and *that's* who you look like, Toby.'

Startled, he gaped at her, then said, 'I do?' He sounded doubtful. 'Are you sure?'

Tessa didn't answer. Instead she opened her desk drawer and took out an ancient photograph of a tall, well-built, darkly handsome man standing next to a younger man in Royal Navy uniform. It was obviously father and son since they resembled each other. She handed the picture to Toby.

He stared down at it with interest, then lifted his head, looked at her. 'Where did you get this?'

'I took it out of an old photograph album in the library at Pennistone Royal a few weeks ago. I was up in Yorkshire, visiting the Leeds and Harrogate stores, and I spent the night there. I was alone, except for Emsie, who was doing her homework, and I went to the library to browse. Actually, I was hoping to find a few pictures of Aunt Edwina when she was young. That's when I came across that particular photograph. I was instantly aware of the striking resemblance you bear to the older man in particular.'

'How do you know it's our great-great-grandfather?'

'Look on the back.'

He did as she suggested, and read out loud the words written in the now-faded black ink. 'My father, Jack Harte, and my brother Winston when he was in the Royal Navy.'

'That's certainly Grandy Emma's handwriting, Toby.'

'So I see.' He offered her the photograph.

Tessa shook her head. 'I don't want it. I brought it for you. Please keep it.'

'Are you sure? After all, it might be missed.'

'Who's going to look through an old album? There are a lot of them in the library. They're all covered in faded red velvet or fancy tooled leather with big brass clasps on the front. Anyway, I think you ought to have it because it absolutely proves you do look like a Harte.' She began to laugh, and went on, 'Like the founding father, actually. Isn't that one for the books?'

'Let's have tea,' Tessa said to Toby as her secretary Claire Remsford came into her office carrying a laden tray. As she spoke she rose and crossed the room, heading for the small seating area near the windows.

'Thanks, Claire,' Tessa murmured, and smiled when she saw the tray. She exclaimed, 'Oh that's so nice! You ordered some chocolate fingers. Mr Harte loves them.'

'Yes, I know,' Claire replied as she went towards the door.

Toby grinned at her, remarking, 'You certainly know how to get to a man's heart, Claire.'

Laughing, blushing, Tessa's secretary exited, and Toby joined Tessa, sitting down in one of the armchairs. 'No milk for me,' he told her, 'and I'll have a sweetener instead of sugar. I'm on a diet.'

She gave him a surreptitious glance out of the corner of her eye. 'But I bet you'll guzzle all of those chocolate fingers.'

'Not all of them. I'll save a few for you,' he shot back, laughing.

'I spoke to my mother the other day,' Tessa confided as she poured the tea. 'About who her successor will be.'

'You did!' Toby sat up straighter in the chair and gazed at Tessa expectantly, his dark eyes suddenly growing more alert. He leaned forward slightly, his face quickening. 'Well, go on, don't leave me dangling. What did she say?'

After handing him his cup of tea, and motioning to the packets of sweeteners in a china bowl, Tessa sat back and said in a low, confidential voice, 'She told me she's not going to name a successor until the day she retires, and that won't be for a long time. Mummy explained that she'd made a promise to her grandmother thirty years ago . . . that she wouldn't retire until she felt she couldn't run the stores properly any longer. Mummy indicated to me that she might stay until she's *eighty*.'

'Like Grandy Emma,' Toby pointed out. 'But you *know* that. And that's *all* she said?' His dark brows drew together in a frown.

'More or less. She was very nice at the end of our conversation, very kind and loving—' Tessa broke off, and took a sip of her tea, reminding herself not to spill the story of her bruised arm to her cousin. She didn't want him to know about that. He would instantly put two and two together, even though her mother obviously hadn't done so. Not yet. Placing the china cup in the saucer, Tessa continued, 'That's about it. The one good thing is she didn't say Linnet was going to inherit. In fact, she said it might not be either of us, but someone else in the family.'

'There isn't anyone else,' Toby asserted, putting his cup down with a clatter. 'And I know it's going to be *you*, Tessa. Aunt Paula wouldn't cheat you out of your right, just as Dad won't cheat me. I'm the eldest and I'm going to inherit the Yorkshire Consolidated Newspaper Company and its subsidiaries. Gideon will continue to run the papers, but *I'll* be the head of the media company in Dad's place. My baby brother will be working for me, just as Linnet will be working for you. That's if she's still at Harte's.'

Tessa frowned, looked at him curiously. 'What're you getting at? Of course she'll be at Harte's. She's very ambitious.'

'And very involved . . . in love with Julian Kallinski. She might well be married and the mother of a brood of bairns by the time Aunt Paula steps down.'

'She and Julian broke up—'

'They're back together, my sweet,' he interrupted.

'How do you know? Oh, I might well ask . . . Gideon told you, I've no doubt.'

'No, he didn't. However, I saw Linnet and Julian having dinner at Harry's Bar the other night. Mind you, Gideon was with them, along with the dark-haired girl—'

'Evan Hughes! I heard on the store grapevine that she's having an affair with Gid. She works fast, doesn't she? She met him in January and it's only the end of March and they're already bedding down together. My, my.'

Toby nodded. 'It looks as if they're very close, from the way they were behaving. Gideon hung on her every word, I've never seen him so . . . well, captivated. It's always been love 'em and leave 'em with him. I used to call him the champion of one-night-standers, don't you remember?'

'Yes, I do. What do you think of Evan?' Tessa asked.

'I've only met her briefly, so I can't really pass judgement.'

'Do you think she looks like Mummy? A lot of people do.'

Toby sat back, his expression turning thoughtful, sipping his tea and then munching on a chocolate biscuit. After a moment, he answered her, saying, 'At first glance Evan is the spitting image of Aunt Paula, but then when one studies her for a few minutes one realizes it's all an illusion. The same exotic, dark colouring, the same height, the same figure, even similar clothes, but there it definitely stops. Because her face isn't at all like your mother's. The shape is different and she doesn't have violet eyes, or the famous Harte widow's peak.'

'Shane himself did a double take,' Tessa announced, giving him a pointed look.

Toby pursed his lips, shook his head. 'I bet he did exactly what I did: looked quickly, registered surprise, and then realized it was only an illusion after a second glance.'

'*I* think she might be related to us.'

'You *do*? But how could she be?' Toby sounded surprised.

'I've figured it out . . . through Paul McGill, Mummy's grandfather. He spent a lot of time in America and Australia, and without Emma. He could easily have had an affair with someone else, probably in America, and that woman could have given birth to a child, and Evan could be an off-spring of Paul McGill's American child. His grand-child.' After this explanation, which she thought was plausible, Tessa sat back. 'Well, what do you think?'

'It's a possibility. I hadn't thought of the Paul McGill side,' Toby answered, 'I must admit that.'

'Maybe she came here to try and get some-thing – you know, some kind of inheritance,' Tessa suggested.

'Don't be daft! It's all tied up, lashed together with steel ropes. Emma Harte saw to that, for the most part, and then your mother, my parents and Aunt Amanda followed her lead and her instruc-tions to the nth degree. In fact, they took many more precautions, as you know. That's why it's a bit of a joke the way the seniors are upset because the notorious Jonathan Ainsley has returned to England. He can't get anything either – well, maybe a few shares of Harte Stores that are traded on the London Stock Exchange.'

Tessa nodded. 'I overheard my mother talking to your mother yesterday. She'd come over for a meeting with Linnet and Mummy about the birthday party in June. Apparently Mummy put a private investigator on him, but nothing untoward has been turned up so far.'

'And perhaps it won't be. Maybe he's just come back to live here because he prefers London, and to be near his father. Uncle Robin's quite frail, I hear. Of course, Jonathan will inherit his father's money, and that's a fortune.'

'But Uncle Robin was a Member of Parliament all his life, a politician. I didn't know he had a *fortune*.'

'Our great-grandmother loved him, despite his misdeeds at certain times. He *was* her favourite son, and I happen to know she not only created a trust for him, but gave him quite a lot before she died.'

'You obviously know more than I do.'

'I do know one thing, Tessa darling. It's going to be you and me running this show one day. You'll be head of the stores and I'll be at the helm of the media companies. We'll rule the Harte empire together.' He smiled broadly, full of confidence.

Rising, Toby went to join Tessa on the sofa. He put his arms around her, pulled her to him, kissed her lightly on the cheek. 'Everything's going to be ours, Tess. Trust me.'

'I do. But my mother's not going to retire as soon as you think, I just told you that. I'll be an old lady when I inherit.'

'Tessa, life is full of surprises. Nobody knows what's in store. Anything can happen, and when we least expect it. Your mother might retire in a few years, for reasons we don't know now, reasons she herself doesn't know now. You see, people suddenly run out of steam, or want to retire after all, want to enjoy life. They might want to have a bit of fun. God knows, our parents have worked like dogs all of their lives, so there are many reasons why they could change their minds. As Ma always says, the only thing that's permanent is change. And she's right. I feel that way about Dad. He could decide he's fed up and pass the mantle to me overnight. *We don't know anything.* So stay cool, my sweet, and for God's sake stop being mean to Linnet. When she marries Julian her life will change, and so will yours.'

'*If* she marries him.'

'Oh she will, take my word for it. The grand-fathers O'Neill and Kallinski are going to push it for all it's worth, now that those two lovebirds are back together. They want the three clans to be forever bound. So please, give Linnet some slack, and stop complaining about her endlessly. It makes you look bad.'

'She irritates me.'

'I know she does, but it gets other people angry with you, and then they favour her, and you can't afford that. You don't need any enemies in the family. You must learn to be like our sainted great-grandmother; you must learn to dissemble the way Emma did.'

'I'll try,' she answered, knowing he was right.

'Good girl.' Toby tightened his grip on her, hugging her warmly.

Tessa flinched.

Toby pulled away, giving her a puzzled look. 'What's wrong?'

She shook her head. 'It's just my shoulder, Toby, I hurt it last week.' She forced a smile. 'In the gym,' she then added swiftly, when she saw that fierce, protective look enter his eyes. Leaning into him she kissed his cheek. 'It's just a bit sore.'

'Are you sure he hasn't hurt you?' Toby demanded, the look he gave her full of concern.

'No, no, he wouldn't do that.'

'I wish you hadn't married him,' Toby muttered when they drew apart, smoothing his hand over her pale-gold hair. He cared about her very much, loathed the idea that anyone could hurt her in any way. 'I can't imagine why you had to make it legal.'

Tessa sighed. 'I wonder sometimes why I did . . .'

They were silent, sitting together on the sofa, their arms wrapped around each other, for a moment lost in their thoughts. Best friends and allies now, they had once been childhood sweethearts, and some of those feelings remained, however much they both denied them. But there had never been a sexual relationship between them. When Mark had suggested otherwise, Tessa had spoken the truth in denying it.

'How's Adrianna?' Tessa asked, breaking the silence.

'Fine. She's still in Hollywood making that movie.'

'Why did you marry her?'

'It seemed like a good idea at the time,' he replied with a rueful laugh.

At the sound of the low buzzing of the phone, Tessa jumped up, hurried over to her desk, lifted the receiver. 'Hello?'

'It's me, Tessa,' Linnet said. 'I wonder if you can spare me a few minutes, please?'

It was on the tip of her tongue to immediately say no, always ready to deny any request from her sister. But looking across at Toby she decided to take his advice. 'That's fine, Linnet. When do you want to come to my office?'

'Well, more or less now, if that's all right?'

'I'm here with Toby. He came in to ask my help about choosing birthday gifts for our fathers, and I suppose he'll be leaving soon.'

'Thanks,' Linnet said and hung up.

'How did I do?' Tessa asked, staring at her cousin, then sitting down at her desk.

'You did good, kid!' he said, adopting an American accent. 'Real good.'

CHAPTER TWENTY-ONE

Toby's manners were excellent, and he rose when Linnet came into the office, moved swiftly across the floor. They met halfway, in the middle of the room, and he gave her a light kiss on the cheek, and asked, 'How's the retrospective coming along?'

'Very well, thanks, Toby.' Linnet smiled at him, then swung around and walked over to Tessa's desk, where she sat down and looked across at her sister, and said in a friendly voice, 'The reason I wanted to see you, Tessa, is actually to do with the retrospective. I was wondering if you'd lend us some of your couture clothes?'

'But I don't have much couture!' Tessa exclaimed, almost too sharply, she realized, and catching herself she adopted a much milder tone. 'Hardly any at all, Linnet, and anyway I don't think the things I have are in good enough condition to be put on display. I've worn them to death.'

'I was thinking of those two evening coats you

296

own. We're still a bit thin on the vintage stuff, and you have that gorgeous coral silk coat with a shoulder cape attached designed by Norman Hartnell. You once told me it was from the 1960s, and there's the Balmain coat Mummy gave you, which belonged to Emma. I think that's from the mid 1950s. Could we borrow those two things, do you think? They would fill a gap if we had them in the show.'

Tessa's first instinct was to refuse. She had grown accustomed to saying no to Linnet over the years. Also, she had genuinely been against the retrospective right from the beginning. She had believed it to be a waste of time, effort and money. But she did not dare display a negative attitude this afternoon. Toby was sitting on the sofa, watching her like a hawk. Anyway, he was right in what he had said earlier. She must be more diplomatic, not so obviously competitive and seemingly against Linnet. She was definitely going to have to watch herself, keep a rein on her temper, and be much more patient in the future. The problem was that she found it hard to pretend, thought doing so was two-faced, even though Toby called it dissimulation and admired anyone who could carry it off.

Pushing a pleasant smile on her face, Tessa said, 'Of course you can borrow them, but I don't know how pristine they are.'

'Oh, thanks very much, Tess!' Linnet said enthusiastically, obviously pleased, and continued, 'I really appreciate it, and don't worry about the condition of the coats. Evan's wonderfully talented when it comes to restoration, and she's very clever at hand cleaning, repairing, steaming and pressing, that kind of thing. She does meticulous work; your coats will come back to you looking like new. You'll be impressed with her work, everyone is.'

'Really,' Tessa murmured and, observing the sudden smile in Linnet's eyes, hearing the warmth in her voice, she understood immediately that her sister admired and liked Evan. They were obviously good friends by the sound of it. I bet she's given Evan Hughes her stamp of approval, as far as Gideon's concerned.

Linnet, in her usual businesslike manner, rushed on, 'Look, I'm very sorry there was a misunderstanding between us recently. About the use of the auditorium. I hadn't realized you had planned a management meeting that morning, and I'd arranged for the space planning company to measure the areas where the platforms are to be built. Since they'd left Leeds, I couldn't stop them from coming to the store. It was already too late.'

'I understand, and it's no problem,' Tessa answered evenly, almost dismissively, endeavouring to appear nonchalant, although at the time she had been furious, had complained to their mother that Linnet had countermanded her orders and commandeered the auditorium. Paula had been so scathing with her about the use of that particular word she had vowed to herself never to use it again.

Watching them from his position on the sofa, Toby was fascinated. It struck him most forcibly that whatever Tessa lacked in the technique of dissembling, her sister more than made up for it. No one will ever know what *she's* thinking when it comes to business, he decided. She was being charming and friendly at this moment, and she had even apologized to Tessa. *Very clever*. No fool, our Linnet, he thought. She had never been his favourite, but he couldn't help admiring her adroit handling of Tessa, albeit grudgingly. He suddenly understood the reason why he had long been wary of her. She was not only crafty but extremely shrewd, not to mention a splendid actress. She ought to get an Oscar for this performance, he thought, his eyes fixed on her.

Although he had never recognized it until this precise moment, Toby now admitted that he was actually a bit afraid of Linnet. And for one very good reason. She was everything their great-grandmother had been at her age: ambitious, driven, hardworking and calculating. A tough cookie. He must warn Tessa to be careful, to watch her back.

Linnet was looking across at him, and saying, 'Would you like to come too, Toby?'

'Er, er, sorry Linnet, I was preoccupied. Come with you where?'

'Down to the storage room where we keep the clothes. We've started to put some of them on the mannequins, you know, the fibreglass dummies. I thought Tessa might like to see our progress, also look at the really beautiful clothes we've assembled so far. And you could come too, Toby.'

'I'd love to, but I'm afraid I can't. I've got to get back to the office. Thanks, though.'

But in the end Toby did join them, changing his mind all of a sudden, wanting to have another look at Evan Hughes, his brother's current paramour. She must have something special to hold Gideon's interest all these weeks, he decided.

Toby had been coming to the Knightsbridge store since he was a child, but he had never been into the famous storage room before today. As he walked behind Linnet and Tessa he saw that it was gargantuan, and he was stunned by its size.

It was a vast, airy space, almost the length of a football field, and it was filled to overflowing with clothes. Some hung on racks aligned side by side, from rods affixed to parts of the ceiling, and some were laid flat on white sheets on top of long trestle tables running the length of one wall.

He could see at a quick glance that all of the clothes which had been assembled were beautiful and obviously costly; the other thing he noticed immediately was the perfect order that reigned within the storage room. No sign of mess or chaos here. It struck him that somebody on this team had good organizational abilities, more than likely India Standish. She had been annoyingly neat and tidy as a child, he suddenly recalled.

'Why are these dresses laid out on tables?' he

asked Linnet, as they walked down to the far end of the storage area.

'Because they're beaded. Gowns with beading are never hung on hangers. You see, the weight of the beads pulls the dress out of shape. Also, it's easier to check for loose beads and damage when the dresses are laid flat. We have a specialist in this kind of beaded embroidery who checks and also does repairs.'

'I thought Evan did that,' Tessa said, a blonde brow lifting quizzically.

'Some of it, but Miriam Flande is the expert who helps out when we need her,' Linnet responded with a small smile.

Glancing around, Tessa suddenly said, 'There're so many clothes here I can't imagine why you want my poor bits and pieces.'

Toby grabbed her arm on hearing these words, and squeezed it. Quickly, she glanced at him, saw his warning expression, and added, 'But of course you're welcome to them, as I said, and naturally I'm flattered.'

Linnet looked at her sister oddly but made no comment.

'Oh hello, India,' Toby exclaimed as his cousin appeared quite suddenly from behind a rack, wearing the white cotton coat favoured by couturiers to protect the new clothing, part of an outfit in her hands. For once he was glad to see her; Tessa could be aggravating at times.

'Hello, Toby,' India answered, then turning to

Tessa she went on, 'I'm so glad you came to visit us. This is all quite something, isn't it?'

Tessa simply nodded, fully aware of Toby's presence right behind her. She did not want to say anything out of place, but inside she was seething with jealousy, envious of what they had accomplished. They were going to pull it off, damn it; contrary to what she had believed, the retrospective was probably going to be a big hit. And this maddened her. Competitive by nature, and extremely so with Linnet, any number of comments flew to the tip of her tongue. But she did not utter any of them. They were all hostile, snide, or critical, and were better left unsaid, she understood that. And so she made an effort to keep her irritation in check, her face neutral.

India hung up the jacket she was holding, then turning to Tessa, she said, 'Come and look at Emma's clothes. Evan's been working on them for the last few weeks and they look brand new – as if they'd been bought yesterday, not fifty years ago.'

'That's great,' Tessa muttered, and fell into step with India, the two of them walking behind Linnet, who was leading the way.

Toby followed behind the three women. He couldn't help thinking how much Tessa and India resembled each other, at least as far as their delicate features and colouring were concerned. That they were related to each other was transparent. The Fairley strain runs through them both, he thought;

from Jim to his daughter Tessa, and from Aunt Edwina to her granddaughter India Standish. He sighed under his breath. What a strange, muddled-up mixture his family was.

These thoughts fled when he came face to face with Evan Hughes, and he found himself thinking at once that she was a true beauty. Suddenly she was standing in front of him, dressed in the white couturier's coat like India, and having appeared from behind a rack just as India had done a moment before. In fact, he almost ran slap bang into her, pulled back just in time, quickly apologizing.

'My fault, suddenly appearing like that,' she said, and thrust out her hand. 'I'm Evan. We met briefly in Harry's Bar the other night.'

He shook her hand, nodding, and then found himself smiling at her. 'Nice to see you again, Evan. Linnet's just been singing your praises.'

'That's kind of her, but she's the one who's responsible for all this – she and India, that is. I haven't done all that much, I've only been here a few months.'

'I know the retrospective has been underway for a year, the planning of it, but Linnet obviously values your contribution,' Toby told her.

She nodded, then explained, 'Today we've been putting some of Mrs Harte's clothes on the fibre-glass mannequins. I think that's where Linnet's leading Tessa. Shall we join them?'

'That's a good idea,' he answered, and together the two of them headed down the centre of the room between the many racks of clothes. Whatever anyone else said, Toby still held to his opinion that Evan Hughes resembled his aunt only at first glance. Up close, as he was now, he could see they were quite different. But, nonetheless, she *was* a knockout, and extremely well put together. Just as Paula O'Neill was; yes, that was part of the illusion: the stylishness. They had that in common, he realized.

Linnet, India and Tessa were waiting for them at the bottom of the storage area. It was here that the team of three had created a makeshift office on the spot, with desks, lamps and telephones. A lot of charts, sketches of the auditorium, lists and photographs of clothing were pinned on several cork bulletin boards, and in general there was an air of high efficiency here.

Tessa realized at once that they were going to give a show. Linnet and India had always been good at that; both rather theatrical in nature, they revelled in presenting projects as if they were on a stage entertaining an audience. She sighed. Well, she supposed they were this afternoon. But it was an audience of two, herself and Toby.

She stole a look at him. He was watching the three young women attentively – or rather, he was watching Evan Hughes. He was obviously fascinated by her, although she knew this was mostly because of Gideon's involvement with her. Her cousin had a reputation for being flighty, and it was deserved, and so not unnaturally the family were intrigued by his sudden and unexpected steadfastness with the American. They all wondered how long it would last. Wouldn't he soon get tired of her as he usually had in the past? She herself didn't particularly care; she had her own problems to contend with.

Linnet, India and Evan were now moving the racks around, swiftly and with great expertise, and as they finally parted them they revealed a series of fibreglass mannequins. There were five of them altogether, and each displayed some of the loveliest clothes she had ever seen. Tessa knew at once that these were her great-grandmother's clothes, and she was stunned by their stylishness, taste and elegance. But then Emma Harte was legendary for her chic appearance, and she asked herself why she was surprised. She ought to have known the clothes would be *haute couture* and gorgeous.

Stepping forward, Linnet explained, 'Tessa, Toby, these are just a few of Emma's outfits. We're going to be displaying fifty altogether, maybe even a few more, and her collection is actually the main feature of the retrospective . . . *she* was the real inspiration behind it.' Linnet looked at India, and said, 'Tell them about the ball gown, India.'

India walked over to the mannequin, explaining, 'We're showing this gown with the back facing out, because very obviously the back is the most spectacular part of the gown.'

'It's beautiful,' Tessa said, moving forward to inspect it closer.

'It is,' India agreed, and continued: 'It's made of cotton tulle, masses of it in the skirt, as you can see, and it's a peculiar green, a sort of greyish-green I would say. It's by Christian Dior. It's from his 1947 collection, created just after the Second World War, which became known as the New Look.' India turned to Evan and beckoned her to come forward.

Evan explained, 'You can see that the narrow, pale green silk belt defines the waist, then comes around to the back and essentially grows into the huge bow. This is, in a way, a kind of bustle with the ends falling to the hem. And it's the trail of pale creamy, slightly pink cabbage roses that give the gown its great style. It was in almost perfect condition,' Evan now remarked, looking directly at Tessa. 'As were most of Mrs Harte's clothes. Very little needed real cleaning or repairs. She took care of her things.'

'Well she would, wouldn't she?' Tessa said. 'Since she came up the hard way, from nothing.'

Whatever Tessa had intended by the remark, it fell into the middle of the group like a large lump of heavy lead. Linnet looked appalled, Evan appeared embarrassed, but India took it in her stride.

With a huge smile, her expression one of immense pride, she said in a smooth and loving voice. 'Our great-grandmother was known to be a perfection-ist, Tessa, and it was her nature to take care of things well. Just as I do. I am thrilled I inherited that trait from her. Emma loved beauty and beautiful things, whether it was clothes, jewellery, antiques or furnishings. Paintings were her joy, as we all know from her many homes and the great art displayed there. So naturally she took care of all of those things . . .' India stared at Toby, who seemed as embarrassed by Tessa's remark as Evan, and then focused on her cousin Tessa. 'And it is because she came from nothing yet created our great business empire and family dynasty that she is an icon, a legend, not only in the family but in the world. Not for nothing is Emma Harte known as a woman of substance.'

Tessa, whose light blonde colouring and delicate features echoed India's, flushed scarlet. 'You don't have to reprimand me in that way, India my dear! I didn't mean anything rude by the remark . . . actually, I was being complimentary.'

'It didn't sound that way,' Linnet muttered, filled with disgust. 'Well, let's get on with it. We don't want to be here all day, and Toby's got to get back to his office. This emerald green cocktail dress is also by Dior, from the fifties. It has a bouffant skirt, shorter at the front to show the legs, and Emma seemingly selected it to wear with her emerald collection.'

Moving to another outfit, Evan said, 'Here is a Balenciaga cocktail dress from 1951. Mrs Harte liked bouffant skirts, and this is made of black tissue taffeta with a ballooning sash.'

It was now India's turn, and she walked over to yet another mannequin, and pointed to the jacket. 'This is Schiaparelli, 1938. It's from her Circus collection, and the amusing pattern of prancing horses reflects this. The pink jacket particularly stands out because it is partnered with a narrow black skirt. Our great-grandmother loved tailored day suits, and this one here in a light herringbone tweed is by Hardy Amies. He designed it in the early sixties for her.' India indicated the suit, then stepped away.

Linnet came forward, saying, 'This is one of Emma's most famous evening gowns. Your mother found it stored away in the attics at the Belgravia house quite a number of years ago, Toby. Aunt Emily pointed us in the right direction, and India and I finally found it up at Pennistone Royal. Look at the beading, Tessa, all these different green and blue bugle beads. The gown is the colour of the sea in the south of France. She also wore this with her emeralds, and we even found emerald green silk shoes from Pinet of Paris to go with it. Evan, come and explain about the restoration of the beading.'

Evan joined Linnet, and took over. 'At first glance, the gown seemed to be in perfect order, as were all the other couture outfits. But then on closer examination I discovered some of the bugle beads were hanging by a thread, and others were missing. It was Madame Flande who did the repair work, and she made a beautiful job of it. The shell of the gown is composed of silk and chiffon, and it was designed by Jacques Heim in the 1940s.'

'Such a lot of evening clothes,' Tessa said. 'She must have led quite a social life, even after Paul McGill was dead.'

Again the three women exchanged startled looks, but said not one word. It was Toby who jumped into the breach, exclaiming, 'This is all wonderful. I'm sure the retrospective will be a smash. Thanks for showing it to me, to us, but I've got to go, I'm afraid.'

'Yes, thank you, it's been very interesting,' Tessa added quietly, realizing her last remark had not gone down well. 'And I have to go, too.' Inclining her head, looking at the three of them, she took Toby's arm, led him away, saying, 'I'll take you down to the David Morris shop. I know you'll find interesting watches there for Shane and your father. They have a great selection.'

'Thanks for your help, Tessa,' Toby murmured, and hurried her away. Once they were outside the storage room he turned to her, and said in a quietly vehement voice, 'My God, Tessa, sometimes you say the worst things! I don't know what gets into you!'

'I wasn't being critical when I said she came from nothing,' Tessa protested, sounding very earnest.

'But it came out that way, and that comment about Emma leading a big social life after Paul's death was just awful. Your mouth is always open and your foot's always in it. You've got to learn to be more diplomatic.'

'I'm trying,' she answered, sounding on the verge of tears.

After introducing Toby to the manager of the David Morris watch shop on the first floor, Tessa went back to her office. On the way up in the lift she thought about the presentation the women had given and envy and jealousy surged through her. But it was envy of their relationship with each other, rather than anything else. What she had seen was their easy way of working together: three young women totally geared to each other's working needs and in perfect sync.

Also, she had picked up on the camaraderie between them, and the loving friendship. Linnet and India, who had been close all their lives, and Evan, a comparative stranger, were obviously on the same wavelength. She had witnessed their knowing glances, their affection, and their devotion. They were a team, and this frustrated her and made her angry. But the most upsetting thing of all was their obvious happiness with their lives. She had wanted to be happy with Mark, to have a good marriage. But both seemed to be eluding her right now. Her sudden bitterness was like a sharp pain in her chest: dismaying, frightening even.

CHAPTER TWENTY-TWO

S arah Lowther was irresistibly drawn to Harte's of Knightsbridge whenever she was in London. Today was no exception. She felt its overwhelming pull as she hurried towards the greatest emporium in the world, founded by her grandmother Emma Harte long ago. Once, she had worked at Harte's for Emma, before taking over Emma's fashion business, Lady Hamilton Clothes, which she had run with great success.

But Sarah had always believed that retailing was in her blood, and over the years she had opened six stores of her own in France. They were actually boutiques selling antique furniture, *objets d'art*, paintings, porcelains, and fabrics of all kinds. She specialized in lovely old silks and brocades, antique *toile de Jouy* and the finest of tapestries, and she had become quite well known for her taste and style in home design and decor.

In fact, the boutiques were now a huge success, and she was very proud of her busy little company, which she had created all by herself. It was apparent to her that her talent for selling had truly been inherited from her grandmother; she was even noticing that same trait in her twenty-five-year-old daughter, Chloe, who was currently running the boutique in Paris where they lived.

Yves Pascal, Sarah's husband and the father of Chloe, had recently remarked about this tendency himself, laughingly adding, 'She takes after you, *cherie*, not me.'

Sarah had had to agree with him. Although Chloe had an artistic bent and a very good eye, she had not inherited her father's extraordinary talent and brilliance as a painter. Today Yves Pascal was considered to be one of France's greatest living artists, renowned throughout the world for his contemporary Impressionist paintings, and in Sarah's eyes he was a true genius.

She glanced around as she walked along Knightsbridge making for the store. It was a beautiful spring day, surprisingly mild for early May and sunny, with a pale-blue canopy of a sky shimmering overhead.

Although she loved Paris, where she had lived even before her marriage to Yves some twenty-seven years ago, Sarah was happy to be back in the country of her birth, if only for a short while. Everything was familiar, and so many fond memories abounded; particularly happy memories of her grandmother, her father Kit, Emma's eldest son, and her mother June. All three of them were dead but they lived forever in her heart, and were very frequently in her thoughts.

As she approached the main doors of Harte's she felt a rush of anticipation, and once she was inside, standing in the middle of the cosmetics department, she experienced a marvellous sense of coming home. It was a combination of excitement, relief to be back in the store, and an awareness of belonging to a greater whole. Walking through her grandmother's renowned emporium was the next best thing to being part of the family.

Leaving cosmetics behind, entering jewellery, Sarah's thoughts were on Paula O'Neill. She had no doubt that her cousin was sitting upstairs in her office, if she was not at one of the stores in Yorkshire. Sarah had to resist the temptation of going up to the executive suite to see her. It was a feeling that frequently overtook her when she was here.

Better not, she cautioned herself – as she generally did – and walked on, admiring everything she saw. The store looked wonderful, as it always had. Nothing had changed . . . except perhaps for the better. It was the greatest in the world, and Paula was obviously carrying on the grand tradition of excellence started by their grandmother.

For years now Sarah had wanted to write a letter to Paula, not one of apology but of explanation. She had long needed her cousin to understand that *she* hadn't done anything wrong all those years ago, that *she* hadn't been treacherous to the family.

What she had done was simply invest some of her money in a company called Stonewall Properties, following the advice of her cousin Jonathan Ainsley. He had not told her that Stonewall was his own company, run by his straw man, Sebastian Cross. Nor had she been aware that Jonathan was cheating the family, diminishing their property interests by funnelling deals which belonged to Harte Real Estate to Stonewall instead.

Nonetheless, she had been blamed along with Jonathan, kicked out of Lady Hamilton Clothes most unceremoniously, and out of the family, by Paula and her father, the late David Amory. That had been the worst part, and it had broken Sarah's heart, and in many ways she had never fully recovered from the blow. It had been, and still was, a cruel and most painful banishment for her.

But she was not a Harte for nothing, Sarah had reminded herself at the time, thinking of her grandmother's favourite 'line', which Emma had applied to so many situations. And she had somehow managed to draw on her considerable inner resources in order to steady herself and keep going. Taking strength from the spirit of Emma Harte that lived on in her, she had started her life all over again and made it work for her.

She had moved to France and built herself a career in the world of Paris fashion, working as a *directrice* at a top *haute-couture* house. It was during this time that she had met and married Yves Pascal, a young artist rapidly gaining recognition.

They had started a family almost at once, and later she had created her own business; today she had a good marriage, a very special daughter, a good life in general, and she was content. And yet . . .

There was a hole in Sarah's heart, a sadness, an awful emptiness at times, despite all of the good things she had. Very simply, she longed to be back in the fold, to be part of the Hartes again, to be friends with her cousins with whom she had grown up and had spent so much of her life: Paula, Emily, the twins Amanda and Francesca, and Winston. And those other two dashing characters from the other clans, Michael Kallinski and Shane O'Neill. *Shane* . . . she had been enamoured of him once, but he had only had eyes for Paula.

Each and every one of them had been part of her existence, her world, and she missed them very much, particularly Emily and Paula. They had had their quarrels, but then what large families didn't have their differences, their disagreements from time to time? For the most part, they had got along, and had never really held any grudges. Linking them was their love for their quite extraordinary grandmother, their shared background, upbringing and experiences. They knew where they belonged . . . they were part of the Hartes, and to be that was something very special indeed.

Jonathan Ainsley had ruined all this for her when he had involved her in his schemes without her knowledge. Sometimes she wondered why she still bothered with him, still saw him. But then there was no other family member left in her life, and she knew she needed that connection to her past, to her heritage. It made her feel whole and special and different from the rest of the world.

Yet it was true that she was frequently troubled by their relationship; she thought of her cousin Jonathan as something of a loose cannon. She never knew what he was up to, what he was going to do. But then weren't these very good reasons to stay close to him?

Jonathan could not help admiring Sarah as she walked towards him down the length of the Grill Room in the Dorchester Hotel. She was an elegant woman, tall, slender and as good looking as ever. Sarah was fifty-nine now and he thought she wore her years well, looked so much younger. Her lovely auburn hair was still the same vibrant colour it had been when she was younger, but it was obviously touched up discreetly. She had the Harte colouring and looks, and had been, and was, proud of this.

The thing that always struck him was her chicness; she had always been stylish and this was most apparent tonight. Sarah was wearing a black wool suit, so beautifully cut and engineered it could only be *haute couture* from a top French designer. On one shoulder she had pinned two flower brooches made of black and white diamonds, and added matching earrings. She looked superb, he thought.

Jonathan stood up as she drew to a standstill, kissed her cheek and greeted her warmly as she took the other chair which had been pulled out by the waiter.

'You're as chic as always, Sarah darling,' he murmured, reaching over, squeezing her arm. 'Nobody holds a candle to you.'

'Why thank you, Jonathan, it's nice of you to say so.'

'A drop of bubbly, or what?'

'Champagne would be nice, thanks. I see you're having a martini.' She smiled. 'Too strong for me these days. Anyway, it's nice to see you.'

He inclined his head, still smiling. 'And you too. Have you had a busy day?'

'Not so bad. I met with an antiques dealer this morning and got a good price on a Georgian desk, and then this afternoon I took a stroll around Harte's.'

'Is it falling down? I hope,' he said dryly, giving her a long, pointed stare.

Although his comment irritated her slightly, she decided to play it lightly, and so she laughed, before saying, 'Don't be so silly, of course it isn't. In fact, it's looking fabulous. Paula's doing a great job.'

Jonathan gaped at her. 'Good Lord, a kind word for Paula! Things *are* looking up.'

'What do you mean?'

'You were always such rivals, for Grandy's approval and love, and for position, power – and Shane O'Neill. I can't imagine what's brought about this change in attitude.'

The waiter arrived with her glass of Dom Perignon;

after they had toasted each other, clinked glasses, Sarah murmured, 'I'm a retailer myself these days and I know what it takes: a great deal of hard work, back-breaking work, not to mention a huge amount of truly smart buying. I suppose I sort of admire her . . . Anyway, all that was long ago. Isn't it better to forget those things?'

Jonathan merely smiled, toyed with the stem of his martini glass, then took a sip. After a moment, he glanced up, gave his cousin a very direct look. 'I'll never know why you go mooching around Harte's, for God's sake. I think it's positively . . . *morbid*.'

'No, it's not! I enjoy roaming through the food halls and cosmetics, the other departments. It's Grandy's store, and I used to work there, and I feel – well, I feel rather at home there.'

He sighed, shook his head, threw her a reproachful look, but she was wise enough not to respond. He knew she was in one of her rather mawkish, sentimental moods, living in the past. Much better to remain utterly silent, at least about Harte's and the family. After a moment, he asked, 'How long are you staying in London this time?'

'Only a couple of days, I'm afraid. I have to go up to Scarborough, or rather, just outside. The outskirts. There's an estate sale coming up, and I understand there's going to be some wonderful eighteenth-century fine French furniture on the block, as well as French silver. Apparently there was a French wife aeons ago, somewhere in the late seventeen hundreds, and she brought a large amount of things with her from France. Part of a big dowry, I suspect. Anyway, it's the kind of stuff that's hard to come by, so I'm going up to Yorkshire for a couple of days, hoping to bid on some of it, then I'm back here for one day before returning to France.'

'Do you think you'll have time to go and see my father?' he asked.

'I might, Jonny, I'll certainly try. And how is Uncle Robin?'

'Not so bad. I was in Yorkshire myself last weekend, staying with friends in Thirsk, and went to see him. He's much better; thankfully he's recovered well from that awful fall.'

'I'm glad.' She took a sip of champagne, and remarked, 'Are you going to look for a country house near Uncle Robin? You said you were thinking about it the last time I was here.'

'Don't know. Not awfully keen any more. My work is suddenly keeping me busy. I have to be in London most of the time, you know.'

'You mean your property company is finally up and running well?' she asked swiftly, although she wasn't surprised. He'd always been a good businessman.

'It is indeed! Are you interested in investing?' he asked, quizzically.

Sarah shook her head. Not bloody likely, she thought, but said, 'Thanks, but not really. I've got my hands full with my own company. I need lots of ready cash to buy antiques. Actually, I do have to carry a lot of stock, make sure I have a big inventory with six boutiques to supply, you know.'

'What do you feel like eating?' he asked, changing the subject, reaching for the menu, studying it.

Sarah did the same, murmured, 'Nothing too heavy. Fish maybe. I prefer something light at night.'

They were halfway through dinner, when Jonathan suddenly looked across the table at Sarah and said, 'One of these days you'll run into one of those damned cousins of ours, when you're flitting about the store, and then where will you be? And what on earth would you do?'

'If that happened I'd just speak to whomever I ran into. I'd say hello, what else? I'm sure much of the animosity has dissolved by now. It probably did years ago. There's no reason we can't be civil with each other.'

He put down his fish knife and fork and leant back in his chair, studying her for a moment.

Sarah stared back at him, thinking that he was better looking now, in some ways, than he had been when he was younger. In her opinion he had always been a bit too pretty when he was in his early twenties and thirties. Blond, with light eyes, not blue but not grey either, a sort of mixture of the two. Tall, slender, dashing, and the spitting image of his grandfather Arthur Ainsley, Emma's second husband. Now in his mid-fifties, he had acquired a certain distinction: the blond hair was touched with threads of silver, the bland and handsome face etched with the lines of a life well lived. She wondered suddenly why he had never remarried. Perhaps the ghastly end of his horrific marriage to Arabella Sutton had scared him off matrimony. Once bitten, twice shy, especially since he had inadvertently married a questionable woman. A shady lady, Sarah called her; Yves, more blunt, dubbed her a *putain*, French for whore.

'You're staring at me, Sarah!'

She laughed. 'Admiringly so, cousin dear. I was thinking how really handsome you look these days. And much more distinguished than when you were merely a pretty boy, a sort of poor woman's matinée idol.'

He grinned at her. 'You do have a quaint way of putting it, Sarah. Now, I haven't asked, but how're Yves and the delectable Chloe?'

'He's painting madly, and sends his best, by the way. He's in the south, at our house in Mougins for a few months. He has a big show coming up and he needs to complete a number of canvases. As for your god-daughter, she's just wonderful.'

'You've been lucky, Sarah darling,' he said, and made a face, then added ruefully, 'Luckier than me.'

'No one special in your life, Jonny?'

'I have a nice girlfriend in Yorkshire' He broke off. 'I don't think I'd better say another word about

Ellie. Every time I boast about a woman she turns out to be a dud.'

'You've just had one bad experience,' she answered, and pushed her plate away, leant against the back of the chair, patting her mouth with her napkin.

'Getting back to the store and the inhabitants therein,' Jonathan said, 'I do want to remind you that they're all as mad as hatters. So you mustn't become entangled with them ever again.'

Sarah stared at him and frowned, her auburn brows pulling together in a jagged line. 'What do you mean? I don't think I quite understand what you're getting at.'

'They're bonkers, darling. Just think about it, cousins marrying cousins *ad infinitum*. Relatives committing suicide, or covering up murders in the bogs of Ireland—'

'My God, Jonathan, that's not true!' she interrupted him, her voice rising shrilly. Sarah blew out air, and shook her head. 'Your imagination's getting the better of you.'

'Then there's that tendency towards immorality . . . Aunt Elizabeth and her *six* husbands, not to mention all of her lovers, most of them members of the bloody British government.'

'I'm not really sure that the latter is true,' Sarah protested.

'It is! Dad told me all about it, and don't forget he was a Member of Parliament most of his adult life.'

'Yes, I do remember,' she murmured, suddenly wondering what had started him off on this rampage about the family.

'Do you want a pudding?' Jonathan asked, after their plates had been cleared away, glancing at the dessert trolley nearby. 'Gosh, they've got bread-and-butter pudding. *Ugh*, not for me. Reminds me of Eton.'

Sarah nodded. 'I think I'll just have herb tea. I'm off coffee, especially in the evening.'

'I still like a cup of coffee after dinner, sort of settles me down.' Jonathan threw her a small smile, motioned to the waiter and ordered for them both. Then, turning to face Sarah again, he went on, 'Then there's the tendency the Hartes have for vendettas: first Emma had one with the Fairleys for years, then Edwina had one with *her* for years. And only God knows who they've got a vendetta with at the moment.'

'Probably nobody,' she shot back succinctly, her eyes narrowing.

'Maybe you're right, but there's a lot of gossip about a newly appointed executive.'

'Who?'

'Her name's Evan . . . Evan Hughes. And she's—'

'Really a boy,' Sarah cut in, smiling. 'Evan is a Welsh boy's name.'

'We all know that, my dear. This Evan is an American. And she's the spitting image of our dear cousin Paula McGill Harte Amory Fairley O'Neill, to give her her full name.'

'She *is*?' Sarah made a *moue*, looking at him curiously. 'Is she a relative?'

'Nobody knows. She arrived as if from nowhere, was taken in by Linnet when she came looking for a job at Harte's, and now everyone's saying she's a McGill.'

'A McGill! That's . . . preposterous!'

'No, it's not, Sarah. Think for a moment. What if the sainted Paul had an American mistress, who gave birth to his child, who grew up and gave birth herself to Evan. Or it could be a boy who was Paul McGill's son, who married and had a child . . . it's a real possibility. After all, he spent a lot of time in New York without Emma when he was building Silex Oil into a major corporation.'

'How do you know all this?'

'I have a . . . *source*, shall we say?'

'Don't you mean a spy?'

'Call it what you will, my dear.'

'Why are you digging up all this old family history tonight, Jonathan, and then relating the current gossip at the store to me? To what purpose?'

His face was very bland as he smiled at her off-handedly, and then shrugged. 'I don't know . . . Frankly, I thought you'd be interested to hear about the new executive who looks so much like your old rival.'

'You're not planning to make any crazy moves against Paula, are you, Jonathan?' Sarah asked, giving him a piercing look through sharp and intelligent green eyes. 'Because if you are . . . I wouldn't, if I were you.'

'How can I do anything to Paula? She's got the business buttoned up like the vicar's little sister's knickers. And you know that from twenty years ago, when I almost sneaked the stores out of her grasp.'

'I know she's made everything very secure. But you and I still get treated properly when it comes to Harte Enterprises. We do get our dividends on time, and Emily's run the company very well. We make a lot of money.'

'Ah yes, she has indeed, and yes we do,' he acknowledged.

Sarah sat back, studying him quietly as he waved elegant fingers at a nearby waiter, who came hurrying over to take an order for a Calvados. Her gut instinct told her that Jonathan was plotting *something* against Paula, although what that was she couldn't possibly imagine. Since business didn't come into it, then it had to be personal. Unexpectedly, Sarah felt slightly bilious.

CHAPTER TWENTY-THREE

Paula O'Neill sat at the small, kidney-shaped Georgian desk in a corner of her bedroom at Pennistone Royal. Her face was thoughtful as she turned the pages inside a manila folder, studying them carefully. After ten minutes she closed the folder and set it to one side, knowing that she would find nothing of any consequence there, even if she read it ten more times.

Sitting back in the chair, she gazed out of the bay window, her eyes on a wooded hillside opposite. In spring it was covered with daffodils, which gleamed in golden streams rippling under the trees in the morning sunlight.

Wordsworth's poem leapt into her mind . . . '*and all at once I saw a crowd, a host, of golden daffodils, beside the lake, beneath the trees, fluttering and dancing in the breeze,*' she said out loud to the empty room. It had been her grandmother's favourite poem, and it had been Grandy who had planted the hundreds of daffodils over there under the trees

326

on the hill. She herself had kept them going over the years. Now, in early May, the bluebells were out, creating another stunning carpet of colour.

Paula let her thoughts drift for a few minutes and then pulled herself back to the present. Opening one of the drawers in her desk, she placed the folder inside, then locked it. There was no evidence in the papers she had been reading to show that Jonathan Ainsley was plotting against her, yet she knew that he was. Even though the private investigator had turned up nothing, it was an instinctive feeling, lodged in the very marrow of her bones. And she trusted it implicitly. What he would do, when he would do it, she did not know, but he *would* move against her. Since he could not strike at her through the Harte holdings or the chain of department stores, it was obvious to her that he would strike at her through her personal life . . . but she could not conceive how.

Life has a funny way of coming at you, she thought. Who could have imagined that Jonathan Ainsley would return to England to live after all those years in Hong Kong and Paris. She did not believe he had come back out of concern for his father; it wasn't in his nature to play the devoted son, therefore there had to be an ulterior motive. In the inner recesses of her mind, Jonathan's voice echoed back to her. 'I'll get you, Paula Fairley. I'll bloody well get you for this,' he had threatened all those years ago. She had never forgotten his words . . . now they had come back to haunt her.

Rising, Paula walked across the room, paused at the large chest of drawers to look in the mirror which hung above it. But she did so absently, her thoughts still focused on her vindictive and treacherous cousin who had been her sworn enemy for so long.

As she half turned away, lost in her reflections, her glance fell on the casket which sat atop the commode, and automatically she smoothed her hand across its lid as she had done so many times in the past, and just as her grandmother had done before her.

It was a beautifully made antique box of highly polished fruitwood, the colour of aged cognac, intricately chased with silver scrolls and interlocking circles. In the centre of the lid there was a silver heart with the initials E.H. engraved upon it. It had been sitting on this chest for as long as she could remember, from the time she had been a young girl visiting her grandmother here at Pennistone Royal.

The box was locked, and there was no key. Seemingly Emma had lost it long ago, but since it was empty she had not bothered to have the box prised open for fear of damaging it. Because it had been thus for fifty years or more, Paula had never seen a reason to tamper with it.

Turning away, Paula walked on into the upstairs parlour which adjoined the bedroom, crossed to the fireplace and stood with her back to it, warming herself.

A few moments later, when she felt less chilled, Paula turned around and looked up at the portrait of her grandfather, Paul McGill, which hung above the fireplace. He wore an officer's uniform; it had been painted in the middle of the First World War when he was in the Australia Corps.

As she stared at the portrait she couldn't help thinking how dashing and debonair he looked. Very handsome with his black hair and bright blue eyes. She had inherited his colouring, his eyes, and also the cleft in his chin and his dimples. There was no mistaking who *she* was descended from. In the picture he was smiling, and Paula knew that this painting had been her grandmother's favourite . . . perhaps because he had looked exactly like this when they had first met and fallen immediately and madly in love. Her grandmother had once told her that he had been irresistible, and Paula could well imagine that he had been.

He had had the world at his feet, or so he believed, Paula now thought. But he hadn't really, because he had not been able to marry Emma Harte, the love of his life. And so, after years of living with Emma in London, he had returned to Sydney to ask his wife Constance for a divorce, determined to legitimize his daughter Daisy by Emma, her mother. By some terrible misfortune he had been in a head-on crash with a lorry on a wet stormy night, and when the lorry driver had managed to extract his mangled body from the wreckage, he was paralysed from the waist down, his handsome face badly scarred, one side ruined beyond recognition.

Paula sighed under her breath, thinking of those awful events long ago. Because there was no way to treat paraplegics in 1939, he knew he would not live very long, that he would inevitably die from kidney failure. And so he had taken his own life. And Emma had never seen him again.

Paula knew from her mother that Emma had almost been broken by Paul's death, and that it had taken her a long time to recover from her terrible grief. But eventually she had managed to pick herself up and go on, for Daisy's sake, hiding her sorrow behind a brave front, finding comfort in her daughter by Paul.

Grandy had taught her that life was hard, and that it always had been, and that the important thing was to keep going no matter what, to fight back, to win in the end, and to triumph over adversity.

She had not had a lot of adversity in her own life, just those horrible problems with the venomous Jonathan Ainsley, and a truly bad marriage to Jim Fairley. For the most part, she had had a relatively easy ride as far as trouble was concerned, and of late things had been running fairly smoothly, both in the business and the family. There had been that great disappointment last autumn when Linnet had made the decision to 'cool it with Julian', as she put it. But now they were back together and all was well between them.

Her daughter Tessa worried her. There was something amiss in her marriage, Paula was quite certain of that; she was also rather curious about the bruised arm and shoulder. She had believed Tessa when she had said she had fallen at home. But how had that happened? Had she been pushed? Or had she and Mark been in a fight? Of course, most accidents did usually occur in the home, and were not always of a sinister nature. On the other hand, Mark Longden had long caused her worry. There was something about him that didn't sit quite right with her, and she found him altogether too obsequious by far. As Emily put it, he was 'a bit of a Uriah Heep'.

That Jonathan had unexpectedly returned and had been seen with Sarah was really upsetting. They had always plotted together, ever since their childhood; their sudden presence in London did not bode well for her, she was sure. Taking Uncle Ronnie's advice she had hired a private detective to investigate him, but the man had turned up nothing. Seemingly her cousin led a blameless life, and Sarah only visited London occasionally.

I wish Jack Figg were around, Paula suddenly thought, remembering how talented and fearless the former head of security for the stores had been. But Jack had retired, more or less, and was enjoying his new home in Cornwall, where he sailed, fished and in general led a happy life by the seashore. She sighed to herself, and went and sat on the window seat, picked up their newspaper, *The*

Yorkshire Morning Gazette, and casually leafed through the pages.

A door slamming somewhere in the distance made her sit up with a start, and she listened attentively, wondering if Shane had arrived. He was driving up from London this morning, and he had told her he would arrive in time for lunch. She looked at her watch . . . it was almost noon.

A look of expectancy settled on her face as she sat staring at the door, but when Shane did not appear she went back to the newspaper and began to read it again.

Quite soon thoughts of Jonathan Ainsley began to infiltrate her mind; she discovered she could not concentrate, and so she laid the paper on the padded cushion of the seat and gazed out of the window, looking towards the moors.

It was still a brilliantly sunny morning, the arc of the sky the colour of speedwells, those tiny blue flowers she loved so much. It was such a pretty spring day outside, and yet she began to shiver involuntarily when an unexpected sense of fore-boding swept through her, taking her by surprise.

Paula jumped to her feet, hating this feeling, and hurried over to the fireplace; she stood warming her hands over the flames flying up the chimney back, still shivering and chilled to the bone.

Deep within herself she was convinced that Jonathan's return signified trouble; she was always just that little bit apprehensive when he was around.

But he can't *do* anything, not really, she told herself, and then thought, but I do have five children and a grandchild, and a husband, not to mention many other family members I am close to . . . accidents *could* be arranged, couldn't they? She had long been aware that he would stop at nothing to wreak his revenge on her for *twice* bringing him to his knees . . .

Years ago her grandmother had said that there was a dazzle to Shane O'Neill, an intense glamour, adding that this sprang not so much from his extraordinary good looks as from his character and personality. Paula remembered Emma's words now as Shane came rushing into the room. He had a bright smile on his face as he walked towards her.

Paula watched him as he travelled the length of the floor, thinking that Grandy's pronouncement, made when he was about twenty-seven years old, still held today. And next month he would be celebrating his sixtieth birthday. What a wonder he was, unbowed by time, hardly aged, tall, broad shouldered, with a barrel chest; a fine figure of a man, as his father was wont to say. Shane's jet-black hair was tinged with grey these days, and there were a few lines around his eyes and his mouth, but otherwise he looked much the same as he had when he was that dashing young man her grandmother had so admired. And he still had that dazzle, the intense glamour.

Even though he was wearing his Saturday casual clothes, he was, nevertheless, still impeccably dressed. Well-tailored grey gabardine slacks were teamed with a red cashmere turtleneck and a black blazer. He looked as smart as ever, right down to his highly polished brown loafers.

His presence filled the room, and she felt that sudden rush of excitement she always experienced when she had not seen him for a while. She stood up and went to meet him, full of genuine pleasure at the sight of him, wanting to touch him, to hold him close. A wide smile enlivened her normally serious face, and he smiled back at her lovingly as he swept her into his arms and brought her closer to him.

After a moment, he held her away, kissed her lightly on the lips, and said, 'Sorry I'm late, darling. Heavy traffic on the way up from London.'

She nodded. 'But you're here now, and it's just wonderful to see you, to have you home at last. I do so hate it when you're in London and I'm not.'

He glanced down at her, a small, puzzled frown pulling his dark brows together in a jagged line. 'I've only been gone a few days. And somebody has to run O'Neill Hotels International, you know.'

'But I always miss you so much, Shane. It seems to get more acute the older I get.'

He chuckled as he walked with her to the sofa where they sat down. 'I would have thought that by now you'd have had enough of me . . . all these years we've been together.'

'All these years indeed! Thirty years married, and the time that went before when we were growing up.'

He smiled and took her hand in his, looked into those unique violet eyes and murmured, 'You sound a little tremulous, Paula darling. Is something bothering you?'

She was not at all startled by his perception; he knew her far too well, and she realized there was no point in denying it. 'I had an awful premonition of trouble brewing a while ago, to do with Jonathan Ainsley,' she admitted.

Chapter Twenty-Four

S hane O'Neill listened attentively to every word
Paula was saying. He always paid attention to
his wife; he both admired and respected her,
and he knew she never made rash statements, nor
did she exaggerate.

But, nonetheless, he was alarmed by what she
was saying, and when she finally sat back on
the sofa and gave him a questioning look, he
exclaimed, 'But Paula darling, Jonathan Ainsley
wouldn't be stupid enough to hurt any of us
physically. He'd be in serious trouble with the
law if he did.'

'I know, but he could hire somebody to do it.'

'He'd still be in trouble, as an accessory to the
crime. No, I really don't think you have to worry
about any of us being harmed, I really don't.'

'He's capable of anything!' she cried.

'Oh, I know that only too well. I remember
when he hit Winston over the head with a cricket
bat when we were little. He could have killed him

actually. He was a nasty little bugger then, and I suppose a leopard doesn't change its spots.'

'Only too true, Shane.' Paula shifted slightly on the sofa, and looked across at her husband, gave him a hard stare, and said, 'I suppose I'll have to try and relax – about Jonathan, I mean. Maybe I'm being overly imaginative because of the past.'

'Perhaps you are, sweetheart.' He reached out, touched her face tenderly. 'Jonathan may be vengeful and devious, but he's by no means stupid, we all know that. He wouldn't do anything to put himself in any kind of jeopardy with the law. And personally I think he came back because he wanted to come home to England, to be close to Uncle Robin, amongst other things.'

Paula shook her head and said quietly, 'I don't agree. He doesn't have a decent bone in his body, not even when it comes to his father. But looking at it objectively, as you are doing, I'm sure he would be careful.' She went on, 'Did you see Philip when you arrived? Was he anywhere around?'

Shane shook his head. 'But when I spoke to him the other night he said he wanted to go riding on the moors this morning. That's why he decided to come to Yorkshire last night, and—'

'But I didn't see him,' Paula cut in. She went on to explain, 'I felt very tired, and I also thought I was coming down with a cold. By ten, when he hadn't arrived, I left him a note and went to bed. And I haven't seen him this morning. So perhaps he did go riding. Margaret said she took a cup of tea up to his room but that he didn't come down for breakfast. She thought she saw him crossing the yard a couple of hours ago. I bet he went up to the moors.'

'I think so. But come on, darling, your baby brother will show up eventually, and I think you and I should go for a walk. It'll do you good, and it's such a lovely day.'

Half an hour later, Philip McGill Harte Amory walked into the Great Hall, his riding boots making a loud clatter against the stone floor.

He made straight for the huge stone fireplace and stood warming himself, trying to thaw out. Whilst it was a beautiful morning – sunny with a blue sky – there was a cold wind blowing across the moors. Even though he had been warmly dressed, with a Barbour over his riding jacket and sweater, he had felt the chill up there under the high fells.

The ride had done him good, and he was feeling better, more refreshed than he had since he had arrived from Sydney at the beginning of the week. Back home in Australia he was on the move a lot, between the city and Dunoon, the family sheep station in Coonamble. There he rode every day and spent a lot of time outdoors on the land.

He loved Dunoon more than any place on earth; it was his true home where he felt the most comfortable and at peace. Perhaps this was because there were many wonderful memories of his beloved Maddy there, although he had also made it his safe haven when he was a boy; had become unusually attached to it early in his life.

The other place where he felt totally at ease and relaxed was this house. Pennistone Royal had been the centre of gravity for Paula, himself and all of their cousins when they were growing up, and they had congregated here around their grandmother. He, in particular, had spent a lot of time with Emma, learning everything there was to learn about the great McGill empire which he and Paula had inherited and he now ran from Sydney. 'I learned at the knee of the master,' he would tell anyone who asked him about his business training, and would then go on to sing the virtues of the renowned Emma Harte.

Tall, slender, dark haired, with the most startlingly blue eyes, Philip was the spitting image of his grandfather Paul McGill. And whilst he had inherited many of Paul's traits, he was also very much a grandson of Emma Harte, and he was exceptionally proud of this. His adored Grandy had been his mentor as well as his very exacting teacher until the day she died. His life was lived on the principles she had taught him.

Moving away from the fireplace, Philip walked over to the table set against one of the end walls. Here Margaret had earlier put out a bottle of white wine in an ice bucket, a jug of tomato juice, a bottle of vodka and a variety of other soft drinks. Philip poured himself a glass of tomato juice and went and sat down on the sofa next to the fire, his thoughts veering to his daughter Fiona, who was an undergraduate at Oxford. She was the light of his life, and now, at nineteen, she had become a unique young woman, in his opinion. Bright, intelligent and mature beyond her years, she made him very proud. He always came to England in the spring to see her, and had done so since she had gone to boarding school.

Fiona had been brought up by him, and she had spent a lot of time with adults, which was probably why she was more sophisticated than most other girls her age, wise beyond her years.

She had his dark colouring, his bright blue eyes, but it was Maddy's face that looked out at him . . . his wonderful, darling Maddy. His true love, who had suffered a fatal brain haemorrhage just before Fiona's birth . . . his exquisite Maddy who had never regained consciousness and had died, leaving him alone. Except for Fiona. Nineteen years ago; it seemed like only yesterday sometimes. He had never remarried. No other woman had matched up to Maddy. Fiona was his only child and heiress to a good part of the McGill empire, which she had been brought up to run one day when he retired. And she would run it well, he knew that. He had instilled Emma's rules in her from childhood.

At the sound of footsteps, Philip looked towards the front door and rose from the sofa, smiling at his sister as she hurried to him, looking anxious.

'There you are, Pip!' Paula exclaimed, rushing to embrace him. 'We wondered where you were.'

After hugging her and shaking Shane's out-stretched hand, he told them, 'I went riding. There's nothing like a good gallop across the moors to blow the cobwebs away. It was great, but a bit chilly, I've got to tell you. Now, can I pour you a glass of wine or make you a Bloody Mary?' He glanced from Shane to Paula.

'I'll have an orange juice, please,' Paula said, and went and sat down on one of the straight-backed chairs.

'Are you having a Bloody Mary?' Shane asked, eyeing Philip's drink.

'No, it's just plain old tomato juice.'

'I'll have the same, thanks. I don't feel like drinking today. Well, maybe a glass of red wine at lunch.' Shane walked across to the sofa.

Philip poured their drinks and carried them over to the fireplace where they were sitting, retrieved his own glass, then joined them. They spoke about a few inconsequential things, and then Philip turned to his sister and said, 'I'd like to discuss some-thing with you . . . something that's troubling me, Paula.'

'Oh dear, Pip, is there something wrong? It's not Fiona, is it?'

'No. It's Evan Hughes.'

As he spoke the name, Paula knew at once that he had heard the current gossip, and was put out by it. She didn't blame him, she herself was annoyed. She wished she knew who had started the unfortunate and galling story in the first place. Taking a deep breath, Paula said, 'I know, I know. The story is that she's somehow related to us, that she's a long-lost McGill, and that she's after *something*. I wish I knew who'd started this: I'd make mincemeat out of them. I believe this came about because some people actually think she looks like me.'

Philip instantly picked up the denial in her voice, and exclaimed, 'But she *does*, very much so.'

'No, she doesn't. We're the same *type*, that's all,' Paula protested, sounding irate. She shook her head vehemently.

Philip, his expression negating what she had just said, remarked, 'You're wrong, sweet 'art. I know you're always right about most things, but this time you're *wrong*.' Philip glanced at Shane. 'Well, she's your wife and you've known her as long as I have. What do *you* think?'

'When I first saw Evan I was struck by a likeness, but on second glance I realized I was quite mistaken.'

'You've seen her then?' Paula asked, giving her brother a long penetrating look.

'You bet! I went over to the store on the pretext of talking to Linnet about something, and I was introduced to Evan in no time at all. She's wonderful looking, very beautiful, no denying that, and personable. And I can understand why people might think she's a McGill.'

'Is that when you heard the story?' Shane asked.

'No, it's not. I heard the gossip on Tuesday, and I heard it in my *own* office.'

'Good God, the gossip has stretched across London to McGill Holdings! I can't believe it.' Paula was astounded.

'You know what they say, gossip travels fast. I also hear she's engaged to Gideon.' Philip looked from Paula to Shane.

Shane began to laugh. 'She's dating him, that's all, and I think things have become overly exaggerated, Philip, I really do.'

'Seemingly so. Nonetheless, I would like to know more about her. Have you had her background investigated?' Philip asked Paula.

'Of course not! I had no reason to, and I still don't,' Paula retorted, looking at her brother askance, suddenly annoyed.

'I do think we ought to know more,' Philip insisted.

'And if we do know more, so what? She can't plunder the McGill empire, or ask for anything, for heaven's sake. Like Emma, Paul McGill tied everything up in trusts and foundations.' Paula shook her head. 'Let's leave things alone, Pip, otherwise there's going to be a real storm flaring up around here. Gideon's very involved with her . . .' Paula didn't finish her sentence, but let the words drift away, dismayed by the conversation.

Shane said, 'I think I have a solution, Philip. Paula, why don't you talk to Evan next week when you're back in London? Ask her a few questions about her parents, her grandparents. You can do that nicely; you might even want to have Linnet in the room with you. That may well make the girl feel more at ease.'

'I don't have to wait until next week, Shane,' Paula murmured, her heart sinking slightly at the thought of confronting Evan. 'She's here,' she added in a low voice.

'What do you mean by here?' he asked, eyeing her curiously.

'Here in this house. She came up with Linnet and India late on Thursday. I'd promised them a week-end here, a bit of R & R. They're all bone-tired, and they've worked so hard on the retrospective I thought it would be nice for them to be pampered a bit by Margaret. And me. They went to Harrogate for lunch. Linnet wanted Evan to see the store there. So I can talk to Evan later. Diplomatically, of course,' she ended on a sigh.

'Excellent idea,' Philip said.

'I hope it's not going to create undercurrents,' Shane muttered worriedly, and gave Paula a questioning look.

'It won't, I promise you,' she reassured him.

CHAPTER TWENTY-FIVE

I t was just turned four o'clock when the three young women came bursting into the upstairs parlour, looking for Paula. She saw at once that they were already full of energy and exuberance again; obviously their trip to Harrogate had been successful. They look *happy*, she thought, and they're such good friends, a wonderful team; this pleased her enormously.

Linnet and India were both shrewd, clever girls, and they would not have taken to Evan Hughes in the way they had if she was at all unsuitable, or questionable. She also trusted Gideon's judgement, and he was smitten with her, wanted to marry her, according to Emily. She was obviously first class.

'Hello, all of you!' Paula greeted them with a broad smile.

'Hello,' they answered, in unison, and Linnet bounded over to the sofa and flopped down next to her mother, kissing her cheek with great affection.

'How was lunch?' Paula asked, warmth echoing in her voice.

'Great,' Linnet replied, smiling broadly, laughter in her green eyes. 'Thanks for the treat, Mums.'

'We took Evan to Betty's Cafe,' India volunteered. 'She was astonished.'

'I loved it, Mrs O'Neill,' Evan said, 'such a quaint place. It reminded me of an old English movie. Oh, and the store is just beautiful.'

'Thank you, Evan. I'm sure Linnet told you we redid it from top to bottom last year.'

Paula poured the tea and Linnet passed the cups around, and then they all sat back, chatting to her, filling her in about their morning and afternoon. India explained how they had given Evan an extensive tour of the lovely old spa city, which a hundred years ago had been a centre of health and revitalization because of the healing properties in the natural water from the underground springs.

As they talked to her, Paula surreptitiously studied Evan, and the more she scrutinized her, the more she recognized that the American girl was not really like her facially. At the same time, she understood why some people thought otherwise. Impressions could be deceptive, and Evan looked like a younger version of her, albeit unwittingly, because their style of dressing was so similar.

At one moment, Evan turned to face her and flushed slightly as she realized Paula's eyes were intently trained on her, steely in their appraisal.

Haltingly, Evan asked, 'Is there something wrong, Mrs O'Neill? Do I have a smudge on my face?'

Paula shook her head and offered the young woman a quick and reassuring smile. Seeing the opening she needed to launch into a conversation with her, Paula said, 'I'm staring at you, aren't I? That's so rude. I'm sorry, Evan . . . you see, a number of people think you look like me, and I was trying to spot a few similarities.'

'We're the same type physically, but that's all there is to it,' Evan replied, relieved that Paula O'Neill had brought the matter up. She had heard the gossip at the store and it both troubled and dismayed her. It also cast a cloud over her, which now worried her because of Gideon.

Linnet said, 'At first glance Evan does have a look of you, Mummy, but she's right, basically you're the same *type* . . . but there the resemblance *stops*.'

'I agree, Aunt Paula,' India volunteered.

'Nevertheless, I would like to . . . well, sort of clear the air, Evan, if you wouldn't mind answering a few questions. I think we would all feel happier if we could put a stop to these silly rumours about you being a long-lost McGill.'

Evan nodded. 'I agree. To be honest, Mrs O'Neill, I'd never heard that name before, not until I came to work at Harte's.'

'Why *did* you come?' Paula asked, leaning forward slightly. 'I mean, what made you choose *Harte's* above all the other stores in London?'

Evan knew there was no point fibbing, as she had to other people, saying she had come to Harte's because she had always dreamed of working there. In many ways her whole future hung on this conversation, and only the absolute truth would do.

Taking a deep breath, Evan said, 'I came to Harte's because of my grandmother. She died last November in New York, in one of the hospitals there. I was with her. We were waiting for my father, her son Owen, to arrive. He was driving in from Connecticut, and he was late – because of the heavy traffic, as it turned out. Anyway, Gran and I talked a little as I sat and held her hand. At one moment she became suddenly revitalized, and she told me to leave New York, to go to London to see Emma. She said Emma Harte was the key to my future. Before I could ask her what she meant, my grandmother died. Then my father arrived, a few minutes too late to see his mother alive, and in all the upset and grief that followed I forgot about Gran's words. Until later, that is. When I repeated them to my father he seemed truly baffled. A short while after, he remembered that my grandmother had met Mrs Harte during the Second World War, and he told me a bit about the store. But he didn't know much of anything.'

Paula nodded. 'I see. So apparently there *is* some sort of connection between your grandmother and mine?'

'I don't think it's a very important one,' Evan answered, speaking with total candour, her honesty reflected on her face.

'What was your grandmother's name?'

'Glynnis. Glynnis Hughes. But before she married my grandfather she was called Jenkins, and she came from the Rhondda Valley in Wales. My grandfather, Richard Hughes, was a GI stationed near London. They got married during the war, here in London, where my father was born. As I was later.'

'When was your father born? What year?' Paula probed, all of a sudden realizing that Owen Hughes's birth date was vital, would clarify a great deal.

'In 1944, Mrs O'Neill.'

Paula felt the tension sliding away, and she exclaimed, 'So he can't possibly be the son of Paul McGill, my grandfather! Because Paul McGill was already dead then. *He died in 1939.*'

Evan nodded, answered in a low, subdued voice, 'I told you, I've never heard that name mentioned in my family. Nor did I ever hear Gran mention Mrs Harte. Perhaps they had only a passing acquaintance. I know Gran lived in London during the war, my grandfather told me that. He'd met her at a canteen for the troops, where she was working with her girlfriends in the evening – entertaining the GIs, he said. And they connected because his forebears had gone to America from the Rhondda Valley. That's where they fell in love, he said.'

'I think we've managed to clear the air rather quickly, Evan,' Paula exclaimed, smiling at her. 'At least I'm satisfied, and we—'

'But Mummy, why did Glynnis tell Evan to come

and see Emma?' Linnet interjected. 'Why did she tell her that her future was with Emma Harte? Doesn't that strike you as odd?'

'No, it doesn't,' Paula shot back impatiently, suddenly wanting this matter finally closed.

'But Aunt Paula, it *is* a bit strange,' India murmured, giving her a hard stare. 'I mean, why would an old lady on her deathbed suddenly tell her granddaughter to seek out a woman in London? *Why?* Think about it. I bet Glynnis and Grandy *were* friends, and that there *was* a connection between them, something important. Perhaps there's something here we're not aware of . . . a secret maybe?'

'If that's the case, why didn't Evan's grandmother explain in more detail, give her the proper information?' Paula asked, first looking at India and then turning to Evan.

It was Evan who answered. 'She was dying, Mrs O'Neill, and she was very weak. I don't think she had the strength to say another word. I was surprised she'd spoken at all. By then she was on her last breath.'

'Obviously your grandmother didn't know Emma Harte was dead, and had been for thirty years,' Paula murmured. 'So tell me, what did *you* think when you discovered this?'

'I was really shocked, Mrs O'Neill. Staggered, actually, and to be truthful I felt a bit foolish that I'd listened to Gran. When I told my father on the phone he said perhaps his mother had been delirious or rambling. And I sort of accepted that.'

'But you still came up to the executive offices to apply for a job,' Paula pointed out, her steady gaze fixed on Evan.

'Eventually. I went and had coffee, and thought about what I'd do, and I realized I wanted to stay in London. After all, I'd given up my job in New York. And I was very taken with the store, impressed with it, and I thought, why not go and apply for a position? And so I did.'

'I think everything has been satisfactorily explained,' Paula announced, looking at each of the young women, again wanting to move on.

Linnet glanced at Evan, and asked quietly, 'How old was your grandmother when she died?'

'Gran was seventy-nine.'

'So during the Second World War, she would have been in her twenties. Correct?' Linnet said.

'Yes,' Evan answered, wondering what Linnet was getting at.

Paula had been thinking the same thing, and asked, 'What's your point, Linny?'

'At the beginning of the war, Emma Harte was forty-nine, fifty, anyway thereabouts, and from what I know about her she didn't have time for a lot of girlfriends, not the way she worked. Besides, there was the age difference between Emma and Glynnis. Could it be that Glynnis Jenkins worked at Harte's during the war?'

Paula was startled, but after giving this suggestion a moment's thought, she said, 'Yes, perhaps. She could have worked at the store, that's quite true.'

Linnet now turned to Evan. 'What did your grandmother do before she was married to your grandfather? Do you know?'

'I'm not sure ... but she could have been a secretary, because she did do all the paperwork for my grandfather's antiques business when I was growing up.'

India sat up straighter and cried, 'That's it! I agree with Linnet. I think Glynnis may have worked as one of Emma's secretaries during the war.'

'But what does that mean, India?' Paula asked, sounding puzzled. 'We've eliminated the McGill connection because of Owen Hughes's birth date. This is finished. We can put a stop to the stories and forget it all.'

'I'm not so sure,' Linnet began slowly, a little hesitantly. 'There's more to this than meets the eye, Mums. I just feel *that* in my bones, and I'm a true Celt like Dad, remember, so listen to me. Anyway Aunt Emily said—' Linnet instantly broke off, immediately regretting these words. She knew she should not have brought Emily into this discussion, that it was wrong, could cause trouble.

'What exactly did Emily say?' Paula probed, frowning, suddenly concerned, as well as surprised.

'I shouldn't have said that, Mummy. Aunt Emily will be angry with me.'

'We can't worry about that right now. Just tell me what she said, Linnet,' Paula demanded, staring at her daughter.

Linnet cleared her throat, and explained in a low,

steady voice. 'Aunt Emily never thought Evan had a connection to the McGill side of the family, nor does she really think she looks like you. But she does believe there might be a connection . . . to *the Hartes*. She says she can't exactly put her finger on it, but that at the edge of her memory there is something she can't quite grasp, a face that won't come into focus. I guess it's like having something on the tip of your tongue.'

Paula was taken aback, and she gaped at her daughter. 'She thinks Evan could be related to the Hartes, and she never told *me*.'

'Don't get excited, Mums,' Linnet said in a placating tone. 'Aunt Emily only mentioned it in passing to me. You see, she didn't want to worry you, add fuel to the fire. That's the reason she didn't say anything, I'm sure.'

Paula sat back against the cushions on the sofa, for once in her life rendered speechless.

Determined to promote her theory about Glynnis having been employed by Harte's, Linnet now said swiftly, 'Mummy, don't look like that, let's try and get to the bottom of this . . . *mystery*. Where are the old employee records kept? I bet they're in the basement storage rooms at the London store.'

'I doubt they still exist, they may have been destroyed when we went to computer,' Paula muttered, feeling slightly put out with Linnet. She had opened up another avenue of possibility, which Paula felt they did not need to cope with at this moment.

'I've just had a brainwave, Aunt Paula!' India sprang to her feet and went and sat next to her on the sofa. 'The diaries! Grandy's diaries, the ones we found in the clothes storage attics months ago, written by Emma in the war years. If there *is* some sort of secret, or something about Evan's grandma, I bet you'd find it in one of those.'

'Perhaps,' Paula agreed, remembering her reluctance to plunge into such a personal area of her grandmother's life. Diaries were always so intimate, meant only for one person's eyes . . . the writer of them.

Evan took a deep breath, and began slowly, carefully. 'I really do think my father *is* who he *is*. He's Owen Hughes, the son of Glynnis and Richard Hughes. He looks like my grandfather, and he's like him in so many other ways . . .' She broke off, gazed at Paula, her eyes reflecting her sadness and hurt.

Paula did not fail to miss this, and she was instantly filled with chagrin, cursed herself under her breath. 'Oh Evan, my dear, how thoughtless we've all been! So unkind, dreadful really, impugning your grandmother's reputation the way we have. How cruel of us to suggest she might have had a relationship with someone else, a man other than your grandfather. I think we've been quite . . . *unconscionable*. I'm so very sorry, very sorry indeed. And I apologize. Yes, we've been quite awful,' she finished softly.

'It's all right, Mrs O'Neill, I haven't taken offence.

I think you all meant well, and that you do want to stop the silly gossip, and it *is* silly. It's all conjecture. But I just want to say this . . . I know I'm not related to any of you. I'm neither a McGill nor a Harte. My grandmother loved Richard Hughes, and she would never have cheated on him. My grandmother helped to bring me up, and she was . . . well, she was true blue, as Linnet would say.'

Later, when they had left, Paula brought out the suitcase which contained her grandmother's diaries written during the war, lifting it out of the commode, carrying it over to the sofa. Placing it on the coffee table, she opened the case and stared at the small black leather books neatly lined up side by side.

She could not bring herself to look at the one for 1939, for she knew from her mother that Emma's grief for Paul McGill had been all-consuming, searing. Her mother had told her that Emma had spent hours writing in her diary that particular year, and Paula could not face reading what she knew would be heartbreaking passages about her grandfather and his untimely death.

And so she skipped the year 1939 and picked up the diary for 1940, began to leaf through this, looking at days here and there, still a trifle reluctant to read her grandmother's intimate and very private thoughts.

The diary fell open at a page, and as Paula glanced down, she read: '*I had dinner tonight with*

Blackie O'Neill. He made me laugh for the first time in months. He is my dearest friend . . .'

Paula heard a slight noise, and as she looked up suddenly there was Shane, standing next to her. She said, 'Here is my grandmother writing in her diary that your grandfather is her dearest friend . . .'

Shane smiled down at her. 'So you finally had the courage to start reading them. Maybe she wanted you to do that, Paula. Perhaps that's why she left them for you to find. She could have destroyed them, you know.' Lowering himself onto the sofa, he asked, 'What year is that?'

Paula glanced at him and said, 'Nineteen forty. She wrote this when she was fifty-one years old. I only knew her when she had become an old woman, and I can't help wishing I'd known her then . . . I wonder what she was like, Shane?'

He put his arm around her and drew her close to him. There was a moment of silence before he spoke, and then he said, 'I bet she was . . . simply bloody marvellous!'

PART TWO

Legend
1940

'She possessed, in the highest
degree, all the qualities which were
required in a great Prince.'
Giovanni Scaramelli
Venetian Ambassador to the Court of
Elizabeth Tudor, Queen of England

Be not afraid of greatness: some men are
born great, some achieve greatness,
and some have greatness thrust upon
them.
William Shakespeare, *Twelfth Night*: II v

CHAPTER TWENTY-SIX

E mma Harte stood in front of the cheval
mirror in her spacious, elegant bedroom in
her Belgrave Square house, regarding herself
thoughtfully.

And she hated what she saw.

Her reflection was of a thin, almost wraith-like
woman, deathly pale, with a mass of red hair
surrounding a tired, sorrowful face like a fiery
halo. The contrasts were stark.

And she hated the dress she wore.

It was a good dress, *couture*, but it was black,
funereal and depressing, and it did nothing for her
except underscore her unprecedented lack of physical appeal. In general her appearance disturbed her
enormously as she studied herself objectively. She
had never looked like this before.

Glancing at the dressing table nearby, her eyes
settled on the photograph of Paul McGill. 'It just
won't do any more, will it, darling?' she said out
loud, talking to his picture as she had done every

day for months and months past. Instinctively shrewd, Emma was aware that the staff thought she was slightly mad these days, the way she talked to herself, quite loudly at that. But she wasn't crazy; she was actually talking to Paul. She knew she always would for as long as she lived. It gave her such comfort, made her feel less alone, less lonely. They had lived together here for sixteen years and his presence was everywhere.

'Nothing for it but a radical makeover,' she continued, and as she walked past the dressing table she touched the top of the gold photograph frame that held his picture, let her hand rest on it for a split second. In the incandescent light from the lamp, the great, square-cut McGill emerald ring Paul had given her after Daisy's birth shone like bright green fire on her small, capable hand.

Moving across the floor rapidly and with the lightest of steps, she took off the black dress and laid it on the bed, put on a silk robe and hurried into the adjoining bathroom.

Without wasting a moment, she found a pair of large scissors in a drawer of the vanity, and with a burst of energy and a great deal of concentration she began to cut off her hair. She did so with much precision and skill, and she did not stop until she was left with a sleek, slightly wavy pageboy, a style that was all the rage at the moment.

Now peering at herself in the bathroom mirror, she saw that the new shorter hairdo so flattered her finely boned face she suddenly looked ten years younger, and somehow much less sorrowful.

Stepping off the bath mat, she bent down and folded it over to trap the discarded hair.

Returning to the bedroom, Emma sat down at the dressing table, regarded her face for a moment or two; then, picking up a large powder puff, she swept it across her cheeks and brow. Next, she added a trace of pink lipstick, smoothed her eyebrows with her fingertips, and brought the black mascara brush to her lashes. Finally sitting back, she saw how her whole appearance had undergone a swift change for the better, and this pleased her. She no longer looked like a demented, mad Ophelia en route to the asylum.

Within minutes Emma had put on a navy-blue dress and stepped into a pair of navy-blue, high-heeled court shoes. Again she regarded her reflection in the cheval mirror in the corner near the window, this time nodding her head in satisfaction. Falling to her ankles, the dress was beautifully made of matte wool crepe. It was by Jean Patou; it was narrow and elegant with long sleeves and a long stole. She had bought it in Paris in 1935 because Paul had loved it, and now she understood why. It was extremely flattering to her slender figure and made her seem taller than she was.

Moving back to the dressing table she put on Paul's square-cut emerald earrings, which matched her ring, and an emerald bracelet, and pinned Blackie's lovely emerald bow on her shoulder.

After spraying Chanel No. 5 at her throat, she went to find a navy-blue bag to match her dress, stole and shoes.

A moment or two later she was ready to go to the Dorchester to meet the boys, as she called them and, as she crossed the bedroom, walking towards the door, she decided they would be pleased that she had put away her mourning black at long last.

Emma stood at the top of the steps for a moment before going down into the street where her car and driver were waiting. She could not help marvelling yet again at the extraordinary weather. It had been glorious all week, and the week before, and it was still the same: a truly gorgeous spring evening, the air balmy and warm, the sky a perfect cerulean blue without clouds.

The worse the news got – of a devastated Europe crumbling under Nazi jackboots, which were aggressively goosestepping into countries too defenceless to withstand them – the more splendid the weather in England was.

And to Emma, now walking down the steps, there was something terribly poignant, almost heartrending, about the radiance of these lovely days and nights, when everything seemed so normal and tranquil under an English heaven. She could not help wondering how long it would be so . . . asking herself when the Nazi assault on her beloved country would begin in earnest. And she knew it would . . . and soon.

Tomkins, her driver, hurried to open the car door for her as she stepped onto the pavement, touching his cap. ''Evening, Mrs Harte.'

'Good evening, Tomkins, I was just admiring the weather. Isn't it a beautiful night?'

'It is, madam, an' a blinkin' miracle, it is that, this luverly warm spell. It's usually still a bit nippy in May.'

After helping her into the back seat, he went around to the front, and a moment later the Rolls was smoothly pulling away from the kerb.

'I'm going to the Dorchester,' Emma murmured, settling back against the leather seat.

'Right you are, madam,' Tomkins answered as he circled Belgrave Square and headed up towards Hyde Park Corner, making for Park Lane.

Emma thought about her destination as the car pushed through the early evening traffic. The Dorchester Hotel had been opened in April of 1931, and from that moment it had been a favourite spot to rendezvous for royalty, the denizens of high society, politicians and the rich and famous. Those in the know who frequented it regularly affectionately called it the Dorch; now it was more popular than ever because it was considered to be the safest hotel in London. This was because it had been built entirely of reinforced concrete, according to Blackie O'Neill. He knew the builder, Sir Malcolm MacAlpine. Blackie loved it as much as everyone else did, herself included.

It was Blackie's favourite place to dine, and

she was on her way to meet him there now, and very much looking forward to seeing him; he had been absent for several weeks and she missed him when he was out of town. He was her true and dearest friend.

Blackie had come up to London earlier in the day, and had brought with him their old friend and long-time companion, David Kallinski. He had been sad and depressed since his wife Rebecca had died, and his emotional state had scarcely been alleviated when he had discovered that his sons Ronald and Mark had suddenly joined the armed forces without conferring with him.

Blackie had told her only last week that David was filled with a deep conviction that his sons would be killed in battle on foreign soil, and that this distressed him.

I'll have to do my very best to pull David out of his black mood, Emma told herself, clutching her bag, now focusing her thoughts on David. He meant a lot to her, and she could not bear to think that he was suffering. They had been in love with each other once, long, long ago, but she had walked away from the relationship because he was married. 'I won't build my happiness on another person's unhappiness,' she had told him at the time. David had eventually accepted her decision, and because they were mature they had managed to preserve both their friendship and their business partnership in Lady Hamilton Clothes over the years.

Quite suddenly his father's face flashed before her eyes, and she thought of Abraham Kallinski, her good friend in Leeds when she was a young girl – alone, destitute and pregnant by Edwin Fairley.

One day, when she had first lived in Leeds, she had tramped along North Street looking for work at one of the clothing factories. It was near there that she had seen a couple of street hooligans throwing stones at a man, jeering at him, calling him a dirty Jew. Injured and bleeding, he had fallen down, lost his spectacles and his loaves of bread.

Without thought to her own safety, she had run to his aid, chasing off the young thugs, shaking her fist at them, saying she would call a bobby, yet ready to take them on single-handedly, forgetting momentarily that she was carrying a child in her womb.

After she had helped the man to his feet and picked up his glasses, she had dusted off the loaves, called challah, and put them back in the paper bag which contained several other items. He had asked her name and introduced himself as Abraham Kallinski, all the while thanking her profusely. And then she had helped him home to his house in Imperial Street. 'A most unfortunate name for that poor little street, considering it is hardly royal in any sense of that word,' he had told her, and she remembered his wry smile even to this day. He had gone on to explain that the street was located in the Leylands, and only then had she been afraid, for she knew that this was the ghetto and dangerous.

But she had taken him home anyway, wanting to be sure he would be safe, and now she recalled the way Janessa Kallinski, his wife, and their two sons had welcomed her. They had taken her under their wing, she, a stranger, and Abraham had given her a job at his little clothing factory and treated her like one of his own.

Having just run away from Fairley village on the Yorkshire moors, she had not known the ways of the big city, nor had she really known what a Jew was, and it was Abraham who had explained about their religion, their customs and their ways. Yes, she remembered all of the Kallinskis with great affection, and she owed them so much for their kindness to her some thirty-five years ago . . .

'Here we are, Mrs Harte,' Tomkins announced, interrupting her thoughts as he brought the Rolls-Royce to a standstill in front of the hotel.

'I'll be a couple of hours, Tomkins,' Emma informed him. 'So if you'd like to go and have supper, that will be perfectly all right.'

'Thank you kindly, Mrs Harte. But I'll stay here, just hang around in the vicinity. I'll be about when you come out.'

Emma nodded and stepped out of the car, assisted by the doorman in his dark green uniform and tall top hat. She walked towards the wall of sandbags, which had been built around the front entrance of the hotel after war was declared on September the third last year. This offered protection, as did the shingles which, according to Blackie, had been added to the roof at the same time; he seemed to know everything about his beloved Dorch.

Making her way across the elegant front hall, Emma was instantly struck by the activity. People were milling around, others standing chatting, bell-boys and porters were rushing about their duties and telephones were ringing insistently.

To Emma, the Dorchester lobby appeared to be busier than usual, a veritable hive of activity. But then the whole of London was hectic these days, teeming with troops, both enlisted men and officers, American war correspondents who were based here, and the sad, rather forlorn-looking refugees who had flooded in from Europe. Many of them were Jews fleeing persecution, and her heart went out to them.

Inclining her head, smiling at the head concierge with whom she was acquainted, she walked on, went through the larger hall, making for the restaurant, unaware of the swathe she cut, the eyes that followed her progress with great interest.

At the restaurant entrance the maître d' greeted her pleasantly, and then escorted her through to the table where Blackie was seated with David Kallinski.

Both men rose as she approached, and they greeted her with much affection, each of them kissing her on the cheek.

Once the maître d' had pulled out her chair and seen that she was seated, he departed discreetly.

Now Emma looked from Blackie to David, and said in a loving voice, 'It's wonderful to see my boys. I've missed you both.'

They both beamed at her, and Blackie cocked his head on one side, his black eyes narrowing slightly as he said, with a small delighted chuckle, 'Well, mavourneen, I can see you've been titivating yourself up a bit, and all I can say is that you're a sight for sore eyes. And a mighty bonny one at that, my lass.'

'My lass indeed! Some lass,' she shot back dryly, but nonetheless her expression was warm and her deep-green eyes were merrier than they had been in a long time. 'Thank you, Blackie darling. You're a sight for sore eyes, too, and so are you, David. It's been weeks since *you* were in town.' Reaching out, Emma laid her hand on his arm affectionately. 'You have to come to London more often, so I can pamper you a little bit.'

'I will,' David replied. 'And I've missed *you*, Emma. Blackie's right, you know.' He cast an appraising eye over her, and added, 'You're bonnier than ever.'

'Sounds to me as if you've kissed that famous stone in Ireland that Blackie O'Neill embraced so enthusiastically donkey's years ago,' Emma murmured. 'But it's a nice compliment, and I thank you. I decided tonight it was time to put away all the black mourning clothes, cut my hair, and titivate myself a bit, as Blackie so aptly calls it. I suddenly realized I had to come back to the land of living, because life *is* for the living. Paul would be the first to say that, David, and so would Rebecca.'

He nodded, and forced a smile. 'I agree with you, and I've managed to bring my sadness to heel . . . at least I hope I have.' He threw Blackie a questioning look.

'David's been wonderful today, Emm. The best I've seen him in a month of Sundays.'

'Your hair is as beautiful as always,' David now said, obviously appreciating her, gazing at her, and when he smiled it was a natural smile, full of love. That he was glad to see her was most apparent. He had always adored her.

And so had Blackie, who asked, 'And now, me darlin', what would you be wanting to drink?'

'Oh Blackie, I think I'd like a glass of champagne. Yes, that would be nice.'

'Right away. David and I are enjoying a drop of good Irish, but we might partake of the bubbly later, so I'll order a bottle. What would you be preferring?'

'Pol Roger is my new favourite, thanks, Blackie.'

Blackie nodded, motioned to the waiter, who was by his side in an instant. After Blackie had given the order, and the waiter was out of earshot, Emma asked, 'How's Bryan? Is he all right?'

'Aye, Emma love, he is, although as I keep telling you, I'm not too happy he joined up so quickly. But these young lads are in such a hurry, wanting to do their bit for their country, full of patriotism, itching to fight the Jerries, just as we were in the Great War.'

'I don't think you were all that keen,' Emma murmured thoughtfully, throwing him a knowing look. 'If I remember correctly, you and Joe were quite late joining up. You both waited to be *called* up, as a matter of fact . . . married men *last*, that was the rule of the day. I'm positive you and Joe joined the Seaforth Highlanders in 1916, after the Compulsory Service Act was passed in March of that year. I've a good memory, you know.'

'I don't be doubting,' he said, 'and aye, you're quite right about the year. Nineteen sixteen it was.'

Turning to David, Emma reached out to him when she said, 'Ronnie and Mark will be all right, David. Try not to worry so much about them.'

'I do try, but it's awfully hard,' he answered, attempting to sound more cheerful, making an enormous effort for her. She was so brave and strong, he didn't want to appear weak in her eyes.

Blackie, listening to Emma comforting David, was suddenly flooded with memories of the Great War. Yes, she was right, he and Joe *had* gone only when they had to, shipping out in 1916, sent to France and the Battle of the Somme. He thought of the rain. And the mud; he had been knee-deep in it in the trenches. He could almost smell the cordite, and the sound of the cannonade seemed to reverberate in his head. Pure hell it had been. The kind of hell he prayed his son would not have to face. *The Battle of the Somme* . . . where Joe had been killed. Emma's first husband, Joe Lowther, the father of Kit. And now Kit was with the British Expeditionary Force, fighting another war with Germany. The last one had only ended twenty-odd years ago. He prayed that Kit, and Bryan and David's sons did not become cannon fodder. He prayed for all of the boys at the front . . .

'Don't you agree, Blackie?' Emma asked.

Rousing himself from his introspection, Blackie muttered, 'I'm sorry, Emm, I missed that.'

'I was just saying to David that when you look around this restaurant you'd never know there was a war on. The women are elegantly dressed and bejewelled, very glamorous looking, and the men arc smart, too.'

'That's true,' he replied. 'On the other hand, those somewhat weary-looking Royal Air Force officers over there at that end table give the game away, don't you think?'

After the waiter had poured a tasting of champagne for Emma she took a sip of it and nodded; he then filled the flute and departed.

Blackie picked up his glass, touched it first to Emma's and then David's, and said, 'Cheers! Here's to old friends.'

The two of them responded to Blackie in unison, and after a sip of the icy-cold sparkling champagne, Emma announced, 'I will never forget the date.' As she spoke she looked pointedly at Blackie and then at David. 'It will go down as one of the most important and memorable dates in the history of

England. Wait, I'd like to amend that . . . the most *momentous* date in the history of our country.'

'Now which date are you talkin' about, me darlin'?' Blackie asked, peering across the dinner table at her, frowning. 'I'm afraid I'm not following you, Emm. Are you, David?'

David shook his head, also puzzled. 'I'm sorry, Emma.'

Emma gave them both the benefit of her lovely, incandescent smile, that famous radiant smile not seen by either of them for a very long time. She explained, 'Friday May the tenth, 1940. *Yesterday's date*, to be exact. You know as well as I do that something truly wonderful happened last night. Winston Churchill walked into Number Ten Downing Street as the new Prime Minister, thank God, and at long last. Now I am absolutely positive we're going to win this war!'

'Aye, Emma, you're quite right in what you say, Winston's the best man for the job, and some job he's got, to be sure. We are in great peril. And we are facing a long road, and it's going to be a bumpy road, but he'll pull us through. We'll beat the Jerries, so long as Churchill is our leader. The country's behind him, even if the politicians in Westminster are not.'

'I endorse that,' David remarked with a quiet authority. 'I must admit, I thought we'd be stuck with Neville Chamberlain and his ridiculous talk of appeasement. Who can appease Hitler? He's voracious for power and world domination.'

Blackie nodded in agreement. 'He wants all of Europe. And England as well. I'll tell you both this, and you mark my words: he'll invade our little island home . . . at least he'll give it a try.'

'He will never succeed!' Emma cried, cutting across Blackie. Picking up her champagne glass, she added, 'Let's drink a toast to the man who can stop him. Here's to Winston Churchill!'

Crystal clinked against crystal, and the three of them repeated his name with genuine enthusiasm and belief. Like Emma, Blackie and David had always supported Churchill and had wanted him back in power for years. He was the only man they trusted in the British government, the only man they believed could lead them to victory against the Nazis.

After a moment, Blackie said slowly, 'To think how they've ignored Winston, all those bloody idiots in the government. He's been warning all of them about the threat of Hitler for years, and not one of them paid any attention. He was a voice in the wilderness, and all the bloody politicians did was cling to the coat-tails of Neville Chamberlain, who would have led us all to doom if he'd remained in office much longer. Just think on this: he makes a pact with Hitler, whose armies have *already* trampled down half of Europe. It's not believable. And there's another thing. Nobody here has done a bloody thing about rearming the country. We're not prepared for war at all. We have no arms, well very few, not many bombs and certainly not many planes. Truthfully, we don't have much to defend ourselves with. I suppose because we've been led by a blind man backed up by his sycophants.'

David nodded vigorously, looked across at Emma. 'Hitler's armies are marching into France at this very moment, and the Gestapo will hot-foot it behind them in order to persecute and murder Jews.' He shook his head sorrowfully, a terrible anguish entering his blue eyes. 'And Chamberlain believes Hitler wants peace! The man's unconscionable! Thank God he's left office.'

Emma said in a low voice, 'There's none so blind as those who will not see.'

CHAPTER TWENTY-SEVEN

'Do I look all right, Mummy?' Elizabeth said, walking into Emma's bedroom.

Emma swung around to face her daughter. Elizabeth gasped, stood staring at her mother open-mouthed.

'Whatever's wrong?' Emma asked, peering across the room at the nineteen-year-old, extremely puzzled by her reaction.

'Nothing's wrong, Mummy, you look absolutely and impossibly *gorgeous*! Whatever have you done since last week?' As she spoke Elizabeth floated into the room on the most beautiful legs Emma had ever seen, adding, 'Well, it's perfectly obvious you've cut your hair, but there's something else . . . you look so *glamorous*.'

Emma began to laugh. 'It's just the suit. I dug it out from the back of my wardrobe. And yes, I did cut my hair, but that's all I've done, darling, I promise.'

'No, it's not, you've stopped wearing *black*. And

so perhaps it is *partially* the suit. Pale blue has always been your colour, it looks wonderful with your red hair. And it's perfect for today, it's like the middle of summer outside. Tony says the worse the news the better the weather.'

'I thought that myself on Saturday night when I went to dinner with Blackie and David. Anyway, darling girl, to answer your initial question, you don't look *all right*: that's the understatement of the year. You look positively beautiful, and if anyone's gorgeous it's *you*, Elizabeth.'

Emma spoke the truth.

Elizabeth Barkstone, Robin's twin sister, was her daughter by Arthur Ainsley. She had spectacular, movie-star good looks. A cloud of shining black wavy hair surrounded an exquisite, delicate face, finely drawn, with high cheekbones, a slender nose, and a smooth wide brow. Black brows arched above clear blue eyes, which were large and set wide apart. She had a slender but shapely figure and those long legs that drew whistles of admiration from men on the street.

Until last year she had been studying at the Royal Academy of Dramatic Art, having long wanted a career in the theatre; Emma had always thought she would succeed, considering her somewhat way-ward daughter to be the consummate actress.

But this past January, Elizabeth had dropped out of the Royal Academy to become a Red Cross nurse. 'I feel I must be part of the war effort, Mummy,' Elizabeth had told her at the time. 'I want to do something worthwhile, especially with Tony up there in the air, fighting the German Luftwaffe.'

Emma had fully understood and endorsed this move on her daughter's part. In December of 1939 Elizabeth had married Tony Barkstone, a great friend of Robin's from Cambridge, who was also in the RAF. They had met through her twin brother, and fallen madly in love. Even though Elizabeth was only eighteen at the time, and Tony not much older, Emma had not had the heart to stop them marrying. As Blackie had said, 'If he's old enough to be sent up into the skies in a Spitfire to defend our country, then he's old enough to get married. And so is she.' And Emma had agreed, seeing the truth in this comment.

The wedding had been small and quiet, because of the war, but lovely in spite of this, and all of the family had been present, except for Kit, who couldn't get leave. Edwina, who was still estranged from Emma, had remained in Ireland but had sent a wedding gift. Emma had always been saddened by the estrangement, and had long wished there was a way to heal the breach. But Edwina was nothing if not stubborn, and she would not bend. It still troubled her that she was illegitimate – to the point of loathing her mother.

Emma said, 'I'm glad you're wearing your uniform, it suits you very well, and you do it justice. But aside from that, I think it's appropriate for this afternoon. It strikes just the right note, and looks patriotic.'

'I would have felt a bit odd not wearing it, Mummy, rather out of place in a suit, or a dress and coat. I'm proud of being a nurse, doing something worthwhile. It's a good feeling, being able to help others.'

'Yes, it is. Now, I just have to put on my jewellery and then I'm ready and we can leave.'

'I think you should wear blue stones today,' Elizabeth ventured. 'The aquamarine pin, perhaps, and the earrings to match.'

Emma paused on her way to her dressing table, glanced over her shoulder at her daughter. 'I'm going to wear my string of pearls and pearl earrings, Elizabeth. I want to keep everything simple.'

'Oh yes, I understand.' Elizabeth strolled over to an easy chair and sat down. 'I spoke to Tony yesterday. He called from the RAF station in Yorkshire where he's gone for special training . . . Topcliffe. He sends his love.'

'Give him mine the next time he phones,' Emma murmured. 'I wrote to him the other day, to all of the boys, in fact. Kit, Robin, Bryan, Randolph, Mark and Ronnie . . . the whole gang.'

'You're just amazing, I don't know how you do it all. Running the stores, Paul's companies, and everything else that's under your control. By the way, I forgot to ask, how's the Little Tadpole?'

Turning around again, Emma said softly, 'She's

fine, and I do wish you wouldn't call Daisy that. You know, it's not really a very nice name, and I'm surprised she doesn't resent it.'

'Oh Mummy, darling, don't be so silly! She knows it's a joke from the days when she loved to play with the frogs in the pond at Pennistone Royal. Anyway, it was Paul who started calling her that, not me.'

'I know.' Emma smoothed her hands over the immaculately tailored Lanvin suit, picked up her handbag and said, 'Well, let's be off, we don't want to be late for the House of Commons. Aunt Jane wanted us to arrive by one-thirty, no later than one forty-five. This is Winston Churchill's first speech in the House as Prime Minister. We must not miss a single word.'

They sat together in the gallery. Three beautiful women: Emma Harte, Elizabeth Barkstone and Jane Stuart Ogden, wife of William Ogden, Conservative Member of Parliament for South-East Leeds. Quite a few pairs of eyes turned to stare, and all of those long stares were full of admiration.

When Jane had heard from her husband earlier in the day that Winston Churchill was to speak in the House that afternoon, she had telephoned Emma to invite her to hear him. It was May the thirteenth, Whitsun bank holiday Monday, and the House of Commons was packed.

Emma was amazed at the reception Neville Chamberlain, the outgoing Prime Minister, was given when he came in. It seemed to her that *everyone* was cheering, and applauding, so much so it was like an ovation. How can they? she asked herself in total bafflement. This man has led us into an abyss of disaster with his policy of appeasement, his reluctance to rearm, his blindness to events in Europe. We are at peril because of him. He has been a disaster for this country and for its people.

These dire thoughts fled, and were replaced with the utmost admiration, when she spotted Winston Churchill entering the Commons chamber. Emma waited for an even greater acclamation than Chamberlain had received, but sadly it was not forthcoming. It struck her that Winston was not particularly well received by his colleagues, and later Jane would tell her that the cheers for him mostly emanated from the Labour and Liberal benches, not his own Conservative Party.

It infuriated Emma that Churchill was being treated in this shabby and mean-spirited way. They just didn't understand, did they? Did not understand either this man and what he stood for, or the mood of the country. The people wanted Winston back, and thank God now they had him.

When Winston Churchill began to speak, Emma Harte leaned forward eagerly, listening to his every word most attentively.

That marvellous voice rang out, mesmerizing in its effect:

'I would say to the House, as I said to those who have joined the government, that I have nothing to offer but blood, toil, tears and sweat. We have before us an ordeal of the most grievous kind . . . You ask, what is our policy? I can say: it is to wage war, by sea, land and air, with all of our might and with all the strength that God can give us: to wage war against a monstrous tyranny, never surpassed in the dark, lamentable catalogue of human crime. That is our policy. You ask, what is our aim? I can answer in one word: It is victory, victory at all costs, victory in spite of all terror, victory, however long and hard the road may be; for without victory, there is no survival.'

Tears filled Emma's eyes, so moved was she, and it took her a moment to bring her emotions under control. This man, whom she instinctively understood was a great man, perhaps even the greatest man in England today, never failed to touch her with his extraordinary words, the sentiments he expressed. No wonder the ordinary man and woman in the street loved him, believed in him, wanted him to lead them.

Later, over tea on the terrace of the House of Commons, Emma turned to Bill Ogden and said softly, 'I don't understand it, Bill, why is there this . . . well, *animosity* I suppose is the best word, towards Winston Churchill? It seems to me they should be rejoicing that he has become Prime Minister.'

'Indeed many Members are, Emma. As I am, and quite a few of my colleagues.' Bill sat back in the chair, steepled his fingers together, looking reflective. 'You know, Emma, Churchill has been a Member of the House for forty years, ever since he was elected Conservative Member of Parliament for Oldham in 1900. It's a very long time, and in those years he's made countless good friends. But also enemies. It's a funny sort of place, peculiar in some ways, and certainly it's full of free-floating . . . *emotions*. I think that is probably the best way to describe what I mean . . . feelings of competitiveness, anger, jealousy, hatred, scorn, not to mention that old bugaboo, *ambition*. And, of course, there are political differences. One of the worst things of all is . . . *envy*.'

'It was the Labour and Liberal benches who were the most enthusiastic, led by Atlee,' Jane pointed out to Emma.

Bill nodded. 'Indeed, Jane. But I never thought for a moment that Clem Atlee would vote for Edward Halifax to be Prime Minister. Although I like Halifax personally, he wouldn't have been right for the job – too much of the order of Chamberlain. Winston was the only choice in my considered opinion.'

'Do they envy him because of who he is?' Emma asked, determined to understand.

'To a degree, perhaps,' Bill responded. 'He was, after all, born in a palace not a pigsty. Blenheim Palace, to be precise. Son of a lord, Lord Randolph Churchill. Grandson of a duke. And a direct descendant of that greatest of generals, John Churchill, the first Duke of Marlborough. So he's truly of ducal descent, enough to cause a bubbling bit of envy in many a chap here. As it so happens, Churchill is the most aristocratic Prime Minister we've had in thirty-five years. And yet, Emma, as you well know, his real power and authority do come directly from the people. One of the reasons he *is* Prime Minister today is because of popular acclaim . . . they love him.'

'But why don't some of the other politicians see that?' Emma asked, her puzzlement still apparent.

'Blind as bats, Emma my dear,' Jane murmured.

'Perhaps not that exactly,' Bill interjected. 'It's partially because their eyes are turned inward upon themselves . . . and on their ambitions, their desires and needs and dreams. In my opinion, I don't believe Churchill has paid too much attention to that ducal heritage of his, not when it comes to his career, at any rate. He's been too single-minded and driven to succeed to dwell on that. I know, and from him himself, that he's always been utterly convinced he was a man of destiny. I know I am right in saying it is a conviction which has never wavered.'

'I've heard that about him.' Emma took a sip of tea, then continued, 'And of course he is *indeed* a man of destiny, we know that now. It's his destiny to lead us to victory . . . Why, his destiny has become a fact.'

'Why have you always been such an admirer of his? Such a strong supporter?' Jane asked as she refilled everyone's cups.

'Partly because of my father,' Emma explained. 'You see, his great hero, when I was growing up, was John Churchill, the first Duke of Marlborough. He thought he was the finest general we'd ever had. And because of this fascination with the general, my father became interested in the general's descendants. He'd read a lot about them in the newspapers and magazines that Cook gave me when I worked at Fairley Hall. He was an admirer of Lord Randolph when he was a Member of Parliament, because he loved his wit.'

Emma looked from Jane to Elizabeth, and smiled at her daughter. 'When my mother, your grandmother, gave birth to her first child, my father was delighted it was a boy and not a girl. Because he'd set his heart on naming his first child after Lord Randolph's son.'

'Now I understand,' Elizabeth exclaimed. 'Uncle Winston is named for Winston Churchill.'

'Yes, he is,' Emma said.

Much later that evening, just before Emma went to bed, she took out her diary, and recorded the events of the day. Carefully, in her neat and gently sloping handwriting, she gave the details of her visit to the House of Commons to hear Winston Churchill speak. And then she wrote:

Parts of his speech moved me to tears. He has such a command of the English language. He convinces. And he inspires; he is the inspiration of this country. He has come to

power in the most dangerous of times and he has inherited
an unholy mess, but somehow he will prevail. He makes me
feel safe. And very proud.'

Emma closed the diary and put it away. Then she
went to bed. She knew that tonight she would
sleep well because at last they had a valiant and
determined leader. And a promise for the future.

Chapter Twenty-Eight

Over the years Emma had mostly walked to Harte's in Knightsbridge, weather permitting. But of late it had become mandatory. She needed to traverse these familiar streets to reassure herself that all was well in this great metropolis of London, a city she had lived in half her life, and which she loved.

It comforted her when she saw the smiling, cheerful faces of the Londoners as they went about their daily tasks. The bobbies on their beat, the newsboys on the street corners yelling the headlines and selling their papers; the cabbies, the milkmen, the window-cleaners and the char-ladies, all of them stalwart and stoic and full of good cheer.

Also out on the streets these days were the Home Guard and the ARP wardens, their presence reassuring but most obviously underscoring the fact that England was at war. Sometimes it did not seem like it to her: there was a normality to daily life, and London was peaceful, still unscarred. There had been no invasion; nothing had happened over these long months since war had been declared last September. That was why so many people now called it the Phony War.

On this Friday morning in late May, Emma crossed Belgrave Square at a brisk pace, once again marvelling at the extraordinary weather. It was a blessing to have these warm, sunny days without clouds or even the merest hint of rain; there were moments when she felt there was a terrible beauty to this unusual summer. It was . . . *unreal*, that was the only word to use to describe it.

Yet the news was very bad indeed.

At this very moment thousands upon thousands of British and French troops were in retreat in France, falling back to the coastline as the advancing Wehrmacht divisions progressed from the Low Countries into the middle of France. The German army, millions strong, was pushing the Allied troops into Calais and Dunkirk, and RAF bases in France had been attacked once again.

Only last night the BBC had broadcast the latest and most dire bulletin: Allied troops would soon be trapped between German artillery and the sea. They would be sitting ducks on the beaches, under gunfire on land and air attack from the skies. The Luftwaffe would be up there in full force.

How do we get them off the beaches? Emma asked herself as she hurried along, her mind preoccupied with thoughts of war. Her eldest son Kit was in France and in danger, and so was Robin, who spent most of his time in the cockpit of a Spitfire, flying over France. As did her son-in-law Tony Barkstone, and Bryan, Blackie's son. He was her surrogate son in a sense, since she had brought him up after Laura's death, when Blackie was away fighting in the First World War.

Ronnie and Mark Kallinski were over there, and so was her nephew Randolph Harte, her brother Winston's son. Her heart sank when she now considered what could happen: the youth of the three clans could so easily be killed. Just like that, in a flash.

France is going to fall, Emma suddenly thought, with a clarity that stunned her. Her step faltered for a moment, and then she took a deep breath and walked on determinedly. England will stand alone, she thought, and we will have to go on alone . . . because we have no alternative. It will be a fight to the death, though. Churchill will see to that.

Yesterday, Blackie and David had come up to London, and she had invited them to dinner at the Belgrave Square house. Because he had business to discuss with her, David had arranged to come a little earlier. At one moment he had expressed his worries about their sons and Blackie's, and they had commiserated with each other, trying to give comfort in these alarming times when so many were in peril.

They had moved on after that, mostly talking about Lady Hamilton Clothes, which was currently producing uniforms for the armed forces instead of ladies' fashions. Emma had not been unduly surprised when he had told her that they had, just the day before, received another large order from the government for winter overcoats for the army and air force.

'As we both knew, Emma, the government are expecting the war to continue through this coming winter and into next spring,' David had pointed out. And Emma had swiftly answered, 'Yes, we're in for a long siege, I'm afraid, David. We must face that now, not have any pipe dreams about the conflict being over soon.' She had sighed and gone on, 'Despite rationing and the blackout, and everything else we're having to put up with, the war hasn't really hit us yet. At least not here.'

Once they had finished talking about their joint business ventures, which went back years, David had suddenly exclaimed that she was looking more like her old self, even better than she had when he had seen her at Whitsuntide, earlier that month.

'You've put on weight, filled out a bit. Yes, you look just wonderful. All you need is a bit of colour in those pretty cheeks of yours, Emma. Perhaps you should come to Yorkshire for a while, get out on the moors. It would be nice for me if you spent more time at the Leeds and Harrogate stores.'

She had not given much thought to his compliments or his affectionate embraces last night, because Blackie had suddenly arrived and had taken over in his inimitable way. And she had been busy helping Grace, and Mrs Coddington, the cook, get dinner onto the table. Podges, her butler of several years, had left to join the Royal Navy, and Rita, the other parlour maid, had joined the ATS. And so she was short of staff. But they had managed very well, the three of them, and her two boys had enjoyed the dinner, relishing the home-cooked meal of Yorkshire pudding and roast beef.

And then this morning, when she was reviewing the evening in her head, she had suddenly wondered if David's interest in her was no longer fraternal, as it had been for years. Did he see her as a potential lover all of a sudden? After all, he was a widower now. But she had no interest whatsoever in rekindling their old relationship, which had died a natural death thirty-odd years ago. However, she knew she must be careful with him. He was a very dear and old friend, and she must not hurt him; on the other hand, she didn't want to give him the impression she was encouraging him. She must walk a very careful line.

Emma sighed under her breath as she pushed open the side door of Harte's and went inside. The last thing she was interested in was an involvement with a man. Those days were over. *Absolutely*.

Emma spent the morning at her desk, going over balance sheets, for the most part. But at one moment she opened a folder which held the inventories of the store's goods in stock. Everything was listed, from clothes to foodstuffs.

As she quickly scanned the first few pages of the

overall appraisals, she was relieved to see that they were in good shape, at least for the time being. But as the war continued she knew most things would be in short supply and difficult to obtain, especially food.

The food halls of Harte's had been impressive from the first day she had opened the store. They were renowned the world over, and, of course, they had always been well stocked . . . stocked to the hilt, in fact, and especially with fresh produce such as baked and boiled hams, meat pies, pâtés, a variety of cheeses, cold meats and sausages, a selection of game pies, smoked salmon, smoked trout and the like. But she knew that these items would soon be in short supply.

I'll just have to cope, she muttered to herself, leaning back in the chair, staring off into space for a moment, wondering where the supplies *were* going to come from eventually. Rationing had already been enforced some time ago.

The phone shrilled, cutting into her thoughts, and she picked it up. 'Hello?'

'Mrs Harte, it's Mr O'Neill,' her secretary Anita told her.

'Oh yes, put him through, please.'

A moment later Blackie's voice boomed over the phone. 'Hello, Emma. Now, shall we have lunch today? Or dinner, whichever you prefer?'

'Just the two of us?' she asked, a lilt of laughter in her voice.

'Sure an' just the two of us! I couldn't get a

word in edgewise last night, I thought David would never stop talking. I love the lad, but . . .' Blackie cut himself off, chuckled. 'I'd like to have you to meself a bit, mavourneen.'

Emma smiled into the phone. 'I think it *will* have to be lunch, Blackie, if you don't mind. I promised Elizabeth I'd spend the evening with her. She's so worried about Tony; a little upset because of the latest news.'

'Understandable, understandable. So, lunch it is, then. How about the good old Dorch? Unless you're getting bored with it.'

Emma laughed. 'Bored with it! I haven't been there since we had dinner together at Whitsuntide. I've not been out, actually, I've been working round the clock.'

'That's your problem, Emm. You're always at it, and you always have been. You've got to slow down,' he told her, his tone chastising.

'Don't be daft,' she exclaimed. 'You should know better than to say that – to me of all people.'

'Aye, I should, considering the length of time I've known you. So, the Dorchester at one o'clock. Can you make it by then?'

'Yes. I'll be there on time.'

'Well, there's certainly no evidence of rationing or food shortages here,' Emma murmured an hour later when she joined Blackie in the hotel's restaurant, and scanned the menu. 'Smoked salmon, smoked trout, cold lobster, Morecambe Bay potted shrimps, roast beef, shoulder of lamp, beef patties, steak-and-kidney pie and roast quail. Good heavens, so many things to choose from.'

'Aye, you wouldn't think we were living in dire times,' Blackie agreed, nodding his great leonine head. 'But all the luxury hotels are still serving three-course meals, and the food is delicious, as good as it's always been. But for how long, I wonder? So, we might as well enjoy ourselves whilst we can. Do you know what you fancy, Emma?'

'I think I'll have the potted shrimps, and then grilled sole, thank you, Blackie.'

'Sounds good to me, I'll have the same as you.' He gave her a broad smile and motioned to the waiter.

Once they had ordered lunch, the two of them talked about the war, mostly the upsetting news they had heard on the radio last night, about the plight of the troops in France.

At one moment Emma said, 'I don't know how we can get them off the beaches, Blackie. Surely the water's too shallow for the destroyers to get in close to the shore, isn't it?'

'It is, and you can bet your bottom dollar that the sea is mined. The Germans aren't stupid, you know.' He shook his head again, his face grave, and then after glancing around the restaurant, he leaned closer to her. He said in a voice that was low, almost inaudible, 'But we're going to start this weekend . . . start doing something—' He broke off as a couple walked past their table.

'Doing what?' Emma asked, drawing closer to him, her eyes on his.

'I can't go into details right now,' he muttered. 'Let me just say this, we'll be using the little boats—' Again he broke off as two army officers sat down at a table nearby.

'How do you know?'

'Oh Emma, *lass*,' he said quietly, 'you know I can't tell you that. And I wouldn't even if I could. Better you don't know who my . . .' He dropped his voice and finished, '. . . government sources are.'

'But what's the plan?' she probed, eager to know, unable to let go.

Blackie realized she would pester him until he gave her more information, but he was reluctant to talk in a public place like the Dorchester restaurant, and so he said, 'I'll walk you back to the store later, after lunch, and we can have a chat then.'

Emma nodded. 'That's a good idea.' She changed the subject, and went on, 'How long are you staying in London?'

'Just for a few days. I have to get back to Leeds. We still have a couple of buildings under construction and I want to get 'em finished as soon as possible. But I really don't know what's going to happen with my business. A number of contracts have been cancelled because of the war.'

'You're not going to close down, are you?' she cut in swiftly, eyeing him, worry settling on her face. She had always been concerned for him.

'Oh no, no, lass, it's not as bad as that. Tell

you the truth, I have enough put away to carry the business for quite a long spell.'

'I'm glad to hear that,' Emma murmured, and was about to say that he should never worry, that she would always be there for him. Then she changed her mind. He was so proud; she didn't want to upset him. Anyway, she was well aware he was a millionaire many times over, because of the success of his building company, his ownership of several office buildings and shops in Leeds, as well as other buildings in Harrogate and Sheffield. He was a fine builder, a brilliant businessman.

After this short silence, Blackie asked, 'Any news from Edwina?' As he spoke he wondered if he'd asked the wrong question.

Emma grimaced, and then shook her head. 'I never hear from her. Never, although Winston sometimes does. She always loved her uncle, you know, and she did invite him to the wedding . . . The trouble with Edwina is that she's stubborn, Blackie, as you well know, and that stubbornness sometimes gets in the way of her better nature. I hope she comes around one day.'

'She will, to be sure.' He looked across the table at her and began to chuckle, his black eyes merry.

'What is it?' she asked, staring back at him quizzically.

'I remember the day we christened her, in the kitchen sink at Laura's house in Upper Armley, because you were afraid to go to the church—'

'I *wasn't* afraid! I've never been afraid of any-thing,' Emma exclaimed, cutting right across him. 'I simply didn't want the embarrassment of the vicar knowing she was illegitimate. And you *know* that, we discussed it at the time,' she finished snippily.

'Aye, I expect we did. And such a little itty-bitty thing you were in those days, Emma, a sprite. You were thin as a rail but so full of vim and vigour. I did admire you.'

'I was strong, Blackie, and that was the most important thing of all.'

He nodded and said nothing, thinking of their early days in Leeds, when he had worked as a navvy, at times building canals, at others working on the railway lines, occasionally doing private jobs for the likes of Squire Adam Fairley. That's how he had first met her, on the way to Fairley Hall. He had come across her hurrying over the moors to that miserable house on a wintry morning. It was there she worked as a maid. Scivvy, more like, he added to himself, the way they treated her. They'd turned her into a drudge, and she only fourteen.

Blackie O'Neill now glanced around the rather grand restaurant of the Dorchester Hotel, marvel-ling to himself that she and he had come so far.

Emma said, 'A penny for your thoughts, Blackie, you're looking so far away.'

He grinned at her. 'Thinking about our early days, that I was – and who would have imagined that you would have become such a grand and elegant woman; a real lady?' He winked at her and added, 'Even though most of the time you're still a drudge, as you were then, working like the navvy I used to be.'

'Nobody ever died of hard work, Blackie.'

'Aye, Emma, I've heard you say that many times before – for the last thirty years, in fact. But sometimes I think you're too hard on yourself. You should take it a little easier; after all, you are fifty.'

'Fifty-*one* on April the thirtieth, Blackie, to be exact. But I don't feel it. I feel like a young woman inside, like a twenty-year-old.'

'And that's what you look like.'

'It's *me* sitting here, Shane Patrick Desmond O'Neill. And please remember that I am fully aware you did your teething on the Blarney Stone.'

'Only too true, mavourneen. Ah, here comes the waiter with our potted shrimps.' He threw her a long old-fashioned look, and winked.

Their walk through Hyde Park was leisurely. Emma had more or less finished for the day, and she was in no hurry to get back to Harte's. And Blackie told her he had no appointments.

As they walked along he confided what he had learned from his contact at the Ministry of Supplies. The rumour in Westminster was that Churchill was going to get the boys off the beaches no matter what, and that there were plans afoot to use anything that floated to do the job. Although she probed and pressed, he genuinely had no other information, and explained that he had told her everything he knew.

'Let's hope it works,' she said as she slipped her arm through his. 'I put my faith in our Prime Minister.'

'And so do I, Emma, so do I,' Blackie readily agreed.

The following evening Blackie and David came to Emma's house in Belgravia, again for a home-cooked supper. Afterward, they adjourned to the library for coffee and cognac, and at one moment Blackie suddenly volunteered, 'I was told last night by one of my government friends that we're assembling quite an armada to get our boys off beaches in Dunkirk. If anyone can do it, the Prime Minister can.'

David and Emma agreed with him wholeheartedly, and later Emma turned on the radio so that they could listen to the nine o'clock news on the BBC. And that night, Saturday May twenty-fifth, they learned that the British Army was now completely isolated; it had been separated from the French. The Germans occupied Boulogne, and the other French ports in the English Channel were falling one by one.

The three old friends sat in silence for a short while after the broadcast was finished, filled with dismay by the report and worried about their sons and the sons of relatives and friends.

It was Emma who finally roused herself and said, 'They're all alone out there, targets for the enemy, I know that. Nonetheless, we must believe they're going to be all right . . . somehow. We can't give up hope. That would be defeatist. No, we must believe all of those boys are coming home. They're young and they're tough and they *are* going to make it.'

Chapter Twenty-Nine

I t was an armada the likes of which the world had never seen before.

But it was an armada of great purpose and an implacable will to succeed. Its aim: to get the British troops off the beaches of Dunkirk and back to England before they were annihilated by the German onslaught.

The armada, and a motley one at that, was comprised of an amazing assortment of vessels, and they had made the hazardous journey across the Channel from every corner of England, sailing to assist the British destroyers and light battleships anchored off Dunkirk. The bigger ships were making desperate efforts to evacuate the men stranded on those wide open beaches, but because of the shallows they could not move in close.

However, the little ships could, and that is what they did: they ferried the troops to the safety of the British Royal navy ships, which in turn transported the men to Deal and Ramsgate.

These little boats were owned and manned entirely by civilians. Volunteers from all walks of life, they were willing participants in the rescue, and none of them would rest until the sons of England were safely home.

And so they came . . . in their little rowing boats and yachts, in sailing boats and fishing trawlers, pleasure steamers and even barges from the canals of England. Anything that could float, and was seaworthy, set sail. There were over a thousand vessels in all, including the British naval ships, and all took part in the most daring rescue ever known.

It went on under heavy enemy fire, and fierce bombardment from the Luftwaffe circling the skies above. But the valiant RAF was up there too, beating back the enemy planes, ensuring they did not have supremacy in the skies.

The whole of Britain waited in suspense.

On Sunday, May twenty-sixth, the weather broke at long last, and it poured with rain for the first time in weeks. Like everyone else, Emma was gloomy and more worried than ever because of this change in the weather, believing it might well slow down the rescue mission.

But the BBC reported that the seas were calm, and this reassured her somewhat. Also, her confidence in Churchill did not wain, and this belief helped to keep her spirits up.

At work as well as at home, Emma was glued to the radio, and she kept it on all the time. By

Monday evening she was thrilled to hear on a BBC news bulletin that 7,000 men had been evacuated by the end of that day, and then the following Tuesday night she learned that 17,000 soldiers had been rescued.

The rest of the week, as the boats and Navy ships ploughed the Channel, 50,000 troops were lifted off the beaches every day. In the end, 200,000 soldiers were evacuated in those four days alone, stunning a nation that was suddenly and unexpectedly joyful.

It was an unbelievable rescue that surpassed anything the Prime Minister and his War Cabinet had expected or thought possible. The epic of Dunkirk gripped the imagination of Britain and her Allies.

Out of hell came back all the little steamers and rowing boats and pleasure steamers, bringing back the living and the wounded. The evacuation had taken eleven days. Some 335,000 Allied troops, including 26,000 French soldiers, had been brought to safety by the time the Germans finally captured the sea town. Their equipment had been abandoned, but thousands of men were safe, and that was all that mattered. Forty thousand were left behind, mostly French troops.

Emma was thankful that she was one of those who could rejoice. On June the third, her son Kit stepped off the barge that had transported him to Deal across a choppy Channel jammed with wreckage and vessels. Many of the small boats, in a hurry, had simply ferried the troops across to the coast of Kent, bypassing the destroyers and bigger ships, anxious to get the boys home without delay. Then they turned around and came back for more.

David was euphoric when he telephoned from Leeds to tell her that both Ronnie and Mark had been amongst the troops who had landed at Ramsgate, and she soon learned from Blackie that Bryan was safe. And so, thankfully, were her son Robin, and Tony, Elizabeth's husband, who had survived the air battles over Dunkirk and were back at the RAF station at Biggin Hill.

Later, when he came home on leave, Kit told her: 'I just made it by the skin of my teeth, Mother. I must have a guardian angel watching over me.' He embraced her tightly and, clinging to him, Emma choked up, thinking of his father, Joe Lowther, who had died in France in 1916, apparently in vain.

On June the fourth Emma was sitting in the gallery of the House of Commons, once more a guest of Jane Stuart Ogden. Knowing how Emma felt about Churchill, Jane had invited her friend of many years to come and hear the Prime Minister speak again. Emma had been thrilled to accept.

Emma noticed that when Churchill rose in the Commons chamber to speak, a different atmosphere altogether reigned. She could almost feel their respect for him, it was a palpable thing, and their confidence in him was apparent amongst the majority of the Members.

Halfway through his speech, Churchill paused for a moment, and then his voice rang out once again, sonorous, filled with emotion as he spoke of the rescue. 'A miracle of deliverance, achieved by valour, by perseverance, by perfect discipline, by faultless service, by resource, by skill, by unconquerable fidelity, is manifest to us all.'

There was absolutely no sound at all in the Commons chamber, and Emma thought that you would hear a pin drop, so quiet was it. As she groped for her handkerchief and wiped the tears from her eyes, she noticed that Jane was crying too. Leaning forward, Emma was attentive, and hanging onto his words as he continued his speech.

Churchill said, 'The Royal Air Force engaged the main strength of the German Air Force, and inflicted upon them losses at least four to one; and the Navy, using nearly 1,000 ships of all kinds, carried 335,000 men, French and British, out of the jaws of death and shame, to their native land and to the tasks which lie immediately ahead. We must be very careful not to assign to this deliverance the attributes of a victory. Wars are not won by evacuations. But there was a victory inside this deliverance, which should be noted.'

His rhetoric was superb as he continued after only taking a short breath, and Emma couldn't help wondering where he got his stamina from; how had he managed to write this speech with all of the other tasks he had? She did not know, but she was glad that he had. It was uplifting, inspirational.

Once more that amazing voice rang out. Not a person stirred or coughed, not a paper rustled. The Commons chamber was absolutely and entirely still, holding its collective breath, waiting to hear more.

'Even though large tracts of Europe and many old and famous States have fallen or may fall into the grip of the Gestapo and all the odious apparatus of Nazi rule, we shall not flag or fail. We shall go on to the end, we shall fight in France, we shall fight on the seas and oceans, we shall fight with growing confidence and growing strength in the air, we shall defend our Island, whatever the cost may be, we shall fight on the beaches, we shall fight on the landing grounds, we shall fight in the fields and in the streets, we shall fight in the hills; we shall never surrender . . .'

His speech had been a long one this time, over half an hour, but he had delivered it with such magnificence the entire chamber was on its feet.

Emma was speechless herself, immeasurably touched by his words: she was certain it would go down in history as one of the greatest speeches ever made in this chamber. His use of language was superb, and he had just evoked so many different emotions in everyone: a sense of duty and patri- otism, a belief in their island race, faith in those young men who were fighting to save freedom and justice, and the young women who stood shoulder to shoulder beside them.

Emma was not the only one moved by Winston Churchill's words, nor was she the only one with tears on her cheeks. Several Labour members cried, and so did Winston Churchill himself.

Emma and Jane later learned from her husband Bill that everyone thought this was a most outstanding and successful performance. A Labour MP called Josiah Wedgwood thought it was 'worth a thousand guns, and the speeches of a thousand years'. Bill also told them that Harold Nicolson had said, 'Winston made the finest speech I have ever heard.'

'How can we fail, Jane, with this man leading us? And our brave boys fighting for us. I know we are going to win. I truly believe that.'

'I pray you are right, Emma. Because if you are wrong, we are doomed as a nation . . .'

'It was Winston Churchill who was *right* when he said we must go to war, that we had no alternative. Because we had to defeat the Germans and *win* the war, in order to crush the terror of Nazism. You will see, Jane, the Prime Minister will be vindicated. Well, actually, he is already, I think. If today's reaction is anything to go by.' She suddenly smiled at Jane, and added, 'And one day he will be considered the greatest Briton of them all. As Blackie would say, you mark my words.'

Jane gave her dearest friend a long, thoughtful look, frowning slightly. Then she said slowly, 'You are very certain, Emma, so very sure . . . of ultimate victory.'

'I am very sure of *Churchill*,' Emma answered, staring back at her friend.

Not for the first time, Jane saw that implacable look settle on Emma's face, and she knew it was wisest to say no more. Emma's mind was made up, and nothing and no one would ever change it. Nor would they shake Emma's unfailing belief in ultimate victory.

CHAPTER THIRTY

'I'm sorry to bother you, Mrs Harte, but I wonder if I could have a word with you?'

Emma looked up from the papers on her desk, and smiled at her secretary standing in the doorway. 'Of course, Anita, come in and sit down.'

The young woman gave her a tentative smile, stepped into the office and closed the door. Then she walked across to Emma's big partners' desk and took the seat opposite her.

After studying Anita for a second, frowning slightly, Emma said, 'You've got a face like a wet week, as my brother would say. Now, Anita, my dear, it can't be all that bad, can it?'

Anita shook her blonde head, and forced a smile. 'It's not, not really. But I think you're going to be upset, Mrs Harte, and the last thing I'd want to do would be to upset you, you've been so good to me, but—' Anita paused, took a deep breath and finished in a rush, 'I'm leaving, Mrs Harte, I want to give you my notice.'

Startled though she was momentarily, it took Emma only a moment to catch on, and she exclaimed, 'Well, I certainly don't want to lose you, Anita, but I think you're going to tell me that you're joining one of the services. Is that it?'

'Not exactly, well, what I mean is, I'm not going into the ATS or the WAFs. I'm joining the Land Army, Mrs Harte.'

'I see. That's very worthy of you.' Emma smiled, put down her pen and leant back in the chair. 'I must admit, it had crossed my mind that you might want to do your bit for the war effort, and of course I think it goes without saying that I'm sorry to lose you. You've been an excellent secretary, and worked very well here.'

'Thank you, Mrs Harte. I love the store, you know. But I just don't feel right, what with my three brothers in the forces and my sister working in a munitions factory. I want to . . . well . . . pull my weight, so to speak.'

'I understand, I really do. All of the young people feel as you do, Anita.'

'I hate to let you down, I know what a lot of work you have.'

'Yes, and I shall miss you, you've been a godsend over the last couple of years. Actually, I don't quite know what I'll do without you.' Emma brought her hand to her chin, her eyes suddenly growing thoughtful. 'What about one of the junior secretaries who work out there with you? Either of them a possibility for me?'

409

'I think Fanny might be . . . in a year. Both she and Lois *are* juniors, Mrs Harte. I give them a lot of the filing, letters to type, small things. Honestly, I don't think they could handle what I've been doing. Not that I want to blow my own horn, Mrs Harte, but, well, they just haven't had my experience.'

Emma nodded, sighed heavily, looking suddenly worried as she thought of what faced her in the next few weeks. 'I suppose you're leaving immediately?' Emma raised an auburn brow as she spoke.

'Well . . .' Anita stopped, and leant forward. 'Look, Mrs Harte, I hope I'm not doing the wrong thing, saying this, but I think you should talk to Mr Harte's junior secretary. He's not in London much these days, since he's been running all the Yorkshire stores, and I don't think she has all that much to do because Brenda Small is the senior secretary. She's a very competent junior from what I've noticed.'

'Perhaps I should talk to her. I doubt Mr Harte would mind, because he *is* away a great deal these days.'

Anita sat up straight. She looked relieved, and she beamed at Emma, pleased that her idea had been received so well. 'Shall I go and get her, Mrs Harte? Ask her to come along to your office?'

'I think I'd better speak to my brother first. He's here in London this week, and he'll be coming to the store today. If he's not already here. And thank you for your suggestion, Anita. By the way, when will you be leaving me?'

'I'd like to give a week's notice, but I can stretch it to two if necessary, Mrs Harte.'

Ten minutes later, Winston Harte was sitting in the chair just vacated by Anita Holmes.

He listened closely as Emma spoke, nodding from time to time, paying strict attention to her words as he always did. He adored his sister, and thought she was the most brilliant person he had ever known.

When she had finished repeating Anita's conversation, he said at once, 'No problem, Emma. It's true, I'm hardly here these days, and one of the other juniors in my office can help Brenda if there's any spillover.'

'If you're sure, Winston. She would be a great help until I can find someone else, a permanent secretary.'

Winston chuckled, his eyes filling with merriment. 'I doubt you'll want anyone else.'

'Oh, she's that good?'

'Yes, she is, as a matter of fact.'

'Glynnis . . . Glynnis Jenkins. Isn't that her name?'

Winston nodded. 'She's Welsh, from the Rhondda, and, quite aside from being a good secretary, she's straightforward. A very nice young woman altogether, Emm.'

Emma's relief was apparent, and it was reflected on her face; her vivid green eyes suddenly looked less worried. 'It's nice of you to do this, Winston.'

'Anything for you, love. I know you're a bit

overwhelmed with work at the moment. The extensive McGill Holdings to handle on top of everything else is a hell of a load for you.'

'Yes, it is, and it's awfully time-consuming. But you'll never hear *me* complain, Winston. When Paul left me everything he made me one of the richest women in the world, and Daisy a great heiress, as you well know. I do my best to look after McGill Holdings properly because the company will go to her one day, and to her progeny: that's what Paul wanted, you know. He wanted Daisy and any children she might have to be safe, and properly taken care of financially. Just as he took care of Constance and Howard in Australia. Those are lifetime trusts he created for them . . . he was very good that way.'

Unexpectedly, a look of immense sorrow fell across her face like a dark shadow, and her eyes turned cloudy. Winston heard her barely perceptible sigh. He asked softly, leaning forward, 'Are you all right, our Emm?'

She stared across her desk at him and blinked several times, then swallowed hard. 'Yes, I'm fine, Winston . . .' Another sigh escaped, and she went on, 'I wish he'd never gone back to see Constance about the divorce . . . he might still be alive if he'd come here from New York with me last year.'

'He had to go because he knew war was coming and he wanted to put his affairs in order, and also make sure his companies would run properly without him. You know very well he thought he would have problems going back and forth to Sydney,' Winston pointed out gently.

'You're right. And yet I can't help thinking if only . . .'

'Oh Emma, darling, life is full of *if onlys*, you know that better than anyone else. And we all think *if only* we hadn't done that, or this . . . it's human nature to react in this way. But what about this . . . if only you hadn't married Arthur Ainsley you'd have had a few extra years with Paul, have you ever thought about that?'

'Of course I have. But if I hadn't married Arthur I wouldn't have had Robin and Elizabeth, now would I?'

'No, you wouldn't.' Changing the subject, Winston now said, 'Is Henry Rossiter all right? I haven't heard you mention him lately. He is working out well, isn't he?'

Quite visibly Emma cheered up, and she exclaimed, 'It's one of the best things I ever did, making him my financial adviser on a permanent basis. He's been extremely smart with McGill Holdings, and he works very well with Mel Harrison in Sydney. Long-distance business relationships are not always successful, but this has been wonderful, and continues to be. As for Harry Marriott in Texas, he and I work well long distance, too. He's running Sitex Oil the way Paul did, and since he's a partner I know he has the company's interests at heart.

'I'm glad to hear all this, but it's still a burden

for you at times. I wish I could help lessen the load for you.'

'Oh Winston, you do. You run the Yorkshire stores, and help me with Harte Enterprises. Frankly, I don't know what I'd do without you. Which is why, right now, I'm wondering how I could be so selfish and take one of your secretaries.'

'It doesn't present a problem, Emma.' Winston rose, smiled down at her. 'I'll go and have a word with Glynnis – and Brenda, of course. And then I'll bring Glynnis in so you can talk to her.'

'Thanks, Winston.' Emma's eyes followed him, and she could not help thinking how handsome he was. Like her, he was all Harte in looks and colouring, and there was certainly no mistaking that they were brother and sister. His devotion to her meant a lot, and she realized, as he closed the door softly behind him, how much she relied on her older brother.

Within fifteen minutes Winston was back in her office, bringing with him Glynnis Jenkins. As Emma stood up, and went to greet her, she found herself marvelling at the young woman's looks. She had forgotten just how beautiful the Welsh girl was. She wasn't beautiful in a classical way: she was too voluptuous for that with her sultry looks and shapely figure. But she had a certain glamour about her, even though she wore a simple, plainly tailored black cotton dress with a white collar and cuffs. Her thick, glossy brown hair, worn in a pageboy style, fell around a full face that was superbly sculpted, and she had a wide forehead, a pert nose, and dimples in her cheeks. Her eyes, large and thickly lashed, were luminous, an unusual smoky grey in colour.

'Here's Glynnis,' Winston said, ushering the young woman across Emma's office.

'Hello, Glynnis,' Emma said, giving her a warm smile.

'Good morning, Mrs Harte,' Glynnis answered rather shyly as she walked forward, trying not to appear nervous.

'Now, let's go and sit down over there on the sofa,' Emma went on, 'so that we can have a little chat. I'm sure Mr Harte has explained that Anita is leaving to join the land army.'

'Oh yes, he has.'

'Would you like to work for me, Glynnis?' Emma sat in a chair next to the sofa.

'Very much, Mrs Harte.' Glynnis cleared her throat and added, 'I think I'll be able to do the job. I've learned a lot from Brenda . . .' She stopped, let her voice trail off, and sat down on the sofa, looking first at Winston who remained standing, and then back at Emma. 'I'll certainly try very hard, Mrs Harte.'

'I'm sure you will.'

Moving towards the door, Winston now said, 'You'll be just fine, Glynnis. And if you'll excuse me, Emma, I'll leave you two alone to talk.'

'I realize you've things to do, Winston. I'll see

you later,' Emma murmured, and turned to the young woman sitting opposite her.

'Let me tell you a little bit about Anita's job, Glynnis. Naturally I realize you know what being a secretary means, the tasks involved. The only difference really, if you work for me, will be the hours. They're a bit longer, but you would be properly recompensed for any overtime. Also, I often work at home, so I would need you to be there with me at certain times. I also give a lot of dictation. You do know how to take shorthand, don't you?'

'Oh yes, I do. As I said, Brenda has trained me for the last year, and I'm a good typist as well. Brenda says I'm a fast learner when it comes to office work.'

'That's good to know. Anita wants to give a week's notice. Today is Monday, so I expect she'll leave on Friday. That only gives you four days with her, Glynnis. However, I might be able to persuade her to stay an extra week. That's really up to you.'

'If I can start working with her this morning, Mrs Harte, I believe I can be ready by Friday to take over . . .' Glynnis stopped, and gave Emma a worried look, biting her lip.

Emma said, 'Is something wrong?'

'It's the other two juniors who work with Anita. Do you think they'll be upset? I mean, about me being brought in?'

'I'm sure not, but you can leave me to handle

things diplomatically. Now, tell me a little bit about yourself, Glynnis. How old are you?'

'I'm nineteen, Mrs Harte, and, as you can guess, I'm Welsh. Mr Harte's always said there's a bit of a lilt in my voice, a bit of the Welsh there. Anyway, I came to work in London in 1938, when I was seventeen. I live with my cousin Gwyneth in Belsize Park Gardens – she's got a little flat there, and I'm sharing with her. My younger brother Emlyn is in the RAF, and my older brother Dylan is in the army. So we're all gone from home at the moment, except for my little sister Elayne, who's back in the Rhondda with my parents.' Glynnis cleared her throat again, and then finished, 'Oh, and I'm single, Mrs Harte.'

Emma nodded. 'Thank you, Glynnis, for filling me in. Now, perhaps we'd better talk to Anita, get you started this morning. The sooner the better.'

CHAPTER THIRTY-ONE

By the end of Tuesday afternoon Emma knew how right her brother had been about Glynnis Jenkins. Aside from the fact that the Welsh girl was willing and efficient, she had a way about her that was most appealing. This had a lot to do with her personality, which was warm and outgoing, and Glynnis had a great deal of natural charm.

Emma found her pleasing to have around. She was lovely to look at, and a deep and sincere person, with nice manners and a gentle, rather quiet demeanour. It seemed to Emma that she was brighter than average, and certainly not afraid of hard work or long hours. 'Glynnis is quite a find,' she said to Winston on the phone. 'And unless I'm very mistaken, I think she's going to be around here for a long time.'

Winston laughed knowingly. 'I told you, Emma, I knew you'd want to keep her. There's something about her that's . . . quite irresistible, that's the only word I can think of, to be honest. I used to believe she was too good to be true, but I discovered she's the real thing: a genuinely *nice* young woman.'

'She has a lot going for her,' Emma murmured. 'I'm grateful to have her, Winston, thanks so much.' Then, changing the subject, she asked, 'Would you like to come to supper?'

'I would. But on one condition.'

'Oh, and what's that?'

'I don't want you faffing around in the kitchen with Mrs Coddington. Let her make the dinner and I'll come.'

'Don't you like my cooking any more? You used to,' she shot back.

'I do, but you work too hard to start preparing meals when you get home. Anyway, what I'd like for dinner is a very simple dish. Cottage pie and peas, which Mrs Coddington can make by herself.'

Emma laughed. 'That's it? Nothing to start with?'

'Whatever you like, as long as it's not soup.'

'I'll see you around six, Winston, and the rest of the dinner will remain a surprise.'

After she had hung up the receiver, Emma stacked her briefcase with reports and balance sheets, and walked across her office. As she went out into the secretarial area adjoining, Glynnis instantly jumped to her feet behind her desk, and said, 'Is there anything I can do for you, Mrs Harte?'

'No, no, but thank you, Glynnis. I'm a little tired today and so I decided to go home early. I can easily do a little work there.'

'Shall I come with you, Mrs Harte?'

'That's very sweet of you to offer, but there's not much you could do for me, to be honest. I'm taking home a pile of reading. But thank you for offering.'

Glynnis gave her a shy smile. 'You just have to say the word, and I'll be there.'

'Thanks again, Glynnis.' Emma smiled in return and left the executive offices.

Tomkins was waiting in front of the store, and as Emma got into the Rolls, assisted by the store's doorman, she picked up at once on the gloomy atmosphere that prevailed. 'Hello, Tomkins.'

'Good afternoon, Mrs Harte.'

'I'm going straight home.'

'Yes, madam.'

'The news is not too good today, is it?' she said, settling back against the seat.

'Never been worse, Mrs H. The whole bloomin' country's been knocked back on its ar—.' He coughed, and swiftly corrected himself. 'Knocked on its behind. Nobody thought the Frenchies were going to . . . collapse the way they did. We're on our own now, madam. It's just us against the Nazis.'

'We'll be all right, Tomkins.'

'We don't have much choice, Mrs H. It's beat them afore they beat us.'

'Are you thinking of leaving me, Tomkins? Joining up, maybe?'

'Oh no, Mrs Harte. I'm not A1 fit, otherwise I

might go in the army. Act'lly, I've got flat feet, Mrs H. Not serious when it comes to driving a car and life in civvie street, but they don't like flat-footed soldiers in the army. Oh no.'

'I understand,' Emma murmured, trying not to laugh. There were times when Tomkins was quite droll; she often had to stifle a chuckle.

But he was right. The news was not only bad, it was disastrous. The French High Command had fled Paris several days ago, and the Germans had marched into the capital and captured Paris without one shot being fired.

They were indeed on their own, as Tomkins had just said so dourly, and the whole of England was traumatized by the news that their only ally was no longer fighting alongside them.

'Hello, Mummy darling!' Elizabeth exclaimed as Emma came through the front door of the Belgravia house. Running across the marble foyer, she embraced her mother most enthusiastically, and then said, 'I hope you don't mind, but I've decided to move in with you. I've come *home*, Mummy.'

'So I see,' Emma replied, smiling as she glanced around at the suitcases scattered across the hall. 'What about your little flat in Chelsea?'

'I've given it up. It was all right for one person, but Tony can hardly *fit* into it, and anyway, he's not likely to get any leave soon, not with what's going on in France.' Elizabeth blew out air, and continued in a rush of words, 'Besides, he'll be much more comfortable *here* when he does get leave, don't you think? And anyway, Mummy, I didn't want you to be lonely.'

Emma glanced away to hide a smile; Elizabeth was so transparent, and at times so without guile. 'I'm happy you've come home. And you're always welcome, darling . . . you're a tonic to have around. Let's ask Grace to help us upstairs with your luggage.'

'Oh, she's up in my room already, unpacking for me, Mummy. I'll carry some more of the cases, don't you worry. We can do it together, Grace and I.' Hurrying to the bottom of the grand curving staircase, Elizabeth picked up two bags and started to climb the stairs. Halfway up she stopped, and turned around. 'I forgot, Uncle Frank called. He's invited himself to sups, and he hopes that's all right. He said Uncle Winston had told him about the cottage pie and peas and he couldn't help but invite himself.'

'I see. I'd better go and talk to Cook, explain about the guests and the cottage pie.'

'Oh, I already did that!' Elizabeth cried. 'I thought I'd better alert her. I hope you don't mind, but Uncle Frank said you'd left the office and I didn't know where you were. Actually, I didn't realize you were on your way home. You're usually so late at the store.'

'I felt a bit tired,' Emma explained.

'Are you all right? You're not ill or anything, are you?' There was a surprised note in Elizabeth's voice, and her expression was worried. She remained standing on the stairs, gazing down at her mother.

'I'm not ill, Elizabeth. Only a bit tired. Now scoot, get unpacked and settled in. Are you sure you don't want me to help you?'

'No, you go and have a rest. I can manage.'

Frank Harte was thrilled to see his sister looking so well tonight. He watched her closely, with much love in his heart, as she moved lithely around the small library of her house.

Emma was wearing a white silk shirt, man-tailored, with long, full sleeves, and a pair of well-cut black linen trousers, and he thought she looked superbly elegant. And glamorous, with her new shorter hairdo and subtle make-up that enhanced her great natural beauty.

When he had last seen her two weeks ago, he had noticed the new hairstyle and also that she had put away her black mourning clothes, and this had made a vast improvement in her appearance. But this evening she was finally back to looking like her old self, he decided, and this pleased him.

He had worried about his sister excessively for the last nine months, ever since he had been the one to break the news to her about Paul McGill's unexpected death. He would never forget that terrible night as long as he lived. She had gone into shock, and at times seemed so demented he wondered aloud to Winston whether she would ever come out of it. The two of them had kept vigil over her for hours, until she had fallen into a drugged sleep.

Emma was implacable, and she had a will of iron, and after weeks of searing grief she had suddenly taken total control of her feelings and pulled herself together.

'I have Paul's child to look after, to bring up,' she had said to him one afternoon. 'Our daughter needs me, and I mustn't fail her, Frank. I'm all she has.' From that moment on she had displayed nothing but self-discipline, unselfishness and practicality. Of course the latter came very easily to her, Frank was the first to know that. Emma was an absolute pragmatist – had been since they were children growing up together in Fairley village on top of the Yorkshire moors.

Fairley village . . . good God, he hadn't thought about that place in years. A series of grim pictures flitted through his head, and he shivered involuntarily. But he knew within himself that the village hadn't been quite so dreadful as he sometimes liked to imagine. It was the circumstances of their life there that had been so disheartening at times. Not inside the cottage, where they had all lived so happily together, but outside, where the disturbances and troubles somehow always affected *them*.

And then there were the memories of the terrible things that had happened . . . memories so clear, so vivid, so heartbreaking: Their mother's untimely death, Winston running away to join the navy when he was underage, then Emma's strange disappearance, and finally his father's tragic and unnecessary death.

In the inner recesses of his mind, Frank remembered with total clarity the day his father had rushed into the burning woollen shed at Fairley mill . . . to rescue Edwin Fairley, trapped beneath burning bales of wool and a fallen beam. Big Jack Harte, their father, had not thought of himself, only of rescuing the young master. He had pulled Edwin out of that fiery wreckage and been badly burned himself in the process. Their father had died a few days later from his burns and excessive smoke inhalation. And Frank had been left on his own; well, not actually alone, since there had been Auntie Lily to look after him.

Deep within himself Frank could not abide the name Fairley, and he had, over the years, secretly and silently cheered Emma on as she had slowly ruined the Fairleys and acquired everything that had belonged to them. She had even bought that hideous mansion, Fairley Hall, where she had once been employed as the kitchen maid. But wisely, Frank had always thought, she had torn that house down, brick by brick, until there was nothing left standing, and all the memories were expunged. And eventually she had turned the grounds of Fairley Hall into a park for the villagers, and named it in memory of their mother, Elizabeth Harte. Today Emma owned Fairley village in its entirety: the Fairley mill, the Fairley brickyard;

everything that had once been theirs was now hers . . .

'Champagne, Frankie?'

He stared at Emma, a brow lifting. She hadn't called him Frankie since he was a boy . . . had she somehow zeroed in on his thoughts, albeit unconsciously? he wondered. 'I'd like that, Emma,' he said at last. 'Do you have any of the Pol Roger left?'

'I certainly do, and it's sitting over there in the ice bucket.' She smiled at him, and glided across to the console, where bottles of alcohol and crystal glasses were kept. She opened the bottle carefully. 'And I think I know who got *you* into the habit of drinking Pol Roger,' she murmured as she popped the cork.

'You like it, too.'

'I do, Frank. But I was referring to the great man. Didn't he start you on this particular brand?'

'By great man, I am assuming you mean the Beaver?'

'Not actually, Frankie, although I'm the first to agree with you that Lord Beaverbrook is a great man and a wonderful newspaper publisher-proprietor. I think the *Daily Express* gets better every day.'

Frank grinned knowingly. 'Now that the Beaver's back in government, the Churchill government to be exact, the slant of the paper is powerfully for Winston, rather than against him. I think that's who you're referring to, isn't it?'

Emma simply smiled again, and carried two flutes of Pol Roger over to Frank, who was sitting next to the open window on this warm June evening. He took one and raised it to her.

They clinked glasses and said 'cheers' together, and then Emma sat down in the chair opposite her brother. 'I *was* referring to the Prime Minister when I mentioned Pol Roger, that's true. You told me he had served that at lunch the day you went to interview him over two years ago, when he was still in . . . *limbo*, I suppose one would call it.'

'He did serve it, yes, and I did acquire a taste for it. You're right . . . what a great man he is, Emm. For six years, no, longer even, he warned us and the world that Germany was rearming and dangerous. Nobody listened—'

'But they certainly do now!' she interjected.

Frank nodded. 'Do you like the way the paper's looking?'

'I do, Frank. It's very modern, very clean. That's Arthur Christiansen's doing, isn't it?'

'That's correct. He's a wonderful chap, we all like him. He's a fine editor, and he has certainly given me my head, with the blessing of the Beaver, of course, who gets to read every piece I write before Chris can let it go. Control, eh?, wouldn't you say? But it doesn't bother me, we're all of like mind these days. Just let's win this bloody war.'

'What's the feeling in Fleet Street . . . about Churchill?' Emma now asked, looking at Frank carefully, giving him a long, hard stare, always keen to get his opinion.

'He's damned popular these days, Winston is.'

'Are you talking about me?' Winston Harte asked, as he came into the room, grinning from ear to ear.

'I was talking about Winston as in Churchill, not as in Harte,' Frank said, jumping up, going to shake Winston's hand. The brothers half embraced, quickly, and Winston moved across the room, went to sit in one of the chairs near a small end table.

Watching him walk slowly, leaning on his stick, Emma decided that his limp was more pronounced than it had been for quite a while. When he was in the Royal Navy he had lost his leg towards the end of the Great War; he had fought to keep it but he had lost the battle in the end. Shrapnel had been embedded in the calf of his left leg; even though the shrapnel had been removed, the leg had not properly healed. Gangrene had set in and travelled rapidly up his leg, and it was only because of Emma's intervention that he had lived. She had forced him to agree to the amputation of his leg when the gangrene was already above his knee and travelling fast. She thought now of the months afterwards and his recuperation, and how he had learned to wear an artificial leg made of aluminium, to stomach the pain of it, to endure the endless, torturous hours of learning to walk on it. Long after those long endless months, she had thought of her brother as one of the bravest men she had ever met. She had witnessed his pain and his suffering and what it had taken, and her heart had gone out to him. But he had mastered the artificial limb, and most people thought he merely had a stiff leg.

Now she said, 'Is your leg troubling you, Winston?'

He shook his head. 'Not really, our Emm. Sometimes it's a bit sore . . . the heat in the summer. It gets to me.' He paused, then added, 'My stump gets sore. But I'm all right, really. However, I would like a drink, love, I'm rather thirsty. It's very close tonight.'

'Winston, I'm sorry darling! Champagne? Or a Scotch?'

'I'll have a bit of the bubbly tonight, it's lighter than Scotch. Not that there's anything to celebrate, not with the current war news. France has gone. It has evaporated as our ally, and we are truly alone now.'

'The Prime Minister is going to broadcast tonight,' Frank announced, looking from one to the other. 'He gave a magnificent speech in the House this afternoon, and he's repeating it later, on the BBC. He wants the whole country to hear it.'

'Oh but we *must* listen,' Emma exclaimed, sitting up alertly.

Elizabeth said, from the doorway, 'Yes, Mummy, it's just been announced again. Mr Churchill is going to be on the radio tonight. At nine o'clock, I think.'

'Come in, darling, and say hello to your uncles.'

Smiling, Elizabeth entered the library as if gliding on air, and Emma's brothers stood up, greeted her affectionately, embracing her with great warmth and love. They each believed that Emma's daughter looked like their mother, Elizabeth Harte, and it endeared her to them even more.

Grace served plates of smoked salmon with lemon wedges, and thin slices of brown bread and butter, and Frank poured white wine in the tall, ruby-tinted crystal goblets. And once Grace had disappeared into the kitchen, the family began to eat the fresh Scottish salmon, as Emma talked about food shortages and rationing, and ate very little.

'Mummy, you sound like the voice of doom,' Elizabeth said at one moment, looking across the table. 'Things seem fine in some areas . . .'

'I'm afraid the difficult days are coming, Elizabeth, and we're going to have to tighten our belts all around. I spoke to Mr Ramsbotham today and suggested that he plant a few allotments at Pennistone Royal. Everybody's starting them, you know; growing vegetables. I also suggested he use the three greenhouses to grow tomatoes and perhaps some soft fruits, rather than orchids and exotic flowers. Much more useful, don't you think?'

'It's amazing, you know, how people *do* pull together,' Winston murmured. 'I know that half the women in the Leeds store have started knitting scarves, mittens and balaclava helmets for the troops in their spare time. I think it's quite remarkable the way everyone has become less selfish.'

'I do, too,' Emma agreed. 'And you've been very unselfish, Winston, letting me have Glynnis.'

'Who's Glynnis?' Elizabeth asked, always curious; she was renowned in the family for asking lots of questions.

'She's my new secretary.'

'What happened to Anita, Mummy?'

'She's going to join the Land Army. She's leaving the store on Friday, and I think it's most commendable of her.'

'Anita in the Land Army! She'll never be able to lift a shovel, she's so delicate and petite!' Elizabeth cried.

Emma chuckled. 'There's a certain truth to that, Elizabeth, but she's very determined, and that can go a long way.'

'So you've discovered Glynnis's qualities in just two days,' Frank murmured, glancing at Emma.

'I certainly have. She's going to be very good for me, I can tell that already, and we have a lot of traits in common.'

This remark startled Elizabeth, who asked swiftly, 'Such as what?'

'She's quick, to begin with, and very willing. Not afraid of hard work. Determined, punctual, well organized, tidy. All the things I am.' Looking across at Frank, she raised a brow and asked, 'Do you know Glynnis, Frank?'

'I don't actually *know* her, Emm. But I've met

her a few times when I've gone to pick Winston up, and he told me that she was now working for you when we spoke on the phone this afternoon.'

'Oh, I see. She's very—' Emma shook her head. 'Appealing . . . no, *beguiling*, that's a better word.'

'I'll say!' Winston exclaimed.

Emma stared at him but made no comment, although she was surprised at the overtones of admiration echoing in her brother's voice.

The four of them talked about things in general after this, and Grace removed the dirty plates, served the cottage pie, and accepted, on behalf of Cook, the praise offered by Emma's brothers. 'Tell her it's as good as the one Mrs Harte usually makes,' Frank said, once they had all finished.

'I will, sir,' Grace murmured as she hurried out.

'It's jam roll with custard for pudding,' Elizabeth announced, looking at her uncles. 'I know you like it . . . Mummy told me.'

'A perfect choice,' Winston replied, smiling at her warmly. Like his brother, he tended to spoil his niece, who bore such a striking resemblance to their mother Elizabeth before she had fallen ill with consumption in 1904. This is how Mam would have looked if she had been well cared for and well off, Winston thought, as he quietly studied Elizabeth. Poor Mam, she never had a chance, what with the poverty and the hard work. Winston pushed aside the sadness, suddenly not wanting to dwell on the past.

'I think we should have coffee in the den,' Emma

said, looking from Winston to Frank. 'After the pudding, of course. We can relax and wait for the broadcast. It's comfortable in there.'

And so as soon as dinner was finished, they all trooped into the den situated just beyond the library. It was a pleasant room of medium size, decorated in shades of dark red and a rich deep green, furnished with comfortable armchairs and two love seats, plus a small Georgian desk where Emma sometimes worked. Silk-shaded brass lamps, a few lovely paintings and decorative objects gave the room a certain cosiness and charm.

Emma turned the radio on as everyone sat down, drinking their coffee as they waited to hear the Prime Minister.

They fell silent as the BBC announcer introduced Churchill. His rich and eloquent voice boomed out into the small den. Emma, sitting next to the radio, concentrated on every word he said. It was a long and detailed speech, and there was total silence in the den as her two brothers and her daughter paid the strictest attention to the Prime Minister's words.

As he came to the end, Emma leaned forward slightly, clasping her hands together, waiting for his final words.

The Prime Minister paused for a split second, and then finished: 'What General Weygand called the Battle of France is over. I expect that the Battle of Britain is about to begin. Upon this battle depends the survival of Christian civilization. Upon

433

it depends our own British life, and the long continuity of our institutions and our Empire. The whole fury and might of the enemy must very soon be turned on us. Hitler knows that he will have to break us in this Island or lose the war. If we can stand up to him, all Europe may be free and the life of the world may move forward into broad, sunlit uplands. But if we fail, then the whole world, including the United States, including all that we have known and cared for, will sink into the abyss of a new Dark Age made more sinister, and perhaps more protracted, by the lights of perverted science. Let us therefore brace ourselves to our duties and so bear ourselves that, if the British Empire and its Commonwealth last for a thousand years, men will still say, "This was their finest hour."'

There was a long silence in the den, and finally it was Frank who said softly, 'Well, he's said it all, as he always does. And he's made it very clear . . . now that France has fallen, Britain does stand alone.'

'I think what he just said is inspiring, and comforting in a way,' Emma remarked, looking across at Frank, flicking the tears off her face with her fingertips. Clearing her throat, she added in a voice full of tears, 'He's told us what we have to do. We have to stand up and fight with all our might . . . and I know we will all do that.'

'Yes, I agree,' Winston interjected. 'And you can bet the entire country listened to him tonight, just as we did. He's all we've got. To inspire us, to lead us, to show us the way.'

'We do have the troops we rescued from Dunkirk,' Frank pointed out. 'They will help to defend us, all 250,000 of them. In the meantime, we'd better prepare.'

'For the Battle of Britain,' Emma said. 'And some battle it's going to be.'

CHAPTER THIRTY-TWO

Later that night Emma was unable to sleep, and she finally got up, put on a dressing gown and went downstairs to the den. She sat at her desk for a short while, reading some of the balance sheets she had brought home with her, but other thoughts soon intruded, and concentration fled.

Thoughts of the war and the invasion were uppermost in her mind for a few minutes, and then, quite unexpectedly, an image of Paul danced before her eyes. She sat back in the chair, staring into space, seeing him very clearly; much more vividly than she had in months. It seemed to her that he was actually in the room with her, coming towards her. She sat very still, waiting. Then the image was gone in a flash, just like that, as if it had never been there.

'Paul,' she said out loud, and rose from the chair, glancing towards the open door as she did. She was quite alone, she knew that, but nevertheless she hurried out to the corridor, looked up and down. Naturally it was empty. And yet she could not shake off the feeling that he had been there with her, if only for a brief second. He had seemed so very real. Nothing like this had ever happened to her before, and she leaned against the door jamb, wondering suddenly if she were losing her mind. But of course she wasn't: it was her imagination playing tricks on her.

Almost against her own volition, she walked down the corridor, opened a door that led to a small foyer and the lift that went down to the bachelor flat which had been Paul's. This was situated on the ground floor of the mansion, with its own entrance at the side of the house. The actual front door in Belgrave Square led into the grand foyer of Emma's maisonette, built on the three floors above the self-contained bachelor flat.

Going down in the lift to his flat, Emma thought of the year he had bought the mansion, given her the deeds, and then set about creating the two apartments within the house. It had been 1925. 'It's much more discreet,' he had explained, and then he had grinned at her in that rather cheeky-little-boy fashion of his, and had added, 'Naturally, I'll be living in the maisonette with you and Daisy. My bachelor flat is for appearance's sake.' She remembered smiling to herself at the time, wondering who on earth he thought he was fooling with two separate establishments. Everyone knew they were together.

But he had used it from time to time, mostly when he wanted to work long hours, or to entertain business colleagues. She had rarely gone down there, and certainly only once since his death. But tonight, somehow, she had a compulsion to be in these rooms. She was not sure why. It would not bring him closer, because he had mostly been in the upper portion of the house with her and their child, and that is where she felt his presence most. And yet . . . something pulled her there . . .

Stepping out of the lift, she turned on the lights in the little foyer and was instantly struck by the wonderful masculine look of the wood-panelled walls, the dark burgundy carpet, the mahogany console table set between two straight-backed Georgian side chairs.

His favourite room had been the library, with its dark green brocade walls and French Empire antiques. He had always worked there, and she walked in, switched on a lamp and stepped across to his desk. She ran her hand along the highly polished mahogany surface, and stared for a moment at a photograph of her and Daisy with Paul, and then she sat down in his chair. Leaning back, she closed her eyes and thought of him, remembering so many things, and for a few minutes so much of the past came rushing back . . . remembrances of little things . . . forgotten things . . . and the tears came then . . . She put her head down on the desk and let them flow unchecked, and she wept in a way she had not wept since Frank had rushed to this house from Fleet Street nine months ago, bringing with him the UP wire story which told of Paul's suicide . . .

'Mummy, are you all right?'

On hearing Elizabeth's voice, Emma slowly lifted her head and looked towards the door, where her daughter was standing. For a moment she could not speak.

Elizabeth came into the library, hesitantly, staring at her mother's tear-stained face, her heart going out to her. 'Oh Mummy, you're grieving for Paul . . .'

Emma simply nodded. She was racked by dry sobs.

Elizabeth murmured softly, 'I woke up, I felt so alone, and worried about Tony. And Kit and Robin, and so I came to your bedroom . . . I didn't know where you were until I saw the door in the corridor wide open.' Moving closer to her mother, she put her hand on Emma's shoulder gently, and whispered against her hair, 'I wish I could help you . . . I love you so much, Mummy . . .'

Turning, Emma put her arms around her daughter's body and held her tightly, trying to control her swimming senses, her emotions. Eventually the sobs subsided, and she pulled away, and said in a choked voice, 'I don't usually let go like that. I'm sorry, darling.'

'You mustn't be sorry. You must grieve, you've got to get it out . . . that's what Uncle Winston said to me months ago. He said I was trying to be far too brave about Paul's death . . .'

Emma looked up at Elizabeth, standing there in her pale blue dressing gown matching exactly the colour of her eyes, and she nodded slowly. 'I know you loved him.'

'I did. He was like a father to me. And to Robin. Certainly more of a father than Arthur Ainsley ever was.'

'I know, and Paul loved you and Robin, thought of you both as his own.'

'Perhaps we'd better go back upstairs.' Elizabeth looked at Emma, her expression one of puzzlement. 'What were you doing down here?'

'I don't really know. I felt I had to come to the library, but there's really nothing here.' She took a deep breath and said in a voice that suddenly faltered, 'All of the memories are upstairs . . . that's where we lived together.'

'Then come on, let's go back. It's silly staying down here, don't you think?'

Emma nodded and stood up, and Elizabeth led her out, turning off the lights as they left the library and then the little foyer, and stepped into the lift.

Once they were back in the maisonette, Elizabeth said, 'Go up to your bedroom, Mummy, and I'll go and make us some hot chocolate. Don't you think that would be nice?'

'Yes, darling, thank you,' Emma replied, suddenly feeling ice cold as she hurried to her bedroom on the next floor.

*   *   *

A short while later, Elizabeth hurried into Emma's bedroom carrying two beakers of hot chocolate on a silver tray. After giving one of the beakers to her mother, Elizabeth took the other one for herself, put the tray on the floor and climbed into bed with Emma.

'The hot chocolate's going to warm you up. You felt very cold downstairs in Paul's flat,' Elizabeth told her, sinking back into the pillows. 'I'm so glad I moved in here today, Mummy. We'll be able to keep each other company when I'm not working at night.'

'It's nice to have you here,' Emma said softly, and took a sip of the hot chocolate. She was considerably calmer, the tears having abated, although she was still somewhat puzzled as to why she had felt impelled to venture down to the ground-floor flat tonight.

After a small silence, Elizabeth said in a tentative, rather nervous voice, 'Mother, can I ask you something?'

'Of course you can.' Emma glanced at her, frowning. 'You sound very serious.'

'It's a serious question,' Elizabeth answered quickly, 'and perhaps I ought not to ask it.' She cleared her throat several times. 'Actually, Mummy, I don't think you're going to like it at all.'

'Well, you'd better ask it and then we'll see, won't we?'

Elizabeth bit her lip, made a small grimace. After

a pause, and a sigh, she said slowly, 'It's very personal . . . perhaps I'd better not.'

'Come along, darling, he who hesitates is lost. What is it you want to know?'

'Well, it's about Daisy.'

'*Oh*. What about her?' Emma looked at her daughter alertly.

'She's not my *full* sister, is she?'

Emma gaped at her.

Elizabeth, seeing Emma's startled expression, hurried on, 'She's not Arthur Ainsley's child, is she?'

It was Emma's turn to hesitate, but only for a split second. 'No, she's not, even though she bears his name. And you're right, she's your half-sister.' Emma answered in a steady voice, knowing only the truth would do now.

'She's Paul's daughter, isn't she, Mother?'

Emma nodded.

'I've thought so for quite a long time, and so has Robin. But we never dared ask you.'

'And what gave you the courage tonight?' Emma stared at Elizabeth, her vivid green eyes narrowing slightly as they grew flinty.

'I felt suddenly very close to you downstairs, Mummy, and I know I'm much more grown-up these days. And the world's falling apart around us, and the boys are in danger; actually, everyone's in danger. And, oh what the hell, Mummy, why does it matter that her father's Paul?'

'I know what you mean, Elizabeth. The times

have suddenly been turned upside down, and the world seems to be in chaos, and we're about to be invaded. Suddenly we all know what our real priorities are. However, I do think it matters to me, and more importantly, to Daisy, because she doesn't know Paul is her father. And you mustn't tell her.'

'Are you sure she doesn't know?' Elizabeth sounded sceptical.

'*Positive*. Why are you staring at me like that?'

'But she *looks* so much like him. Don't you think she realizes that, Mother?'

'No, I don't. Now you must promise me that you will not betray my confidence in you by telling her,' Emma insisted.

Elizabeth exclaimed irately, 'I would never break a confidence, Mother! You always taught me to be honourable. And I won't tell Robin, if you don't want me to.'

'I'd prefer to tell him myself when the time is right,' Emma replied.

'You *are* going to tell Daisy who her father is, was, I mean, aren't you?'

'Yes, when she's older. She's only fifteen, Elizabeth. Sometimes I think you forget that.'

'Well she seems a lot older, perhaps because she was always with you and Paul, and never with children her own age.'

'That's silly, she was with you and Robin a great deal of the time.'

'But we were away at school . . . latterly, anyway.'

'That's true. And of course I will tell her, how could you ever think I wouldn't? Any child would be proud to claim Paul McGill as their father.'

'I am,' Elizabeth said, and squeezed her mother's hand. 'He was so good to us . . . Robin feels the same way.'

'Yes . . .' Emma's voice trailed off, and she put the beaker down on the bedside table, leant back against the mound of pillows, closing her eyes.

Elizabeth now fell silent, and so did Emma, and mother and daughter were lost, for a while, in their own thoughts. It was Elizabeth who broke the silence between them when she said, 'I think Edwina is being rather beastly, the way she is hiding herself away in the bogs of Ireland, incommunicado. I do think she could have brought her husband to meet us, and brought the baby over, too. After all, you're the child's grandmother. Don't you agree, Mummy?'

'It would have been nice, Elizabeth, but Edwina's rather angry these days, and most especially with me. I don't think we'll be seeing her soon, I really don't.'

'It's her loss, and she's such a fool. I don't think she has a right to be angry. You've been a wonderful mother to all of us. We've been lucky.'

'I'm glad you think that, darling.'

'Why did Paul kill himself?'

The question, coming out of the blue, shocked Emma, threw her, and it took her a few moments to recover. 'This is the first time you've ever admitted you knew that . . . I thought you all believed Paul had died of his injuries.'

'Not really, Mummy.'

'He knew he wouldn't have long to live . . .' Emma began. 'There was no way to treat him. He would have died of kidney failure in a few months . . . he knew he couldn't get back here in time to see us. I suppose he wanted to take control of his life again . . . his destiny.'

'I see.'

Emma was silent, thinking about Paul's last letter, wondering if she should show it to Elizabeth. She was a married woman now, and living with the dangers of war, and much more grown-up than she had been even a few months ago. And yet Emma hesitated. The letter was so very personal, meant for her eyes only. And perhaps one day for Daisy's. No, she would not get it out of the casket. Not yet, not tonight . . .

But much later, when she was alone, Emma got out of bed and went to her dressing room. She unlocked the fruitwood-and-silver casket which stood on a chest and took out the letter which had arrived from Australia just after Paul's death. Then she returned to the bedroom.

Sitting down on the bed, she took the letter out of its envelope and read it again, as she had read it so many times before:

My dearest darling Emma:
You are my life. I cannot live without my

445

life. But I cannot live with you. And so I must
end my miserable existence, for there is no
future for us together now. Lest you think my
suicide an act of weakness, let me reassure you
that it is not. It is an act of strength and of
will, for committing it I gratefully take back
that control over myself which I have lost in
the past few months. It is a final act of power
over my own fate.

It is the only way out for me, my love,
and I will die with your name on my lips, the
image of you before my eyes, my love for you
secure in my heart always. We have been lucky,
Emma. We have had so many good years
together and shared so much, and the happy
memories are alive in me, as I know they are
in you, and will be as long as you live. I thank
you for giving me the best years of my life.

I did not send for you because I did not
want you to be tied to a helpless cripple, if
only for a few months at the most. Perhaps I
was wrong. On the other hand, I want you to
remember me as I was, and not what I have
become since the accident. Pride? Maybe. But
try to understand my reasons, and try, my
darling, to find it in your heart to forgive me.

I have great faith in you, my dearest Emma.
You are not faint of heart. You are strong and
dauntless, and you will go on courageously.
You must. For there is our child to consider.
She is the embodiment of our love, and I know

446

*you will cherish and care for her, and bring her
up to be as brave and as stalwart and as loving
as you are yourself. I give her into your trust,
my darling.*

*By the time you receive this I will be dead.
But I will live on in Daisy. She is your future
now, my Emma. And mine.*

*I love you with all my heart and soul and
mind, and I pray to God that one day we will
be reunited in Eternity.*

I kiss you, my darling.

Paul

Emma sat for a moment, holding the letter in her
hands . . . such small hands, Paul had always said
to her. The tears rolled down her cheeks, and
she thought her heart was breaking once again.
But deep within herself she knew she had been
correct to read yet again his last letter to her. It
had reminded her of her duty to Daisy, and to her
other children as well. And it had also reminded
her of the stuff she was made of: *steel*.

Once she had returned the letter to the casket,
locked it, and pocketed the silver key, Emma went
to the desk in a corner of her bedroom. After sitting
down, she took out her diary and opened the page
for 18 June 1940.

She made a short entry:

*The Prime Minister spoke tonight. He reiterated that France
has fallen, and warned us that the Battle of Britain is about*

to begin. We cannot allow ourselves to be broken by Hitler. We must not be defeated. Those were the sentiments he expressed. And so we must be courageous, stalwart, dauntless. Paul's last letter to me reminded me of that when I re-read it tonight. We must draw on our inner resources. We cannot fail or we are lost. Churchill will show us the way. I have faith in him.

My beautiful Elizabeth moved back home, so that we can share our loneliness, help each other in these difficult times. She is a good daughter. I am lucky to have her. I have decided Daisy must stay at boarding school. She is safer in the country. Winston and Frank came to supper. What would I do without my loyal and loving brothers? We must pull together now that we are about to be invaded.

Emma closed the diary and put it away. Then she went to bed. But she did not sleep. Her mind was too preoccupied with thoughts of the days ahead, and the plans she would have to make for her family, her employees and the stores themselves. Everyone and everything had to be protected. The defence of Britain was about to begin.

She tossed and turned all night, and only fell asleep finally as dawn broke.

CHAPTER THIRTY-THREE

'Come on, Glynnis, we'd better make a run for it!' Emma cried. 'They're going to start dropping their bombs any minute.' As she spoke Emma rushed across Belgrave Square, making for her house on the far corner.

Glynnis followed in her wake, her high heels clattering against the pavement as she raced to catch up, all the while marvelling at Emma Harte's fast sprint across the square. Her boss was quite extraordinary.

The sirens were wailing, warning them of an imminent air raid, but in fact the Luftwaffe was already immediately overhead, the planes roaring across the skies of London on one of their day-light raids.

The ARP warden on the corner caught sight of them both, and shouted out, 'Hurry up, Mrs Harte! Go inside as quick as you can. Get down in your cellar! It's the safest place.'

'We will, Norman, you can be sure of that,'

Emma called back. 'And if you need to shelter, please come and join us.'

'Right, I will, Mrs H.' The warden indicated that they should be quick, waving his hands at them, shooing them on, before turning away, his attention suddenly caught elsewhere.

Glynnis hurried after Emma up the steps of the house and through the front door, closing it behind her. They both stood for a moment in the grand marble entrance foyer, catching their breath.

'I think we made it just in time,' Emma muttered at the sound of a loud explosion not far away, and then the shattering of glass. A split second later there were several more explosions and Emma and Glynnis exchanged apprehensive looks. 'They've made several hits,' Emma said, shaking her head, looking alarmed. 'But so far they've managed to miss us. Keep your fingers crossed.'

The entrance foyer was devoid of furniture, except for an ornate French console table set against a side wall under a French gilded mirror, and a French Louis XV bench on the opposite wall. A crystal chandelier hung from the slightly domed ceiling, and a grand curving staircase led up to Emma's maisonette.

Aside from the front door, there was only one other door in the foyer, and this was set in the wall underneath the staircase. Emma now hurried to this door, opened it and went down a steep flight of steps. Glynnis followed; the stairs led them to the small hallway of Paul's bachelor flat.

'From here we take the lift to the cellar,' Emma said, and beckoned to Glynnis. Together, the two women rode down to the basement; when the lift stopped they stepped out into Paul McGill's extensive, well-stocked wine cellar.

Glancing at the walls and walls of wine racks, Emma said, with a small sigh, 'I think I'd better have my brothers come for some of this. It's all vintage, much of it very rare. I'd much rather they and their friends drank it than have the Germans drop bombs on it. Now . . . we go through this arch, Glynnis, and here we are in the air-raid shelter.'

'Is that you, Mrs Harte?' a voice called out nervously, echoing hollowly in the vaulted cellar, and all of a sudden there was Grace peering at them from behind a pillar.

'Yes, it's me, Grace. I have Glynnis with me.' Emma hurried through into the new air-raid shelter, which had recently been built by Blackie O'Neill. It was completely reinforced using steel girders and concrete-and-steel pillars; sandbags had been stacked against all of the walls as an extra precaution. 'Are you alone?' Emma asked, looking at Grace.

'Yes, Mrs H. Wot 'appened is this. Mrs Coddington never come in today. The docks was bombed again last night, ma'am, and parts of the East End, and 'er sister Ethel's gone and got bombed out. So she went to 'elp her,' the maid explained. 'She phoned, but you was gone . . . to the shop.' Stepping aside, so that Emma could walk over to the desk she had recently brought down to the cellar, Grace continued, 'Cook'll be in termorrow, so she said, ma'am.'

'I understand, and I do hope her sister's family is all right. Nobody's been hurt, have they?' Emma asked anxiously.

'No, her sister was there with their mother, and they're both all right, Mrs H. Ethel's five sons are in the army, the navy and the air force, and her two daughters, Flossie and Violet, are in the land army, so they wasn't there to be 'urt, was they?'

'That's true, Grace. That's one family which is truly doing its bit for the war effort! Most commendable. Goodness, yes!' Emma glanced around and, turning to Glynnis, she said, 'It's not too bad down here, you know.'

'I think it's very nice, Mrs Harte,' Glynnis responded swiftly, 'Air-raid shelters are usually sort of . . . *dismal*. Certainly this is a lot more comfortable than those Anderson shelters everyone's building in their back gardens. My Da has copied the neighbours', and now we have one too. Mum's quite chuffed about it.' Surveying the cellar a little more thoroughly, Glynnis sat down in a chair, and added, 'You've certainly thought of everything. A primus stove for cooking and boiling a kettle. Electric fires for the winter months, plenty of chairs, a rug underfoot, and lots of blankets and pillows.'

'I've also ordered a number of camp beds,' Emma told her.

'And there's a big stock of tinned stuff,' Grace

interjected in a proud voice. 'Baked beans, sardines, red salmon, corned beef, Spam, tomato soup, and a lot of candles, just in case the lights go.'

'Did you get a first-aid box?' Glynnis asked, glancing across at Emma who was already sitting behind the rather ugly, very utilitarian desk.

'Yes, we have a couple down here, but perhaps I'd better order some more. You never know.'

'I'll make a note of it,' Glynnis murmured, and took out a shorthand pad.

In her usual businesslike way, Emma now concentrated on her work. She took a stack of papers out of her briefcase and was soon absorbed in them.

Grace picked up the ladies magazine she had been reading before, and Glynnis pulled out her knitting; she was making a khaki scarf, her second in a week.

The two young women focused on what they were doing, knowing better than to waste their time with idle chatter in front of Emma Harte. In any case, they did not dare say a word to each other when she was working.

As she knitted, Glynnis thought about the war, wondering when it was really going to end. Mrs Harte had told her it would last for quite a few years, and although she hoped Emma was wrong, Glynnis believed her boss was probably right. Emma was a genius when it came to everything else, so how could she be wrong about the duration of war?

The Battle of Britain had begun in June, just after France had fallen, but so far not a lot had happened. The bombing raids had been rather sporadic, and during June and July the whole country had been working hard to ensure the safety of Britain. People were building air-raid shelters in their gardens, reinforcing their cellars, piling sandbags around their shelters and in front of exposed entrances. Candles were bought up in case of electrical shortages; tinned food was stacked up in homes from Dover to the Hebrides. People thought of everything they might need in emergencies and went out and bought it if it was available. Already there were shortages. Gas masks were issued to every citizen, and many people made sure they had tin helmets to protect themselves from falling rubble.

Not many civilians had been killed thus far, either in June or July, but in August the figures had started to rise as the Luftwaffe stepped up its efforts, flying in from its northern French bases to bomb London and the surrounding counties of Kent, Surrey and Sussex. Hitler's aim was to destroy the RAF, now Britain's only real defence, both in the air and on the ground, and also to demolish the factories where the production of Hurricanes, Spitfires and bombers was already in full swing. Daylight raids such as the one today had been relatively infrequent, the German air force preferring to bomb the British Isles at night under cover of dark.

But things had begun to change, and Emma kept telling anyone that would listen that things were going to get worse. And in the next few days she was to be proved right.

After two and a half hours the all-clear siren sounded; even though they were sitting in the cellar under the house they heard it, albeit somewhat faintly, when it went off.

'That's it!' Emma exclaimed, and immediately put her papers back in the briefcase. 'We'd better go up and see what the damage is. Glynnis, Grace, come along.'

Emma was relieved that her house had not been hit, and she was fairly certain that Belgrave Square remained undamaged. Nonetheless, it was with trepidation that she opened the front door and looked out. She was pleasantly surprised to see that the square was entirely intact, although the air was acrid and filled with smoke, and there was the sound of falling rubble from the streets beyond. Obviously many buildings nearby had been heavily bombed.

'I'd better phone Harte's,' Emma said to Glynnis as she stepped back inside and closed the front door. She hurried upstairs to the maisonette and made for her den; within seconds she was talking to the operator at the store. 'It's Mrs Harte, Gertie. Is everything all right?'

'Oh yes, Mrs Harte. The Jerries missed us this time, thank God.'

'I'm glad to hear it. I'll see you on Monday. Have a nice weekend, and a safe one, hopefully.'

'Thanks, Mrs Harte, and the same to you.' Emma turned to Glynnis, who had followed her into the small room she used as an office, and nodded her head. 'The store's still standing, and that's a plus. But there must be an awful lot of damage out there, especially on the docks.'

'Yes, and perhaps some of the factories were hit. We know the Germans are hell-bent on destroying them, slowing down the production of planes,' Glynnis reminded her quietly, looking as worried and concerned as Emma.

'I wonder if there is anything we can do to help?' Emma murmured, but before Glynnis could answer, the phone rang. Emma, who was sitting at the desk, picked it up. 'Hello?'

'Hello, Emma, it's Jane.'

'Jane darling, how are you? I hope everything's all right with you. You haven't been bombed, have you?'

'No, no, fortunately we've escaped again, thank goodness. But Bill just heard that the docks and the East End have taken a terrible beating. Horrendous. Seemingly there's a massive clean-up starting, but he thinks those poor people are going to need help tomorrow.'

'What about right now?' Emma asked swiftly.

'I believe they're going into the tube stations soon to take shelter for the night, and the Red Cross, the St John's Ambulance Brigade and several other agencies are doing quite a lot. But I can't help thinking about tomorrow. It's Sunday, and it seems to me they will need food.'

'Jane, you're right! And I'm on board, if that's what you were going to ask.'

'Well, yes, I was, Emma. I'm going to start making sandwiches tonight, and I thought you could do the same.'

'Of course, but we'll need more than sandwiches. I'll phone Harte's and have the manager of the food halls bring over a few hampers of food. Now, what time are you setting off tomorrow? And where should I go?'

'I'll come around at nine o'clock in the car, and Tomkins can follow me. We'll be going to the East End. And Emma, thank you for this. You're a good woman.'

'I'm glad to help,' Emma murmured, and glanced at her watch. 'I'd better go, Jane, I need to speak to the store, arrange for the food.'

An hour later, Jack Field, the manager of the food halls at Harte's and a favourite of Emma's, stood in the middle of her kitchen in the maisonette, explaining what the collection of wicker hampers contained.

'Every kind of pie, Mrs Harte. Game, chicken, veal-and-ham, and a lot of the small individual pork pies we sell. Cornish pasties, sausage rolls, cold meats for sandwiches, cold chickens, tea biscuits, eggs, mayonnaise, like you requested, and bags of fresh sausages as well as sausage meat.'

'That's excellent, Jack. Now let's unpack the sausages and the ingredients for the sandwiches first . . . oh, and the eggs. I want to make a big batch of egg salad.'

As she moved across the kitchen, Emma beckoned to Glynnis and Grace, and told them, 'Let's get to work. You can get the eggs boiling, Grace, and Glynnis, why don't you help me to fry the sausages? Jack, you can assist with the sandwiches, if you don't mind.'

'Mrs Harte, it's a pleasure to do anything I can, and I'll be here tomorrow morning with the van and driver to go with you to the East End.'

'Thanks, Jack, I appreciate that very much.' Emma, who had earlier changed into a shirt, trousers and flat shoes, now donned an apron, and handed one to Glynnis. 'Thank you for staying,' she said to her secretary. 'It's very good of you, especially on a Saturday night.'

'Oh, Mrs Harte, I'm pleased to be of help. I'd nothing to do that was special. My cousin and I talked about going to the pictures, but we can do that another night.'

Emma was always fast, whatever she was doing, but in a crisis she became a dynamo. And such was the case on this September Saturday night, as she and her team of helpers fried sausages, made Scotch eggs, and prepared hundreds of sandwiches, which they wrapped in dampened white linen napkins to keep them from drying out and going stale overnight.

'These 'ere napkins'll be ruined,' Grace muttered at one moment, looking at Emma reproachfully.

'For heaven's sake that doesn't matter, there's a war on, Grace! I can't worry about napkins at a time like this!' Emma exclaimed, shaking her head, rolling her eyes at the ceiling. 'Just let's keep going, and once we've finished you should all sit down and eat some of the sandwiches and sausages, or the Scotch eggs. And Grace, you must make a pot of tea.'

'That sounds grand, Mrs Harte,' Jack said with a laugh. 'I must admit, I'm getting a bit peckish meself.'

Emma glanced at her watch. 'I'm not surprised, it's turned eight o'clock already. Well, we've almost finished, and you've all done a wonderful job. Thank you very much.'

'We want to help, do our bit,' Glynnis said warmly, smiling at Emma.

'Yes, we must do everything we can to help those who've been bombed out,' Emma answered. 'And Glynnis, please take a taxi home.'

'I will, Mrs Harte. Will you need me tomorrow?'

'It's nice of you to offer, but you must have a rest, it's been a very busy week. I can manage with Jack and Tomkins, I'm quite sure.'

'I can bring one of the chaps from my department,' Jack volunteered. 'Dennis Scott's a good lad, he'll be happy to oblige.'

'That's a good idea, Jack. And now I'll say goodnight to you all.'

'Don't you want a bit of supper, Mrs Harte?' Grace asked.

'Not right now, thanks. I have some work to finish.' She smiled at them and made her way across the kitchen.

'Good night, Mrs Harte,' they chorused as she left.

The following morning Emma set off with Tomkins to the East End, following Jane and Bill Stuart Ogden in their car. The green Harte van, stacked with the hampers and carrying Jack Field and Dennis Scott, was at the rear.

When they arrived at their destination Emma was speechless, as were the rest of their group. The onslaught of bombs had been massive, and the Luftwaffe had done its work well. The streets were levelled, rubble piled everywhere. It was the most horrendous devastation the likes of which none of them had ever seen or indeed even envisioned.

They picked their way slowly and carefully over the rubble, passing out the food, saying comforting words to the men and women who were working in the piles of bricks and dust which had once been their homes.

'Thank you, thank you,' a woman said to Emma at one moment. 'It's right good of you to come and help us.'

Emma's eyes filled, and she was unable to speak; she simply touched the woman's arm gently and walked on.

And yet, despite the loss of their homes and the suffering they had endured, there were cheery smiles on many of the faces, and a frequent disparaging quip about the enemy would ring out, causing much laughter amongst them all.

'How strong our people are,' Jane said as they continued to pick their way across the rubble-strewn streets, distributing the food with Jack Field and Dennis Scott.

'And brave,' Emma added. Suddenly she came to an abrupt halt and grabbed hold of Jane's arm. 'Look! Over there! Everyone's cheering. Isn't that Winston Churchill?'

'Oh my God, it is. Bill, it's the Prime Minister. Look! Look! He's standing over there on that pile of rubble, wearing a funny-looking hat and smoking his cigar.'

Bill Ogden followed Jane's gaze and saw for himself that it was indeed Winston Churchill, a man whom he had admired and been devoted to for many years, always supporting him in the House of Commons.

'Come along, ladies,' Bill said. 'I shall take you over there to have a word with him.'

And this he did.

A few minutes later Bill was greeting the Prime Minister, an old friend and colleague, who turned, smiling, and shook hands with Bill and Jane, and then Emma was introduced to him.

She was so awestruck and overwhelmed Emma could barely speak, but after shaking his hand she managed to say, 'Thank you, Mr Churchill, for inspiring us . . .'

'And thank you,' he answered, obviously realizing what their mission was this morning in the rubble-strewn East End streets.

Later one of the air-raid wardens told Bill that Winston Churchill had had tears in his eyes when he had first viewed this terrible devastation. Emma nodded, knowing that everyone loved him that much more because he was not afraid to show his emotions.

That night, when Elizabeth finally got home from the hospital, Emma saw how tired her daughter looked, and she fussed over her for a while.

'There have been a lot of casualties,' Elizabeth explained, as she and Emma finally sat down to eat sandwiches and drink a cup of tea in Emma's den. 'And this is just the beginning of the Blitz, Mummy. You've been saying it was going to get worse, and you were right.'

'*Unfortunately*. Frankly, I wish I'd been wrong. Our boys are up there in the air every night, fighting the Luftwaffe, and now they'll have to be up there during the day as well.'

'Yesterday's raid was catastrophic,' Elizabeth murmured. 'But we're going to win, Mummy, you've instilled that in me.'

'No, Winston Churchill has, and our fighter pilots are very brave.'

'I'll never forget what Mr Churchill said last

month, when he spoke about the fighter pilots. You won't either, will you, Mummy?'

'No, I won't. Actually, I wrote it in my diary to remind myself. He said, "Never in the field of human conflict was so much owed by so many to so few." As always he got it exactly right, and he said it in his own inimitable way.'

'They will be all right, won't they?' Elizabeth now asked, looking at Emma intently. 'Tony and Robin and Bryan?'

'Yes, they will. I believe that, I truly do, darling. I must believe it, Elizabeth, because if I have any doubts about them surviving this war I'll fall apart . . .' Tears sprang into Emma's eyes, and she blinked them back. 'Years ago I taught myself to be positive in the worst moments of my life. That's what kept me going when I was a young girl, out on my own, struggling to make a living. You see, I couldn't afford to have any negative thoughts then . . . and *we* can't now.'

'It's nice to see you, Frank,' Emma said, smiling at her brother. 'But you look awfully tired and pale.'

'I've always been pale, Emma, even as a child. Don't you remember how you used to fuss around me and wrap me up in scarves. And send me out onto the moors to "get some colour in your cheeks", you used to say.'

She laughed. 'I know I did, and you used to get very upset with me. But you *are* all right, aren't you, Frankie?'

'It's *Frankie* again, is it? Do you know you hadn't called me that for years until quite recently?'

'Because you told me not to when you were young. You said our mam had told you that you were a big lad, and Frankie was a baby's name. But I like it, perhaps because it's affectionate.'

Frank gave her a long, loving look, but said nothing. These two were very close, and he had always believed that his sister could read his mind. Whether she could or not was beside the point; she was certainly on the same wavelength as he was. 'I am a bit tired, Emma, you're right about that. Mostly because I've been working hard at the *Express*.'

'How's the great man?'

'Which one? Beaverbrook or Churchill?'

'Either. Both.' Emma leant forward now, her face lighting up as she exclaimed, 'Frank, I met Winston Churchill. Finally and at last.'

'When? And where?' he asked, fully understanding her excitement. He knew it must have been a thrill for her. Churchill was her great hero.

'I met him last Sunday, September the eighth . . . only four days ago, to be precise. In the East End. I'd gone with Jane and Bill Stuart Ogden to take food to those poor people who had been bombed out, and he happened to be there. Bill introduced me. He's just extraordinary.'

'That he is, and he often goes out to inspect the bomb damage, to talk to people. They love him for that, for his immense humanity. He reaches out to common folk, and he touches and moves them in a way few politicians can. And, of course, Bill has always been a supporter of his, so no doubt the PM was glad to see him, to see all of you. Especially since you were being so kind, and helping. We're all going to have to pitch in now that the Blitz has started.'

'I was so overawed I could hardly speak,' Emma admitted with a small, embarrassed laugh.

'I know what you mean. It's easy to be over-whelmed by him these days. He's a monumental man. And you'll see, one day, in the not-too-distant future, he'll be thought of as a legend, Emm.'

'To me he's a legend now. I hope he's well protected . . . he is, isn't he, Frank?'

'Oh yes, of course he is. He spends most of his time in his various bunkers.'

'What do you mean *bunkers*?'

'He's got a lot of sort of . . . underground bolt holes, where he works and lives and sleeps. He's not really at Number Ten Downing Street, you know. I think he pops in and out, but it's far too dangerous. He could be so easily bombed there. Mostly he's in the War Cabinet rooms. When he saw the room which was to be his he apparently said, "This is the room from which I will direct the war." And that's what he's doing.'

'Where are they, these War Cabinet rooms?'

'I don't know. Only the most privileged know that, Emma, but making a guess I'd say they're somewhere in Whitehall.'

'I'm glad to know the Prime Minister is in a safe place. But getting back to you, Frank, why do you have so much work at the moment?'

'That's a daft question for someone as smart as you, Emma. Because a lot of our young journalists have left. They've joined the armed services. So I've been writing more than usual. I enjoy it, though. I suppose the reason I'm also a bit more tired than usual is because I'm writing another novel and—'

'Oh Frank, that's just wonderful!' Emma interrupted enthusiastically. 'I love your books. What's this one about?'

'The war. What else?' he said, and smiled at her. She was his biggest fan.

'Do you think America's going to come in to help us, now that we stand alone?' she asked, changing the subject.

'I'm not sure. I hope so. President Roosevelt's a good man, and he and Churchill do seem to have a certain rapport. But he's answerable to the American people, and they don't want to go near this war. Oh no.' Frank bit his lip. 'Incidentally, the daylight bombing's going to get worse, so be alert, Emma.'

'You know I always am.'

'How's Elizabeth doing?'

'She's working hard. Thousands and thousands have been hurt in the last few days, you know, and she's run off her feet at the hospital. Now she's talking about helping out at the London Bridge tube station, where 8,000 people gather every night for safety.'

'You can't let her do *that!*'

'I don't know how to stop her. So I think perhaps I'd better go with her, to keep an eye on her, and to help those who are sheltering there.'

'Oh, our Emma, you're too much!'

'Come on Frank, let's go to lunch.' As she spoke she rose, and together they left her office at the top of the store. 'I think it's a no-choice lunch today in the café.'

'What on earth is that?'

'Exactly what it says. No choice. Tomato soup followed by bangers and mash with fried onions. Not bad really, not when you consider there's a war on.'

CHAPTER THIRTY-FOUR

Winston Harte nodded when Emma had finished speaking, and said swiftly, 'I think you're absolutely correct, we do have to make changes at Yorkshire Consolidated, and this is what I propose. Let's promote Martin Fuller to managing editor, and Peter Armstrong to managing director.'

'But *you're* managing director, Winston!' Emma sat up straighter on the sofa and stared at her brother, frowning, her eyes turning anxious. 'Please don't tell me you want to leave the running of the newspaper company to someone else?'

'No, not at all. Sorry, I don't think I made myself quite clear. I ought to move up, too, become co-chairman with you, if that's all right. I'll still supervise, be on top of everything. But I'd feel much better knowing we had a managing director sitting at the main office in Leeds, and a managing editor alongside him. Both of them handling the day-to-day stuff right on the spot.'

'Then we'll do it, Winston. And frankly I've been worried about you lately. You're burdened down between the Yorkshire stores, the Fairley mill, and the newspapers. And there's also your involvement with Harte Enterprises. It's too much.'

Winston began to laugh. 'Listen who's talking. There's nobody busier than you, and on top of your work you've taken on so much else – you volunteer for so much war work. I don't know how you do it all. You're running yourself ragged.'

'When I think of what our troops are doing to keep us safe and win this war, my burdens seem light.'

As she spoke, Emma picked up the silver Georgian teapot and poured another cup of tea for her brother and herself.

The two of them were sitting in front of the fire in the upstairs parlour at Pennistone Royal. It was 1942, and a freezing afternoon in the middle of December. Emma had been in Yorkshire for a week, reviewing her business interests with Winston, and checking out the situation on her Yorkshire estate.

Although Leeds, Bradford and Sheffield, and many of the other industrial cities in the north, had been bombed, Ripon and the Dales remained unscathed for the most part, although some Royal Air Force bases at Topcliffe and Dishforth had been near misses when the Luftwaffe had flown over. As far as Pennistone Royal was concerned, things were relatively normal, except for the food, petrol and other shortages affecting everyone in Britain.

As he sipped his tea, Winston went on, 'Marty and Pete are good chaps, talented and hard working, and devoted to you and Consolidated. It's going to be fine, Emma.'

'As long as you're sitting on top of them, then I feel secure about things, although I do agree with you that they're *both* smart and dedicated.' Emma shook her head and made a small *moue* with her mouth. 'I always hoped Frank would take over the running of the newspaper company, but it's just not for him is it, Winston?'

'No, it's not. He's never been interested, not even when you bought up the Sheffield papers in 1935 and started Consolidated. You offered him the top job and he said no. So that's that. He's a journalist, not a manager. To each his own, Emm.'

'He loves the *Express* and working for Lord Beaverbrook and, let's face it, Winston, Frank is the golden boy on that paper, a favourite of the Beaver and of Arthur Christiansen as well.' She put her cup down in the saucer, and gave Winston a long, thoughtful stare. 'I suppose Edwin Fairley will try to cling to the *Yorkshire Morning Gazette* until the day he dies.'

Winston nodded. 'That newspaper's been in the Fairley family for three generations; you don't think he'll ever let go of it willingly, do you?'

'No, I don't suppose he will. But the paper's lost a lot of its circulation.'

'That's because we've been giving it a run for its money. We've taken a lot of readers away.'

'I know,' Emma said with a small, satisfied smile. 'But Edwin Fairley should stick to the law. He's a much better barrister than he is a newspaper-owner, don't you think?'

'Remember, that plays in our favour. He'll have to sell one day, and you'll be able to buy it . . . for a song.'

'Let's hope you're right. Talking of Frank, he said he and Natalie won't be able to spend Christmas with us in London, because of her family. Do you think you can talk him into it?'

'I do,' Winston responded, but he looked slightly puzzled. 'However, I don't think I'll have to, Emm. Frank told me only the other day that he has to be in London. He said Beaverbrook needs him for something special during Christmas, and that it's mandatory.'

'Oh, I'm glad. Then he will be able to come on Christmas Day after all. He's probably not got around to telling me yet.'

'Perhaps that's so.'

'You and Charlotte are coming, aren't you? And Randolph?'

Winston's face changed, lighting up at the mention of his son, his only child. 'We're keeping our fingers crossed that he'll get leave, if only for a few days. His battleship's up at Scapa Flow at the moment. But yes, we're coming. What about your boys?'

'I think Robin will be getting a two-day pass, and hopefully Kit will, too. I know he's anxious to see June and the baby.'

Winston's expression changed yet again, and he almost chortled as he said, 'And what a smashing little redhead Sarah is ... there's no mistaking that she's a Harte and *your* grandchild. She looks just like you – well, at least her colouring is the same.'

'I can't believe I have a second grandchild ...' Emma stopped abruptly, and sadness settled on her face as she looked across at Winston and asked, 'Have you heard from Edwina lately? How's her marriage, and how's my first grandchild?'

'I did get a short letter recently,' Winston admitted quietly. 'But she didn't say very much. Little Anthony is flourishing, and Jeremy is fine. I thought he was a splendid chap, Emma, when I went to the wedding. Please don't worry about Edwina. I'm sure she's happy, and she'll come round one day.'

'I don't know about that. Maybe it's wishful thinking on my part.' Unexpectedly, her face lit up with the extraordinary radiance that had always captivated everyone. 'Just think, Winston, I've got a grandson who's a lord ... Lord Anthony Standish.'

He smiled, enjoying this sudden flash of pleasure in his sister. Wanting to prolong it, he moved away from the discussion of her recalcitrant and difficult daughter Edwina, and said, 'How's Daisy?'

'She's just a miracle! Of course, even though she's now left boarding school, there's no way she can go to a finishing school in Switzerland as Edwina and Elizabeth did. Because of the war. But she doesn't seem to care. She's perfectly happy living at home with me and Elizabeth, and thank God they've always been the closest of friends. The house is very harmonious.'

He nodded, relieved that her other two daughters were so devoted to her. Edwina irritated him at times; she was bearing a grudge that went back to her childhood, and she a woman now in her mid-thirties. Ridiculous, he thought, and made up his mind to write a stern letter to his niece. Or perhaps he would phone her at Clonloughlin in Ireland, where she lived with her husband and little son. He would talk to Frank about it; get his brother's advice.

'Blackie's also coming on Christmas Day,' Emma said, interrupting Winston's thoughts. 'And hopefully Bryan will get leave.'

'What about David? Is he coming up to London too?'

'Naturally. He's always attended my Christmas Day lunch, you know that, Winston. The three clans are always together, it's the one day we celebrate our long friendship. Blackie O'Neill, Emma Harte and David Kallinski. The Three Musketeers, that's what Frank used to call us . . . such a long time we've been friends. Blackie and I met when I was only fourteen and a half, almost fifteen . . . in 1904. And I met the Kallinskis about a year later. Thirty-eight years or more . . .'

'Of great devotion, loyalty and love between the three of you. Do you know how remarkable that is, Emma?'

'Yes, I believe I do.'

After her brother had left to drive back to Leeds, Emma remained in the upstairs parlour, drifting with her thoughts for a while, enjoying this time of repose and reflection. She had not been here in this house for some time, caught up as she was with the store and her worldwide business enterprises in London. And the war.

She had missed Pennistone Royal, and she had missed this room. She had always thought it was distinguished by a gentle beauty. It was understated, and not at all pretentious, and yet she knew only too well that its very simplicity was deceptive. It had been achieved by a great expenditure of money when she had decorated it in 1932; she had also been both skilful and patient when she had sought out furniture, knowing that only the very best antiques would do for this splendid and ancient room.

Now, as she glanced around, she saw how well everything had held up, how beautiful it still looked after ten years. Pale yellow washed over the walls, and this soft, radiant colour gave the room a truly sunny feeling, even on the dullest of overcast Yorkshire days. A dark, highly polished wood floor gleamed against the antique Savonnerie rug that splashed its pale colours into the middle of the room. She had always loved beautiful crystal and silver, and her favourite pieces sparkled against the rich, mellow patinas of the Georgian tables, consoles and chests.

Two long sofas faced each other in front of the fireplace of bleached oak, and were covered in a colourful floral chintz with a white background. Emma smiled to herself, knowing how right she had been to buy numerous bolts of this fabric. Every few years she had the sofas reupholstered, so that the same pink, yellow, blue and red floral pattern could bloom afresh. Once she had created a decorative theme for a room she rarely changed it, simply refurbished it when this was required; always using the same decorative elements for the identical effect.

Her eyes roamed around, noting how fine the Rose Medallion china looked in the elegant Chippendale cabinet, and then she focused for a moment on the priceless Turner landscape above the fireplace. It was redolent with misty greens and blues; its poignant, bucolic setting never failed to stir her. And yet she had decided only the other day to hang it elsewhere. Certainly there was plenty of wall space, and she wanted to put a painting of Paul over the fireplace. It was the perfect spot.

She wondered which to hang there, and decided it should be the one of him in his officer's uniform. He had sat for it after the end of the Great War, and she had always thought this one in particular bore the greatest likeness to him . . . the way he looked when they first met.

Rising, she walked across to the leaded windows and stood looking out. The hillside opposite was covered in snow, but in spring the daffodils bloomed, and were such a wondrous sight to her, always evoking in her mind the lovely Wordsworth poem. Sighing to herself, she turned away and went back into the room, walking over to the large Queen Anne chest. It stood under a mirror, and it needed something to finish it, some sort of decorative object to give it a completed look. The fruitwood-and-silver casket, she suddenly thought. I'll bring that up here the next time I come. It will look beautiful on top of the chest.

Moving across the floor, she went and sat down at her large desk, took out her diary for 1942, found today's date, and wrote a few lines about her meeting with Winston and the decisions they had made about the Yorkshire Consolidated Newspaper Company. And then she put the pen down and sat back, thinking about the *Yorkshire Morning Gazette*. She had always wanted that paper, and one day she *would* own it. Edwin Fairley did not have the financial resources to keep it going. It had had staggering losses over the last few years;

she was using her own Yorkshire newspapers to run his into the ground. It was the only Fairley business she did not own ... once she did, her revenge would be complete.

All of a sudden she heard Blackie's voice in her head, echoing to her down the years; he was quoting the Bible to her. 'Revenge is mine, sayeth the Lord, and that's the truth, Emma.' At the time she had laughed and answered, 'And Shakespeare wrote that revenge is a dish best served cold.' That day she had shaken her head and laughed hollowly again, had added, 'I want to enjoy my revenge. I'm not leaving it to the Lord or anyone else. And I'm certainly not going to serve it cold.'

Emma knew deep within herself that Edwin realized she had deliberately set out to ruin the Fairleys, and that he did not care. He knew they deserved it, and that his brother Gerald had been as responsible for their downfall as she had. In his own way, Edwin had prospered as a barrister, specializing in criminal law. The newspaper was his great folly ... and he was playing into her hands, just as Gerald had done before him.

Edwina was the fruit of their brief union when she had been a servant girl at Fairley Hall and he the son of the squire, Adam Fairley. She had always done her best for Edwina, even gone that step further, and yet Edwina hated her because she had not been able to give her daughter the one thing she had always wanted: legitimacy and the Fairley name. Emma longed to see her first-born child, and her first grandchild, little Anthony Standish . . .

The jangle of the telephone interrupted her thoughts.

'Hello? Pennistone Royal.'

'Hello, Emma. It's Frank. I just spoke to Winston, and he asked me to let you know about Christmas. We'd love to come, all of us. Is that all right?'

'Of course it is! Oh Frankie, I'm so pleased you're able to make it after all. This means the family will be together . . . well, almost all of us. If the boys get leave.'

Thoughts of Edwin Fairley and his betrayal of her vanished. Bleak, dark memories of her terrible and painful past were expunged. And a rush of real joy at the prospect of spending Christmas with those she loved galvanized her.

Emma jumped up, almost ran out of the upstairs parlour, down the stairs, through the Stone Hall and into the kitchen.

'Hilda! Are you here?' Emma called out, glancing around.

A split second later her devoted young house-keeper hurried out of the stone storage larder at one end of the kitchen, carrying two bottles of preserved plums and pears.

'That's just what I need,' Emma exclaimed, laughter echoing in her voice.

'Bottled fruit, Mrs Harte? Whatever for?' Hilda

looked slightly puzzled as she put the bottles down on the large wooden table in the centre of the kitchen. 'Do you mean you'd like some for supper? With custard?'

Emma shook her head. 'No, Hilda, not for supper. I've just had the most wonderful news! Both my brothers and their wives are coming to dinner on Christmas Day. It looks as if I'll have the whole family with me – if the boys get leave, of course. Hopefully Mrs Lowther will come with baby Sarah. And there will be Mr O'Neill and Mr Kallinski, and with a bit of luck their sons too. So you see, Hilda, I'm afraid I'm going to have to raid your larder.'

Hilda beamed. 'Oh Mrs Harte, that's luvely to hear! I sort of hoped you'd be having a family gathering this Christmas. It was awful for you the year of the Blitz, and last year as well, what with the boys away fighting. So I did prepare some nice things for you to take back to London with you, on the off chance you'd need them.' Hilda paused, and finished, 'Would you like to come into the stone larder? You can look at everything.'

'I would indeed. And I might have known you'd be thinking ahead to Christmas in the summer. Did you bottle a lot of fruits?'

Hilda nodded. 'Pears, damsons, plums from the orchard. Gooseberries and blackberries – we had some luvely ones in the garden this summer. I also bottled some of the tomatoes Mr Ramsbotham's been growing in the greenhouses.' Hurrying over to the larder, Hilda added, 'And I've made things like chutney, and done a lot of pickling. Onions, beetroot, gherkins, and your favourite, piccalilli, Mrs Harte.'

Walking across the kitchen, following Hilda into the stone larder full of floor-to-ceiling shelves, Emma said, 'Thank you. And I'm fairly certain you made some Christmas cakes and Christmas puddings as well, didn't you?'

'Oh yes,' Hilda answered, beaming at her. 'Christmas wouldn't be the same without a bit of your fruitcake, would it, Mrs Harte? I always use your recipe.' Hilda indicated the large round tins stacked on one of the many shelves. 'These are the cakes. I put lots of fruit in, just the way you like, and sherry, plenty of that. And down there are the puddings in the white basins tied with cheesecloth. I've also got jams and jellies made, all your favourites, madam, and lemon curd, as well.'

'Thank you for preparing all these wonderful things, Hilda, I really appreciate it.' It was cold in the larder and Emma was shivering as she hurried back into the warmth of the big family kitchen. She went and stood in front of the fire blazing in the hearth.

'Cook taught me well before she retired, Mrs Harte,' Hilda murmured, walking over to the table.

Emma's face changed slightly, her eyes turned anxious. 'How *is* Mrs Walton doing? Is she any better?'

'Yes, a bit. It's the gout, a'course, in her right

foot. Too much acid or summut. Anyways, it makes standing and walking right difficult for her.'

'Give her my best, Hilda, when you see her.'

'Oh I will, madam. She always asks about you.' Hilda sighed and, giving Emma a long pointed stare, she said, 'I do wish you could all spend Christmas here at Pennistone Royal. That'd be luvely, it would.'

'I'm afraid it's quite impossible.'

'But it's right dangerous in London, what with all the bombing, madam. If you don't mind me saying so, I was thinking only the other day that it'd be right nice for Miss Daisy and Miss Elizabeth if they were in Yorkshire. *Safer*, madam.' Her voice faltered and she wondered if she had spoken out of turn, crossed a line she knew she should never cross.

'Well, what you say is true, Hilda. I agree with you that it's safer up here, and calmer.' As she spoke Emma was reminded of the screaming sirens, the deafening sound of the anti-aircraft guns in Hyde Park, the bombs exploding, the searchlights at night, and the general air of chaos, although things were becoming a bit better.

Returning Hilda's steady, questioning gaze, she felt the need to explain. 'The problem is they want to be in London with me, Hilda. As you know, Miss Elizabeth is very committed to her nursing. Also, her husband is stationed at Biggin Hill, which is much closer to London than it is to Yorkshire.' Emma shook her head. 'Not that he's been on leave lately. Those boys are always up in the air, in combat.'

'Perhaps things'll get a bit better now that the Americans are in the war,' the young housekeeper suggested.

'Let's hope so, Hilda, let's hope so. And, speaking of the Americans, what have you planned to do for Christmas for the American pilots stationed around here?'

'Well, I was going to speak to you about that before you left,' Hilda replied. 'Joe and I thought we'd do a nice buffet for them in the Stone Hall, with your permission, that is. It'd be luvely for the young lads to have a bit of Christmas fare, sort of remind them of home, don't you think, madam?'

'I do, Hilda, and naturally you have my permission. Don't skimp either: make sure it's a proper treat for them. I remember how much they enjoyed the July the fourth party we gave this summer.'

'And the bowling on the lawn,' Hilda reminded her. 'They enjoyed that. And the dancing later with the girls from the village. *You* were a big hit, Mrs Harte, you really were. Especially with that nice young major.'

'Come along, Hilda, don't be so silly,' Emma murmured, and quickly changed the subject.

CHAPTER THIRTY-FIVE

Blackie O'Neill stood with his back to the blazing fire in the beautiful drawing room of Emma's Belgrave Square house, waiting for her to come downstairs.

'Mrs Harte'll be down in a minute,' Grace had told him after she had ushered him into the room. 'Wot she said was to fix yerself a drink. Do yer want me ter do it for yer, Mr O'Neill?'

He had declined. Now, as he glanced at the clock on the mantel shelf, he saw that the minute had stretched into ten. He was just about to walk over to the console where there was an assortment of drinks, to fix himself something after all, when he heard Emma's high heels clicking against the parquet floor of the hallway outside. He swung around to greet her, and then said not a word, just stood there open-mouthed, staring at her, utterly speechless for a moment.

'What's the matter, Blackie?' she asked, walking into the room. 'You're gawping at me.'

'Aye, I am that, Emma Harte. And everybody else that comes here today will also be . . . *gawping* at you.' He chuckled. 'I do love that funny Yorkshire word of yours.'

Coming to a standstill in front of him, she smiled a little coquettishly for her, stood on her tiptoes and kissed him on his cheek. 'And why will they be doing that? Why are you doing it, Blackie darling?'

'Oh, Emm, you know very well *why*. You know exactly how you look this afternoon,' he answered, chuckling again. 'And if you don't, mavourneen, then it's a new pair of glasses I'll have to be buying you.'

'My eyesight's perfect,' she shot back.

'Aye, I know it is, so you must know that you look positively beautiful. In all the forty years I've known you, I've never ever seen you look better or bonnier. And that's the God's own truth, me darlin' girl. You've outdone yourself, Emm.'

'Thank you, Blackie. It's an *old* dress, you know. I've had it since 1937. You like it, do you?'

'Aye, I like it. Very elegant it is.'

Emma had spoken the truth when she had said it was old. It was from Paris, designed by Lanvin, and it was a cocktail dress. Made of exquisite black cobweb lace mounted on emerald-green silk, the silk showed through the lace for an unusual effect. It had a full skirt, a Vee neckline, long sleeves, and was sashed in emerald-green silk. The full skirt and tight bodice flattered her youthful figure and long, shapely legs. She wore very high black silk court shoes by Pinet, her favourite shoemaker.

Still eyeing her with the utmost admiration, Blackie said, with a huge smile, 'I'm glad to see that you're wearing my emerald brooch. It goes well with your frock.'

'Yes, it does, doesn't it? I've always loved my emerald bow. Do you know, Blackie, I still have the original one you gave me.'

'You *do*?' He sounded surprised and yet also pleased. 'I can't believe it . . . all these years you've kept it, since you were a little sprite of a girl, only fifteen. My little green glass bow?'

'That's right. And by the way, I've known you since I was fourteen and I'm now fifty-three, so actually I've only known you thirty-nine years, not forty.'

'Splittin' hairs are we now, mavourneen?' he asked, his black eyes narrowing.

'No, I'm just teasing you, my dearest friend. Now, would you like champagne? Or a drop of Irish?'

'I think I'll be having a drop of whiskey, Emma love. And I can fix it meself, you know.'

'No, I can do it for you. But perhaps you can open the bottle of champagne, please.'

'It'll be my pleasure, Emma. And isn't it grand Bryan got leave, and the other lads. It's a jolly Christmas night we'll be havin' with our families.'

A few minutes later he was pouring her a flute of champagne and handing it to her, and she gave him his Irish whiskey in a crystal glass.

'Here's to you, me darlin' Emma, the most beautiful woman I know.'

'And to you, Shane Patrick Desmond O'Neill, the young spalpeen who became a great gentleman and a toff and who has always been my best friend.' She laughed. 'You used to say to me years ago . . . "I'm going to be a toff one day." And you are! And I'm so proud of you.'

They touched glasses and Emma hovered next to him in front of the fire, as they waited for her children and his son and her other guests to join them.

At one moment, after a short silence, Blackie said, 'I'm glad Frank could come after all, he might have some news about the war . . . you know, inside stuff.'

'He might, but I doubt very much that he'd tell us,' Emma murmured. She knew Blackie liked to pick her brother's brains, as she did herself, but Frank could be extremely close-mouthed. Above everything else, he was discreet and trustworthy, as his boss Lord Beaverbrook knew very well.

Emma looked towards the hallway as she heard running feet, and suddenly there was her daughter Daisy, rushing into the drawing room like a young colt, flying to her Uncle Blackie, who was one of her favourites.

'A little decorum: walk, don't run, Daisy,' Emma admonished gently, but her eyes were loving, her smile benign.

'And if it's not me darlin' little Daisy, the prettiest

flower in the world,' Blackie said, hugging her close, then holding her away. 'You've sprung up in the last week, little one,' he murmured with a frown.

Daisy, dark-haired and blue-eyed like her father Paul McGill, laughed uproariously. 'Oh Uncle Blackie, don't be silly! I'm wearing high heels.' As she spoke she spun around, her dark blue velvet dress billowing out like a bell.

'Aren't I the foolish man!' Blackie laughed, and then looked at the door as Elizabeth came in clutching the arm of her young husband, Tony Barkstone. She wore a red silk dress and pearls, and he was resplendent in his Royal Air Force blue uniform, and Blackie couldn't help thinking what a handsome couple they made: Elizabeth, a stunning dark beauty; Tony a blond blue-eyed Englishman, the bloom of youth still on his handsome face. Why are they always so young, those who defend us? he wondered.

After greetings had been exchanged all around, Elizabeth went over to Emma and said, 'Mummy, you look gorgeous.' She stood staring admiringly at her mother's red hair and perfect pink-and-white complexion, the vivid green eyes that matched the exquisite emeralds at her ears, on her shoulder and hands, and she found it hard to believe she was gazing at a woman of fifty-three. Emma looked so much younger. Leaning into her mother, Elizabeth whispered, 'Mummy, you don't look a day over thirty-nine.'

Emma threw back her head and laughed. She was happy this afternoon. In fact, she had not felt this happy in a very long time, not since Paul's death almost four years ago. She knew it was because her children and family and friends would all be with her today. They gave her such joy and comfort, and she was proud of them.

In the distance, she heard the faint cry of the baby, and she hurried to the hallway as Kit and June came towards her. June was carrying the newest redhead in the family, little Sarah Lowther, not yet a year old but making her presence felt.

Emma kissed her baby granddaughter, touched her fat little cheek, then kissed her daughter-in-law June. Finally she turned to her eldest son, Kit, son of Joe Lowther, her first husband. She thought he looked a lot like Joe today: blond, fair of complexion, grey-eyed, a solid-looking young man wearing his army captain's uniform proudly, grinning from ear to ear and showing his perfect white teeth and dimples.

Taking hold of Emma's arm, Kit drew her towards him and hugged her tightly. He had always adored his mother, and now he said against her auburn hair, 'I'm thrilled the baby looks like you, Mother, just in case you didn't know.'

Emma drew away from him, touched his cheek. 'So am I, Kit darling.'

'I'm not the last, am I?' Robin cried, running down the stairs, walking swiftly across to join the small group in the hallway.

'No, no, we're still waiting for a few others,' Emma murmured, smiling up at Robin. He was her favourite, but never once had she shown this. She had not believed in playing favourites in the family; had treated them all equally and in the fairest way she knew how.

As she watched Robin shaking hands with Kit, and kissing June, who had only arrived from Leeds a short while ago, Emma could not help thinking that Robin resembled her brother Winston more than he did his father, Arthur Ainsley. He was tall and dark-haired like Winston and his twin Elizabeth. Tonight he appeared more dashing than ever in his Royal Air Force blue. He was a pilot, and something of an ace flyer, and had recently been promoted to captain. She suspected he might be a daredevil and a risk-taker, and she worried excessively at times when she thought of him up there in his Hurricane flying over enemy territory. In order to keep her sanity, she tried not to think about what Robin did in the air.

Grasping her hand in his, Robin twirled her around, almost but not quite jitterbugging, and whistled, 'Wow, Ma, you look like . . . a film star. If some of our chaps could see you now they'd be fighting over who got to be your escort.'

'Indeed they would,' David Amory said as he came down the stairs and stepped into the hall where they were still standing chatting.

'Good evening, Mrs Harte,' he said, as he joined them.

'Good evening, David,' she responded, steeling herself, smiling warmly, trying not to stare too hard at him. It would take her a while to get used to this young man who bore an odd likeness to Paul McGill. She had been floored last night when he had arrived with Robin and Tony, and two other young pilots, all members of the 111th Squadron stationed at Biggin Hill.

'They're going to bunk in here with us, Ma, is that all right?' Robin had asked, and she had been happy to acquiesce. For several years now Robin had been bringing his squadron mates home, and she had willingly opened her door and her heart to these brave and dauntless young men who were constantly in danger defending their country.

But throw her off balance he did . . . because he reminded her of Paul. He was tall and dark, with a flashing smile and bright blue eyes. Yet David was not as outrageously handsome as Paul had been as a young man, nor did he have his massive size and audacious personality. But he certainly struck a chord in her memory of Paul as he had been in the First World War when they had met. David had an engaging manner, and last night he had charmed her at once. She was glad that he was staying with them for Christmas. However, she was also already concerned about his presence here: Daisy had seemed mesmerized last night. Her seventeen-year-old daughter had not been able to take her eyes off David, who was twenty-four and something of a war hero already, and a new addition at Biggin Hill. David had seemed taken with Daisy also.

'Well, let's not stand here,' Emma now said, taking hold of David's arm, leading him towards the drawing room. 'And where are your friends?' she asked, looking up at him.

'They'll be down in a few minutes, Mrs Harte,' he replied and, bending closer, he added softly, 'They're enjoying the luxury of your bathrooms, Mrs Harte. They're rather different from those in our billets.'

Emma laughed as they went into the drawing room together, where she introduced him to Blackie, and then watched as Daisy glided towards him looking as if she were floating on clouds.

June went to sit on a sofa with baby Sarah, and Kit helped Robin to pour champagne, while Blackie engaged in a conversation with David Amory, whom he had instantly taken to and was chatting to like an old friend.

Emma swung around as Winston and Charlotte came into the drawing room, and hurried over to them. She was disappointed to see they were alone, but kept her expression neutral. After kissing first Charlotte and then her brother, she stepped back and said to her sister-in-law, 'How lovely you look, Charlotte. The deep burgundy velvet is so becoming on you.'

'Thank you, Emma, and I must say you're as elegant as always.' The two women, who were good friends, smiled at each other warmly and then Winston said, 'But where are Randolph and Georgina? Haven't they arrived yet?'

'No, they haven't,' Emma answered, relieved to hear her nephew had been given leave after all; Winston would have been glum company otherwise, and so would Charlotte.

Frank and Natalie, with their daughter Rosamunde and son Simon, arrived on the heels of Winston, and once more greetings were exchanged, compliments given. Emma then led her brothers and their wives into the drawing room, and said to Frank in a low voice, 'I did manage to get extra staff today, but not really enough. So could you help Robin and Kit with the drinks, darling?'

'No sooner said than done,' Frank murmured, and went to join his nephews at the console.

Emma took hold of Natalie's arm and led her over to the fireplace to introduce her to David Amory. Frank's wife was lovely: rather delicate and ethereal looking, with a finely drawn face, swan-like neck and very slender figure. Her hair had turned colour years ago, and she was prematurely white, but the silver tone suited her and somehow did not age her.

'I'd like to introduce you to my sister-in-law,' Emma said, smiling at David, who turned to greet Natalie and gave her the benefit of his considerable charm.

Blackie drew Emma away from the fireplace, and said in a worried voice, 'I can't imagine what happened to Bryan and Geraldine. I told them to be here by five, and it's almost twenty past.'

'Since he's already in London you know they're coming, Blackie, so do relax, darling. It's not as though he had to come from Scapa Flow like Randolph.'

'I believe Randolph got here in the early hours of the morning,' Blackie informed her. 'So Bryan told me.' Once again Blackie looked towards the hallway and suddenly began to laugh. 'And speaking of the two young devils, here they are,' he added, clasping her hand in his, leading her out into the hallway at the top of the stairs.

'There you are, lads, just in time for a drop of the Irish before dinner,' Blackie said, throwing his son an affectionate look and embracing Randolph, of whom he was exceptionally fond. He then went to kiss his daughter-in-law Geraldine who had baby Shane in her arms. Turning to Randolph's wife Georgina, he kissed her also, and glanced at the little boy in her arms . . . Winston the second, they called him.

'Now come along, ladies, and you too, Bryan, Randolph. You all look a bit nithered; what you'll be needing now is a drink and your backs to the fire for ten minutes. It's hellish cold out there today.'

'I'm just going to pop into the kitchen to make sure everything's all right,' Emma murmured to Blackie, and glided away. He watched her go, his love and adoration of her written all over his face for all the world to see. Then he marched across to the console table and filled two crystal glasses with Irish whiskey, saying to Frank as he did, 'Anything new? What's happening in the world today, Frank?'

'Not a lot, thank heavens,' Frank answered, and gave Blackie a knowing look. 'And I hope it stays that way, at least for Christmas Day. Oh look, Blackie, here's David and the boys.'

As soon as they spotted Blackie and Frank, David and his sons came over to greet them, and a moment later Robin was dashing across the room to welcome the two young pilots from Biggin Hill, whom he had invited to spend Christmas with them.

Leading them around the drawing room, Robin introduced Matthew Hall and Charlie Cox to everyone present before going to get them both glasses of champagne.

A few minutes later, when Emma finally returned to the drawing room, she first went to greet David, Ronnie and Mark Kallinski, and then floated over to talk to the two young pilots, wanting to make them feel welcome and at home.

Frank, watching her from the sidelines, as always the astute observer, could not help admiring her. His sister was charming and gracious this afternoon, not to mention staggeringly beautiful, and he was proud of her, proud of everything she had become. To Frank, Emma was, at fifty-three, a great lady ... soignée, sophisticated, knowledgeable about countless things, exceedingly intelligent, a fountain of information about everything from *haute couture* and jewels to great art, eighteenth-century French furniture, porcelain and silver and Georgian antiques.

When he thought about their early years, so poverty-stricken and isolated in Fairley, it was miraculous to him that she had become this most extraordinary woman. She was also a tycoon par excellence, renowned in international business circles, and a power to be reckoned with. In certain ways it beggared belief; she was, to him, a phenomenon.

He shifted his eyes from Emma, who was busy being the perfect hostess, and let them roam around the drawing room. Frank thought it was one of the most beautiful rooms he had ever seen, and she had designed and decorated it herself, just as she had her other homes.

The walls were a funny sort of colour – not quite blue, not quite pale green, but a mingling of both shot through with a hint of grey. The billowing silk taffeta draperies at the three tall windows were the identical colour, and this same shade was repeated in French chairs and a sofa, while a love seat was covered in pale blue; another series of four French chairs were in pale green. Jade and crystal lamps, shaded in cream silk, stood on various eighteenth-century French tables and chests, and the whole was pulled together by the faded antique Aubusson carpet underfoot.

Emma had acquired any number of beautiful objects, but the art was perhaps the most stunning element in the room: two Renoirs, a Sisley, and a Monet; all of them in pale pastel colours that added to the soft quality of the room awash in pale greens and blues, creating a misty effect.

She taught herself everything, he reminded himself. But she always had great taste.

CHAPTER THIRTY-SIX

Jack Field and Dennis Scott, both single with no immediate family in London, and nowhere to go on Christmas Day, had been willing and happy to help Emma with her holiday dinner – flattered to be asked, in fact.

Promptly at six o'clock Grace came into the drawing room and whispered to Emma that the buffet table in the kitchen had been completed and the helpers were waiting to serve.

Emma, who was standing next to Blackie, asked him to announce that dinner was ready, and he did so, his deep voice booming out across the room. He repeated what Emma had just asked him to say, but of course it was in his own words.

'Ladies and gentlemen, our Christmas fare awaits us in the kitchen. Emma has had everything set out on a grand buffet table, but you will take your places in the dining room once you have your food. Now, let's be going into the kitchen before everything gets cold.'

Jack, Dennis, Grace and Mrs Coddington, the cook, all stood behind the buffet table, which was grand indeed. Covered in a white damask cloth, it had two silver candelabra holding red candles at each end and was groaning with food: two large delicious-looking boiled hams from Yorkshire, three roast turkeys and three roast chickens, all browned to perfection and steaming, a selection of vegetables, also from Pennistone Royal, a huge platter of roast potatoes, bowls of sage-and-onion stuffing, smaller crystal bowls of relishes such as piccalilli and chutney, as well as the pickled beetroots and onions, all from Hilda's larder, and several gravy boats of Emma's special gravy.

Once everyone had been served, they trooped out, following Emma into the dining room, which looked very festive, filled with seasonal touches. Again she had used red candles in the silver candlesticks on the long mahogany table, and in the centre was a large crystal bowl filled to overflowing with red, silver, gold and green Christmas tree baubles, which she had used instead of a floral arrangement. On the sideboard were matching crystal vases filled with red Christmas berries, sprigs of holly and mistletoe, flanked by more red candles in silver sticks; standing on a chest was an artificial Christmas tree glittering with gold and silver ornaments and big gold bows. Next to the chest Emma had placed a double crib for the baby boys, Winston II and Shane.

Everyone found their seats, thanks to Emma's

table plan. Kit, Robin, Bryan and Randolph were assigned the task of serving the red and white wines, which they promptly did, moving briskly around the table. Once they had finished and were seated, everyone began to eat.

As always, Emma ate sparingly, and as the meal progressed she was gratified to see that all of the young men were tucking in, relishing the wonderful home-cooked meal. Her eyes settled on each one of them in turn . . .

Tony, sitting next to his beloved Elizabeth, his face so open and easy to read, without guile, blessed with blond good looks, his air-force blue uniform echoing the colour of his eyes.

And Kit, on the other side of his sister Elizabeth, so proud in his army captain's uniform, and adoring of June and their baby Sarah, who gurgled in the small crib Emma had placed against the wall, just behind June. He was the same type as Tony, fair skinned, with light brown hair and a pleasant, honest face. No mistaking *his* heritage either. He was true blue English.

Bryan, alongside Geraldine, also in air-force blue, and as proud as the others to be serving his country. He was the spitting image of Blackie, just like Blackie had been as a young man. Tall, broad of chest and shoulder, he had the same merry black eyes and a fine head of curly black hair. He looks *exactly* the way Blackie did the day I met him on the moors above Fairley, Emma thought, smiling inwardly. Bryan was her surrogate son, the child she had raised after Laura's death when Blackie was away fighting, and she loved him like one of her own. Her eyes moved on.

There was her darling Robin, handsome as the day was long, very dashing in his air-force uniform, his sensitive, finely drawn face quick and alert as he listened to everyone and talked to everyone, as usual the genial and articulate host. Robin sat between his sister Daisy and his Aunt Charlotte, who had always been drawn to him because of his similarity in appearance to Winston.

For a moment her eyes rested on her elder brother, and her heart overflowed with love for him. He had always been her good right hand: devoted, loyal and hardworking. How happy he looks tonight, she thought, because Randolph, Georgina and baby Winston are here. He loved his family deeply.

Now it was her nephew's turn to undergo a moment of her fixed scrutiny. Randolph, sitting next to his wife, was tall, a little broader in the chest than Winston, and good-looking; it was obvious he was a Harte from the shape of his face and his colouring. He had eyes only for Georgina. A lieutenant in the Royal Navy, he wore his uniform with great aplomb.

And so did Ronnie and Mark, David's sons, who were both in the army, and seated on either side of Natalie. Handsome young men, dark-haired, with lively, intelligent blue eyes inherited from their grandmother Janessa Kallinski. How good that family had been to her when she had had no one except Blackie.

David caught her studying his sons, and he smiled at her and winked. She was seated at the head of the table, and he was on her left. Blackie was on her right, as he usually was.

'Quite a gathering of the clans, Emma,' David murmured. 'We're all enjoying this wonderful meal, it's delicious. And just look at all the boys ... they're practically smacking their lips. I bet they haven't had food like this in a while.'

She laughed, her green eyes sparkling. 'I'm quite certain it's a bit different from their usual fare,' she murmured and, hearing Daisy's sudden lilting laughter, she looked down the table, saw the fervent happiness on her daughter's face, and her heart sank. Daisy was sitting next to David Amory, and she was absolutely fascinated by him, totally absorbed in the young Royal Air Force pilot. And I fully understand why, Emma thought, for a moment concentrating on him.

David Amory was undoubtedly a charmer, and his looks were guaranteed to make him a target of women. Robin had described him as 'a real pin-up boy, Ma, but he's genuine, very sincere'. Robin had grinned at her and added, 'It's Daisy you should watch.' It was his uncanny likeness to Paul which had first startled Emma when he had arrived with Robin last night. But slowly she was growing accustomed to him. It struck her again that he was as interested in Daisy as she was in him, and she wondered if he knew her daughter was only seventeen. She would make sure Robin pointed that out to him later. David was quite obviously well-bred, with impeccable manners, and Robin had told her he was from an old Gloucestershire family.

As for Matthew and Charlie, the other two pilots from Biggin Hill, they were having a wonderful time, she could see that. Matthew had made her laugh uproariously earlier, when he had given her a rave review about the bathroom adjoining his bedroom, which was on one of the upper floors of the maisonette. He kept going on and on, exclaiming about the marble walls, the size of the bath, which he pronounced gargantuan, and the *hot* water. Not to mention the *heated* towel rail. 'A bit different from our billets,' he had explained.

Matthew Hall, a lanky young fellow with brown hair and a sensitive face, seemed much more serious than the others. And yet he did have that lovely sense of humour, a wicked grin and a somewhat wry approach to life. She had taken to him immediately.

Emma's eyes moved to his friend. Charlie Cox, who was seated next to her niece Rosamunde, was obviously an experienced raconteur, and he was engaged in a long story which Rosamunde was listening to with obvious interest. He was a pleasant-looking, clean-cut young man, with the same fair-complexioned English colouring as Kit, and deep brown eyes, rather soulful. Emma decided that his quiet, almost ordinary looks belied a fatal charm. He's deceptive at first glance, she thought, but she liked him.

The quietest person at the dining table was her nephew Simon, Frank's son, and as her eyes slid to him in concern Emma realized that he *was* enjoying himself after all. She saw how much he was appreciating the food, really relishing it, and there was a happy expression reflected in his light-grey eyes. He was a clever and studious boy, she knew that, and Frank and Natalie had great hopes for him – were planning to send him to Oxford. He looked more like his mother; there was not much Harte in him, she could see that most pointedly tonight. Although he did have Frank's eyes and his finely wrought mouth and high cheekbones. As for Natalie, Emma decided she had never seen her looking prettier. She wore a silver-coloured silk cocktail suit, beautifully cut and very understated. It suited her extremely well, but Emma couldn't help thinking how unusually thin Natalie was, and for a moment this troubled her.

And then her attention was caught by Jack Field, who had appeared in the doorway of the dining room, inviting them to come back to the buffet table in the kitchen to select their desserts.

'There's quite a lot to choose from,' Emma told Blackie and David Kallinski as they escorted her to the kitchen. 'Hilda's bottled fruits with hot custard, Christmas plum pudding with a brandy sauce, Christmas cake full of sultanas, currants, candied peel and sherry.' She threw Blackie a quick glance, and added, 'Just like those fruitcakes Mrs Turner used to make in that other life of ours.'

Blackie looked down at her, and put his arm around her shoulder, almost protectively, as thoughts of their past came flooding back to him. 'I think I'll be having a bit of each . . . I won't be able to resist, and neither will David.'

'Only too true,' David Kallinski agreed. 'But I've always loved your fruitcake.'

After dinner, when everyone was replete with food, Robin ushered everyone into the drawing room. 'For a sing-song, Mother,' he told Emma, and thought to add, 'Oh, by the way, I invited some other chaps over for drinks later, Ma; some American pilots I got to know recently. I hope you don't mind.'

'Of course not, Robin,' she said, well used to the way her younger son did things on the spur of the moment. Long ago she had decided it was part of Robin's charm, that spontaneity of his. He had an outgoing personality, a friendliness about him, and he enjoyed meeting new people, making new friendships. He definitely had a 'hail-fellow-well-met' air about him.

Coffee was served in the drawing room by Grace. Georgina, Geraldine, Elizabeth and Daisy passed the cups around; Kit stoked the fire, piling more logs onto it, and Blackie walked over to the baby grand, lifted the lid and tinkled on the keys for a few seconds.

'It's in fine tune,' he announced to the room at large, and then realized, much to his embarrassment, that this was rather a silly comment on his part. Anything to do with Emma Harte was always in fine tune, so to speak, whatever it was . . . exactly the way it should be.

Robin, Bryan and Randolph acted as bartenders, pouring cognac for Blackie, Winston and Frank, and a crème de menthe for Charlotte. The other women declined, staying with the coffee.

'There's quite a lot of sheet music in the piano stool,' Emma began, and stopped as the doorbell pealed loudly.

'It's my Yanks!' Robin exclaimed, hurrying across the floor, out into the hall and down the stairs three steps at a time.

Within a few minutes he came back, escorting the three young American pilots who entered the drawing room rather shyly, Emma thought. Her heart went out to them as they came over with Robin to be introduced to her. They were just boys.

'Gee, thanks for having us, Mrs Harte,' Harry Trent said after Robin introduced them, shaking her hand enthusiastically, smiling. He was so tall she had to really crane her head to look him in the face.

'It's great to be with a family for Christmas,' Phil Rodgers murmured, glancing around. 'Beautiful place you have, Mrs Harte, and thanks for having us. It's just like being at home.'

'It's kind of you to have us over, ma'am,' the

third pilot, Harvey Wilson, said. 'This is better than the officers' club any day.'

Emma smiled and nodded and ushered them over to various chairs and asked them if they wanted anything to eat, as usual being her gracious and thoughtful self. None of them were hungry, it seemed, but they did accept the drinks Bryan and Randolph offered, and jumped up when Elizabeth, Daisy and Rosamunde came to speak to them.

'Would you be excusing me, mavourneen,' Blackie murmured, bending over Emma who was now seated with Winston on one of the sofas. 'I think it might be a good idea for me to get this sing-song of Robin's going, sure an' I do.'

'Oh yes, do do that, Blackie darling. It'll be lovely. I know everyone's going to enjoy it.'

Striding over to the piano, Blackie sat down, made himself comfortable, and announced, 'I'll start this sing-song off then, and you must all join in . . .'

'Go for it, Uncle Blackie!' Kit called out, grinning.

'I will, I will, lad, just give me a moment.'

Blackie looked through the sheets of music, and then sat back, and began to play . . . it was a haunting melody, and everyone fell silent, touched by it, waiting for him to begin singing.

In an instant Emma recognized it, and as Blackie started to sing the words her throat tightened with emotion, and she leant into the cushions and closed her eyes, let herself be carried back to the very first day she had met him. And she remembered what a shabby, starveling little creature she had been as she had hurried over the cold and windswept moors. And how he had come across her, as he walked out of the mist, asking the way to Fairley Hall. He had frightened the wits out of her . . .

Blackie's wonderful baritone rang out, filling the room. ' "The Minstrel Boy to the war is gone, in the ranks of death you'll find him. His father's sword he has girded on, and his wild harp slung behind him . . ." '

Not one voice joined in.

The drawing room was totally silent as they listened to his wondrous voice, and so he sang another verse, and then moved on quickly, thinking that perhaps this first Irish ballad had been overly poignant. And so he sang an Irish jig full of tongue-twisting names, and once again Emma recognized it immediately. He had also sung this jig on that long-ago day, and he had made it his second one then. After the jig he sang 'Danny Boy', a ballad that was one of Emma's favourites – and apparently everyone else's, too, since they sat listening raptly, not moving.

Finally, changing the mood, Blackie launched into one of the most popular songs of the day when he began to sing: ' "There'll be Bluebirds over the white cliffs of Dover, tomorrow, just you wait and see. There'll be love and laughter, and peace ever after, tomorrow, when the world is free." '

As he started the next verse, Blackie lifted his right hand and waved it around, motioning to the others to join in. Elizabeth leapt to her feet and ran to the piano, and Daisy immediately followed. A second later, David Amory was standing next to her, his arm around her waist, Emma noticed.

Others came too . . . Harry and Phil, the young American pilots, Robin and Kit, and then Bryan walked over and stood behind Blackie, his hands on his father's shoulders.

They all sang along with Blackie as he started another verse, and then they repeated it, since everyone loved this particular wartime song.

When Blackie paused for a moment, Elizabeth bent down and said, 'Uncle Blackie, could we have a Vera Lynn favourite? I know all of them, and I can sing, too.'

'That I know, me darlin',' Blackie said, and began to play the song he heard her singing all the time. Elizabeth accompanied him, her voice quite lovely, just as he knew it would be.

'"We'll meet again, don't know where, don't know when, but I know we'll meet again some sunny day. Keep smilin' thro' just like you always do. Till the blue skies drive the dark clouds far away."'

The entire room had listened attentively without joining in, and now there were shouts for more, and clapping, but Elizabeth simply smiled and demurred, all the while looking across at Tony.

Phil began to sing 'Paper Doll', and Blackie picked out the tune, and many sang with him; then Matt asked Blackie to play 'There'll Always Be An

England', and everyone sang enthusiastically, and continued to do so with many more of the tunes Blackie and then Bryan played.

Listening to them, watching them enjoying themselves, Emma's heart was full to overflowing. How handsome the boys look in their different uniforms, she suddenly thought. It had often struck her that there was something rather glamorous about uniforms, and a man wearing one was usually lethally appealing to women. But there was nothing glamorous about their jobs . . . what they did was terrifying. And they're all so very, very young . . . some of them no more than boys. Why is it always the flower of a nation that has to go to war? she asked herself. Her heart clenched as her eyes swept over them, knowing what it was they would be doing tomorrow and the day after. And she looked at Blackie and her brothers, and thought: The young *have* to go, it's always been so, because our other men are too old to fight; they could not stand the rigours of war. So it must be the young who put their lives on the line for us . . .

It was Charlotte who suddenly spoke up, and said, 'Blackie, can we have a Christmas carol?'

'Sure, me darlin', and why not?' Blackie answered, smiling broadly. 'Come on, Bryan, me lad, and you too, Randolph. I know you two have often sung together: let's have a bit of harmonizing here.'

Bryan and Randolph came around the piano and stood together facing the room, and the others moved back a little to give them space. And as

Blackie struck a few chords, Emma recognized the first strains of the carol he had chosen for Bryan and Randolph to sing.

'"Silent night, holy night,
All is calm, all is bright,
Round yon virgin mother and child
Holy infant so tender and mild
Sleep in heavenly peace,
Sleep in heavenly peace . . ."'

CHAPTER THIRTY-SEVEN

It was a glorious day in early October 1943, an Indian summer day. The kind of day Emma Harte could not resist. Golden sunshine streamed in through the leaded windows of the upstairs parlour at Pennistone Royal, flooding the room with incandescent light.

Emma had been writing in her diary, as she did each day, and now she put down her pen and closed the black leather book. Locking it in her desk drawer, she pocketed the key and stood up, walked across the room, and stood gazing out of the soaring window that faced the moors.

The sky was a lovely cerulean blue, filled with puffy white clouds, an unusual sky for October. Even in the summer months it was frequently overcast, bloated with dark clouds, as rain blew in from the North Sea. Such was the Yorkshire weather. Today was an exception.

The heather's still lingering, she murmured to herself, noting the purplish tinge on the rim of the hills, how they beckoned her . . . She was a child of those stark implacable moors, had grown up amongst them under the high fells and great black rocks that rose like monoliths to touch the heavens. It had been her world, her most beloved world, and she was always drawn to it, yearned to be up in that desolate country, which was so glorious to her.

On an impulse, suddenly unable to resist, she hurried out and ran downstairs to the Stone Hall. After changing into a pair of her flat walking shoes which she kept in the armoire, she slipped into a loden-green wool coat and headed towards the office at the end of the hall.

As she went in, Glynnis looked up from her typewriter and gave Emma a small smile. 'I was just going to come up and see you, Mrs Harte. I have your letters ready to sign, and—'

'Would you mind if I did it later, Glynnis? I need a breath of air to clear my head. I'll only be gone a short while, a quick walk on the moors.'

'That's fine,' Glynnis murmured, turning back to her typewriter.

'Is everything all right?' Emma asked, frowning, staring hard at her secretary. 'You seem a bit wan today.'

'I'm fine.' Glynnis smiled at her once more.

Emma noticed at once that it was another faltering smile, but she made no reference to it. Glancing at her watch, she said, 'Why don't you go to the kitchen, Glynnis dear? Hilda will make you a little lunch, a cup of tea. It's almost one o'clock, you know.'

'Thank you, Mrs Harte, I think I will.'

Nodding, smiling at her secretary, Emma closed the door behind her as she went out. Once outside she walked off in the direction of the moors, passing the beautifully designed parterres as she did so. She paused for a moment to inspect them with her eagle eye, but they were perfect today; she had always loved their geometrical designs, which did need intense care and weeding. As she moved on she saw Mr Ramsbotham, the head gardener, in the distance. He was with his young nephew, Wiggs, who one day would take over from him. She waved to them. They both waved back, and Mr Ramsbotham, who was wearing a cap, doffed it to her.

Within minutes Emma was heading up the steep path, making for her favourite spot under the 'monoliths', as she always called them. Although she had not been up on the moors for several months, she did not find the climb hard – quite the contrary. At the end of April she had been fifty-four, but she knew she did not look it and she certainly did not feel it. Thank God I'm so fit and healthy, so strong, she thought as she pushed on up the steep incline. She was anxious to reach the summit, where she felt she could touch the sky if she stood on tiptoe and reached up a little bit.

She smiled inwardly, thinking of her brothers and Blackie, and how the three of them had always teased her about the moors, and her unwavering passion for them. Long ago she had stopped trying to explain what they meant to her. How could she put into words this almost mystical feeling she had about them? Sometimes she felt as though they belonged to her and her alone . . . they were a safe place . . . her haven. Whenever she was troubled she came up here to think, to sort out the problems in her head; sometimes she just came because she loved to walk across them. There were times she craved their solitariness and the solitude that abounded here.

After a twenty-minute climb she finally reached the huge pile of black rocks, which seemed so precariously balanced they looked as if they could topple over on a windy day. But they had been here for aeons and aeons, she knew that.

It was windy up here and she quickly slid into the niche between the two rocks. She sat down on the stone she had once had a gardener place there as a seat for her. That had been in 1932. Eleven years ago now, she thought . . . how time flies . . . like those birds on the wing soaring into the sky. They were in a 'V' formation. 'V' for victory, she murmured to herself, and no sooner had that thought entered her mind than she spotted the bombers coming in, flying low across the blameless blue sky in the same 'V' formation. 'V' for victory, she thought yet again, smiling, filled with relief and joy. They'd made it *home* . . . were coming back to their airfields, Dishforth or Leeming, or perhaps Topcliffe, where Tony had been stationed for special training at the beginning of the war. Obviously they had been on a bombing raid over Germany . . . they were home safe. As they droned overhead, she stood up and found herself saluting them . . . the sons of mothers just like her. Her heart swelled with pride.

Emma sat for a while, staring out at the vast panorama that spread itself in front of her: the valley below, and beyond the continuation of the endless moors, empty, desolate, solitary and without life. Except for the larks and linnets with their joyous songs . . . the tender little birds of her childhood days.

It seemed to Emma that time had just sped by since Christmas. So much had happened in the last ten months. The war was progressing quite well . . . it had become a world war in 1941 after Germany had invaded Russia and the Japanese had bombed Pearl Harbor. The Americans had been fighting alongside them for some time now . . . in Europe, North Africa and the Far East. There had been defeats, but triumphs, too, for the Allies, and everyone was optimistic.

Emma believed they would win the war, just as Winston Churchill had always predicted, especially now that they had the valiant and courageous Americans on their side. She thought of the young pilots she had met through Robin, and here in Yorkshire, and she had been impressed with all of them. Her sons were still safe and unharmed, as were all of the sons of the three clans, and for that she was thankful. They were all thankful.

The spring had passed quickly this year, with Robin coming and going, bringing his comrades-in-arms to 'bunk down' with them, as he called it, and with David Amory always tagging along. There had been much laughter and gaiety, the sound of the gramophone playing constantly, the clink of glasses, the peals of laughter, the songs around the piano. She had loved those months: their youth and high spirits had drowned out the wail of the sirens, the harsh gunfire from the anti-aircraft guns in Hyde Park, the deafening sound of exploding bombs.

She had taken them all under her wing, loving them, spoiling them, and most especially David.

It had come as no surprise to her when he had approached her this past May and asked her permission to marry Daisy when she became eighteen. 'But that's next week!' she had exclaimed, and he had answered, 'Yes, I know, Mrs Harte, but there's a war on.' She had been unable to refuse them, they were so much in love. And she approved of young David with his boundless charm and sweet nature. Besides that, Emma knew that she had set her own precedent by allowing Elizabeth to marry Tony at eighteen. There was no way she could say no to her most beloved child, the love child of Paul McGill. And their wedding had turned out to be the happy event of the summer of 1943.

She herself had been somewhat bogged down with work since the beginning of the year, as she invariably was. But she refused to give up her war efforts, even though Winston was always on her back, telling her she was exhausting herself. Emma felt honour-bound to pitch in and do her bit, that was her nature. And she often went with Elizabeth to London Bridge tube station to bring food, kind words and comfort to the Londoners who were sheltering there. Daisy was a willing volunteer as well. Emma also gave money to various needy causes, and raised money for them, and ran a canteen for the troops.

Suddenly she began to laugh, remembering how Jack Field had protested when she had decided to use the basement of Harte's for the canteen, asking her if she had a permit to do such a thing. Jack's objections, albeit uttered in mild tones, had surprised her. She had glared at him most ferociously and snapped, '*Permits? Who needs permits?* There's a war on. And anyway, in case you've forgotten, this is *my* store. I own it, and if I want to have a canteen in the basement, I'll have one!'

Within ten minutes, after she had calmed down, she had been chagrined, filled with the utmost remorse at the way she had spoken to Jack, one of her most loyal and devoted employees. And she had run down to his office behind the food halls and apologized most profusely; he had been relieved that she was not going to give him the sack, that she was so forgiving. 'There's nothing to forgive, Jack,' she had told him softly. 'Well, let's put it this way, *you* have to forgive *me* for speaking to you so harshly, and so very rudely. I value everything you do for me. I'm so sorry.'

He had nodded and smiled and explained, 'I was just worrying about things like fire regulations, Mrs Harte, and the number of people we are allowed to have there, and whether the canteen would affect store security in any way.'

Emma now understood that he had only been doing his duty, and she had castigated him for it. She had listened to him most carefully as he had outlined the inherent problems, and of course he was right; she had been wrong, carried away in her enthusiasm and desire to help the fighting forces. Instead of using Harte's basement she had bought a warehouse just off Fulham Road, and this had been turned into a canteen for the troops. It had become a great success, and she and Jack had remained good friends and colleagues. He even elected to work at the canteen once a week, as she herself did. They both enjoyed it.

A sudden smile illuminated Emma's face, and in an instant she was transported back to a memorable evening at the canteen, not so long ago that she didn't remember the details. The weeks and months fell away . . . she stepped back into her memories of the recent past . . .

'Mummy, look, over there, at Glynnis dancing with Bryan,' Elizabeth said, tugging at her arm, 'isn't she a wonder, the way she's jitter-bugging. Gosh, they're like Ginger Rogers and Fred Astaire. They ought to be in the pictures together.'

Emma followed the direction of Elizabeth's gaze and she had to agree. Her daughter was correct, Glynnis really was a fantastic dancer, whirling around on her high-heel wedge shoes, her dress flaring as Bryan spun her around and out, then pulled her back to him and twirled her again. It was obvious they were enjoying themselves, intent on their dancing.

'The two of them do look very professional. My goodness, I've never seen anyone dance together the way they do, except on the silver screen,' Emma murmured. 'They're a perfect team, just as you said.'

Emma and Elizabeth were standing near the bar in her canteen on the Fulham Road, watching the young Englishwomen and servicemen of various nationalities jitterbugging. Earlier, the two of them had made stacks of sandwiches and served them to the boys, along with cups of tea and coffee, lemonade, Tizer pop and beer. And quite a few glasses of Paul McGill's vintage wine. Jack Field had managed to get Emma a liquor licence for the canteen, and now they could serve alcoholic beverages. 'And what better way to dispose of some of that wine?' she had asked her brothers Winston and Frank, who had agreed with her wholeheartedly.

Frank and Winston were with them at the canteen tonight, along with Robin, who had been given a two-day pass unexpectedly, as had Elizabeth's husband, Tony Barkstone. Emma liked coming to work at the canteen, to talk to the boys from the different services, to give them a bit of mothering, comfort and encouragement. And it warmed her heart to see how much they enjoyed being there having a little fun.

Tony, who had been playing darts, now came over and joined them, putting his arm around Elizabeth's waist, drawing his wife closer. Suddenly the jitterbug music came to an end, and Emma noticed Frank was at the gramophone, putting on another record. Within seconds the strains of Glenn Miller playing *Moonlight Serenade* was filling the canteen with the captivating swing; music popularized by Glenn Miller's big band.

Bryan began to lead Glynnis around the floor at a slower pace, obviously reluctant to release her, but he had to do so when Frank tapped him on his shoulder, cutting in. It was Frank's turn to sway to the music with her.

Emma smiled to herself when she spotted Robin making a beeline for them, and she knew her son was about to cut in, just as Frank had done a moment before.

'I must say, Glynnis is very popular,' Emma said to Elizabeth and Tony. 'I bet she'll dance with almost every serviceman tonight, she's such a good sport.'

Tony agreed, and added, 'Anyway, she happens to be the best dancer who comes to work at the club. She's as light as a feather on her feet.'

'Have you heard her sing, Mummy?'

'No, I haven't, Elizabeth.'

'She's got a golden voice, very lovely.'

'The Welsh are wonderful singers,' Tony informed them. 'They have very special vocal chords.'

Emma stared at her son-in-law in surprise. Tony constantly amazed her; he was always full of tid-bits of information. But there was some truth to what he had just said. 'Yes, the Welsh choirs are renowned,' Emma murmured, looking past him at Frank, who was strolling over to join them.

A moment later Winston came and stood with their group. Placing an arm around Emma's shoulders, Winston whispered, 'That's the one thing I miss, Emm. Dancing. I used to love it so before I lost my leg.'

Slipping her arm through his, she whispered, 'Yes, I know. But let's just remember that if you hadn't had it off when you did you wouldn't be alive.'

'That's true.' Winston was staring at Glynnis and Robin on the dance floor together, and he suddenly said, 'She's turned out to be the best secretary you've ever had, hasn't she?'

'Indeed she has,' Emma answered and then laughed, as she watched an American flyer cut in on Robin, who had no option but to relinquish Glynnis. Her son loped over and exclaimed, 'Why are you standing, Mother, let's all sit down, shall we?' He pulled out a chair for Emma and they all seated themselves at a table near the edge of the dance floor.

Jack Field was standing at the gramophone now, and he changed the record this time. The strains of Glenn Miller's band playing *Fools Rush In* floated into the air, and Emma leaned back in the chair, her mind on Paul McGill. She had not ceased to miss him, and now she felt a pang in her heart, understanding at this moment that there would never be another man in her life. Paul had been her great love, and would remain so always.

When the music stopped, Glynnis glided across the floor, and Emma said, 'Do sit down, Glynnis dear, and catch your breath.'

'Thanks, Mrs Harte. I am a bit puffed. But it was lovely, I'm crazy about dancing.'

'Would you like a glass of lemonade, Glynnis?' Bryan O'Neill asked, hovering around her solicitously.

'Oh yes, I would, thanks, Bryan.' Turning to Emma, Glynnis went on, 'I was hoping my nice GI friend Richard Hughes would be here, but I haven't seen him. Have you, Mrs Harte?'

'I haven't, I'm afraid, but it's quite early, and the canteen is full tonight, so it's hard to spot everyone.'

Winston said, 'How's everybody in the Rhondda, Glynnis? Family all right, are they?'

'Oh yes. Mum worries a lot about my brothers,

off in the war. But then we all worry these days don't we? There's a great deal to worry about, as a matter of fact.'

Winston nodded, lit a cigarette, sat back relaxed, sipping his glass of red wine.

Robin bent towards Glynnis and asked her if she'd like another turn around the dance floor, but she declined. And she also said no to Bryan's invitation when he returned with her lemonade. 'I'm just a bit tired right now,' she murmured, smiling at them in turn, dimpling, her eyes full of sparkle, her cheeks flushed from the exertion.

Watching the men ogling Glynnis, smiling at her, trying to win her favour, Emma saw her objectively, viewing her in quite a different light than she did at the office. There had never been any question about Glynnis's good looks, but studying her intently tonight, watching her brothers, her son and Bryan O'Neill surrounding her like bees around a honeypot, Emma had become acutely aware of her sexuality. Glynnis was . . . *luscious* . . . as well as sultry and glamorous. She had long, very beautiful legs, an ample bosom, a small waist, and the most luxuriant dark hair.

She's definitely a knockout, Emma thought. No wonder they all want to get her in their arms on the dance floor. But that's the only place they will get her . . . she's such a nice girl, not a flirt, not coy, not coquettish, not leading them on. Glynnis is a good girl. I hope her nice American GI comes tonight. She'll be disappointed if he doesn't show up.

No sooner had Emma thought this than Richard Hughes appeared out of the blue, striding over to the table. He nodded to everyone, stretched out his hand to Emma. 'Good evening, Mrs Harte.'

'Hello, Private Hughes. It's nice to see you.'

Glynnis looked up at him, her large blue eyes shining, full of laughter. 'There you are, Richard. I've been wondering where you were?'

Richard gave her a long intense look, obviously smitten with her, and stretched out his hand. Glynnis took it and he pulled her to her feet.

'Please excuse us,' he said to the group at large, nodding to them politely, and then he led her away to the dance floor.

'He seems like a nice chap,' Frank observed, lighting a cigarette. 'She deserves only the best, she's a special girl.'

'Yes, she is,' Emma agreed, her gaze following them. The dance floor was now crowded. There was a happy feeling in the air tonight, a low excited buzz below the sound of the music . . . laughter, voices in conversation. She filled with gratification all of a sudden, pleased that she had started this servicemen's canteen. It did such a lot to boost the morale of the troops . . . troops of all nationalities. British, Canadian, Australian, American, French, Polish . . . young men of spirit, courage and daring, all fighting to free the world of tyranny.

Feeling the cold wind biting into her bones, Emma pushed the memories away, stood up, casting a lingering glance at the high-flung fells, and

then began to make her way down the path returning to Pennistone Royal.

'Have you seen Glynnis?' Emma stood in the
doorway to the kitchen, looking across at Hilda
who was scraping parsnips at the sink.

Her housekeeper swung around, startled, and
exclaimed, 'Oh Mrs Harte, you did make me jump!
I didn't know you were standing there. And yes, I
saw her about half an hour ago. She had a sandwich, here at the kitchen table. And a cup of tea.'

'Was she all right, Hilda?'

'I think so,' Hilda began and stopped, bit her
lip, looking suddenly hesitant. 'Well, madam, as
I say that, I realize I don't rightly know. Glum,
she was, and – well, it's a funny word to use, but
I thought she seemed to be a bit downhearted . . .
perhaps even troubled.'

'I see.'

'Why do you ask, Mrs Harte? Isn't she in that
there little office at the end of the Stone Hall?'

'No, Hilda, she's not, and there's a half-typed
letter in her machine. I came to the kitchen thinking
she might be here, still having lunch. Although it's
not like her to leave a letter in the typewriter.'
Emma paused, threw Hilda a baffled look.

'I asked her about her boyfriend, the nice GI she
told me about the last time she was up here, and
she gave me such a funny look. Right queer it was,
madam.' Hilda shook her head, and announced,
'There's nowt so queer as folk, Mrs H.'

Smiling knowingly, Emma exclaimed, 'I know all of those Yorkshire sayings, Hilda, don't think I don't ... There's nowt so queer as folk, except for thee and me, and thee's a bit odd. You should have finished it, you know.'

Hilda just laughed, thinking you never knew what Mrs Harte was going to say. Putting the parsnip down, she wiped her hands on the tea cloth and said, 'Speaking of lunch, madam, I notice you haven't had anything to eat since that bit of toast for breakfast ... you'll not get fat on that, you know.'

'You can make me a cup of tea, Hilda, that would be nice, but just at the moment I'm not hungry. Now, getting back to your mention of the boyfriend, do you think that perhaps there's trouble between him and Glynnis?'

'Ooh, I just don't know about that. But she did act a bit queer ... as I told you.'

'Perhaps she's not feeling well. She looked a little peaked earlier. I'll just pop up to her room. In the meantime, you can put the kettle on, Hilda.'

'Oh right away, madam.'

Glynnis was occupying a guest room on the floor above the upstairs parlour, and as Emma climbed the stairs she couldn't help wondering about Glynnis's boyfriend, the nice American she had met at the canteen in Fulham Road. Like herself and Jack Field, Glynnis worked there with some of her girlfriends, wanting to do something for the war, like everyone else. He had appeared to be pleasant. Had they broken up? she asked herself as she came to the door of the Blue Room.

Before she even knocked, Emma heard the muffled sobs, and she hesitated, wondering what to do. And then she rapped on the door, deciding that perhaps Glynnis needed help of some kind.

A moment later, Glynnis was staring at her from the entrance. She was as white as bleached bone, her eyes red-rimmed from crying.

'Whatever's the matter?' Emma asked in a gentle voice.

When Glynnis did not respond, Emma went on, 'May I come in? I can't bear to see you like this, so very upset. Perhaps I can be of help in some way . . .'

Still Glynnis did not speak. She merely opened the door a little wider and stepped back so that Emma could enter the Blue Room.

As Emma glanced around she saw that the bed was rumpled – apparently Glynnis had been lying on it, crying. Moving towards the seating area in the bay window, Emma lowered herself onto the sofa and said, 'Come and sit with me, my dear. You don't have to talk if you don't feel like it, but at least I can try and give you a bit of motherly comfort.'

Standing in the middle of the floor, staring at Emma, Glynnis immediately burst into tears, covered her face with her hands and just stood there, shaking and sobbing.

Emma was on her feet at once, and she guided

Glynnis across the room, helped her to sit down, and then took the armchair opposite. 'Take your time, my dear, try and calm down. Would you like a glass of water? A cup of tea?'

Glynnis shook her head and groped in her pocket for her handkerchief, pressed it to her swollen eyes. After a moment or two she took a deep breath, and said in a choked voice, 'I'm so . . . so . . . sorry to break down like this . . . I've tried to be brave, but it just got to me today.'

'What did?' Emma asked quietly.

Glynnis shook her head, bit her lip, looking worried.

Emma said, 'Is it something to do with your nice GI boyfriend? *Richard*? Have you quarrelled or broken up?'

'Oh no, Mrs Harte,' Glynnis whispered between dry sobs.

'But there is something terribly wrong, something that's disturbing you, Glynnis dear, and I don't want to pry, but I do want to help. Don't you think you can trust me? I can assure you no one will ever know what you tell me. I would never break a confidence.'

Glynnis took a deep breath and tried to get the heaving under control. Finally, in a tearful voice, she blurted out: 'I'm going to have a baby, Mrs Harte. And I don't know what to do.'

For a second or so Emma was speechless. Far away in the past she heard a poor little servant girl saying, 'I'm going to have a baby, Edwin, and I don't know what to do.' And her chest tightened as memories of that day in the rose garden at Fairley Hall swamped her. But then determinedly shaking off the past, she reached out and took Glynnis's hand in hers.

'Oh Glynnis, no wonder you're so upset,' Emma consoled. 'But what about your friend, Richard? Surely he's going to do the right thing by you. I thought he seemed quite taken with you the night you introduced him to me, and I've noticed, subsequently, how lovely he is with you. He seems very caring, very protective.'

'Yes.'

'Doesn't he want to marry you, Glynnis? Is that the problem?'

Glynnis bit her lip, looking suddenly flustered.

Emma frowned. 'You have told him, haven't you?'

Glynnis could not speak. She just shook her head, her face whiter than ever, and there was a stricken look in her lovely eyes.

'But Glynnis, you must tell him, my dear—'

'It's not his,' Glynnis whispered, interrupting Emma.

Emma sat back in a sudden movement, staring at her secretary, her expression extremely troubled. 'Then have you told the man who *is* the father?'

Glynnis nodded, and began to cry, tears gushing down her cheeks.

'He doesn't want to marry you, is that it?'

'Yes. He can't.'

'Is he married?' Emma asked, giving the young woman a long, knowing look.

When Glynnis remained totally silent, Emma murmured, 'Oh Glynnis, my dear, getting involved with a married man only spells trouble. They rarely, if ever, leave their wives . . .' Emma broke off, wondering why she was giving this poor girl a lecture about married men when she needed comfort and guidance.

Glynnis began to weep once more, and Emma rose and went to sit next to her on the sofa. She put her arms around her, held her close, and eventually, as Glynnis calmed down a little, Emma told her firmly, 'We must make a plan, Glynnis. I will help you in any way I can. I don't suppose you want to go home to the Rhondda Valley?'

Glynnis pulled away with a jerk, and gaped at Emma askance. 'No, no, Mrs Harte, I can't! My Da will kill me, or he'll die himself. For one thing, he couldn't stand the shame, me giving birth out of wedlock.'

'Sssh, my dear, I understand what you're saying,' Emma murmured, and she surely did, for hadn't she said the self-same thing to Edwin Fairley when she was fifteen years old?

'Would you like me to speak to the man in question?' Emma said softly, understanding her predicament and wanting to be gentle, sympathetic.

'I don't think it would . . . make any difference,' Glynnis said in a low, choked voice.

'Who *is* the father, Glynnis dear?'

There was a moment's hesitation on Glynnis's part, and then she told her.

Emma simply stared back at her, flabbergasted. For once in her life she did not know what to say, and she sat there, speechless, staring at her secretary. *Disaster*. I'm facing a disaster, Emma thought, and closed her eyes.

But quickly recouping, she opened them, took hold of the girl's hand, and said in a steady voice, 'I think perhaps you'd better tell me all about it.'

And Glynnis did.

It was an old, old story, as old as the world, of a man and a woman, and Emma Harte was only too familiar with its many different interpretations. An instantaneous attraction, a *coup de foudre*, overwhelming passion, a falling in love so hot and obsessive it obliterated everything else. A kind of insanity, a madness, a love so intense it transmuted the ordinary into the sublime . . . for a time. She knew all of the words and phrases Glynnis was uttering. And then tragedy, heartbreak and pain . . . as the man cooled when she told him her sorry tale of woe . . . informed him she was carrying his child. His bastard, was the way Glynnis had just put it.

Yet Emma now noticed that speaking about it seemed to have calmed Glynnis. The tears had ceased to flow, her voice no longer quavered and her excessive trembling had unexpectedly stopped.

Emma had been attentive to the young woman's

every word, concentrating on the details of the over-charged romance now gone wrong. And she fully understood that nothing was going to change. Not now. The man had vacated her life; he would not come back. And Emma was quite certain that Glynnis was well aware of this.

When Glynnis finally finished, she sat back, paused for a second, then murmured in a subdued voice, 'Now you know it all, Mrs Harte. You know my terrible predicament.'

'Indeed I do, Glynnis,' Emma answered, and thought: Only too well do I know what you are facing, but said, 'Basically, you are on your own. At least that is what you believe. But you're not, in fact, because you have me, and I am going to help you through this tough time in your life. I'm going to make sure you have a proper doctor, wages while you take maternity leave, a job waiting for you after the baby's born. This I promise you.'

Glynnis, taken aback by Emma's sympathy, kindness and generosity, was silent, staring at this powerful woman, an uncomprehending expression in her eyes. At last she said slowly, 'Why would you do this for me, Mrs Harte? Don't think I'm not grateful, because I am. But *why*?'

'Because I'm fond of you, Glynnis, and because once, long ago, when I was only a girl, much younger than you, I was in a similar position. I had no one to help me at one particular moment, and so all I craved was money, because I knew money would be my salvation, the salvation of my child. I knew money would protect the baby, protect me, and I strove hard to acquire it. A lot of it. So you see, I *know* first-hand that money is the most important thing to a single mother, as well as a little understanding and kindness from others, if it's available. But it isn't always, you know. Most people turn a blind eye, or treat you like a leper.'

'That's true, I'm sure.' Glynnis took a deep breath. 'I don't know what to say, Mrs Harte. *Thank you* doesn't seem quite enough.'

'Oh it is, Glynnis, of course it is. I just want you to try not to worry now that we've had this talk.'

'I do worry, I'm afraid it's my nature.' Glynnis stopped, bit her lip, and said in as steady a voice as she could summon, 'Mrs Harte, a while ago you spoke about Richard Hughes, my GI boyfriend. You said he seemed attentive and caring, protective even . . .'

'Yes, I did say that. And it was my honest observation, Glynnis.'

'Richard loves me, and he wants to marry me, and I was thinking that perhaps . . . well . . . actually, I wondered what *you* thought about it? I mean about me marrying Richard? Wouldn't it be a solution . . . to my *predicament*?'

Emma, momentarily startled though she was, kept her face neutral, displayed nothing as she sat back in the chair, giving Glynnis a keen and somewhat appraising look. 'Do you have any feelings for him, Glynnis? I thought you were so madly in love with the other man that you couldn't see straight.'

'That's true, Mrs Harte, I just told you, I loved *him* too much. But I like Richard a lot, you can't *not* like him, he's so kind and good-natured. And he's crazy about me, so I suppose I could grow to care for him in a *good way* ...' Her voice trailed off when she saw the stern look settling on Emma's face. 'What's wrong, Mrs Harte? Why are you looking at me like that?'

'I was thinking that – if what you're saying about Richard is true – you cannot possibly deceive a man as good and kind as him. It would be dishonest, and dishonourable. You cannot let him think this child is his.'

'Oh, but I wouldn't do that!' Glynnis cried, her voice rising shrilly. 'Anyway, it couldn't be his, because we ... well, we haven't, you know, done anything like that.' Glynnis stopped abruptly, her face now scarlet with embarrassment. 'I'm not promiscuous.'

'Forgive me, Glynnis, I didn't mean to imply that you were. However, you did appear to be rather close to him when I saw you together at the Fulham Road canteen, so I made an assumption. That was totally wrong of me, and I apologize. I would never cast aspersions on your morals, my dear. I understand life too well to do that.'

'It's all right, Mrs Harte, please don't get upset.' Glynnis swallowed hard and, dropping her voice, she added *sotto voce*, 'I was a virgin until I fell in love with *him* ... he was the first man I ...

knew.' Her voice was lower, as she added, 'You *know* what I mean.'

'I see.' Emma rose, went to look out of the window, staring down at the parterres. 'Best seen from above,' the young Wiggs was always telling her. He was such a sweet little boy . . . they were all sweet when they were boys.

Returning to the chair, Emma now continued: 'So . . . how will you go about this, Glynnis? Are you simply going to accept Richard's proposal, and then tell him you're pregnant? Explain to me how you intend to proceed.'

'I don't know,' Glynnis said quietly, looking suddenly more subdued and downcast than ever. 'Perhaps I should just tell him the truth, say that I'm pregnant, that the man's not standing by me, and ask him if he still wants to marry me. That *I'd* be willing, if he is.'

Emma said nothing, turned this over in her mind, her eyes narrowing.

'What do you think, Mrs Harte?'

'I think it's the only way to approach it, I really do,' Emma replied finally. 'I think in this particular instance, honesty is your best policy.' Leaning forward, focusing on her secretary, Emma explained: 'You have nothing to lose. If Richard turns you down and walks away from you, then you have your fall-back position. *Me.* You know I won't break my word to you, Glynnis. I will help you all I can, and for as long as you need my help. I promise you that.'

'Thank you, thank you very much. And will you promise me something else, Mrs Harte?'

'If I can keep the promise, then of course I'll make it. What is it?'

'Whether I marry Richard or not, I don't want anyone to know who the father of my child is, not ever. You must promise me that you'll never tell a soul.'

'I promise I won't tell anyone *ever*, Glynnis, not as long as I live.'

Glynnis sighed in relief. 'You see, if Richard doesn't marry me, I'll figure out a story about the father of the baby. It's 1943 and there's a war on, and there are a lot of dead heroes already . . . I'll invent a good story to protect my child . . .'

Emma nodded, but remained silent.

'Perhaps it doesn't sound very nice, but it's only a sort of . . . well, a white lie, isn't it? You see, I wouldn't want the world to know that *he* had . . . abandoned me. It would be humiliating. Do you understand that?'

'I certainly do. However, remembering how beautifully your nice GI treats you, I feel certain he'll marry you. Why wouldn't he? You're very lovely, Glynnis, and a very nice girl. He'd be a fool not to marry you.'

CHAPTER THIRTY-EIGHT

Emma picked up the silver-framed photo-graph of Daisy and David, taken at their marriage in May of 1943, and breathed on the glass. Then she rubbed it with the yellow duster she held in her small hand, removing the fingerprints.

There, that's better, she murmured to herself, staring down at the picture, thinking how lovely Daisy looked in her wedding dress. It was made of pale blue silk and she wore a matching picture hat, and carried a nosegay of summer flowers. Almost two years ago. Now she was a mother, having given birth to a baby girl in January of this year, 1945.

Stepping closer to the long library table in her Leeds office, Emma put the photograph back in its place, and picked up the latest one of her newest granddaughter.

Paula McGill Harte Amory. How surprised Emma had been the day of her granddaughter's birth, when she had gone to the London Clinic to see Daisy. 'I've chosen the baby's first two names, Mummy,' Daisy had announced. 'I'm going to call her Paula McGill. After my father.' Emma would never forget how flabbergasted she had been. Daisy had simply laughed and said, 'Don't look so *shocked*. Honestly, Mummy, for a woman as sophisticated as you are, you can be awfully naïve sometimes. Did you think I didn't know Paul was my father?'

Emma had not known what to say, how to answer her. Daisy had gone on to explain that she had worked it out for herself when she was quite a small child. 'And anyway, I realized how much I resembled him physically. And when I was twelve he told me himself. He told me he was my biological father.' She had been stupefied, had gaped at Daisy, who had laughed again, but very gently this time. And then Daisy had told Emma how much she loved her and Paul; that they had been the best of parents. But now Emma recalled that she had remained a little flustered all that day.

His heiress, Emma thought, as she put the picture back on the table and reached for the one of her first grandson, Alexander Barkstone. Elizabeth had given birth to him in February of 1944. He was a handsome little devil, gurgling there at his christening, the spitting image of his father Tony. She set the photograph down, and leant closer to the table, now looking at the wedding picture of

Robin. He had married Valerie Ludden in January of 1944, a nursing friend of Elizabeth's, who had been their matron-of-honour. They look well together, Emma decided, and she'll be perfect for him, good for his career. The right choice. She stared at her favourite son. How good-looking and clever he was. Recently he had told her he was going into politics after the war.

After the war, she thought, moving away from the table; how glibly we say that these days. But the end *was* near. Everyone knew it. And Churchill kept saying it. They *were* winning the war, with the help of their greatest ally, the Americans. Thank God the Yanks, as Robin called them, had come in to fight alongside their troops. They might not have made it without them. And certainly not without Winston Churchill, the greatest leader their country had ever known. Deep in her heart Emma believed that Churchill had been their salvation, and that it was he who had brought them to victory, a victory hard won and honourable.

Walking back to her desk, Emma suddenly thought of Glynnis Jenkins, with affection. Eventually Glynnis would go to America as a GI bride.

She was Glynnis Hughes now, having married her nice GI boyfriend in December of 1943. The wedding had been at a local chapel in her home town in the Rhondda Valley, and everyone had had a grand time, Glynnis had told her afterwards. Especially the Jenkins family. They had discovered that Richard's forebears had come from that part of Wales before emigrating to America a century before.

Glynnis's son had been born in April of 1944, and they had called him Owen, a favourite Welsh boys' name. He was just a year old this month. Emma made a mental note to send him a card and an appropriate present. She and Glynnis had stayed in touch; there was a deep friendship between them. And without knowing it, perhaps, Glynnis had averted a disaster.

Marriages and births, that's what make the world go around, Emma thought, and then looked at the door as it burst open, startling her.

Her brother Winston hurried in, moving so rapidly she thought he might trip. From the look of him she thought something dreadful must have happened, perhaps to one of their boys. His face was drained of all colour and stricken, and his eyes were dark with pain.

Automatically, she jumped to her feet, all of her senses alerted to trouble. 'Winston, whatever is it? You look . . . *demented*.' She took a deep breath and steadied herself for bad news. 'It's not one of our boys, or Blackie's or David's, is it?' she asked, her voice faltering slightly.

'No, no,' he was swift to answer, wanting to reassure her, seeing the fear in her eyes.

'But what is it? You seem so perturbed, so distressed.'

'I am. And so will you be. It's hard for me to explain here. You have to *see*. You have to come across the street to the *Evening Standard*. They're waiting for you. We have some important decisions to make. About what to put in the next edition today. The first one's already on the street. I want you there because the decision will be yours ultimately. It's your newspaper, you own it, and you've got to call the shots today, Emma. The editorial shots.' He grabbed her arm and started to pull her away from her desk. 'Come on, it's urgent!'

'But for God's sake, Winston, tell me what's wrong? What is this all about?' She struggled to free herself from his grip and stared into his face, trying to understand. 'Please tell me before we go over to the paper. You owe me that.'

'I do.' Winston Harte took a deep breath. 'American troops marched into Buchenwald yesterday . . . Thursday the twelfth of April, 1945. Don't forget the date. What they found boggles the mind. Prisoners in such appalling and horrendous condition the Americans thought they were *dead*. But they weren't. Just tortured beyond belief. It's been wholesale murder for years. The Nazis have committed the most vile atrocities imaginable. They've murdered millions. It's genocide . . .' Tears were running down Winston's face, but Emma was sure he didn't know, so emotionally disturbed was he. He stared at her, then brushed his face with his hands, absently. 'David Kallinski was always right, Emma, when he told us the reports were toned down, minimized. *Millions and millions.* The Nazis have murdered *millions* of Jews . . .'

She was looking at him almost uncomprehendingly, and then she said, very slowly, 'But Winston, they wouldn't dare.'

'They dared,' he said.

They walked across Commercial Street to the back entrance of the newspaper company, which faced the front of Harte's store, the most important and imposing in Leeds. They entered the building through the circulation department. Here the vans waited to be loaded with the newspaper's edition, which was then distributed throughout the city and suburbs, as well as outlying districts and other nearby towns.

The familiar smells of damp newsprint and ink greeted them as they went in, making Emma feel instantly at home. These were her newspapers and she loved them; she nodded to the men who turned to greet her, wished them good morning.

As they went up the back stairs to the offices of the *Yorkshire Morning Standard* and its sister paper, the *Evening Standard*, Winston suddenly drew to a halt and took hold of Emma's arm.

They had barely spoken since leaving the store a few minutes earlier, both caught up in their troubled thoughts. Now he said, very quietly, 'Brace yourself, love. You're in for a shock.'

She simply nodded and they continued on up the stairs, through the linotype room, where the typesetters waved to her or called out greetings. Finally they came into the corridor of the editorial offices and hurried down to Martin Fuller's office. It seemed to Emma that an air of gloominess pervaded the newspaper company this morning. Usually she was energized by the activity and excitement of news-gathering; today it was oddly absent.

Just before entering Marty's office, Emma straightened her black jacket, adjusted the collar of her white silk shirt. Then she nodded to Winston. They went in.

Only twenty-seven, Marty was a boy genius in Emma's eyes, very much from the same school as Arthur Christiansen, editor of the *Daily Express*, where her brother was the leading columnist. Chris, as he was called by everyone, had changed the look of the *Daily Express*. Marty had done the same with the *Yorkshire Morning Standard* and the *Evening Standard*.

Marty was on the phone, but he said goodbye and instantly hung up at the sight of Emma, and Winston, his immediate boss.

After they had greeted each other, Emma said, 'Winston tells me the news is horrendous.'

Marty nodded, but said nothing.

She suddenly noticed the strain on the managing editor's face, his pallor. 'We'd better get to work. It's a matter of urgency because of the next edition, isn't it?' she said.

'I had to let that one roll, Emma. It's got to be on the streets at ten o'clock and it's already nine-twenty. It's printing now as we speak. If we make some quick decisions I can revamp the front page, maybe more, for the noon edition.'

'Let's go to the newsroom then,' Winston said.

'I've got everyone working at the conference room table. The editor, the chief sub, the news editor, the pictures editor, my layout man, several of our top reporters . . . it seemed easier to have them all together, Emma.'

Emma sat in the midst of Marty's team, a group of hardworking newspapermen with their sleeves rolled up ready for action, their eyes on her, but also occasionally glancing at the big clock on the wall opposite. The deadline for the next edition was creeping closer and they were all fully aware of that.

'Some of the national dailies have carried stories this morning, but not too many pictures. Remember, they were going to press last night, and in the early hours of this morning, when the story was breaking,' Eric Knowles, the editor of the *Evening Standard*, reminded her. As he spoke he pushed the papers towards her, but she barely glanced at them.

'Are you telling me we have much more information already?' she asked Eric, pinning her eyes on him intently.

He nodded, and turned to the news editor, Steven Bennett. 'Tell Emma what we have.'

'Loads of stuff has been rolling in all night, from Reuters and the other wire services and our own correspondents. We certainly have a lot more information now than was available last night. It's still coming in. And we have the pictures.'

Jack Rimmer, the pictures editor, interjected, 'They're horrific, Emma. Almost unbearable to look at.'

Swallowing hard, she said, 'I'd better see them, Jack.'

He pushed a pile of wire service photographs towards her, and she began to shuffle through them. Horror spread across her face and her eyes held a stunned expression as she looked up, and stared for a moment at the pictures editor. She couldn't bear to look down again at the photographs spread out before her, but she knew she had to do so. They wanted her to make the decision about what went in the paper . . . it was clear that, in this instance, it was her responsibility.

Finally she lowered her eyes again and focused on the pictures once more.

They were graphic; told a foul and inhuman story of torture and the most unspeakable brutality and cruelty ever known to man. It was mass murder of innocent people on a grand scale, a scale so vast it stunned in its magnitude, and Emma was speechless with shock. Naked and half-naked people, emaciated beyond recognition as human beings, were hollow-eyed and without hair, living skeletons as they stared out at her from tiered bunks and from behind the barbed-wire fences of the camps. The images were chilling.

There were more photographs equally as disturbing and horrific, of gas ovens and torture chambers and piles and piles of dead bodies dumped carelessly like so much rubbish in mass graves. All victims of the highly efficient and relentless Nazi death machine . . . She was nauseous, could think of no words strong enough to describe this atrocity, so appalling was it.

Emma could not stop trembling and her eyes filled with tears. She compressed her mouth and snapped her eyes shut for a moment, striving for control, not wanting to break down completely in front of these tough newspapermen. But when she finally opened her eyes a moment or two later and looked at them she saw their sombre, ashen faces and the horror and pain in their eyes also. Groping for a handkerchief in her pocket, she wiped her eyes and blew her nose, but the tears started again and it took her a moment to compose herself.

Taking a deep breath, she said, 'This has to be the most heinous and barbaric crime against humanity that has ever been committed in the history of the world.'

'It is,' Marty agreed. 'Millions have been killed. And the wire service stories now coming in are predicting a lot more dire news. Other camps are being liberated by American and British troops as we are speaking . . . they're starting to go into Dachau, Belsen, and Ravensbruck, to name only a few. God only knows what other atrocities they'll find.'

Winston glanced at his watch and said, 'Do you

have some front pages for us to take a look at, Marty?'

The managing editor nodded, and beckoned to Johnny Johnson, his brilliant layout man. 'Bring those front pages over here, Johnny, for Emma and Winston to see.' As he spoke Marty also looked at the clock on the wall. 'Time is ticking,' he muttered.

The layout editor spread the first mock-up in front of Emma and Winston, who was sitting next to her.

Emma stared down at it, and shuddered involuntarily. There was a large photograph of the skeletal prisoners staring out hollow-eyed from behind barbed wire, and a banner headline of one word only: GENOCIDE.

The next mock-ups they were shown were of a similar nature, a shattering, graphic photograph with a damning headline. She read: CRIME AGAINST HUMANITY. And then looked at the next one, which announced MASS MURDER, and at a third, NAZI DEATH MACHINE.

Emma did not have to ask anyone's opinion or discuss it. She knew very well which banner headline had the most impact, and swiftly she said, 'I think we must go with this one. *Genocide*. It says it all. Now what are you carrying inside, Eric?'

The editor told her, 'We've a number of stories, very detailed, about the camps, and we can keep updating the stories for later editions as the news keeps breaking.'

'Good.' She took another deep breath, and continued, 'I don't think you should pull any punches, either in the text or in the pictures. Our readers have to be told about this in detail. Unflinching detail.'

'Leeds has a big Jewish population,' Marty remarked. 'They'll want to know.'

Emma looked across at him and nodded. 'That's true. But even if there were no Jews living in Leeds, I'd still play this to the hilt. The whole world must know what was perpetrated by Nazi Germany. We're in the business of news, so let's do our best to present this most . . . heartstopping story . . .' Her voice unexpectedly broke, but she recovered fairly swiftly, and finished, '. . . in the most dignified way we can, but without minimizing it to protect people's feelings. The pictures are horrific, harrowing to look at, heartbreaking, unbearable. *But we must show them.* One picture is worth a thousand words, so I'm told. We have to run with this, give it our all. And use everything. Cut down on local news, if that's necessary.'

Eric Knowles jumped up, and exclaimed, 'You're right, Emma! And I'd better go with Johnny and get things rolling. Genocide it is, right? That's the headline you want?'

'Yes. It says it all in one word.' Emma then asked, 'Will we make the noon edition?'

'Just about.' He ran out, followed by Johnny Johnson, the news editor, and the reporters.

Emma stared at Winston, then focused on Marty.

'I want a special edition devoted entirely to this story.'

'When for?' Marty asked, staring at her worriedly.

'Can we get it out today?'

'Not if we want to do the story justice. There's a lot more coming in on the wires out of Germany, as I told you earlier, not only from Reuters but also from the Associated Press. Obviously all of the wires are carrying it. And we have our own reporters on the job in London. Let's face it, it's the biggest story of the century.'

'Of any century,' Winston murmured. Turning to Emma he said, 'Let Marty and his team do the story *right*, Emma.' Addressing Marty, he suggested, 'Why not do a special edition for the weekend?'

'Good idea,' Marty exclaimed.

Emma said, 'I agree.'

Later, when she was back at the store, Emma wept in the privacy of her office. The horror of what she had just seen would not leave her consciousness and the images in the photographs kept floating in front of her eyes. And she would begin to weep again.

But eventually she gained control of her swimming senses and picked up the telephone and dialled David Kallinski's number at his office.

'David, it's Emma.'

'Hello, Emm. How're you?'

'So so. Can I come and see you?'

'Is something wrong? You sound upset.' His voice echoed with sudden concern.

'David, some of the national papers carried stories this morning . . . about the Americans liberating the concentration camps in Germany. Did you see any of those stories?'

'No, I left for the office very early, and the paper hadn't arrived.' There was a small silence, then he said, 'It's . . . bad, isn't it?'

'Very bad. Worse than bad. *Horrendous.*' She tried to swallow. Her mouth had gone dry. 'Let me come and see you, David darling . . .' With one hand she flicked the tears from her damp cheeks.

'Yes, I'd like that,' he said in a voice that was suddenly hoarse. 'You've always been a comfort to me, Emma.'

CHAPTER THIRTY-NINE

'Isn't it wonderful, Winston, that the war's over!' Emma ran across to her brother as he came into her Leeds office, grinning, his face alight with happiness, relief reflected in his eyes.

'Thank God, that's all I can say.' Winston hugged her to him, kissing her on the cheek. 'All of our boys are safe and soon they'll be coming home, and finally, at long last, we can get back to normal.'

It was Monday 7 May, 1945. That morning, in the early hours, at 2:41 a.m. precisely, General Alfred Jodl, the representative of the German High Command, and Admiral Hans von Friedeburg, empowered by the Grand Admiral Karl Doenitz, the designated head of the German state, signed the act of unconditional surrender of all German land, sea and air forces in Europe to the Allied Expeditionary Force and simultaneously to the Soviet Union. The war with Germany was suddenly and finally at an end.

Walking with Emma to the small seating area

near her library table of family photographs, Winston went on, 'Marty called me a few minutes ago. Apparently it's now official. It's been declared V-E Day in Europe . . . tomorrow May the eighth. So we can all celebrate. I thought it might be a nice idea to throw a little party for the boys over at the news-papers. They'd love it, I know. I tested the waters with Marty, and he reacted in a very positive way.'

'Then do it, Winston. Let's show our appreci-ation. Have Marty arrange it.' She frowned. 'But where will they have it? In one of the pubs?' She shook her head. 'No, it wouldn't work. Perhaps a private room in a restaurant?'

'That sounds better, but don't worry about it, Emma. Marty will handle it. I just wanted to be sure the idea had your approval.'

'Of course it does. They all deserve it. They've worked like demons all through the war years, done a terrific job, considering they've been under-staffed. And the special editions they did in April, when the death camps were liberated, are master-pieces of twentieth-century journalism. I'm very proud of the staff, and of the specials.'

'Yes, they were superbly handled,' Winston agreed. 'Are you staying in Leeds for the rest of the week, Emm?'

'Yes, I am, Winston, why?'

'Well, since it's V-E Day tomorrow, I thought you might like to celebrate with me and Charlotte.'

'There's nothing better I'd like to do. Thank you.'

* * *

It seemed to Emma that the city of Leeds went crazy on V-E Day night. The red, white and blue Union Jack hung out of every window, fluttered from every flagpole, and was waved in the hands of most children and adults as they crowded into the streets. The air of festivity was beyond belief.

People danced and sang, cheered each other and laughed; they hugged and kissed, strangers as well as friends; and they shouted out their pride and happiness at their victory over tyranny. They were jubilant, full of high spirits.

Streaming rivers of light, from windows no longer blacked out against enemy bombers, illuminated the streets like sunshine. Bonfires blazed on every corner, as if it were Bonfire Night in summer, and effigies of Hitler were sacrificed to the flames.

The pubs were filled to overflowing, the customers spilling out into the streets, and everywhere there were patriotic songs, and toasts to the brave boys in blue and khaki and navy, and cheers for Winston Churchill. 'Long live Winnie!' they cried, affection filling their voices. 'He's brought us through. Our British bulldog has brought us through. Long live Winston Churchill!'

Charlotte had cooked a wonderful dinner, and when Emma arrived at their lovely house in Roundhay she felt her nose twitching. For the first time in weeks she was suddenly hungry.

After Winston had opened a bottle of champagne, they toasted each other, and their sons, and finally Emma said, 'Here's to our Prime Minister, the greatest leader *we've* ever had.'

The following morning she thought exactly the same thing, experienced the same sentiments as she opened the *Yorkshire Morning Standard*, and saw his speeches printed on the front page. She had asked Marty to make sure the paper carried them in full, and the managing editor had obliged.

As she began to read the report of the event she truly wished she could have been there. Thousands had assembled near the House of Commons, and they had roared their approval of Churchill as he had appeared with some of his colleagues on the balcony of the Ministry of Health in Whitehall. He made two brief speeches to the vast crowd. After the words, *'This is your victory,'* the crowd had roared back, 'No, it is yours.' According to the correspondent of the *Morning Standard*, who was covering it, this response had signified an unforgettable moment of love and gratitude.

She read on, savouring every word Churchill had said last night:

'God bless you all. This is your victory! It is the victory of the cause of freedom in every land. In all our long history we have never seen a greater day than this. Everyone, man or woman, has done their best. Everyone has tried. Neither the long years, nor the dangers, nor the fierce attacks of the enemy, have in any way weakened the independent resolve of the British nation. God bless you all.'

According to the reporter, a respectful hush had fallen over the crowds, and they had stood in silence, waiting to hear him speak again, seemingly unable to get enough of him.

Emma began to read the second speech he had made to those crowds, and her heart swelled.

'My dear friends, this is your hour. This is not victory of a party or of any class. It's a victory of the great British nation as a whole. We were the first, in this ancient island, to draw the sword against tyranny. After a while we were left all alone against the most tremendous military power that has been seen. We were alone for a whole year.

'There we stood alone. Did anyone want to give in?' The crowd shouted 'No.' 'Were we downhearted?' 'No.' 'The lights went out and the bombs came down. But every man, woman and child in the country had no thought of quitting the struggle. London can take it. So we came back after long months from the jaws of death, out of the mouth of hell, while all the world wondered. When shall the reputation and faith of this generation of English men and women fail? I say that in the long years to come not only will the people of this island but of the world, wherever the bird of freedom chirps in human hearts, look back to what we've done and they will say "do not despair, do not yield to violence and tyranny, march straightforward and die if need be – unconquered." Now we have emerged from one deadly struggle – a terrible foe has been cast on the ground and awaits our judgement and our mercy.'

Emma sat for a few moments on the sofa under the leaded window in the upstairs parlour, thinking about Churchill's words and of the past six years. Last night everyone had celebrated, but her uppermost emotion had been relief. Relief that her sons had not been killed, that her son-in-law and her nephew, and the sons of Blackie and David Kallinski had managed to cheat death also. Thankfully, they had their futures ahead of them, and that was something to celebrate, wasn't it?

Walking over to her desk, she clipped the speech from the newspaper, put it in an envelope and stowed it safely away in the fruitwood casket scrolled in silver. It was worth keeping, something to savour again later.

It had been sunny all day, remarkably balmy for May, and to Emma's surprise it stayed warm well into the early evening.

She sat on the long terrace at Pennistone Royal, waiting for Blackie O'Neill to arrive. He had been in London on business on V-E Day, and so he had not been able to celebrate with them in Leeds. But now that he was back in Yorkshire they would have their own celebratory dinner tonight, just the two of them.

Her thoughts drifted . . . events of the last seven years sped through her head like a reel of film unwinding before her eyes. Paul's death, her overwhelming grief, the perils of war . . . the Blitz, the dreaded V1s, those deadly, pilotless bombs that had devastated and decimated London. Their young at risk in the air and on land and sea. But the triumphs, too. Dunkirk and other victories . . . so many good things mixed in with the heartache: her children's marriages, the birth of three grandchildren.

How time passes, and so swiftly as we get older, she thought. She had been fifty-six at the end of April . . . it didn't seem possible to her. In a few years she would be sixty. Yet she felt so *young*. Young at heart and in spirit, and her strength and energy and vitality were the same as they had been when she was ten years younger.

I have been lucky, she thought suddenly, and more so than some, her mind turning to the mothers and fathers who had lost sons in the conflict, like those of young Matthew Hall, Robin's friend from the 111th Squadron at Biggin Hill, shot down over France. Killed in action. A smile touched her mouth when she thought of him, but her eyes were moist. So young, too young to die.

A fragment of Rupert Brooke's famous poem ran

through her head . . . If I should die, think only this of me: / That there's some corner of a foreign field / That is for ever England. There shall be / In that rich earth a richer dust concealed; / A dust whom England bore, shaped, made aware, / Gave, once, her flowers to love, her ways to roam, / A body of England's, breathing English air, / Washed by the rivers, blest by suns of home . . .

She heard his step, and then his familiar voice, calling, 'Are you out there, mavourneen?' and she quickly brushed the tears from her cheeks before she stood up and swung around, went to meet her oldest friend.

Blackie put his arm around her and they walked back down the terrace, and sat together on the wrought-iron garden seat. He said, 'I'm sorry I missed all the excitement in Leeds. Winston told me it was quite something to behold.'

'It was, the town went mad.'

'Aye, the whole of Britain went mad with joy.' He looked into her eyes. 'We've been lucky, you and I. And Winston and David Kallinski. Our sons are safe. Some not so lucky, eh?' He touched her damp cheek with a fingertip. 'You've been crying, lass.'

'I was thinking of that nice young man, Matthew Hall, just before you arrived. Robin's friend, and Bryan's, from the 111th Squadron.'

'It's a tragic thing, the loss of our young. Bryan's been devastated that Matt didn't make it.'

'I spoke to David today, Blackie. He was so sad

about his cousin Ruth. She married a Frenchman, if you remember, and went to live in France. She just vanished during the war, and he has worried about her so much. Poor Ruth. He never knew her fate, but now he surely does.'

'There are a lot of broken hearts around these days, me darlin', but we must not dwell on sadness this evening. You and I have such a lot to be thankful for . . .' His eyes grew warm, very loving, as he asked, 'And how's the bairn?'

Emma's face lit up. 'She's just wonderful. Daisy was concerned that her eyes would change colour, but they haven't. They're still that lovely deep blue, so deep in colour they're almost violet, like pansies.'

'Aye, I noticed that when we saw her two weeks ago. And she has Paul's black hair. She's a McGill, all right.'

'I have a good feeling about Paula. She's going to be my girl.'

'Nay, lass, you can't be taking her away from her mother,' he admonished, looking at her askance.

'I didn't mean that she'll be mine *physically*, to bring up. I'm leaving that to Daisy and David for a few years. I meant she would be mine *spiritually*. Neither Elizabeth nor Daisy wanted to come into my business, but I'm hoping Paula will.'

Blackie began to laugh, shaking his head. 'There you go again, thinking about business, as you have done all of your life. But then a leopard doesn't change its spots, I suppose. Still, she is only five months old, Emma. Give her a chance, let her have a childhood!' He continued to laugh, highly amused.

Emma joined in his laughter, and then, sobering, she said softly, 'Paula is my future, Blackie, she surely is. Mind you, I suppose we *will* make an odd couple: the little girl and the old lady . . .'

'You're not *old*, Emma Harte! Why, you'll never be old, me darlin'. You'll always be *my* young colleen of the moors, that little sprite of a girl with her big green eyes and bright red hair shot through with gold . . . Why, I can see you now, Emma, in my mind's eye . . . such a powerful *being* you were, even then.'

Emma sat back in her chair. 'Thank you, Blackie, for always being here for me, for being my very best friend, my dearest friend.'

'And I thank you Emma, for the same . . . it's been a privilege to know you, mavourneen.'

They sat together in silence. After a moment Emma looked up at the sky. It was a deep pavonine blue, turning deeper as twilight now descended, tinged with gold on the rim of the moors. A gentle sky tonight. Reaching out she took hold of Blackie's hand and held it in hers. He looked across at her. She gazed back at him intently for a long moment, and then she smiled her incomparable smile, which illuminated her face with radiance.

'Hearts at peace, under an English heaven,' she said.

PART THREE

Legacy
2001

The legacy of heroes is the memory of
a great name and the inheritance of a
great example.
   Benjamin Disraeli, British statesman
        and twice Prime Minister

I charge you to hold my dream.
                    Emma Harte

CHAPTER FORTY

'I didn't find any secrets,' Paula said, leaning against the door jamb, watching Shane change his shirt, tie and suit in his dressing room which adjoined their bedroom in the Belgrave Square maisonette.

'*Nothing*?' he asked, glancing across at her, a surprised look on his face as he buttoned his fresh shirt.

'Well, let me amend my statement. There is definitely a secret to do with Glynnis Hughes, and it's a name. But that name is not in any of the diaries. Grandy never wrote it down.'

'Who is it the name of?'

'The real father of Owen Hughes.'

'Oh, so Richard Hughes wasn't his biological father after all?'

'No.' Paula adjusted her stance against the door-frame, and went on, 'Whilst you've been out of town, I've done nothing but read Emma's diaries in the evening – well, I skip-read some of them. And very interesting reading they make. Emily agrees. She had to help me out at one point. As I mentioned on the phone to you, Glynnis was Emma's secretary during the war years. She mentions her a lot in the diaries, but she was awfully closed-mouthed about her private life: *protective*, I'd say.'

'But do you think Emma knew the name of the man involved?' Shane asked, his curiosity getting the better of him.

'Oh yes, I'm certain she did. Emma wrote something in her diary, the day Glynnis broke down in tears and told her about her predicament. It was at Pennistone Royal, she used to take Glynnis up there with her from time to time. Actually, Shane, she promised Glynnis she'd never reveal the name of the baby's father as long as she lived, and she didn't. You knew my grandmother, and what she was like. Integrity was her middle name.'

'Yes, Grandfather always said she was the most honest person he had ever known, man or woman. But getting back to Glynnis, she and Grandy must have been quite friendly.'

'I believe there was a deep affection there. I think Glynnis hero-worshipped Emma, and my grandmother was certainly exceedingly fond of Glynnis – favoured her.'

'So the mystery man made Glynnis pregnant, probably refused to marry her, so she married Richard Hughes . . . Do you think that's the true story, Paula?'

'More or less.'

Shane threw her a questioning glance and frowned. 'You sound doubtful.'

'From what I gather, Glynnis knew Richard for some time. They'd met at Grandy's wartime canteen for the troops—'

'Emma had a canteen for the troops,' he cut in. 'Well, I'll be damned!' A surprised but pleased expression crossed Shane's face. 'Well, why am I sounding surprised? That's just like Emma. I wonder why Grandpops never mentioned the canteen to me?'

'It was so long ago, darling, water under the bridge to them. Grandy never mentioned it to me, either. Anyway, Richard was crazy about her, and had proposed, according to Grandy's diary for 1943. She told Glynnis to tell him the truth, explain that she was pregnant, and suggest marriage. If he walked away, Grandy said she had her for a back-up position. That she'd help Glynnis financially.'

'That was generous . . .' Shane threw Paula a pointed look.

'Just Grandy remembering Edwin Fairley, and her own predicament, that's all, I'm sure. Nothing else behind her helping Glynnis. Anyway, the reason I looked a bit doubtful is this . . . I'm not certain the man involved *could* marry Glynnis.'

'Oh, I get it. A married man?'

'Possibly.'

'You've got a funny look on your face, Beanstalk,' Shane said, reverting to his childhood nickname for her. 'Come on, spill it.'

'It's only a thought . . . but maybe Uncle Winston

565

was the father. Emma's brother was awfully high on Glynnis, singing her praises constantly. Grandy even remarks on it in her diary.'

'You can't be serious!' Shane exclaimed, reaching for a blue silk tie, threading it under his collar, beginning to make the knot, staring in the mirror as he did.

'It's just a thought that crossed my mind, because Grandy mentions her brother Winston making extremely flattering remarks about Glynnis. Apparently he really liked her.'

Shane swung around to face Paula. 'But why would Emma give the game away? If her brother was the culprit, why make comments about him liking the girl? Isn't that like . . . spelling it out?'

'I suppose you're right.'

'So Glynnis married her GI and went off to America. End of story.'

'Not quite. As you well know. On her deathbed, Glynnis instructed her granddaughter Evan to go and find Emma Harte because Emma was the key to her future.'

Shane took his jacket off the hanger and slipped it on, then opened a drawer looking for a silk handkerchief for his breast pocket, saying as he did so, 'The dying meanderings of an old lady, most probably.' Then he suggested, 'Look, we've established Evan Hughes is not a McGill. Your grandfather had been dead for several years when Owen was conceived. Let's just assume she's not a Harte either. Therefore, case closed.'

'I agree, and so does Emily. She went through some of the diaries, as I told you. She came across nothing, no reference to the mystery man. She thinks I'm wrong to even consider Winston the first. She says it's well known in the family that he adored Charlotte, and would never have so much as glanced at another woman. So, case closed it is. And naturally I'm not going to mention a word about Glynnis to Evan. There's no reason for her to know about her father's illegitimacy . . . why hurt her?'

'You're right, darling. All you have to do is kill the gossip about Evan being a long-lost McGill.'

'Philip and I will do that, don't you worry. Now, are you ready? We don't want to be late for the retrospective.'

'That's right. How do I look?'

Paula smiled at him. 'Not bad for a man who's spent half a day on a fast plane and in a fast car, trying to get here at breakneck speed.'

'But I did make it in one piece.'

'And some piece it is,' she laughed.

Reaching out, Shane pulled her to him and held her close in his arms for a moment. Then he held her away, looking into her violet eyes that were truly the colour of pansies. 'You're beautiful, and I love you. And I think we're going to be very proud of our daughter tonight, and what she's accomplished.'

'I agree with you . . .' Paula slipped out of his arms and went to pick up her black silk evening purse, then turned to look at him. 'I'm very worried about Tessa, Shane. I think she's being abused.'

He gaped at her. 'Why do you say that?'

'Because she has all the symptoms of a battered wife. I've always thought Mark caused that problem with her shoulder. And I think that psychologically she's unbalanced.'

'If it's true then she'll have to leave him! I won't allow a man to beat her, you can be damned sure of that.' His face had turned grim, and there was a hard glint in his black eyes. 'We're going to have to get to the bottom of this, Paula!' he exclaimed, and she saw how angry he was.

'It won't be easy. Battered wives don't always want to talk. Or leave a dangerous situation. I thought we could take her to dinner with us tonight, Shane, after the retrospective. In fact, I invited her already.'

'Isn't Mark going to be there?'

'Apparently not.'

Shane nodded. 'Perhaps we'll find *something* out. We can certainly try. Anyway, who else is coming to dinner?'

'Winston and Emily. Uncle Ronnie and Michael Kallinski. India and a boyfriend of hers – nobody serious, I understand. Linnet and Julian. Evan and Gideon. Lorne and Mummy. Your father. Aunt Elizabeth and Marc Deboyne. And Amanda.'

'So we won't be able to have a serious talk with Tessa, but we can try to glean something from her. Certainly we can ascertain her state of mind, her mood. How has she been at work?'

'That's just it, Shane, she's not been particularly well, in my opinion. Impatient, irritable and not cooperative. Linnet said she's been very moody, combative, worse than ever.'

'This is a priority . . . we must get to the bottom of it and as soon as possible. But now we'd better go, we won't want to be late,' he said.

India Standish glided down an aisle between two fashion displays, looking stylish in a multicoloured chiffon dress with a narrow torso, bell-like sleeves and a flattering, feminine skirt that fell to her ankles. Some of the pink, yellow and pale blue flowers in the chiffon's pattern were lightly embroidered with tiny bugle beads. It was a stunning summer evening dress that emphasized her slender figure and height.

'You look fabulous, India,' Evan said admiringly, walking over to join her. 'And I love your Manolo Blahniks. I almost bought the same pair.'

India grinned. 'I know, Linnet told me, and you could've you know, I wouldn't have minded at all. And Evan, you look really beautiful. What a lovely colour this delphinium blue is on you.'

'Thank you. It was Linnet who made me buy the dress, but, to be honest, I'd fallen in love with it anyway. I've never had anything quite as stylish before.' Or as expensive, Evan thought, but she did not say this. Her dress was slightly off-the-shoulder, with tiny cap sleeves and horizontal pleats of chiffon from the neck to the mid-calf hem. It was by Chanel, and only someone of Evan's height and willowy figure could have carried it so well. She wore silver strip sandals with high heels, and a pair of diamond stud earrings from Gideon.

The two colleagues and good friends walked around the auditorium, looking at the different displays of *haute-couture* clothes on mannequins, which stood on slightly raised platforms for perfect viewing by the public. There were different sections. Some were devoted to famous designers and their clothes from the 1920s to 2000, with huge blow-ups of the designers on the walls behind the platforms.

There was a section which featured Fashion Icons, the chic and stylish women who had agreed to lend some of their couture pieces, and be part of the retrospective. Their large photographs were displayed on easels in front of their clothes.

And finally there was the biggest and most beautiful display of all, which was entirely devoted to the clothes of Emma Harte, the collection dating from the 1920s to the late 1960s, all designed by world-famous couturiers.

Silk banners bearing the words EIGHTY YEARS OF FASHION: A RETROSPECTIVE hung down from the ceiling in different areas. The entire space was well-planned; designed to allow the maximum number of people to walk around comfortably, looking at the clothes without impeding the view of others.

'Those space-planners from Yorkshire did a really great job!' Evan exclaimed at one moment. 'Gee, India, I sort of hate to say this myself, but I think the whole auditorium looks smashing. Congratulations to you, to us!'

'I agree. You know, we've really pulled it off,' India murmured in a pleased voice. 'It's simply splendid. And the clothes are divine.'

'Oh look, here's Linnet with one of the press people.' As she spoke Evan waved, and Linnet hurried over. She was wearing a black lace dress with green silk showing through the cobweb lace, and when India stared at her, frowning, she said quickly, 'It's a *copy*. The original's still over there somewhere in Emma's collection.'

India and Evan both laughed, knowing she was making a reference to Emma's Lanvin, and Linnet said, 'I'd like to introduce you to Ms Barbara Fitzpatrick. She's the editor of *Chic* magazine, and she wrote that lovely story about the retrospective, which appeared last month.'

After the three women had exchanged greetings, India and Evan moved on, leaving Linnet to talk to the editor and escort her around the show. 'It was really nice of you to come back to see the retrospective finally finished,' Linnet said, smiling at Barbara Fitzpatrick.

'I wouldn't have missed seeing this,' she answered. 'I think you've done a superb job. In fact, I don't think I've ever seen anything quite so well mounted ever before.'

'Thank you again for saying so. I must say we've had some really talented people working on it. Anyway, you'd said on the phone that you wanted to see the Emma Harte Collection again, now that it's really and truly in place. Properly in place.'

'Yes, I would. I've always been a great admirer of your great-grandmother. I think she blazed the way for women in business, in the boardroom. In fact, my mother told me she knew her vaguely in the Second World War. They worked at some charity together. In any case, she was a legend in her own time, everyone knows that. So naturally, I'm interested in the clothes she chose, and wore. Apparently with great aplomb.'

'It's just over here,' Linnet murmured, and ushered the fashion editor, renowned in London for her style, down one of the aisles. They came to a stop at the largest display, composed of a dozen or so platforms. Laughing all of a sudden, Linnet said, 'My cousin India was startled a moment ago when she saw me in this cocktail dress. She thought I'd nicked Emma's Lanvin. But as you can see, Ms Fitzpatrick, there it is in all its glory.'

Barbara Fitzpatrick followed the direction of Linnet's gaze, then stepped closer to look at the black lace dress on the mannequin. Glancing back at Linnet, who stood behind her, she said, 'Someone made you a wonderful copy of this, I must say.'

'I know. I couldn't quite get over it myself. The person who made it copied it right down to the last little detail. The emerald bow on the shoulder of the dress on the mannequin is costume jewellery, of course. But my great-grandmother had a real emerald bow.'

'Yes, I've seen photographs of her wearing it. In fact, there it is on that blow-up of her. Oh my goodness! You do look like her, don't you? You're the spitting image.'

'That's what everyone says.'

At five-fifty exactly, a cadre of good-looking young women, all wearing identical black trouser suits – smartly tailored jackets with slim trousers – moved discreetly through the exhibition. Approaching the members of the press who were attending the Press Preview, they explained that the cocktail reception was about to start in the adjoining area. Would they please move forward into that area to partake of the refreshments.

Once the exhibition hall was empty, Linnet went out and locked the glass doors herself, and gave the key to her secretary, Cassie Littleton. Then she asked one of the Harte's security guards to put the red rope in place. Turning to Cassie she said, 'A little later you can have them put out the "No Food, No Drinks" signs outside these doors, which can be opened again at exactly seven-thirty so that the public can go through to view the clothes. That's what they paid for, after all.'

'And the cocktail reception too, Linnet,' Cassie said. 'The evening's a total sell-out. We could easily have sold two or three hundred more tickets.'

'But then it wouldn't have been *exclusive*, it would've been a bun fight,' Linnet answered, laughing. 'Limiting the event to four hundred people at a thousand pounds a ticket means that Breast Cancer Care benefits to the tune of four hundred thousand pounds – because Harte's is absorbing all the costs, don't forget. It's going to be a good evening, with a celebrity-filled crowd. *Hopefully*. They did all finally accept, didn't they?'

'Oh yes, and Lorne helped with the actors and film stars. We've got a whole lot coming – big names, too.'

'I knew he wouldn't let us down.' Glancing around, Linnet nodded to herself. 'Thanks, Cassie, for working so closely with the floral people. I think the reception area looks beautiful with all the orchids and the orchid trees. They've done a fantastic job.'

'Everybody's really got behind the retrospective, Linnet.' Cassie turned her head when she heard her name being called, and said, 'Oh, that's the reporter from the *Mail* who's assigned to cover the evening. I'd better go and help him. Excuse me.'

'Fine, I'll see you later. Oh, and you said I'm to go to the podium at about seven-twenty, to announce the opening of the retrospective?'

'That's right.'

Cassie hurried away and Linnet meandered around for a few minutes, checking on last-minute details, and then spotting India and Evan on the other side of the room, she went to join them. Over the last five months they had become inseparable friends as well as colleagues, and she wanted to be with them now, to savour the success of the evening.

CHAPTER FORTY-ONE

Jonathan Ainsley considered promptness on
social occasions plebeian; he preferred to be
fashionably late by at least fifteen minutes.
And so it was six-twenty when he nonchalantly
sauntered into the charity cocktail reception in
the auditorium at the top of Harte's in Knightsbridge.

He had not been inside his grandmother's store
for years, and he was only here tonight because of
his rampant curiosity. He wanted – no, *needed* – to
see his nemesis, his cousin Paula O'Neill. And her
family. After all, he *was* in the process of destroying
them, her husband Shane O'Neill included, and he
had the irresistible desire to gloat.

After a moment or two, moving around the
periphery of the room, he realized it was a smart,
indeed very fashionable, crowd assembled tonight,
quaffing champagne and nibbling on fancy hors
d'oeuvres of all ethnicities, including a large variety
of Asian tid-bits. That was one of the things he

missed about Hong Kong: the food. And certain other aspects of that notoriously tantalizing city of limitless pleasures.

Jonathan Ainsley now slipped his hand into the pocket of his dark-blue suit jacket, his long fingers curling around the Imperial jade disc. His talisman. Good joss, he thought, *this* piece will bring me good joss.

Long ago, he had had another favourite talisman, a smooth pebble of mutton-fat jade. But in the end that had brought him only bad joss, and twenty years ago he had flung it out of the car window as he had sped through the London traffic to Heathrow, on his way back to Hong Kong. And bad trouble.

He rubbed the Imperial jade piece between his fingers, almost sensually, and he knew in his bones that this special and expensive disc was lucky. It had been blessed in a very unique way by an extraordinary woman.

A waiter passed by and Jonathan took a glass of champagne, murmured a thank you, but declined a miniature spring roll offered by a delectable Oriental girl in a black cheongsam. He loathed getting his teeth messy at cocktail parties like this; one never knew who one was going to run across. His eyes lingered on the Chinese girl as she proffered her tray to other guests; he wondered what different wares she might be prepared to offer later. He considered trying to get her number, then dismissed the idea. He had better fish to fry.

Glancing around, seeking Sarah and Chloe, who were his guests tonight, he realized they had not arrived yet. Suddenly, his eyes fell on a tall, handsome young man standing just across the room, only a few feet away. He was elegantly dressed and Jonathan recognized him at once. It was a well-known and much-loved young actor who trod the boards very regularly in the West End. *Lorne Fairley*. Paula's son by Jim, once a friend of his. And there was no question that the woman standing next to him, clinging to his arm, was his twin, Tessa Fairley, Mark Longden's wife. No mistaking her; she resembled her twin too much for that.

Appears to be a bit wan tonight, the beautiful Tessa does, he thought. Pale, obviously highly strung, nervous. Poor girl. Was she having marital problems? He'd heard that Mark Longden was a bit of a devil, and on the fast track these days. *Pity*.

Now, who's this? Jonathan asked himself as another blonde young woman joined Lorne and Tessa. He peered at her over the rim of his glass, his eyes narrowing. It took him a moment before it hit him. She looked a bit like the other two, like a Fairley. So she had to be India Standish, the daughter of his cousins Anthony Standish and Sally Harte, Winston's sister.

Disgusting, he thought, all this intermarrying. He was surprised they weren't all bonkers by now, stark raving mad.

And here was the famous Linnet Harte O'Neill

arriving. Jonathan had no trouble in recognizing her. She was the reincarnation of Emma Bloody Harte, his sainted grandmother. And by God the resemblance was terrifying. It wasn't just the red hair, it was everything about her. He was close enough to see the vivid green eyes, the perfect complexion, the shapely figure. *She* must have looked like this at her age, he thought. And he had to admit that Linnet O'Neill was beautiful. But then his grandmother had been beautiful, and also the devil incarnate. He had ended up hating her.

So focused, so concentrated was he on his relatives, that he did not see his cousin Sarah Lowther approaching him.

But Sarah noticed Jonathan. In fact, she paused, her eyes widening as she followed the direction of his intense, unblinking gaze. Immediately she saw Paula's three children standing with India Standish, the four of them chatting and laughing, obviously enjoying themselves.

What fine-looking young people they are, Sarah thought admiringly, smiling. Rather like my lovely Chloe. She wished Chloe knew her cousins. That was something her daughter had always missed: siblings, and an extended family. How she longed to give her that.

Sarah took a few steps towards Jonathan and then unexpectedly faltered. Her eyes were on her cousin, and her blood ran cold when she saw the expression on his face. It was one of pure malevolence. She felt an icy chill run through her, and suddenly she knew what he was going to do, how he would seek revenge on Paula. He would do so through her children. He would hurt them somehow.

So sure was Sarah of this that she wanted to turn around and leave. But that would be cowardly, she told herself. No, she must stay, play him at his own game, find out everything she could. Be his friend. That was the only way she could help her cousin Paula. And help her she would. More than anything else she wanted to be accepted back in the family, not only for her own sake but also for Chloe's. Besides, Paula's children were innocent, and in a way so was Paula.

'Hello, my darling Jonny,' Sarah said a moment later, touching his arm, smiling up at him.

Instantly his face changed. The hard and dangerous expression disappeared, was replaced by a warm, friendly smile. 'Sarah, my dear, as beautiful and chic as always. I like this cocktail dress. Very fetching. Whose is it?'

'Balmain.'

'The royal blue flatters you. Where's Chloe?' he asked, looking beyond her, frowning, as he sought out his god-daughter.

'She couldn't come, Jonathan, I'm so sorry. She sends her apologies. And where's Uncle Robin?'

'Dad wasn't well enough to come up to town. He's stuck in Yorkshire. A bad back. His ticket was a waste of money, and apparently so was Chloe's, unless you've given it away.'

'No, I haven't, and I'm so very sorry about this. Look, I'll reimburse you.'

'Don't be silly, I don't want your money.'

'Oh, and I thought you did. I was under the impression you wanted me to invest in your new company, Jonny.' She made a *moue*. 'I guess I was mistaken.'

His face lit up, and he exclaimed, 'If you want to, I'd be glad to have you invest, Sarah. You'd be onto a good thing, too; have a very profitable return on your money.'

Smiling back, she took hold of his arm affectionately. 'Then we must talk about it over dinner. You can tell me about it, and I'll make a decision. After all, I was a very good partner in the past, wasn't I?'

'Certainly. Mind you, I'd only let you in on this deal because you're family, you know.'

'I understand, and I'm very grateful. I've always been grateful to you,, Jonathan, for letting me into these little deals of yours. Thank you for the opportunity.' She wondered if he'd forgotten all the money she'd lost with him.

He half smiled, and then drew her attention to the family members nearby. 'See that group over there, Paula's little gang. And look at the flaming redhead like you . . . that's Linnet O'Neill.'

Sarah merely nodded, and took a glass of champagne from a passing waiter.

'She's going to be the one to inherit it all,' he whispered, leaning closer. 'Even Pennistone Royal.'

Startled, Sarah looked at him intently. 'How do you know that?'

'A little dickybird told me,' he answered with a laugh.

Sarah shook her head. 'I wouldn't be too sure of that.'

'Well, well, well!' Jonathan exclaimed, suddenly grabbing hold of her arm fiercely. 'Enter a blaze of princes!'

Sarah stared at him, frowning, and then swung her head towards the entrance. Coming through the double doors, entering the auditorium, were her cousins Paula, Emily, Amanda and Winston. And Shane O'Neill accompanied them, looking more handsome than ever to her. Well, she had loved him once.

She heard Jonathan sniggering. 'Who the hell do they think they are?'

But Sarah paid no attention. She felt a surge of love for them all, and a sudden, long-absent sense of absolute pride. Four of those five people entering the room with such dignity, such elegance, were Hartes. Just as she was a Harte. And she felt herself standing just a little taller. A blaze of princes indeed. Emma Harte's princes.

'Just look at bloody Paula O'Neill, dripping in Grandy's emeralds!' Jonathan muttered angrily. 'A bit overdone isn't it, rather vulgar, what?'

'No, not vulgar at all, Jonathan. I think Paula looks beautiful in the white satin jacket and black skirt. That outfit also happens to be a Balmain, and the emeralds are fabulous on the white satin.'

'Oh God, are you getting all sentimental on me, Sarah? Bloody mawkish again?' he growled.

'No, not at all,' Sarah answered quickly, and reminded herself to be careful. She did not want to annoy him; she wanted to get as much information as she could from him.

The moment Paula saw Evan Hughes, she excused herself from the others and hurried over to her. 'Good evening, Evan,' she said, smiling at her warmly.

'Hello Mrs O'Neill. You look *fantastic*. If you don't mind me saying so, you'll be the star of the show tonight.'

'Thank you, Evan, that's nice of you, but I think there are *three* genuine stars here. You, India and Linnet. You've done quite the most extraordinary job, all of you. And I'm proud of you.'

'We've tried very hard ... I'm glad you're happy.'

'Evan, I've got some wonderful news for you. There's no mystery, no secret in my grandmother's diaries. I've read most of them, and Emily helped me by reading some of the others. Yes, your grandmother, Glynnis, did work for Harte's during the war. She was Emma Harte's favourite secretary. My grandmother was very, very fond of her.'

'And that's all? There really is no terrible secret buried in those pages?' Evan asked, her eyes on Paula.

Paula shook her head. 'Just mentions of them

working together, at the store, at the house in Belgrave Square, and up at Pennistone Royal. Actually, what I thought was really interesting is that your grandmother met Richard Hughes, your grandfather, at the canteen for the troops that Emma started in Fulham Road.'

Laughter flooded Evan's face, and she exclaimed, 'That's what grandfather told me! That they'd met at a canteen. Just imagine, he must have known Mrs Harte too.'

'I believe he did.'

'So I can relax, Mrs O'Neill. I'm not a McGill. And I'm not a Harte either.'

'That's correct,' Paula replied. 'Now, if you'll excuse me, Evan, I see my mother standing over there with Grandfather O'Neill. I need to speak to them.'

'Thanks so much for going to all that trouble, Mrs O'Neill,' Evan said, and then she exclaimed, 'Oh, there's Gideon, I think he must be looking for me.'

CHAPTER FORTY-TWO

E van walked along the beach, kicking a stone,
feeling miserable. She had never been one
for confrontations, and she loathed them,
tried to avoid them whenever she could. But Gideon
had been in a terrible mood, not only last night but
this morning. And his attitude disturbed her.

Sighing under her breath, she walked over to
an ancient stone wall and sat down, wondering
how to bring their relationship back to where
it had been before, how to get it on an even
keel.

Even keel, she thought, and suddenly smiled to
herself. She hadn't thought of that phrase for years.
Her grandfather had often used it. He had loved
boats, and had frequently taken her out on his
sailboat when she was a child; she had thoroughly
enjoyed every moment of sailing with him.

The wall she was sitting on overlooked the Irish
Sea, and she realized that was why the phrase had
popped into her mind. The view was beautiful, and

it was a lovely sunny day, pleasantly warm. Not a day for rows or upsets, not at all.

It had all begun last night, at the retrospective at the store in London. Towards the end of the evening, a strange man had come up to her and engaged her in conversation. He had wanted to know who she was, if she was related to Paula O'Neill, and he had even tried to ask a lot of other questions.

Momentarily startled, she had suddenly resented the intrusion, had excused herself and hurried away. A moment later Gideon had been by her side asking her what the man had been talking to her about. He had been upset, a little angry.

She had explained everything to him but he hadn't seemed satisfied, and somehow the incident had cast a pall over the dinner later.

Even this morning, on the private jet flying to Douglas in the Isle of Man, he had been a little curt with her, and moody. After they had checked in at the hotel he had disappeared almost at once, telling her he had to meet with Christian Palmer. She had fully understood – that was the reason they had flown over to this little island in the middle of the Irish Sea – yet it had upset her because he was so . . . *cold*. Yes that was it, that's what bothered her. His coldness. Until last night he had always been warm, loving and considerate.

She wondered if he wanted to break up with her, and then dismissed that thought at once. After five months, almost six, she knew him well. He was too straightforward and open to play games. If he wanted to end the relationship, he would. He would tell her in his usual frank way, which she had found refreshing and disarming. Some men were devious. Not Gideon Harte. He was almost *too* honest at times.

He had told her he would be back after lunch, and would meet her at the hotel. It was called The Nunnery, and if she hadn't been so upset she would have teased him about the name. After all, he had signed them into a suite as Mr and Mrs G. Harte.

Did she want to be Mrs Gideon Harte? She wasn't sure. Yes, she wanted Gideon, the man, but her father had tried to put her off him, telling her she wasn't in his league, that he was a Harte, and came from a different world. It struck her again that her father had been strange on the phone in the last few months, especially when it came to that particular family.

Jumping up, Evan shrugged into her cotton windbreaker and, shoving her hands in her trouser pockets, walked along the pretty beach, wishing they could stay in the Isle of Man for the week-end and work things out. But they had to go to Yorkshire.

Lifting her head, she glanced up. The sky was a lovely blue, filled with hazy clouds, and out on the bay there were sailboats and several yachts. It was a charming spot, and she certainly wanted to come back. There were quaint little houses and shops, and ancient-looking pubs, and she had noticed that the surrounding landscape was quite breathtaking. Did it remind her of Nantucket, this unique spot? Or somewhere else? Somewhere she had been with her grandfather when she was young? Somewhere in France, she thought.

Paula O'Neill had been so nice last night, and Evan was relieved that those now-famous diaries contained nothing odd or unpleasant about her darling gran. Glynnis Hughes had been the centre of her world when she was a child, and she had loved her deeply, looked up to her. She couldn't have borne it if there had been something wrong about her gran.

The sunny weather, the pretty surroundings, helped to calm Evan, and soon her morose mood fled. Blown away by the Irish wind from across the sea, she thought, and taking a deep breath she decided she was going to be . . . *on an even keel* when Gideon returned from his meeting. She hoped that the famous and brilliant newspaperman would agree to come back to work for the Hartes . . . certainly that would put Gideon in a better mood, if nothing else would.

Leaving the beach, Evan wandered up into the town, and soon found a charming little café for lunch. After ordering a bottle of still water, she looked at the menu, and when the waitress arrived she ordered fish and chips.

Gideon found Evan sitting in the garden of The

Nunnery when he returned from his meeting with Christian Palmer. She was reading a magazine, but put it down when she heard his step.

Looking up at him, smiling, she said, 'I hope everything went all right, Gideon. Is Christian coming back?'

'Yes and no,' he said, sitting down next to her in one of the garden chairs. 'It's a kind of compromise.'

'What do you mean?' she asked him, genuinely interested in his work.

'He's coming back part of the time. It's not exactly what my father wanted, but it's better than nothing, I suppose. He just loves it here in Douglas so much he doesn't want to be anywhere else. What we've agreed is that he works for three weeks and then gets a week off. Also, quite a few free months in the summer. He loves sailing, the beach life.' Gideon sighed. 'I'm going to have to cover us by finding a really bright young journalist to train, somebody who can fill the gap when Christian's away.'

'Yes, I understand.'

Gideon fell silent, lost in thought.

Looking across at him, Evan said, 'Can we talk about last night, Gideon? *Please?*'

'If you want to, yes,' he agreed in a neutral tone.

'I do. Not that there's a lot to talk about . . . I just don't understand why you were so angry . . . about that guy speaking to me.' She shrugged, half laughed. 'He didn't mean any harm.'

'How do you know?' Gideon asked, sitting up straighter, giving her a hard stare. He didn't want to tell her how angry his father had been when he had seen Jonathan Ainsley and Evan chatting. Ainsley's presence at the retrospective had infuriated Winston, and then he had suddenly grown suspicious, asking him if Evan knew Ainsley from somewhere. But basically, deep down, Gideon knew it was an innocent encounter on her part. On the other hand, a Harte didn't talk about a Harte to somebody who wasn't a Harte. Family rule. Emma's rule. And so he didn't mention his father being upset, just fudged it a little and finally said, 'The man who came over to chat to you is a somewhat disreputable member of our family. His name's Jonathan Ainsley, and I was upset that he was . . . *accosting* you, Evan. And curious to know what he *actually* talked to you about.'

'But Gideon, darling, I *told* you,' she responded, being careful to keep her voice soft, very low. 'He asked if I was related to Paula O'Neill, who I was, did I work at Harte's, what I did there. And so I told him, but then I began to think he seemed a bit . . . *creepy*, you know, *really weird*, so I edged away. And then suddenly you were at my side and steaming.'

He nodded, realizing he had perhaps been out of line a little last night. Forcing a laugh he said, 'Hasn't it occurred to you I might have been jealous?'

Evan started at him askance, and grinned. 'But

he's old enough to be my father! This Jonathan Ainsley guy is easily sixty! Really, Gid!'

'Ainsley's not a nice man. If you ever run into him again, walk in the other direction. And walk fast.'

'I won't run into him again.'

'You never know.'

Evan decided he was goading her again, and she said quietly, 'Enough of this relative of yours. Are you angry about something else?'

'Not angry. No. Just disappointed,' he admitted.

'In *me*?' she asked, her voice suddenly rising an octave.

'No, not actually in you. I'm disappointed that you seem to be pulling away from me . . . I've never been in a serious relationship before, Evan. *I am serious about you* . . . I'd hoped that you would have been able to commit to me, as I have to you . . . but you're so *elusive*.' He sighed. 'Don't you feel the same way any more?'

'Oh Gideon, yes, yes, I do. I just want to be sure. We've only known each other five months . . .'

'Sometimes you can know someone all of your life, and never *truly* know them . . . then again, you can know someone totally in only a few days.'

'I do love you, Gideon . . .' Her voice trailed off.

'But there's a *but*?'

'Not really. It's my father—' She cut herself off, shocked that she had mentioned his name, and stared at Gideon, unexpectedly lost for words and furious with herself.

'Your father doesn't even know me. Are you saying he objects to me?'

'No, no, not at all!' she cried, her expression earnest, seeing the colour flooding into his face. She knew he was a very proud man. 'He thinks that we're from different worlds, that it might not work out in the long haul.'

'That's your father. What do you think?'

Evan did not speak for a moment; she sat in the other chair, looking at him, loving him, knowing now that if she wasn't careful she would end up losing Gideon Harte. And that she did not want to risk.

'I don't think it matters at all that we're from different worlds.' Reaching out, taking hold of his hand, she smiled at him.

He stood up, went over and tilted her face to his, kissed her cheek. 'Let's not quarrel any more.' Pulling her to her feet, he added, 'I just can't stand it when we do.'

CHAPTER FORTY-THREE

A shaft of bright light suddenly cut through the dim greyness of the bedroom, and Tessa blinked and endeavoured to sit up. She saw Mark silhouetted in the doorway, and instinctively she knew he was in one of his hostile moods. Over the last few weeks she had grown more and more atuned to him, knew what to expect.

Taking a deep breath, she said in a steady voice, 'Hello, darling. We missed you tonight.'

'Where were you?' he asked in a dull, low tone, coming into the room, closing the door behind him.

Reaching out, Tessa turned on the little brass lamp she used for reading. But it cast only a small pool of light near the bed, and she could not quite make out the expression on his face. He remained standing near the door.

'It was the retrospective at the store,' she explained. 'The fashion retrospective. I kept thinking you would arrive.'

'I told you I wouldn't be able to make it,' he muttered.

He had done nothing of the sort, but Tessa ignored this and said, 'Never mind. We did miss you at dinner, though. My mother was asking for you.'

'I left you messages.'

This wasn't true either. However, she went along with it, having learned of late not to argue, exclaiming, 'Oh dear, and I never got them. Were you working late, Mark?'

'Yes, at the office.'

'Haven't you had any dinner? Do you want me to go downstairs and make you something?' She pushed herself up in the bed, her eyes on him. She was suddenly wary.

'No. I've eaten.' He slouched into the room, beginning to undress as he did, throwing his jacket on a chair, pulling off his tie, stepping out of his trousers and underpants. Then he went into the adjoining bathroom and closed the door.

After a moment Tessa heard the toilet flush, the water running. She stared at the door, her mind racing, wondering about his condition. He hadn't been drinking, she was fairly certain of that, but there *was* a strangeness about him. He spoke in a mumble, and he had moved in slow motion. It alerted her. Was he on something again? Feeling suddenly extremely vulnerable in bed, Tessa threw back the bedclothes and got up.

At that moment the bathroom door flew open

and Mark stepped into the bedroom. There was an aura of anger around him.

They stared at each other across the bed.

Mark spoke first. 'Why did you get up? Don't you want to share my bed anymore? Perform your wifely duties?'

Tessa forced a faint laugh before saying, 'Don't be silly, Mark, of course I do.' She laughed again even more weakly and added, 'I was just going to check on Adele.'

'Why?'

'I thought I heard a noise.'

'No you didn't! You just want to leave my bed. Who are you screwing these days? Is it Toby Harte? Are you still having it off with your cousin?'

Tessa tensed up, but she kept total control of herself, edged toward the door.

'Answer me!'

'You know there's no truth in what you suggest,' she replied, keeping her voice low, controlled, taking a few small steps again.

'I don't trust you, you bitch!' Mark rushed to the door, locked it, and then moved in on her, his fury finally coming to the surface, bursting out of him.

Tessa backed away, but he was fast, and he suddenly had his hands on her shoulders. Pulling her toward him roughly, he brought his mouth down hard on hers. She struggled, trying to avert her face without much success; he gripped her even tighter, and pushed her up against the wall, then slammed her back against it as she tried to push him away again, wanting to escape him. But tonight he was stronger than usual. Now he flattened his body against hers, brought his mouth to hers, pushed his tongue in it, then with one hand he sought her breast. She tried harder to extract herself, and almost did, but he lunged at her, snatched at the neck of her nightgown, and ripped it down to the hem. Grabbing her arm, he dragged her to the bed, threw her on it, and flung himself on top of her. As his face came down to hers, he mumbled, 'You're not going to get away from me.'

'Please, Mark, don't do this. I don't want you to make love to me like this. You're hurting me. Please, Mark, calm down. I'm saying no, to you, Mark. No. No. *NO*. Please stop!'

'It's Toby you want. I know that. Everyone knows that. The whole world knows that. But you can't have him. I won't let you. You're mine, bitch. And you're going to submit to me.'

'No, Mark, no. Not this way. This is rape, Mark.' Tessa began to sob, and tried once more to slither out from under him, but he was a dead weight on her body. She could not move, could barely breath.

His face, hovering above hers, was engorged, and there was a look of pure hatred in his eyes. Unexpectedly, he threw back his head, and a shout of laughter escaped him. 'Rape? You call this rape? Then you'd better get used to it, you little whore.

Because this is the way it's going to be from now on. You must submit to my will, submit to whatever it is I want from you.'

'Oh please, don't do this,' she cried, tears running down her face. She grabbed at his shirt, tried to pull herself upright.

Mark Longden paid no attention to her pleas. Instead he plunged into her, forcing himself inside her, thrusting against her, making grunting noises as he did, his breathing ragged.

Fight though she did, Tessa was no match for him, and she finally gave up, exhausted. She lay still, let him have his way with her, vowing it was never going to happen again. He was raping her for the last time.

Finally he rolled off her, fell into a deep sleep almost immediately, breathing heavily.

Tessa waited for a while and then she turned off the small brass reading lamp, slid out of bed and crept towards the door. Unlocking it as quietly as possible, she slipped out into the corridor, shut the door softly behind her. After looking in on Adele, checking that she was asleep, Tessa went down the corridor to her own private suite of rooms.

After taking off her torn nightgown, and throwing it in the wastepaper basket, she stepped into the shower and let the hot water sluice over her for some time, leaning against the tiled wall in the showerstall, sobbing as if her heart would break.

But after a while the tears ceased, and she shampooed her hair, washed herself thoroughly, wanting to remove all traces of Mark. And she was thankful that she had started to use birth control pills again ... the last thing she wanted now was to find herself pregnant by him again.

After drying herself and her hair, Tessa got dressed, pulling on tights, a pair of grey lightweight gabardine trousers, and a white cotton top. Pushing her feet into a pair of comfortable brown loafers, she began to pack a few clothes to see her through the weekend. Later she would prepare a case for Adele, whilst Elvira got herself ready and packed for a trip to the country.

Later, sitting at her desk in her office in the private suite, Tessa wracked her brains, wondering where to take her daughter and the nanny. Certainly she did not want to go to Yorkshire; she didn't want her mother and Shane to know about Mark's treatment of her. She was far too humiliated to confide in them. I'm an abused woman, and I'm fitting the profile perfectly. Hide the facts. Don't tell a soul. Forgive him. Accept his contriteness and apologies. Until he does it again. And again. And again. Until he kills you.

Tessa had now read enough about abuse to understand ... and she did understand many of the reasons for it. And yet Mark did not exactly fit the profile of an abuser. She knew without a doubt that he was on something, drugs of some kind. And he was drinking.

Sitting back in the chair, staring blankly at the computer screen, Tessa unexpectedly had a moment of absolute clarity: yes, there was only one place for her to go: *Pennistone Royal*. There was nowhere else she was truly safe from Mark Longden. For undoubtedly, he would try to find her and their child. He would come after her with deadly intent in his heart.

Anyway, she belonged there, didn't she? Belonged in her mother's house.

It struck her that she knew exactly who she was at this precise moment in time. She was the daughter of Paula O'Neill, the great-granddaughter of Emma Harte. She was very much a Fairley in many ways, but she *was* a Harte. And therefore she must stand tall, be strong, take control of her life. And it must be a life without Mark Longden.

CHAPTER FORTY-FOUR

P aula stared at her pad, scanning the list of guests she and Shane expected at Pennistone Royal for the weekend. It was more than she had originally thought.

Some of their children would be there. Emsie; Desmond, who was coming home from boarding school and Linnet. And Linnet had invited Evan Hughes, and so she wrote Blue Room next to her name, and moved on to Julian Kallinski. He would be comfortable in the Gold Room, she decided. Grandfather Bryan came to stay with them every weekend these days, so he had his permanent suite, which he loved. He would stay put.

Smiling, feeling a sudden surge of happiness, Paula sat back in the chair, thinking about her daughter's forthcoming engagement to Julian. How happy Grandy would have been, and David Kallinski, Emma's dear old friend. Emma, in particular, had longed for the three clans to be joined in matrimony, and finally it was going to happen. She and

Shane had elected to announce the engagement and throw a family dinner the night before the upcoming birthday party for Shane and Winston, two weeks from now.

Aside from Evan Hughes, all of the guests at the dinner would be family members. She hoped there would be no family squabbles . . .

There was a knock on the door and Margaret walked in, looking apologetic. 'I'm sorry to disturb you Mrs O'Neill, but there's a young woman downstairs in the Stone Hall asking to see you.'

'Who is it, Margaret?' Paula asked, looking puzzled. 'I'm not expecting anyone today.'

'She didn't tell me her name. She has a letter for you. She showed it to me but she wouldn't give it to me. She says she was instructed to put it in your hands and yours only. Very adamant she was.'

'I suppose I'd better see her then.'

Margaret was staring across the room at the long library table which held a large collection of family photographs, and Paula glanced at the table herself. It had come from Emma's Leeds office years ago. 'What is it, Margaret? What's bothering you?'

'The girl downstairs has red hair. Almost the same colour as Miss Linnet's. I think she might be a relative.' Walking across the room, Margaret stopped at the library table and touched the top of a silver frame. 'She looks a bit like her.'

Paula was startled and she stood up, shaking

her head, nonplussed. 'It can't be . . . why would Sarah Lowther's daughter be here?'

'I don't know, Mrs O'Neill. But she is . . . she's downstairs. I'm sure of it.'

'Please bring her up. Straightaway, please.'

Margaret nodded and hurried out, and Paula went around the desk, crossed the room to the library table. It was jammed with Emma's collection of favourite pictures which Paula had never had the heart to put away. Her grandmother had bought the table from the Leeds store over thirty years ago, and the photographs, all in silver frames, had been her pride and joy. She had often held a picture in her hand and talked about the person in it to Paula. She was always warm, always loving, never critical about any of her children or grandchildren. Except Jonathan Ainsley. Emma herself had removed his photograph just months before her death; she had come to the conclusion he was double-crossing her. And how right she had been.

Focusing on Sarah's photograph, Paula wondered if it really was Sarah's daughter downstairs. She knew Sarah had married a famous French painter, Yves Pascal, years ago, and had made a success of her life and her business in France.

She wondered if Shane had really spotted Sarah at the retrospective; he had insisted several times that she'd been there. With Jonathan Ainsley. Winston had definitely seen *him*, and had been outraged. 'What temerity he has,' Winston had spluttered to her later at the dinner. 'How dare he show his face to us!' Emily and Gideon had managed to calm him down, but he had really seen red the other night, had been apoplectic.

Turning away from the library table, Paula walked over to the long sofa in front of the leaded window, and stood waiting. A moment later Margaret was ushering the young woman into the room. With a slight nod, her housekeeper disappeared.

The young woman walked forward, held out her hand and said, 'Good morning, Mrs O'Neill. I'm Chloe Pascal, Sarah Lowther's daughter. Please forgive this intrusion, but my mother wanted you to have this. I'm to wait for your answer.'

After returning her greeting pleasantly, and accepting the envelope, Paula indicated that Chloe should be seated. Then she walked over to her desk, slit the envelope with a paperknife and took out the letter.

The stationery was expensive and it had her cousin's professional name engraved across the top: *Sarah Harte Lowther*.

Paula scanned the letter quickly. It said:

> *Dear Paula:*
>
> *I am sending this note by hand with my daughter Chloe because I want to get it to you quickly, whilst I am still in England. I must see you urgently. I have vital information which*

concerns you. I am nearby, and if you will see
me now, Chloe will come for me.
    Sarah

Walking back to the seating arranged under the
leaded window, Paula lowered herself into a chair
and said, 'Where is your mother, Chloe?'

'She's sitting in the car further down the driveway, just beyond the curve. You can't see the car
from here.'

'I know. Would you please go and get her, ask
her to come and see me. From what she says in
her note we have to talk.'

Chloe jumped up. 'Right away. I'll be back in
a few minutes, Mrs O'Neill.'

Paula nodded, watched her hurry out. The girl
looked like her mother, with the same burnished
auburn hair that was such a Harte family characteristic. It was a warm June day and Chloe wore a
stark black cotton suit and simple gold jewellery,
but she had that distinctive French chic which was
so hard to imitate.

Rising, walking across to the leaded window,
Paula looked down, saw Chloe heading for the
driveway. She turned away, went back to her desk,
putting the letter in a drawer. She had a gut instinct
that her cousin Sarah wanted to tell her something
disturbing about Jonathan. But why? Had they
had a falling out? Or had Sarah had a twinge
of conscience? It had to be something of vital
concern to *her* or Sarah would never have asked to

see her, made these moves. She felt herself tensing, suspecting that Sarah had only bad news. Paula took a deep breath, steeling herself for trouble.

A few minutes later, Margaret came into the room, escorting Chloe and her mother.

Walking forward, Paula said, 'Hello, Sarah. This is a surprise,' and stretched out her hand.

Sarah shook hands with her. 'Thank you for seeing me. And please excuse the way I've handled this. But I needed to see you quickly before I return to Paris. And I thought if I telephoned you might—'

'Hang up?' Paula said, cutting across her. She shook her head. 'No, Sarah, I *would* have taken your call. In fact, I've often thought you would be in touch over the years . . . I sort of expected it, actually.'

This comment startled Sarah, and she exclaimed, 'If only I'd known. I've wanted to speak to you, just to explain one thing. And it's this. I never knew Jonathan was cheating the family, hurting Harte Enterprises. I did invest in his company, that's true, but I thought everything was above board. I only found out how wrong I'd been the day your father fired me, and you threw me out of the family. I trusted Jonathan and I shouldn't have. I think I was rather naïve, looking back. But I swear on my child's head that I never knew what he was doing.'

'I realized that a long time ago, Sarah. I came to understand that you were innocent of any wrong-doing.' Paula paused, pursed her lips, shook her head sadly. 'What a waste of the years . . . Well, that's all water under the bridge . . .'

'Yes, it is,' Sarah agreed, and went on swiftly, 'And I didn't come here to explain, or to try to exonerate myself. I came to warn you.'

'Let's sit down,' Paula murmured, indicating the seating in front of the leaded window. 'Can I offer you anything? Tea? Coffee? Water?'

'No, thank you,' Sarah said, sitting down in a chair.

Chloe, lowering herself onto the sofa, simply shook her head.

Leaning slightly forward, looking at Paula intently, Sarah began: 'I've suspected for a long time that Jonathan wanted to get back at you, hurt you in some way. He has always believed you were his nemesis, that you destroyed him. He cannot get at you in business any more, you've seen to that, but he can hurt you through your children. The other night I was at the retrospective and I saw something that frightened me. It also alerted me. At one moment he was staring very intently at your children, and he had a look on his face of pure malevolence. Evil. I knew instantly that he was up to no good, and I was afraid for you and yours. I didn't know what he planned, but I made up my mind to find out as much as possible.'

'Did you think he would simply . . . *confide* in you, Sarah?' Paula asked, giving her a long hard stare.

'No, I didn't, he can be very close-mouthed even with me. But Jonathan likes his wine and he likes to boast . . . and he has a tendency to boast when his tongue has been loosened by a good French vintage.'

'Are you saying you got him drunk?' Paula raised an eyebrow quizzically.

'No. But I had invited him to dinner, and I ordered a very expensive bottle of Mouton Rothschild, which he loves. And I asked the right questions.'

'What's he planning to do? How will he hurt my children?' Paula asked, alarm making her voice sharp.

'He's already hurt one of them I'm afraid, Paula.'

Holding herself very still, staring across the coffee table at Sarah, Paula asked, 'Tell me . . . tell me the worst. Who has he hurt? And how? Why don't I know?'

'Indirectly he's hurt Tessa, through her husband Mark Longden. Mark is Jonathan's architect . . . on the house he's building near Thirsk.'

'My god, none of us knew *that*!'

'No, you didn't, because Jonathan and Mark invented a phony name for the new client. William Stone.' Sarah shifted slightly in the chair, and explained, 'Mark told Tessa his new client was a tycoon, a very rich tycoon, that his name was William Stone and that he was building a house in the Midlands. Your daughter had no reason not to believe Mark.'

'I understand. But how has Jonathan hurt Tessa?' Paula demanded.

Sarah hesitated, and then explained in a quiet voice, 'I got the feeling the other night that Jonathan is getting Mark hooked on drugs and drink, and other women. And that he's enjoying doing so. I've long suspected Jonathan was a little depraved under that sparkling, gentlemanly exterior of his. I truly believe Mark Longden is now in his clutches in the worst way. Jonathan was laughing about Mark and his weaknesses. He made some remark about that marriage going south sooner than anyone had expected. He even commented on Mark's mistreatment of Tessa . . . physical mistreatment.'

Paula was aghast, and turned very pale. 'No man would boast of abusing his wife.'

'I don't think Mark *did* boast, Paula. I'm putting two and two together. Jonathan told me that Mark had said to him he was teaching Miss Moneybags who wore the trousers in the family; that she'd feel the back of his hand on her if she didn't behave.'

'I've suspected he was abusing her,' Paula confided in a shaken voice. 'And thank you for warning me, Sarah. I now know what to do.'

Nodding her head, Sarah cautioned, 'If I'm to continue helping you, then you must leave my name out of it. Jonathan mustn't find out.'

'I understand.'

'There's one other thing you must know, Paula. At the retrospective Jonathan made a comment about Linnet. He said she was going to inherit everything, including Pennistone Royal. I was so taken aback I retorted that I didn't believe it, and asked who'd told him. He said "a dickybird", and he had a very smug, knowing look on his face.'

'Oh, but he's completely wrong about that!' Paula shook her head vehemently. 'Completely.' She wondered where the leak had come from, her mind racing frantically.

It was almost as though Sarah had read her cousin's mind when she remarked, 'I think you've got a problem in your office. At the Leeds store, I suspect. Jonathan is having an affair with an old friend of his, a woman called Ellie. I think she works there.'

'Eleanor Morrison! That's who it must be. She's one of my secretaries in Leeds. But she doesn't have access to my private papers – and anyway, I told you, it's not true.'

'Don't give her the sack,' Sarah warned.

'I wouldn't dream of it,' Paula said. 'It would only make Jonathan Ainsley suspicious.'

'Just be very careful . . . about anything confidential, any private papers.'

'I always am,' Paula answered, wanting to kill any ideas about who would inherit what. But she knew she would have to keep a sharp eye on Eleanor. Sarah was correct, she couldn't sack her. But she could render her useless to Jonathan.

Standing up, Sarah said, 'That's it. I've told you everything I know, Paula. I hope it helps you.'

Also rising, Paula answered, 'It does.' She stared

at Sarah in the most penetrating way, and confided, 'I've had an instinctive feeling lately that Jonathan Ainsley would do something to injure my family. Ever since he came back to live in London . . . even Sir Ronald warned me.'

'Uncle Ronnie was always smart. Grandy said he took after his father. Anyway, I'll keep my eyes and ears open. I usually see Jonathan when I come to London . . .' Sarah did not finish her sentence. She glanced around the room and then addressed her daughter Chloe. 'This is the upstairs parlour I've often spoken to you about. My grandmother's favourite room . . . everybody's favourite room actually, Chloe. We had wonderful times here when I was growing up.'

'Mother, there's your photograph! Over on that long table.' As she spoke, Chloe hurried to the library table and picked it up. 'You look so beautiful. Come and look, *Maman*.' Walking across the room, Sarah joined her daughter and they stared at the photograph together, then Chloe put it back.

Sarah and her daughter now moved in the direction of the door; Paula followed them. Sarah turned around, just before leaving, and said, 'The room hasn't changed. It's exactly the same as I remember it. It's full of wonderful memories for me, especially of Grandy.'

Returning her very direct gaze, Paula saw the tears in Sarah's eyes, and she was filled with compassion for the cousin she had banished so many years ago. Had she been too harsh? Perhaps. But at the time she had thought she was doing the right thing. She had truly believed that Sarah had betrayed the family. Her view of things had slowly changed over the years, but she had done nothing about bringing Sarah back into the fold.

'I don't know how to thank you for what you've done today, Sarah. I'm so very grateful to you. As our grandmother used to say, forewarned is forearmed. Now that I'm alerted I'll be on my guard.'

'That's wise, I think.'

'I hope we'll see each other again soon. I want you to know, you're very welcome . . .' Paula's sentence trailed away as she stepped forward and embraced her cousin.

Sarah clung to her, swallowing her tears. 'And I don't know how to thank *you* . . . It makes me so happy to know I'm welcome . . . in the family again.' Stepping away from Paula, Sarah shook her head. 'Just as long as Mr Ainsley doesn't know.'

Once she was alone, Paula tried to reach Tessa. She rang her at the Knightsbridge store only to discover she had been in her office earlier, but had suddenly left. She tried the house in Hampstead and was surprised that there was no answer. Finally, she punched in the numbers of Tessa's mobile phone. Still her daughter did not respond, so she left a message and hung up.

Paula looked at the carriage clock on the desk,

and was taken aback to see that it was only noon. Tessa was probably out to lunch, and Elvira had more than likely taken Adele for a walk on Hampstead Heath. She must try not to worry about Tessa's whereabouts; she knew her daughter would call her back as soon as she had read her message. In the meantime, in order not to become hysterical about Mark Longden and his mistreatment of Tessa, she would concentrate on the plans for the weekend. But first she must straighten those picture frames on the library table. Chloe had moved them around to pick up Sarah's photograph and now they looked muddled. She hated mess.

It struck her that Sarah had been so proud her picture was still so prominently displayed at Pennistone Royal, when she herself had been in disgrace for years. I just hadn't noticed it was there, Paula muttered under her breath as she crossed the room, began to move the frames around. Soon order reigned; Sarah's photograph was back in its given place.

The phone began to ring and Paula rushed to her desk, knocking a photograph onto the floor as she did. She heard the glass shatter as she grabbed the receiver.

'Hello?'

'Mummy! It's Tessa.'

'Darling, where are you? I've been trying to reach you?'

'I know, I got your message. I'm in a limousine. Just leaving London. With Adele and Elvira. I'm being driven to Yorkshire. I'm too exhausted to drive myself. Mummy, I've left Mark.'

'Thank God for that!'

'I'm never going back to him. I'm getting a divorce.'

'I'm relieved to hear it. When will you arrive here at Pennistone Royal?'

'It'll take us a good four hours, maybe a little bit more.'

'I'll be here waiting for you, darling.'

'Bye, Mummy.'

'See you soon, Tessa.' Paula hung up, filled with relief. Thank God her daughter was out of that house and away from Mark Longden's presence. And thank God for her cousin Sarah and her sense of decency and duty.

Paula got up and returned to the library table, picking up the photograph frame which had fallen on the floor as she had brushed against it.

The glass was broken. She tried to slide the pieces out without success, and so she went and sat at her desk and carefully took the frame apart. As she slid the velvet-covered back out of the frame and then the piece of cardboard, she noticed two envelopes taped to the inside part of the cardboard. She wondered what they contained and opened one. Inside was a silver key. Paula knew at once that it belonged to the fruitwood casket scrolled with silver. It had never been lost, but hidden. She felt a sudden rush of excitement, and opened the second envelope. It contained a photograph of a young woman, probably taken in the middle of the fifties. She was holding the hand of a small boy. Her grandmother held the child's other hand. Paula turned the snap over. On the back was written: *Glynnis, Owen and me.*

Paula placed the snapshot on the desk, and finally took out the eight-by-ten photograph, one she had looked at so many times over the years. And with a small shock she knew at last who the father of Owen Hughes was.

CHAPTER FORTY-FIVE

P aula put the snapshot in her desk drawer, and then walked over to the Queen Anne chest where the fruitwood casket embellished with silver had stood for her entire life. So many times she had asked her grandmother what had happened to the key, and so many times Grandy had told her it was lost. But it had been carefully hidden, not lost at all.

With shaking hands Paula put the elaborate silver key into the equally elaborate silver escutcheon, and turned it. The casket opened easily. Lifting the lid she looked inside, almost afraid of what she would find. She saw at once that the casket contained a bundle of letters tied with blue ribbon. All of them were addressed to Mrs Emma Harte at Pennistone Royal. Turning one over, she read the sender's name: Mrs Glynnis Hughes, New York City.

After reading a number of the letters, although not all of them, she had a fairly good understanding of everything, and she knew what she had to do. Locking the letters in the casket which had kept them safe for over forty-odd years, and pocketing the key, Paula ran downstairs.

Crossing the Stone Hall to the kitchen, she put her head around the door and told Margaret that Tessa, Adele and the nanny Elvira would be arriving in time for tea. 'I'm going out for a while, Margaret,' she added. 'I should be back within an hour or so, if anyone should call.'

Margaret nodded her understanding. 'What time will Mr Longden be arriving? Or isn't he coming tonight?'

'No, Margaret, he can't make it this weekend,' Paula replied. Or any other weekend, she thought, as she headed towards her car parked in the cobbled yard near the stables, trying to douse her anger towards him. The bastard, she thought, cursing him under her breath.

Thirty-five minutes later Paula was driving through the tall, wrought-iron gates of Lackland Priory in Masham. She had always liked the appearance of this old stone manor, once a priory before the Dissolution of the Monasteries, that period when Henry VIII had destroyed so much church property because of his anger against Papal Rome.

Fortunately, Lackland Priory had not been destroyed. It had gone into private hands, and so had avoided being turned into a ruin like Fountains Abbey.

It was a graceful house made of local grey stone, with a series of beautiful windows perfectly aligned across the front façade. It was symmetrical, and she liked its simplicity and its plainness. It stood in the middle of perfectly flat green lawns; it was not surrounded or backed by stands of trees as so many manor houses in Yorkshire were.

After parking in the cobbled yard near the kitchen, she walked around to the front door and rang the bell. She had only a moment to wait before Bolton, the butler, appeared at the door, staring at her in surprise from the threshold.

'Miss Paula! Good afternoon. Are we expecting you?' As he spoke he opened the door wider and ushered her inside.

'No, you're not, Bolton,' she answered, offering him one of her most charming smiles. 'I thought it would be nice to give him a surprise. He once told me he had always liked surprises.'

'Indeed he does. Come along, Miss Paula. I'll take you to him. He's in the library.'

'How is he?' she asked, following the butler across the polished parquet floor.

'I'm pleased to tell you he's a lot better. Still not quite his old self, but he will be in a week or two. He's made wonderful progress.' Opening the library door, Bolton said, 'Sir, it's Miss Paula, she's driven over to see you.'

The man, who had been sitting reading by the window in a wing chair, put his book down and stood. 'My dear Paula, what a lovely surprise.'

Paula glided across the Savonnerie carpet towards him, thinking how marvellous he looked. Bolton had been right: he had made a wonderful recovery. She had known him all of her life, but now she tried to see him through objective eyes, assess him, giving him an appraising glance as she finally drew to a standstill. He was still good-looking; he must have been quite devastating when he was younger.

She gave him a radiant smile, stood on tiptoe and kissed his cheek. He held her against him for a moment, his face against her hair, and then as they drew apart he said, 'Your hair has always had the most lovely smell, ever since you were a child, Paula.' He smiled at her, and indicated a chair. 'Now, to what do I owe this honour, my dear?'

'I haven't heard a word from you about the birthday party for Shane and Winston. You are going to come, aren't you?'

'I do believe I am. I think it would be rather jolly to see all of you. We might even have a turn on the dance floor, you and I.'

Paula leaned back in the chair and crossed her legs, studied him for a moment.

Becoming aware of her rather fixed scrutiny, he said, 'Is there something wrong, Paula? You're giving me rather sharp looks.'

'Oh, I'm sorry. I was just thinking about something I recently discovered. I was reading my grandmother's diaries and I discovered she started a canteen during the Second World War. In the Fulham Road.'

He nodded, his eyes lighting up. 'That's true. She did.'

'Did you ever go there?'

'Indeed I did. We always had a lot of fun.'

'Did you meet your wife there?' she asked, her head on one side, watching him closely.

'No, as a matter of fact, I didn't. But why do you ask this, Paula?'

'I know you met a young woman there, and I wasn't sure exactly who she was. This young woman . . . she was very beautiful. My grandmother thought she was so glamorous . . .'

He sat back in the leather wing chair rather suddenly, jerkily, and he turned his head, looking out across the lawns. He did not speak, merely sat there, staring through the window as if he could see something quite unique that was not visible to her.

What a marvellously patrician profile he has, and such a splendid head of white hair, Paula thought. And she waited. Waited for him to speak.

At last he turned back to face her, and she thought his face was sad, sorrowful. He seemed to ponder for a moment, and then he said, 'Her name was Glynnis . . . Glynnis Jenkins. And she was beautiful, and glamorous, just as you said a moment or two ago, quoting your grandmother's diaries, I've no doubt. But Glynnis was much more than that . . .' He stopped speaking, shook his head. 'She was very loving, passionate, sensual.'

'You loved her.'

'Oh yes, I did.'

'And you made her pregnant.'

'Yes. That's true, Paula, I did,' he answered without hesitation.

'But you didn't marry her.'

'No.'

'But why not?'

He let out a long sigh. 'Our relationship was passionate, but it was also highly charged and extremely volatile. We could fight as quickly as we could make love. In the vernacular of today, it was over the top. I was aware that a passion like that could just as easily burn out as fast as it had flared. Or it could consume me. And—'

'You couldn't afford that,' she cut in peremptorily. 'You had to protect yourself, didn't you, Uncle Robin? Because of the career you planned.' She spoke softly, kindly, and finished, 'I do understand.'

'You are quite correct in your assessment, Paula. But let me explain . . . I broke up with Glynnis before I knew she was pregnant. And soon after that I became engaged to Valerie Ludden, a young woman I'd known for a while and of whom I was very fond. Of course, it was not the same kind of relationship I had with Glynnis. It was much calmer, more stable. I loved Valerie in a different way, and we were ideally suited. She was right for me, for my future in politics. Whereas Glynnis and I would have been consumed by each other, destroyed by each other.'

'But Glynnis was pregnant, and in those days that was a terrible stigma.'

'I'm aware of that, and I offered to support Glynnis. But she refused any help from me.'

'I see.'

There was a silence between them, and then Robin Ainsley said, 'So you found Emma's old wartime diaries. Apparently she wrote about my love affair with Glynnis?'

'No, she didn't, Uncle Robin. There is one entry in October of 1943, about Glynnis's predicament. But you are not mentioned as the father. No one is named, actually. Your mother protected you and she protected Glynnis. Anyway, Glynnis Jenkins never wanted you named as the father of her child either.'

'Then how do *you* know?' he asked, frowning, giving her a baffled look.

'Because today, utterly by chance, I found some old letters from Glynnis Hughes, as she had become, to Grandy. I read several of them in which you were mentioned as being Owen's father. She wrote to Emma for years, you know, and Emma even met your son by Glynnis.'

'My mother supported Glynnis for a long time . . . sent her money on a regular basis, even after Glynnis had gone to America,' Robin said. 'So I'm not surprised Glynnis wrote to her. I'm just surprised my mother kept the letters.'

Paula nodded. 'I know what you mean.'

Leaning towards her, Robin now asked, 'Why

have you come to tell me about this today, Paula? What's this visit really all about? I know you very well, and there's a reason behind it.'

'You have a granddaughter called Evan Hughes . . . she's the daughter of your son Owen. And she's living in London, Uncle Robin. I thought you might want to know that.'

'A granddaughter . . .' He paused, his expression becoming thoughtful, and he was silent for a while, once more staring out of the window, his eyes suddenly full of sadness, perhaps even regret.

Watching him, waiting for him to say something, Paula thought of his long career in politics. He had been a popular Member of Parliament, had served in the British government several times, and Emma had always been proud of him. He had lived the life he had envisioned for himself, and he had been successful. So perhaps he had made the right choice.

Finally, Robin shifted in his wing chair and gave Paula a long, penetrating look. 'How do you know this young woman . . . did she come looking for me?'

'No, she didn't. She didn't even know about you. Let me explain everything.'

Robin listened to Paula attentively as she spoke at length, his expression revealing nothing. When she had finished he said, 'And so you want me to meet her, is that it?'

'That's up to you, Uncle Robin. *You* must decide.'

'I think I would like to meet her. From what

621

you've just said she sounds very nice. Very appropriate.'

Paula laughed. 'Indeed she is, and beautiful. Oh my God! I've just realized who she has a look of: Aunt Elizabeth, your twin. And everyone has been saying she resembles me.'

He smiled. 'Then she must be quite lovely. Elizabeth is a beauty. Perhaps you should arrange a meeting, Paula.'

'Whenever you want. At the birthday party, perhaps. She will be coming with Gideon.'

'Gideon?' He stared at her, puzzled. 'Why Gideon?'

'Because she has been seeing him . . . they're involved.'

'I wonder why it is that Hartes are always attracted to Hartes.' He shook his head, nonplussed for a moment. 'It's like the pharaohs in ancient Egypt, don't you think?'

Paula burst out laughing. 'Oh Uncle Robin, you are a hoot at times.'

'Anyway, that is a good idea. I could meet her at the party for Shane and Winston. Yes, indeed, most appropriate.'

Nodding, Paula then leant closer to her uncle, and said in a low voice, 'I don't think you should mention anything I've told you to Jonathan. It might upset him. He *is* your only son, and heir, and since he's never given you grandchildren he might resent Evan.'

'Oh my goodness, *yes*. You are quite right, Paula. He might regard her as some sort of threat.' His eyes narrowed. 'Jonathan has been a great disappointment to me. I know he has no love for me, nor does he care a jot about my health, my life today. I've hardly seen him since his mother died; he didn't come much when she was alive either, though Valerie was the best mother in the world. You'd think he'd pop by occasionally; after all, I am eighty, you know. But he never does, not even when he goes to see his fancy woman in Thirsk.'

Taking a deep breath, Paula plunged in. 'I think Jonathan is dangerous, Uncle Robin. I want to warn you about him.'

He listened as she recounted everything Sarah had told her.

'I'm not at all surprised,' he said quietly, when she had finished. 'I have begun to think, recently, that he's a sociopath. He has no morals; actually, he's *amoral*, and he believes he's above the law. He never thinks he is doing anything wrong. He is indeed dangerous, Paula, you are right there. He will not hear about Evan Hughes from me.'

It seemed to Paula that the next two days were hectic, between settling Tessa in, calming her, and listening to her dreadful stories of life with Mark Longden. She backed her daughter to the hilt as far as a divorce was concerned, but purposely did not mention Sarah's visit. She had to protect her cousin against Jonathan Ainsley's wrath. And they had enough evidence of mistreatment; plenty of grounds for divorce without involving Sarah.

Then there were the plans for the weekend to finish: menus for the meals from Friday through Monday morning, plus seating plans for the lunches and dinners. But as usual she pushed ahead determinedly, and Tessa helped her by writing the place cards and doing other small tasks.

By the time Linnet, India and Evan arrived on Friday afternoon, Paula was just about finished with everything, and ready to relax with them over tea in the upstairs parlour. They had lots to recount to her: the success of the retrospective, the number of people visiting the exhibit, the great press coverage, the accolades, and a sudden surge in business on the fashion floors.

'It's a triumph for you all,' Paula said, smiling at them when they had finally finished. 'I have a feeling the retrospective is going to be a permanent fixture in the store for quite a long time. Well done, all of you. Now I want you to relax, forget work, and enjoy the weekend.'

Linnet stood up, and headed towards the door. 'I want to go and unpack.'

'I should do the same,' Evan said.

'Oh please don't go, Evan. I'd like a word with you,' Paula murmured, reaching out, touching her arm.

Evan looked at her questioningly, and sat down.

'I have to iron a dress,' India said, jumping up. 'It's chiffon and so it must be ironed. I can't use a steamer on it.'

Linnet pretended to shudder. 'Never. Come on then India, let's go.'

Once they were alone, Paula said, 'I have something to tell you, Evan, regarding your grandmother. But I think for the moment what I'm going to say must remain confidential. I don't want it spreading through the family. Not just yet.'

'You found something in the diaries after all?' Evan asked alertly, leaning forward anxiously.

'No, I didn't. But I did find some old letters from your grandmother to my grandmother here at Pennistone Royal the other day, quite by accident. In several of the letters Glynnis refers to Owen's father ... his biological father.' Paula paused, smiled gently at Evan, and continued, 'Richard Hughes married Glynnis when she was pregnant by another man during the war. He did not care because he loved her so much, and he loved the child she bore: he brought him up as his own. He was a good man, and a very good father to Owen.'

Evan was flabbergasted and she sat staring at Paula in stunned silence. After a moment she swallowed hard and said in a low voice, 'You're telling me my father is *illegitimate*?'

'Technically, yes.'

'Who was Dad's father? Who is Dad really? Who am I?'

'Owen's father is Robin Ainsley, who is my uncle, and Emma's favourite son. He's a Harte. And so are you, Evan. Emma Harte was your great-grandmother.'

'Oh my God!' Evan had turned very pale and she

sat back against the cushions on the sofa, gaping at Paula, lost for words. Suddenly she burst into tears and brought her hands to her face.

Paula rose and went to her desk, brought a box of tissues to Evan, sat down next to her on the sofa. 'I know it's a shock, suddenly finding out that things are different from what one thought. But please don't cry, Evan. All of this happened fifty years ago, you know.'

Blowing her nose, wiping her eyes, Evan nodded. 'Yes, I realize that. I looked up to Gran. I believed she was the most wonderful woman . . .' Evan paused, stared at Paula, the tears welling again.

'You mustn't let this make a difference in the way you think about Glynnis. She must remain the same wonderful woman in your memory – because she was exactly that, Evan. I am going to give you her letters to Emma, and when you read them you will understand so much more.' Paula sighed, and took hold of Evan's hand. 'We must always take into account human frailties, and remember that *none* of us is perfect.'

For a moment Evan was silent, her mind awash with innumerable thoughts, and suddenly she exclaimed, 'I'm related to Gideon! *We're cousins.*'

'Several times removed,' Paula pointed out.

'Does my real grandfather know about me . . . ?'

'Yes. I told him on Wednesday, the day I found the letters.'

'What did he say? Does he want to meet me?'

'Yes, he does. Do you?'

'I don't know . . . well, yes, I guess I do . . .' she murmured, sounding hesitant.

'There's a slight problem we have to overcome,' Paula said, playing it down so as not to alarm Evan. 'Robin Ainsley has one son, Jonathan Ainsley. Amongst other things, he is my enemy, and that's why Gideon was upset the other night when he came over to speak to you. Jonathan was married and divorced, but he never produced any grandchildren for his father. So more than likely he will see you as some sort of threat, since you are Robin's granddaughter. Because of his inheritance—'

'I don't want anything!' Evan interrupted. 'I don't want Robin Ainsley's money.'

'I know. But things have to be dealt with properly, in a businesslike way. Firstly, Jonathan Ainsley has to be informed by his father of your existence, and he must be told that you do not affect his inheritance in any way, that you will not be in Robin's will. Once Jonathan knows this, we can tell the family . . . about the new development, about who you actually are. Do you understand?'

'Yes, I do.' Evan had calmed down, and after blowing her nose again, she asked quietly, 'Can I tell Gideon?'

Paula had already foreseen this and dealt with the issue. She said quickly, 'Tomorrow evening before dinner Shane and I are going to have Gideon and his parents for a quick drink here in the upstairs parlour. You are invited too. But that's all, no one else.'

'What about Linnet?'

Paula shook her head. 'I want to keep this very quiet. Linnet will know next week, once Uncle Robin has spoken to Jonathan. Do you understand?'

'I understand.'

Paula rose and went over to her desk, took out the bundle of letters tied with blue ribbon. 'These are for you, Evan dear,' she said, returning to the sofa, handing them to her. 'Your grandmother's letters.'

Evan took them from her, and walked across the room. She paused at the door, and said, 'Thank you for these. And I'd like to meet my grandfather this weekend. Do you think that's possible?'

Paula looked across at her, frowning, and then exclaimed, 'I don't see why not. I'll phone him.'

CHAPTER FORTY-SIX

E van sat waiting for Paula in the Stone Hall. She felt a little anxious about the meeting with Robin Ainsley, which was due to take place in less than an hour. She glanced at the tall grandfather clock in one corner, saw that it was almost ten. She knew that Paula would arrive at any moment, to drive her over to Lackland Priory where he lived.

Last night, just before dinner, Paula had drawn her aside, and told her in a low voice that Uncle Robin had agreed to meet her on Saturday morning. She had worried about it all night, worried mostly about their reaction to each other; but she had also worried about what to wear, wanting to make the right impression.

This morning she had dressed in a beige trouser suit with a cream silk shirt, deciding it was casual enough for the country but a little bit smarter than a skirt and sweater, which she had originally been going to wear. A pair of gold shrimp earrings and her watch were her only pieces of jewellery, but she had tied a beige, red and blue Hermes silk scarf around her neck.

Last night, after reading many of her grandmother's letters to Emma Harte written over the years, she had understood so much. At first, when Paula had told her about Glynnis and Robin yesterday afternoon, she had been upset. But in the middle of the night, she had come to love her grandmother more than ever. For as she had read the letters she had begun to realize what a good person Glynnis had been, a truly kind and generous woman who had not wanted to hurt anybody in any way whatsoever.

Seemingly, when Robin had rejected her during the war, she had stepped away from him, and with dignity. And she had been honest and open with Richard Hughes, had told him the truth. The letters had been poignant, happy, sad, positive, optimistic. Seemingly, her grandmother had run the gamut of emotions over the years. But one thing was certain, she had managed to live her life to the fullest and without regret. And she had remained devoted to Emma Harte until her death.

There had been a moment during the night when Evan had almost picked up the phone to call her father, but then she had decided against it. She wanted to meet *his* father first, give Robin the once over before telling Owen anything at all about these new developments. Another thing had shone through the letters most forcefully, and that was

Glynnis's devotion to Richard Hughes. Theirs had been a very successful and happy marriage, and Evan was glad of that. But she had known this anyway, hadn't she? Certainly they had never been anything but serene with each other in front of her, and Glynnis had told her so many times how important compatibility was in a marriage, as well as love.

In one of the letters her grandmother had discussed money with Emma, and now Evan knew where that large legacy had come from originally. Emma Harte had sent money to Glynnis for many years, and Glynnis had saved most of it and rather frugally so, rarely spending anything unless it was really necessary. Apparently Richard had insisted on supporting Owen, whom he considered to be his son, and he had done so with a great deal of pleasure and gratification.

There were still a number of letters to read, and she planned to look at them this afternoon. In the meantime, she would soon meet her biological grandfather. She took a deep breath and stood up as Paula O'Neill came down the stairs, greeting her with, 'Good morning, Evan.'

'Good morning, Mrs O'Neill.'

Paula laughed as she came to a standstill next to Evan, and took hold of her arm, kissed her cheek. 'I think it might be a good idea for you to call me Paula, since it turns out we're related. I've been trying to figure it all out, and you're my cousin several times removed. I think.' She laughed again.

'I was trying to do the same, Mrs O'Neill, I mean Paula, but it's been quite a lot for me to absorb since yesterday afternoon.'

'I know it has, Evan. Come on, we can talk as we drive over to Uncle Robin's.'

They walked out of the Stone Hall together, and went around to the kitchen side of the house to the back yard, where the garages were located. Evan waited in the cobbled yard while Paula drove the car out of the garage, and then she got in, saying as she did, 'I read a lot of Grandmother's letters last night, in fact, I was up half the night poring over them.'

'I thought you might be. I didn't actually read many of them, Evan, only enough to find out who Glynnis's wartime lover had been. I just want you to know that.'

'Thanks for telling me, but you could have read them. They're yours really, since they were sent to your grandmother.' A sudden thought struck her, and Evan exclaimed, 'I wonder why Emma kept the letters? I mean, to what purpose?'

'Evan, I've no idea. I thought of that myself, when I found them, and I wondered why she had left the key in the back of the frame holding Robin's picture. And the photograph of Glynnis, Owen and herself. And I could only come to one conclusion.'

'What's that?' Evan asked, an eager expression settling on her face.

'I believe Emma Harte wanted the key found,

and she bargained that I would be the one to find it. Since I'd always pestered her about that casket from childhood she knew I'd know at once that that particular silver-scrolled key was for that special box.'

'Why not just keep the letters in a safe, or tell you about them?'

'I wish I could answer you, but I can't. Perhaps she hid them the way she did because she didn't want them found while she was alive. And then possibly she forgot about them. She died rather unexpectedly you know. Shane has another theory: he thinks she kept them because it gave her a sort of hold over Robin. But I'm not certain he's right. However, their discovery and the advent of Evan Hughes is certainly going to upset Robin's son, Jonathan Ainsley.'

'Yes, you explained that last night. Why is he your enemy?'

'Basically, he believes he should have inherited much more than he did from Emma, and most certainly the department stores. He's been very disgruntled about everything to do with her legacy since her death. He feels cheated. And at one moment he really did Harte Enterprises harm financially, through the real estate division he ran, and he tried to grab the stores by buying up a lot of stock, and also getting voting control of more shares through a friend. But he didn't succeed. Anyway, Evan, he's bad news, take my word for it.'

'Gideon sort of indicated that after the retrospective. We went to the Isle of Man for twenty-four hours, and he was upset that I'd been talking to Jonathan Ainsley. But I had no idea who he was.'

'I realize that.' Paula glanced out of the window, and said, 'We're going to a lovely little village called Masham. Uncle Robin has lived at Lackland Priory for many, many years. It's a beautiful old place, you'll be struck by its simplicity, and yet it's an architectural gem.'

'I can't wait, but I am a bit nervous about meeting Robin . . . my grandfather.' Evan made a face. 'That sounds funny, saying *grandfather* when I think of my grandfather as Richard Hughes and he's dead.'

'You don't have to be nervous, Evan, I think Uncle Robin is rather pleased to know you exist. Jonathan has been a genuine disappointment to him . . . I do believe he thinks of him as rather strange, to use a nice word.'

'What do you think of him, Paula?'

'Naturally I detest him, because he's damaged us. I think he's a rather sinister presence in the family . . . and just a little bit dangerous. So we must be careful how we handle this news of your existence. Ah, look, Evan, just ahead. Those are the gates of the hall. We'll be there in a few minutes.'

Once they had driven through the gates, Evan gazed at the beautifully kept lawns, the copse of trees to the right of the house, and the house itself standing at the edge of the main lawn. Solitary. Simple. And yet so beautiful, as Paula had said a short while before. Evan loved the grey stone which was used so much in Yorkshire; Gideon had told her it was a local stone taken from the nearby quarries.

Paula pulled up at the front door, glanced at her. 'Are you ready, Evan?'

'Yes.' Opening the door, she got out of the car and followed Paula to the front door, swallowing hard as she did, and straightening her jacket.

Within seconds the door was opened by the butler. 'Good morning, Miss Paula,' he said, opening the door wider. 'He's waiting for you in the library.'

'Thank you, Bolton. And this is Miss Hughes.'

The butler inclined his head; Evan smiled faintly, and the two women followed him across the entrance hall, walking in the direction of the library.

Robin Ainsley was sitting in the wing chair by the window; there was a book on the Queen Anne tea table, but it was closed, and it occurred to Evan that he might have been dozing in the chair.

The butler cleared his throat. 'Miss Paula has arrived, sir. With Miss Hughes.'

'Ah yes, thank you, Bolton.' Robin immediately rose and turned to them, his eyes on Evan as the two women walked toward him.

Likewise, Evan's eyes were on him. She saw a tall, slender, white-haired man, rather elegant and refined in appearance. He wore an old tweed jacket with leather patches on the elbows, grey slacks, a pale blue shirt and a brown knitted tie. In a peculiar way, he reminded her of Richard Hughes, and she smiled inwardly, thinking that perhaps Glynnis had been drawn to the same type of man.

Paula kissed his cheek, and introduced her. 'This is Evan, Uncle Robin.'

He stretched out his hand, gazing at her. 'I'm very pleased to meet you, Evan.'

'As I am, Mr Ainsley.'

A faint smile touched his mouth. 'Why don't you call me Robin, my dear? Much friendlier.'

'If you'd like that?'

'I would. Now, can I offer you something? Tea, coffee, sherry perhaps?'

Paula said, 'I'd love a glass of fizzy water please, Uncle Robin.'

'So would I, thank you,' Evan murmured.

Robin Ainsley looked across at Bolton, hovering in the doorway, and said, 'Two glasses of fizzy water, and sherry for me, Bolton. Thank you.'

The butler departed discreetly, closing the door behind him, and Robin said, 'Why don't we sit over there near the fireplace? I know it's June, but there's still a nip in the air up here, and I do like a fire even now. I feel the cold in my bones rather a lot these days. Getting old, living on borrowed time.'

Paula smiled at him, slipped her arm through his and walked with him to the fireplace, indicating with her eyes that Evan should follow.

Once they were seated, Paula said, 'Evan asked

to meet you today, Uncle Robin, because she's going back to London tomorrow, and she won't be here again for two weeks. For Linnet's engagement dinner, the night before the big birthday party.'

'I'm glad she suggested it.' He turned his gaze on Evan. 'To be frank, I wanted to meet you at once, but I thought that perhaps I should leave the decision to you.'

Evan cleared her throat, still feeling somewhat nervous, and said softly, 'It seemed rather silly to wait. I really didn't have to think it over much. I wanted to meet *you*, too.'

'Have you informed your father of this . . . development?' Robin asked, eyeing her thoughtfully.

'No, I haven't. I did think about it last night, about calling him, but I changed my mind.'

'Oh, why is that?'

'I wanted to look you over first,' she blurted out before she could stop herself, and felt herself blushing.

Even before she could say anything else, Robin laughed. It was a deep-throated laugh, and he was obviously highly amused. Glancing at Paula he said, 'Evan sounds like Emma . . .' Addressing Evan, he continued, 'My mother was always rather blunt, spoke her mind, and much to my consternation at times.'

'I'm so sorry, I did sound rude, didn't I? But I just felt we ought to meet before I told my father anything. Besides, it's a bit difficult to discuss on the phone. I think I'd prefer to tell him face to face. He's supposed to come over in a couple of months. On vacation.'

'Is he now?' Robin pondered this for a moment, and was about to say something when Bolton came in with glasses on a silver tray. After the drinks were passed around and they were left alone again, Robin said, 'What do you think his reaction will be?'

She shook her head. 'I don't know, honestly I don't.'

'It will be a shock, I suppose,' Paula said. 'After all, he grew up knowing another man as his father.'

Robin was silent; he took a sip of dry sherry.

Evan shifted slightly on the sofa, and said quietly, 'I think he might suspect something . . .'

Robin glanced at her swiftly. '*Oh.*'

'What makes you say that?' Paula asked, filled with curiosity. *This* was a new turn of events.

'His attitude really. He wanted me to come to London originally. And then he seemed to change his mind, especially after I started to work at Harte's. I think he might have found something after my grandmother died last November. *Some papers.*' Looking at Paula, Evan added, 'The way you found the letters from Glynnis to Emma.'

Paula was thoughtful, her brows drawing together.

Robin said, 'I understand from Paula that on her death bed your grandmother told you to come and find Emma Harte, that she was the key to your future. But they were close friends, surely she knew Emma was dead?'

'I'm sure she did, Robin,' Evan replied, saying his name for the first time. 'I think she wanted to put me in your orbit – by that I mean in the orbit of the Hartes. Perhaps she knew people would think I looked like Paula, and that something would happen . . . I'm just not sure.'

'And we'll never know, will we? On the other hand, I think you're probably right.' Settling back in the chair, Robin gazed at Evan for a long moment, studying her once more. Then he said, 'You don't look like Paula. You have a strong resemblance to my sister Elizabeth.' Glancing at Paula, he continued. 'You mentioned that the other day.'

'I know I don't look like Glynnis,' Evan announced.

Robin inclined his head. 'No, you don't. I think perhaps they threw away the mould. Glynnis was quite the most extraordinary looking woman I've ever known . . .' His sentence remained unfinished.

Paula said, 'Uncle Robin, do you mind if I pop out into the garden for a moment? I want to look at those plants I sent you the other day, to be sure they're in the beds correctly.'

He was about to tell her his gardener knew what he was doing when he realized she was being discreet, leaving them alone together for a few moments. He nodded. 'Of course, do go out to the garden, Paula, my dear.'

He smiled at Evan a few seconds later. 'She's a bit too obvious at times.'

Evan smiled back at him. 'But she's thoughtful.'

'Oh yes.' He seemed to ruminate on something for a short while, as if having a tussle with himself, and then he said, 'And do you hate me, Evan, for not marrying Glynnis Jenkins?'

'No. It's so long ago ... something like sixty years.'

'Yes, indeed. It wasn't that I didn't love her, because I did. I just loved her far too much. And she loved me in the same way ... too much. We would—'

'Oh my God!'

Robin stared at Evan. 'What is it? What's wrong?'

'My grandmother said something ... *I loved him too much*, that's what she whispered on her deathbed. I thought she was referring to Owen, her son, my father. But perhaps she was referring to you ... do you think?'

'Maybe she was. That was our problem. Too much passion and too much possessiveness. Our love would have burnt out, or we would have killed each other. Do you understand what I'm saying?'

'Yes, of course.' Evan gave him a long, hard stare. 'Were you happy in your marriage?'

'In many ways I was. However, to be truthful, I missed *her* always, missed the passion, the sensuality, the charm of her, and her beauty. Glynnis

Jenkins was the most enchanting woman I ever knew. Yes, I missed her . . .'

'Glynnis was happy, you know,' Evan told him. 'Very happy with Richard Hughes, and they had a good marriage. But she was always drilling something into me . . . the importance of compatibility, as well as love. You two weren't very compatible, were you?'

'No. But that didn't stop me loving her.'

There was such a strange note in his voice, a gruff undertone, that Evan glanced at him swiftly, and she saw that there were tears in his eyes. On an impulse, without thinking, she jumped up, and went to him, put her hand on his shoulder. 'Oh Robin,' she murmured. 'I do understand . . . and I don't blame you.'

He gazed into her face and for a split second he saw not Evan, nor his sister Elizabeth, but Glynnis. And without thinking he pulled Evan into his arms and held her very close. Within a few seconds he released her, and said in that same gruff voice, 'Forgive a very old man.'

'There's nothing to forgive,' she said and returned to the sofa.

Pulling himself together, Robin reached for the glass of sherry and tossed it back. Sitting up straighter, he asked, 'So, my dear, do you think you and I can be friends?'

'Oh yes, I hope so.'

'And your father?'

'That I don't know.'

641

'Mmmm. I understand. Do you plan to stay in England?'

'I want to, yes.'

'So I'm likely to see you again?' Robin raised an eyebrow.

'Absolutely.'

There was a little silence.

Evan broke it. 'Robin, why do you think Emma kept the Glynnis letters, yet hid them in that strange way?'

He let out a deep sigh. 'I just don't know. It's a mystery to me.' A smile broke through and he exclaimed, 'But I'm damned glad she did.'

'Who did what to whom?' Paula asked, coming back into the library.

'Emma. She kept the letters, and you found them, and I've found my only grandchild. You are the *only* one, aren't you?' He shot a glance at Evan.

She smiled. 'I am. I do have two sisters but they're adopted.'

Paula said, 'You two are looking very pleased with each other, Uncle Robin, Evan. But I want to caution you both . . . there's Jonathan to contend with.'

'Ah yes.' Robin sat back in the chair, steepled his fingers, brought them to his mouth. 'I shall talk to him next week, explain everything. As long as he knows that I am not going to change my will, everything will be all right.'

'I don't want anything!' Evan exclaimed, and then blushed when he gave her a stern look.

Paula said, 'You know that, Uncle, and I know it, but will Jonathan believe you? Will he accept your word?'

'I shall make him believe me.' Robin rose, went and sat next to Evan on the sofa, took her hand in his. 'You and I don't actually know each other, we've only just met, but you are my grandchild, and I am going to create a Trust for you. Immediately. I shall attend to it on Monday. But remember, this is between the three of us.'

Evan nodded, not daring to say a word.

'What a good idea, Uncle Robin. And you don't have to worry about me. I'm not going to tell anyone, not even Shane,' Paula promised.

Later that day Evan read a lot more of her grandmother's letters to Emma, and was instantly engrossed in them. Glynnis had written in great detail, giving Emma colourful descriptions of her life in New York with her son and her husband Richard. Evan found them fascinating. She also understood that the two women had grown closer over the years, sharing a special bond because of Owen.

Putting the last one she had just read back in the bundle and tying the blue ribbon carefully, Evan placed the letters under her sweaters in a drawer, knowing she wanted to peruse them again, perhaps tonight after dinner.

As she showered and washed her hair, Evan thought of Glynnis. Her admiration of her gran had grown and grown in the last twenty-four hours, because of her dignity, kindness and the way she had led her life. She had even brought Owen to London on several occasions when he was a little boy, and Emma had met him. Didn't her father remember these occasions? Perhaps he did, but had preferred not to tell her. Or maybe he had simply not understood who Emma was, or forgotten or blocked them out.

Stepping out of the shower, Evan dried herself, put on a terrycloth robe, and stood in front of the mirror drying her hair with a blower, thinking now about Robin. She had liked him almost instantly, had found him warm, kind and very courteous, and she was quite certain he liked her. Of course, they had to get to know each other properly, and that would take time, but instinctively she felt they would have a worthwhile relationship eventually.

Naturally Robin had been concerned about her father, and she was too, truly unsure of the way he would react to the news. She had made up her mind not to telephone him in Connecticut; at least if she did she would not tell him about the sudden startling development in their lives. She knew him well, and she believed his reaction would be very mixed. He had been devoted to Richard Hughes, who had brought him up, and whom he regarded as his father. Well, of course Richard had been his father. Her grandmother had once said something to her . . . that any man could get a woman pregnant but it was what a man did with a child later that made him a true father. She had often thought about her gran's words, and now they made perfect sense. Glynnis had been thinking about Richard when she had uttered them.

After brushing her hair and putting on a little makeup, Evan moved into the bedroom where she quickly dressed, choosing a silk dress of pale aquamarine, a colour which suited her perfectly. She fastened Glynnis's string of small pearls around her neck, and put on the matching earrings, then slipped her feet into low-heeled silk shoes that matched the colour of the dress.

She was the first one to arrive in the upstairs parlour, and she went and stood at the leaded window, looking out towards the hillside opposite, and then she turned to go back into the room. She saw the photograph at once, recognized Robin immediately, Robin as a much younger man, perhaps in his thirties. Picking it up, she saw that the broken glass Paula had referred to had been replaced. She held it for a moment, staring at the face, seeing her father and herself reflected there. Odd, though, that Robin Ainsley had a look of Richard Hughes . . . She smiled to herself as she put the photograph back in its place amongst the other framed photographs of Emma Harte's family.

Even though it was early June, these old country houses were cool, she had noticed, and she made for the other side of the room where a fire blazed in the hearth. A moment later Gideon came in, his eyes lighting up the moment he saw her.

Hurrying over, he brought her into his arms,

645

kissed her cheek and then stood away from her, exclaiming, 'You should always wear that colour. You look wonderful in it!'

'Thank you, kind sir,' she said, smiling up at him.

'My parents will be here in a moment, but what's going on? My mother said Paula wanted to talk to the three of us privately, with just you and Shane also present. Why not Linnet and Julian?'

'We must wait for Paula, Gid, she will explain everything.'

He frowned, said in a low voice, 'Don't tell me the mystery of your ancestry has been finally solved?'

Evan threw him a cool inscrutable look, but made no comment.

When Emily and Winston came in, Emily hurried over to her, kissed her on the cheek, and said, 'It's lovely to see you, Evan. And I must congratulate you again: the retrospective was so well mounted.'

'Thank you.'

Winston joined them, also kissed her on the cheek. 'It goes without saying that I agree with Emily. My wife is always right. Now, what's all this about, Evan, do you know?'

'I'm about to tell you,' Paula announced from the doorway, gliding into the upstairs parlour, followed by Shane. 'Let's sit down,' she said, and lowered herself onto one of the sofas near the fire. Once they were all seated she proceeded to explain how she had knocked Robin's photograph off the long library table, taken it apart to remove the broken glass, found the key for the silver-scrolled casket, and the photograph of Glynnis and Owen with Emma.

'The casket was full of letters from Glynnis Hughes to Emma, and it became instantly clear to me that Robin Ainsley was the father of Glynnis's son, Owen, who is Evan's father.'

'Oh my God!' Emily cried. 'Then you *are* one of us, Evan! Oh, *of course*. Now I know who it is you look like! My mother when she was young, about your age. Goodness me, you're a *Harte*.'

Winston said, 'Well, my dear, welcome to the family. You're going to make a wonderful addition.'

Gideon simply sat there, staring at her, his face quite unreadable.

Shane said, 'Paula went to see Robin the other day, told him everything, and he confirmed that he had been involved with Glynnis during the war. That in itself is another story for later, however. Paula also informed Evan when she arrived yesterday, and this morning she drove Evan over to the Priory to meet Robin. Seemingly it went very well.'

Emily asked, 'Did you like him, Evan? And how did he react to you?'

'I liked him, yes, he was very courteous,' Evan answered. 'So very nice, and I'm sure he reciprocated my feelings.' She looked across at Paula questioningly.

Paula nodded and told them, 'I do believe Robin is truly thrilled. He didn't say that exactly, but he was very keen to know Evan better and to meet her father eventually. And we all know what Jonathan is . . . yes, I think Robin is over the moon that he suddenly has a grandchild.'

Gideon, recovering from his initial surprise, gave Evan a long, loving look, and said, 'I second my father, Evan. Welcome to the family, yes, welcome, welcome!'

There was a little amused laughter amongst the others, and Paula continued, 'For the moment, this must remain confidential. It's between the six of us only. No one else in the family can know. Not until Uncle Robin has told Jonathan, and reassured him that Evan's advent in his life is not going to affect Jonathan's inheritance.'

'I hope he believes it!' Emily exclaimed.

Shane said, 'I know what you mean.'

Winston looked thoughtful, pondering for a moment, and then he nodded to himself. 'Uncle Robin is not Emma Harte's son for nothing. He's as shrewd as she ever was. And let's not forget he's a barrister, well schooled in the law, and that he was a Member of Parliament and a member of the government for years. He's not going to fumble this one, rest assured. He's going to use the right words, come up with all the right answers when he sees Jonathan.'

'And when is that going to be, do you know, Paula?' Emily asked.

'Uncle Robin said he was going up to London on Monday. To see his solicitor. Perhaps he wants his advice about handling Jonathan.'

'Possibly,' Winston said. 'But it's more than likely he wants to draw up some sort of legal papers that give Jonathan the guarantees he'll probably want.'

'I agree with you, Winston,' Shane said, standing up, pulling Paula to her feet. 'Now, let's go downstairs and have a drink. The others are going to wonder what's going on up here.'

Paula said, 'Remember everyone, not a word to anyone, not even Linnet. We know what Jonathan is, we don't want him going wild before Uncle Robin has placated him. And it's funny how gossip spreads in this family.'

Winston and Emily nodded, and followed Shane and Paula out of the upstairs parlour.

Gideon said, 'We'll be down in a few minutes.'

When the others had left, Gideon went and sat next to Evan on the sofa. Taking her hand in his, he looked into her large soulful eyes and said softly, 'So how does it feel to know that we're related?'

Evan sighed, her face serious. 'It startled me at first, of course, but when I got used to the idea it didn't bother me. Does it bother you, Gid?'

'No, why should it? I was taken aback, I must admit that, because there had been talk about you being a long-lost McGill. As it happens, you're a long-lost Harte actually.' He laughed, then leaned into her, and kissed her on the mouth. Her arms went around him and they kissed for a long moment, intimately and with passion.

Finally Evan pulled away. 'I think we'd best go downstairs, don't you?'

Leering at her a little theatrically, Gideon shook his head. 'I'd much prefer to stay up here with you, doing this. But I suppose we have to display a little decorum and join the others for drinks. Later, after dinner, I'll take you for a drive, so that we can be alone. All right?'

'Very all right,' she answered, happiness flooding her face.

It seemed to Evan that the following ten days passed in a flash. She was very busy at Harte's. The retrospective was a huge success, so much so they were innundated with requests for interviews from newspapers and magazines, and there was quite a lot of interest from foreign publications. This aside, they were starting to do record business on the various fashion floors.

Evan sat at her desk in her office on Wednesday afternoon, going over her appointments for the rest of the week. Thankfully things had eased off a little for her personally, and she only had two photographic sessions to supervise. One was set for tomorrow afternoon, and the second on Friday morning. Leaning back in the chair she thought about the weekend. It was going to be very special. On Friday evening Paula and Shane were giving an engagement dinner for Linnet and Julian at Pennistone Royal; only the three families were invited, the Hartes, the O'Neills and the Kallinskis. And then on Saturday night the sixtieth birthday party for Shane and Winston would take place in the gardens of the ancient house.

Everyone was excited about the upcoming weekend, and she was driving up to Yorkshire on Friday afternoon with Linnet and India. They had toyed with the idea of taking the train to Harrogate but in the end had settled on the car because it was more convenient.

As thoughts of the weekend ran through her head Evan glanced at the dresses hanging on the rack at the far end of her office, and she stood up, went over to look at them. For the engagement dinner she had bought a lovely, pale-grey silk slip dress with spaghetti straps, very simple and elegant, but she was uncertain about what to wear on Saturday night for the birthday party. She knew Gideon loved her in light blues and aquas, and her first choice was a floating chiffon dress in a mix of those colours, with long, full sleeves and an ankle-length skirt. Now, as she looked at it again, compared it with the rose-coloured silk India had picked out for her, she knew the blue chiffon was right for her. There was something delicate about it: and it was soft, feminine and romantic.

The shrill of the phone made her jump, and she hurried back to the desk, picked it up. 'Hello? Evan Hughes here.'

'Hello, darling. It's Gid.'

'Yes, I know.'

'I'll pick you up at six-forty-five tonight. Is that all right?'

'Yes, of course. I'll see you then,' she answered, then made a kissing sound against the receiver.

'Many kisses in return, my Evan,' he said, and hung up.

As she began to move towards the rack the phone rang again. She snatched it up. 'Evan Hughes,' she said into the receiver.

'Hello, Evan. It's your father.'

'Hi, Dad, thanks for calling back. How're you, how's my mother?'

'Doing much better, Evan. She's not so depressed at the moment, we're going out more often and she's even been into New York with me this past weekend.'

'Oh Dad, that's so wonderful. I'm really thrilled.'

'I got your message that you wanted to talk to me urgently. Is everything all right?'

'No problems, no problems at all, I just wondered if you'd made any plans to come to London? Remember you said you were thinking of taking a vacation here this summer.'

There was a small silence, a hesitation at the other end of the phone, and then Owen cleared his throat, and said, 'I couldn't make it before August. Yes, I *was* thinking of August. It'll be lovely to see you Evan, I've missed you.'

She caught the sudden wistfulness in his voice and for a moment she almost told him about Robin, but caught herself just in time. She was worried about his reaction and informing him about the letters, all they had revealed, over the phone would not work. And so she bit back the words, and said, 'I can't wait to see you, and I've missed you too. Will Mom be coming with you?'

'I'm not sure. Certainly I'll bring her if she's well enough.' Owen chuckled. 'That's where we first met, honey.'

'I know. How's business, Dad?'

'Can't complain. And I know you're just thriving, I can hear it in your voice.'

'I am. I love London, and I love working at the store.'

'Still being nice to you, are they?'

'Very much so, and as I told you last week, the retrospective was a huge success.'

'Congratulations again, honey. I'll call you soon. Or call me when you've got a moment. At home. Your mother loves your calls, Evan.'

'I will Dad. Love to Mom and the girls. Love you.'

'I love you too, Evan.'

They hung up, and she stood looking at the receiver for a moment, her mind full of Robin and everything that had happened in the last ten days. How her life had changed . . .

It was six-fifteen when Evan left Harte's through the staff entrance, and she knew at once that she was going to have trouble finding a taxi. There were none in sight. She glanced up and down, and then decided to walk. It was a nice evening, quite warm, and although it was a good twenty minutes from Knightsbridge back to the hotel, she knew it was wiser not to dawdle, looking for a cab. Anyway she might easily pick one up on the way home.

Striding out, she hurried on past the back of the store and a small parking area, so intent on getting back to the hotel as quickly as possible she did not notice two men and a woman loitering just beyond the parking lot. It was only when one of the men grabbed hold of her arm, that she saw them, startled, her eyes widening. The woman lurched at her, punching her in the stomach; Evan gasped, doubled over, dropping her briefcase in the process.

Evan felt a hard blow in the middle of her back and her legs gave way. She fell onto the pavement, gasping even harder, her breath strangled in her throat. The woman grabbed her handbag, and one of the men leaned down over her, showing a knife. She recoiled, terrified, certain he was going to stab her. 'Please don't hurt me,' she whispered, barely able to speak.

'Gimme the earrings,' the thug bending over her hissed, 'c'mon, gimme the pearls.' He kicked her thigh with a booted foot and bending closer he pressed the knife point at her throat.

Shaking now, and filled with spiralling fear, Evan pulled off the earrings, fortunately clip-ons and dropped them on the ground. The other young thug pounced on them, and the one with the knife at her throat said, 'The watch. Gimme the Rolex or I'll cut yer.'

With trembling hands Evan took off her watch and threw it down, shrinking into herself, doubling over, bracing herself for another kick from the booted foot. But nothing happened. She lay there curled in the foetus position, hardly daring to breath. Suddenly she felt the boot smash against her side, and the thug kept on kicking her, while his partner bent even closer to her body, pressing the knife point on her neck, breaking the skin. 'I'm gonna cut yer . . .'

'Hey, what's going on!' a woman's voice shouted, echoing down the street.

Evan heard running feet and she opened her eyes, saw her three attackers fleeing; a moment later a young woman was bending over her, asking her if she was all right.

'I think so,' Evan whispered hoarsely, touching her neck, then looking at her fingers. 'He cut my neck,' she said, sounding surprised. 'He drew blood.'

'So I can see.' The young woman hunkered down, stared into her face. 'Do you think anything's broken?'

'No. One of them kicked me in the thigh and the side, the others hit me on my back and stomach. But I guess I'm okay.' Evan swallowed, tried to sit up, but found it difficult.

'Here, let me help you.' The young woman put an arm around her and somehow levered her to her feet.

Evan leaned against her for a moment, trying to gather her swimming senses. She began to cough; her throat felt dry and she coughed again, holding her hand to her face. Finally, she straightened and looked at the young woman. 'Thank you. I think you saved me from being badly hurt.'

'I'm glad I was around to help. Can you stand? Do you think you're really all right?'

Evan nodded. 'Sure. My legs are a bit wobbly, but I'm fine, honestly. Please, tell me your name, I'd like to—'

'No, no, that's not necessary,' the young woman answered, giving her a quick smile. 'I'm just glad you're all right.' She hurried off, obviously wanting to go about her own business.

For a moment or two Evan leaned against the wall, and then she looked down at her beige trousers, brushed the dirt off, started to walk. She was shaken up, and nervous, could hardly walk steadily, but she had no choice but to do so if she wanted to get home.

Spotting a taxi at last she flagged it down, told him where to go and got in, leaning against the seat, filled with relief. Tentatively, she touched her neck, saw blood on her fingers again, and groping around in her pocket she found a tissue. She pressed it to her neck, endeavouring to steady herself.

When the taxi pulled up in front of the small

hotel, Evan saw Gideon standing on the steps, looking up and down the street, obviously wondering where she was.

She got out, moving slowly towards him, explaining, 'I've been mugged. Could you please pay the cab-driver, Gid.'

He was horrified. Grabbing hold of her, he held her against him, took a ten pound note out of his pocket and gave it to the cab-driver. Then he led her inside, concerned, solicitous, and seething that this had happened.

'I have to sit down a minute,' she said, as they went through the entrance foyer, and indicated the sitting room. 'Let's go in there.'

The room was empty, and Evan sank onto a sofa, stared at Gideon who was hovering over her anxiously. 'What happened? Are you up to telling me?'

'Yes, I am. But could you please get me a glass of water first, my throat feels so dry.'

He nodded and disappeared, returning a moment later with a glass of fizzy water. 'Would you like a brandy? Would that help?'

'No, thanks, this is fine.' She took a long swallow, looked at Gideon and burst into tears.

'Oh darling,' he said, sitting down next to her. 'I'm so sorry this happened to you. London's become such a dangerous city. Muggings happening in broad daylight like tonight.' He gave her his handkerchief and she dried her eyes, then pressed it against her neck.

'He cut me,' she muttered, taking the handkerchief away. 'Is it a bad wound?'

Gideon leaned closer, examined her neck. 'Thankfully, it's just a nick. Are you sure you're not hurt? Do you want to go to Emergency?'

'No, no, I'm okay! I am, Gid, honestly. They kicked me, punched me, took my briefcase and my bag. And one of them made me give him my pearl earrings, and my Rolex.' Tears sprang into her eyes again. 'The earrings were my grandmother's.'

He put his arms around her and soothed her, and when she was calm she was able to tell him what had happened. 'The thug with the knife really frightened me,' she finished. 'I thought he was going to kill me. I was fortunate that the young woman came down the street when she did. She scared them off, they fled at the sight of her.'

'You're lucky she stopped to help, some people wouldn't have,' Gideon told her.'

'I guess you're right.' Leaning back against the sofa, Evan went on. 'Fortunately there wasn't much in my handbag – makeup, a little money. My passport and credit card are in my room here. Linnet warned me ages ago not to carry too much unless I was sure I needed it.'

'I'm glad she did.' Gideon brought her close, held her in his arms. 'I couldn't bear it if anything happened to you, Evan. You're the most precious thing to me.' He stroked her head, and went on, 'Perhaps we ought to go up to your room, look at your knees. You said they were hurting you.'

'Yes, let's go upstairs. Do you mind cancelling the reservation at the Ivy? I don't think I'm up to going out. And we could eat here. You said you liked the dining room.'

'That's a good idea. Come on.' Gideon stood up, helped her off the sofa, and putting his arm around her he led her to the lift.

Once they were in her room Evan took off her jacket and trousers, and sat down. Gideon examined her knees. 'They're grazed, that's all,' he murmured. 'Nothing serious. Stand up, let me look at your back.'

She did as he asked, and flinched slightly when he touched it. 'That hurts. He hit me in the middle of my back. But the more I think about it, the luckier I feel, Gid. I got away with a few scratches and bruises. I could have been seriously hurt.'

'That's true. But don't stand here talking. Go and have a hot bath, it will help you ease the pain a bit.' He kissed her on the forehead. 'Go on, scoot.'

She did as he asked, disappeared into the bathroom and closed the door. Gideon sat down in the big easy chair in the seating area, picked up the phone and dialled the restaurant, and after cancelling his reservation, he switched on the television set. But he found he could not concentrate. His mind was awash with thoughts of the mugging, her lucky escape. It struck him as odd that the mugging took place so close to the store, but then there was no saying where they would happen these days. They were so prevalent they were becoming a nightmare.

He thought then of Jonathan Ainsley and sat up straighter in the chair, his eyes narrowing. Paula had called him dangerous and Gideon believed she was correct. Jonathan already knew about Evan, knew that his father had a grandchild. According to his mother, Robin was in the process of drawing up certain legal documents with his solicitors, in order to satisfy several demands Jonathan had made. His inheritance was in no way jeopardized, and he was totally aware of that.

On the other hand, might he not bear malice? Might he not want to hurt Evan in some way? Out of spite? A mugging could be arranged, couldn't it?

Gideon pushed these thoughts away, not wishing to think that Evan had been a target. Better to believe this incident had been random.

Chapter Forty-Seven

They were all assembled in the great Stone Hall of Pennistone Royal. The Hartes, the O'Neills and the Kallinskis ... the three clans.

The men looked splendid in their dinner jackets, the women elegant in their evening gowns and jewels. And there was a feeling of festivity in the air as they mingled with each other and sipped champagne.

Paula, wearing a gown of pale green chiffon and Emma's emeralds, slowly moved around the hall, speaking to everyone. Her brother Philip had arrived back from Paris the night before, and had been amazed when she had told him the story of Uncle Robin, Glynnis and the hidden letters. He stood with his daughter Fiona, here from Oxford, and Uncle Robin, chatting amiably with Evan and Gideon. Those two seemed joined at the hip, she thought, going over to speak to them all for a moment, and then moving on. She paused to kiss her mother Daisy and aunt Elizabeth.

Uncle Ronnie spotted her and waved, and she glided across to him. He was with his son Michael, Julian's father, and they both planted kisses on her cheek and told her she looked wonderful.

'What an occasion this is,' Sir Ronnie said, beaming. 'Finally they are to become engaged.'

Paula laughed. 'It's fantastic.'

Sir Ronald Kallinski drew her closer, and whispered against her ear, 'I heard from my bankers in the City that Jonathan Ainsley has put his new company on the market. Apparently he's about to return to Hong Kong. Permanently. That should please you, Paula.'

'It does,' she murmured, and as she walked on she felt as though a burden had been lifted, and so unexpectedly.

Everyone who had been invited had come, and, most importantly to her, Aunt Edwina was there. She was Emma's first-born child, over ninety now, and the Dowager Countess of Dunvale. And what a countess she makes, Paula thought admiringly. Edwina was resplendent in purple silk and a necklace of diamonds, and looked every inch the aristocrat. 'She's something else,' Paula murmured to Shane who drew to a standstill next to her.

'Who is?' he asked, putting his hand under her elbow.

'Aunt Edwina. Doesn't she look perfectly . . . wonderful.'

'Yes, but then all of the ladies do. Come on,

darling, let's not stand here. We've something to do now.'

'Yes, I know.' She looked up at him. 'I wish Grandy and Blackie were here.'

'Maybe they are,' he answered. 'Watching over us.'

Together Paula and Shane walked into the middle of the Stone Hall, and were joined by Linnet, radiant in pale yellow silk, her red hair a burnished halo. She held Julian's hand tightly, and he looked so proud of her. Within seconds the group was silent, waiting for Shane to speak.

'In 1905, ninety-six years ago now, three ambitious young people living in Leeds became friends,' Shane said. 'Emma Harte, Blackie O'Neill and David Kallinski. They remained friends all of their lives, and it was always their hope, their dream that the three clans would be united in marriage. Tonight their wish is finally fulfilled. Let us toast their descendants, their great-grandchildren Linnet and Julian, who will soon be joined in holy matrimony.'

ACKNOWLEDGEMENTS

Firstly, a word about this book. It is the fourth in the series which began with *A Woman of Substance*, followed by *Hold the Dream* and *To Be the Best*. Those chronicled the rise to power of three families, beginning at the turn of the nineteenth century in England. This novel picks up the story in 2001 with the current families, the descendants of Emma Harte, Blackie O'Neill and David Kallinski.

By popular demand I have brought back my most beloved character, Emma Harte, the protagonist of *A Woman of Substance* and *Hold the Dream*. To do so I had to return to the 1940s and the tumultuous war years in Great Britain at one point in this story. In order to give a sense of time, place, mood and historical events of that period, I have used as a leitmotif segments of the great rhetorical speeches of Sir Winston Churchill. Apart from being my own personal hero, I believe that it is to him we owe the survival of Western Civilization.

Without his extraordinary leadership during the Second World War, when he fought appeasement of Germany, Nazi terror and the evil of Hitler, the world would be a very different place today. Certainly we would not have freedom, justice and the decencies of life we have come to cherish. We all owe him so much.

In a long and complex novel many people give assistance in different ways. I would like to acknowledge the debt of gratitude I owe to my friends Edwina Sandys and her sister Celia Sandys, the granddaughters of Winston Churchill. Edwina generously gave me twelve never-released discs of the great Churchillian speeches, which were invaluable. Her sister Celia arranged a private tour of the Cabinet War Rooms in Whitehall which was most edifying. I must thank Phil Reed, Curator of the Cabinet War Rooms, for being a most articulate guide.

My friend Jane Ogden is owed my thanks for being a patient listener and for sharing her memories of growing up during the war years. Susan Zito of Bradford Enterprises gave me enormous help with research and proof reading, and she knows how much I appreciate her involvement in all my novels. I owe a really big thank you to Liz Ferris of Liz Ferris Word Processing, who coped with a long and complex manuscript with great diligence, at top speed, and presented a meticulous manuscript.

I wish to thank my literary agents Morton Janklow

and Anne Sibbald of Janklow and Nesbit, who have represented me since 1981, and have always been there for me. And thanks also to my long-time British editor Patricia Parkin, of HarperCollins, UK who has worked with me since *A Woman of Substance*, and thanks to my editor in the US Jennifer Enderlin of St Martin's Press, New York.

Finally, but by no means least, I must thank my husband Robert Bradford, not only the greatest sounding board and intelligent critic, but my most enduring and loving supporter.